THE CRAXTON-LANGS

THE CRAXTON-LANGS

VOLUME 1 TALBOT ROAD

ALAN DENT

No-one should marry who is not accustomed to loneliness. Chekhov

PENNILESS PRESS PUBLICATIONS

GRAPPENHALL WARRINGTON

www.pennilesspress.co.uk/books

Published by

Penniless Press Publications 2018

© Alan Dent 2018

ISBN 978-0-244-70104-8

Cover:L.S. Lowry – Frith Street

CONTENTS

CHAPTER ONE – TWO WOMEN   7

CHAPTER TWO – A PERFORMANCE   27

CHAPTER THREE – BULL'S EYE   60

CHAPTER FOUR – SATURDAY AFTERNOON   95

CHAPTER FIVE – A POT OF HONEY   132

CHAPTER SIX –AGREEMENT   162

CHAPTER SEVEN – SUGAR   196

CHAPTER EIGHT – BABIES   234

CHAPTER NINE – THE MIND DOCTOR   269

CHAPTER TEN – JUDITH   291

TWO WOMEN

The shabby little terrace shared a wall with the mill so the drumming rattle of the looms was always slightly audible; the pot Spaniels on the mantelpiece would wobble, the chiming clock shift as if some tiny creature were beneath it and the cockroaches run from behind the fire surround. Bert filled a few empty minutes chasing and crushing them with his clog. When his grandparents weren't at work, they were in the pub; and when they weren't working or drinking they were sleeping. Cleaning the house they didn't have time for, so it stank. So did Bert as his clothes were washed infrequently and the house had only one cold tap on the big, square, white sink in the kitchen.

The other kids, who were hardly on intimate terms with soap and water, called him Pongo. It hurt him to the depths of his being and opened up a chasm of incomprehension. Why had his mother left him? Why were his grandparents always drunk? Why did he sometimes have to go barefoot? Why did the other children behave so cruelly? The one small, solid little island in this quagmire of humiliation and loneliness was school. He was top of the ragged class and even though he stank, his pals had to respect that. As soon as he understood he was better than the other kids at spelling, sums and composition, he worked like an ant. School might be a field of nettles; you might get the leather strap across your tender palms for whispering; Mr Colenso might enjoy grabbing a boy by his soft ear and dragging him to the front or whacking him on the back of head with his great, bear-paw hands; but it was the only place where he could feel good about himself. It became an obsession to be first in every test and never drop a mark. If he got nineteen out of twenty for spellings, even though the next best was eleven, he chastised himself for laziness and stupidity; if Mr Colenso picked on him and asked him what was half of three eights and he couldn't answer, he lay in bed reciting fractions to the early hours.

He would have had a place at the grammar school easily, but his grandparents drank away the money and couldn't pay for the books or uniform. At thirteen he started work in the mill next door and he hated the world so much for denying him, he could have murdered everyone in it.

7

He was saved by Adolf Hitler.

He was seventeen in May 1939. In September he signed up for the RAF. He was sent to Italy. The war didn't interest him but the language, the beautiful women and the elegant clothes the wealthy men wore did. When he came home in 1945 he was determined to get an education, make money and find a beautiful woman. He voted for Attlee because he knew poverty. He wasn't mean-spirited. He wanted money, nice clothes, a big house, a car, pretty women; but he didn't want to deny anyone else. Prosperity for all. The good life for all. Anything that tasted of aristocracy or privilege was bitter. It was what had been denied him. It was a fixed, closed world from which he was excluded. No. Men like him needed a society that was opened up, democratic, egalitarian, so long as there was scope to use your brains and your energy to make a good life for yourself. But at the heart of him was the humiliation of poverty; that child Pongo who had wanted to die when the mocking voices followed him down the back alley, and he would not have that inflicted on anyone.

He had to find a job. He discovered having been in the RAF made employers complaisant. Somehow they thought it meant intelligence and competence. He got a place in the accounts office of a building firm, Edmund Cropper & Co. The proprietor, Cecil Cropper, was a Catholic and refused to employee Protestants. Bert thought he was crazy.

"But if a man's a good joiner," he said to Harry Clow, the accounts manager, "what does it matter where he prays? Why employ a lazy Catholic when you could hire a hard-working Protestant?"

"It's the boss's way. He's a Catholic and that's that."

Bert thought it summed up all that was wrong with society. His grandparents were Catholics so he'd been sent to *Sacred Heart*; but what good was their Catholicism? It was mere fearful superstition. They were as scared of the priest as of the boss. Bert thought that craven and silly. He didn't care a donkey's fart for religion. Was there a god? The idea seemed mad to him when he thought of the war, of that overgrown baby Hitler bringing the world to the edge of ruin. What god would make a world in which such things could happen? No, it was men that mattered. It was the choices we made for ourselves that shaped the world. War was just the daftest thing he'd ever seen and Hitler should never have been allowed the weapons.

8

Just as men like him, men from the bottom, needed a world of democracy and equality if they were to flourish, so they needed peace. The only people who got rich from war were the toffs, the high-ups. All men like him got were a bullet through the brain or a bayonet up the arse. Stuff that. No. Peace, prosperity, opportunity, democracy, equality, these were the things that excited Bert. And women. Pretty women.

He asked Harry what he needed to do to qualify as an accountant. Harry laughed.

"You didn't even finish school."

"Never mind. I can catch up."

"Takes years."

"Doesn't bother me."

"You could do something at night-school. Double entry book-keeping and so on."

"I can do that already," protested Bert. "Child's play. I want a proper qualification like you."

" I went to university," said Harry.

"Then so will I," said Bert.

Harry looked at him askance with a little smirk of derision. Yes, that's right. He was an upstart. He was a kid from the drains whose clothes always stank and who didn't wear socks till he joined the forces but he'd show the world. He'd seen those men in Italy who took as much care over their clothes as any woman. He'd admired the shadow-check suits, the tooled leather shoes. He could dress like that. He could take a shower every day, put on aftershave and talc. He understood elegance could be bought and he was going to earn the money to buy it.

Harry sneered at him because he didn't believe men like him could come through; the opportunities were apportioned to those higher up the cliff-face. He was at the bottom and that's where he should stay. Double-entry book-keeping? Double-entry up your arse. Bert knew well enough he'd been competing against other gutter kids at school; he knew the middle-classes got a better start and moved on faster; but he didn't believe they were more intelligent. He'd never come across anything that turned his intellect to water; he could do maths,

9

he'd picked up Italian, he read Shakespeare and Chaucer with no difficulty, and even Einstein, who everyone had told him was impossible to understand, he had a go at it by poring over the astringent explanations of the Special Theory.

Yes. He was cocky. There was no doubt about that. People didn't like it. People who thought the opportunities were for them. No. They didn't like it one bit. But why should he apologize? The world had made him cocky. It was the only way he could survive. All those toffs and middle-class folk who voted Tory to keep people like him in their place, they'd made him what he was; and if they didn't like him cocky they'd have to lump him.

So he signed up for a night-school course in accountancy, and though he found it tedious, it wasn't hard. He went along twice a week to the big, high-ceilinged room in *The Harris College*, and sat at the same desk on the front row on the right. The teacher was a tall, spare, droning man called Biswell, who could have sucked the excitement out of England beating Brazil at Wembley. Bert would look at him and wonder; what kind of life did he have? How could such a man feel passionate about anything? He could go on like an idling bus engine, but there was never any fizz, any vim, he was as flat as a paving stone and about as interesting. Bert found it odd that the world was full of people whose minds didn't pop like his. Life was just endlessly fascinating. There was always something new to see or hear. Why were people so dead? Why did they drag themselves through life as if it was a burden?

One of the fascinating things to see and hear was the unattainable Mrs Bruzzese. She was a couple of years older, married to an Italian who ran a little restaurant in a converted basement near the town hall, very handsome, well-dressed and with a slow smoky voice that made him think of her in her bra and knickers, black and lacy, enticing, tempting, a cigarette burning between the long fingers of her slender hands, its tip as red as her nail varnish when she drew hard on the filter and blew aromatic clouds into the room. He spoke to her one night as they were leaving at nine and the rain was punishing the pavement and threatening to crack the windows.

"Far to go?"

She looked at him, self-possessed and perfectly capable of flattening him with a disdainful remark.

"St Thomas's square."

"You'll get soaked."

"Bus stop's only over the road."

"Want a lift?"

She paused and stared at him.

"You have a car?"

"I do. Nothing fancy. Austin seven. Dry though and quicker than the corporation."

He was a little embarrassed by the modesty of his car. He'd bought it from an old RAF mate who was one of those men who can fix anything. Forever with his head under a dangerously propped bonnet or sliding beneath a car tilted up on little metal ramps, he fitted reconditioned gearboxes, replaced cracked cylinder heads, welded exhaust pipes and renewed suspensions on bangers he picked up for a nursery rhyme and sold on for an old whore's profit. Bert bought his for twenty quid and though it sometimes spluttered and wheezed on a cold morning and the right trafficator periodically refused to stand up, it was a start. It was a car. He was making his way by small steps and this was one of them.

"Does your husband have a car?" said Bert.

" Why not me?"

Bert laughed and looked at her.

"Can you drive?"

"Can you fly a plane?"

"No."

"Could you learn?"

"I reckon."

"So do I. I reckon."

He laughed again. She had a bit of spirit and a bit of wit and he liked that.

Her house was on the little square by St Thomas's church, just on the outskirts of town where the wide road began to take traffic away to the suburbs Bert hoped to live in one day. At either side of an oblong of grass enclosed by black railings they'd built two rows of su-

11

perior terraces; three-bedroom houses with a little garden at the front and a yard at the back, attractive stained glass in the windows and a good bit of space inside. Bert had moved on from the house by the mill and was lodging with his auntie Alice in a clean, comfortable terrace in Talbot Road. Unlike his grandparents his grandfather's sister was as strict as gravity and as self-denying as a stone. She'd never touched alcohol in her life, wouldn't eat so much as an apple between meals, was always in bed by ten and up at five, cleaned the house from top to bottom every day, including her front step, and never missed the ten o'clock service on Sunday. After the dirty, drunken chaos of his childhood, her home appealed to him.

He had the tiny second bedroom. She cooked for him and washed and ironed his cheap shirts. He shaved at the kitchen sink and filled the bath with too-hot water to within two inches of rim while she was singing Charles Wesley's hymns and praying for his soul. She was the only person close to him he'd ever been able to respect. He didn't share her religion or her temperance, but he admired her adherence to principle and the kindness that lay beneath her severe, quiet ways. He handed over his board every week. She nodded in appreciation and put the folded notes in her apron pocket. In the evening she would listen to the radio, knit or embroider. Sometimes he sat with her, reading the paper or a novel by Nevil Shute or Alistair Mac-Lean, but she had no conversation; she was as frugal with words as with money, so as often as he could he went out leaving her to the iron silence of her stern widowhood.

She had little contact with her brother and spoke of him only once when she said: "A man who can't resist drink is a worthless fool." Bert understood and didn't mention him. Seeing Mrs Bruzzese's house made him disappointed and his disappointment sparked his ambition. He would have his own house as soon as he could. A good house like one of these. And then he'd move on to a big four-bedroom with a garden and garage. He thought of his auntie Alice and said to himself he'd offer her a room.

"Nice spot," he said.

"I like it. Handy for town. Want to come in for a cup of tea?"

"Won't your husband mind?"

"Only if he finds out."

Bert laughed again. He felt he'd found a fellow spirit.

The place was very neat. They'd spent a bit on the furniture: a three piece suite in maroon fabric with little cream dots, little wooden wall fittings in the alcoves, an inviting matching rug in front of the coal fire. In the corner was a small television. Yes, he must have a television soon. He wondered if he should suggest it to Auntie Alice.

This was a home. It struck him he'd never really known one. The filthy, stinking place where he'd grown, where the floors were bare flags or boards, the furniture sparse and cheap, the curtains frayed and grubby, was a shelter but not a home. In the care and comfort of this place was love and he envied Mr Bruzzese his luscious, obliging wife and his homely comforts.

She came from the kitchen with a white pot of tea, cups and plate of biscuits on a gold tray.

"Warm enough for you?"

She bent forward to put the things down on the coffee table and he saw the great, inviting chasm of her cleavage. His experience with women was paltry. The war had dragged him away at seventeen. Whores hadn't appealed to him because he felt they had power: some of his mates had gone to brothels in Italy but he resisted because he couldn't see himself handing over money. The women were using the men and what kind of experience would that be? He didn't have unduly romantic notions about women, but he did have a fierce pride about not being hoodwinked: if you bought your shoes from a back-street, pay-no-tax cobbler you'd expect sore feet, and the humiliation of handing over money and being cheated could have driven him to murder. So all he'd known was a bit of tame kissing and some fumbling petting and now he was faced with this big, luxurious, dark, slow-voiced woman whose motivation was a mystery.

"Yes," he said, "nice and cosy in here."

"Glad you like it."

"Lovely little house. I'd like a place such as this myself."

"Where d' you live?"

"With my grandfather's sister."

"Is that all right?"

"For the time being. She's a good-hearted soul but I'm ambitious. I want a nice big house. Somewhere I can spread myself out."

"Me too."

"This is fine. I'd be happy in a house like this. For a start."

"What I'd like," she said sinking into the sofa, "is a nice big back garden."

"You're right."

"Nice and private."

"Of course. Somewhere for the kids to play. Do you have children?"

"No."She became serious and distant for a moment. "We can't."

"Oh, sorry to hear that."

"My husband. Doesn't fire on all four cylinders you might say."

"That's a shame."

He sipped his tea and feeling the silence was painful to both of them said:

"You could adopt."

"Not the same."

"No."

"I'd like to bring a child into the world."

"What woman wouldn't?"

"My husband agrees."

"Sorry?"

"I told him, you see. I can't not have a child so it's either divorce or I get pregnant."

Bert took a custard cream and bit into it so the dryness stopped him replying for a moment. Mrs Bruzzese threw back her head and shook her great ton of black curls. She lifted her right foot onto the sofa and let her knee sway. Bert slurped his tea.

"And he's happy with that?"

"Happy? God, happiness would be too much to ask wouldn't it? He accepts it as inevitable."

"He's a liberal bloke."

"He's in love with me."

"I'm sure."

"And I was in love with him till I discovered he was firing blanks into me."

"Really?"

"You're surprised?"

"I wouldn't've thought you'd stop loving him."

"Well I did. I don't know why. We don't know much about our feelings do we? They come and go and there we are. We have to deal with them. But the thought of the barrenness and his responsibility for it....Unfair aren't I?"

"Not for me to say."

"You should've been a diplomat."

He laughed.

"You have to go to a fancy school and university to do that."

"You must've gone to school."

"Not for long."

"But now you're studying."

"I reckon I can get a decent job if I qualify in accountancy. If you think about it, everything runs on finance. Every factory, office, garage, school, everything. You just can't do without people who can get the numbers right."

"So you like numbers?"

"Not at all. I'm a words man. But who's going to pay me for that?"

"You could've have studied journalism."

"Aye, but things are against blokes from my background. I reckon I've a better chance in accountancy. Not controversial, is it? You get the numbers right. That's the point."

"I find it boring but I'm doing it for my husband's business."

"He's a lucky man."

"That's what I keep telling him."

Bert laughed again, but his mind was working as fast as a piston: was she suggesting he should make her pregnant? He couldn't believe it. Yet the more he ran her words through his head, the more it seemed impossible to come to any other conclusion. It terrified him. Had she been making it clear she wanted to go to bed with him, he would have reciprocated; but making a married woman pregnant was a whole different matter. The child would be his. It might look like him, share his tastes and inclinations. He'd want to bring it up. Surely a man couldn't just fire his spunk into a woman, watch her belly swell and then walk away. He'd always be thinking about the kid. But what rights would he have? If she simply seduced him and once she was pregnant shut the door on him, what could he do? It flew in the face of all he believed about women. It was frank and cynical and accepted the brute facts of biology in a way he'd been raised to imagine women didn't. They were supposed to be romantic, to want everything shrouded in love, to glow with gentle desire over candlelit dinners; to rest a hand as soft as calf's leather in yours as you walked together on a balmy evening by a lisping sea over which an eternal sun was setting, spreading a red glow as warm as their hearts. They were supposed to be modest and bashful, to shade their eyes from the insolent glances of opportunistic men like the succulent heroines of Hollywood movies.

Yet here was this dark, tall, slim, splendid woman with narrow ankles and broad thighs, hair as luxuriant as thick grass on the river banks in May, white teeth as regular as day and night, lovely long fingers and nails filed into gentle points, who was apparently talking about the facts of reproduction as if they were as straightforward as boiling an egg. His attraction to her fought his terror and terror was a hawk against a pigeon. He was finishing his tea when her husband walked in. He was a big, smiling Italian with black hair combed into a great quiff, wardrobe shoulders and that immediate impression of *chic* in his smartly pressed trousers and well-tailored jacket which had so captured Bert's imagination during the war. He shook Bert's hand, kissed his wife on the cheek and sat next to her on the little sofa. She let her weight fall against him, as if she really was in love with him.

"Bert hopes to find work in finance," she said.

"Is good. Is very good," said Gino. "Make a lotta money," and he rubbed together the thumb and middle-finger of his right hand laughing as if making money was the most carefree activity in the universe and humanity liberated by property.

Bert noticed how strong yet elegant his hands were and how carefully tended his finger nails. He was thinking, at one and the same time,

16

that he was one of those men who take great pleasure in knowing they look good, men whose minds aren't preoccupied with great questions but who live in a perpetual present of tasks to be done and pleasures to be had and who can find enough to propel them through the most frustrating day simply by catching sight of their handsome profile in the mirror; and also that his hands were powerful enough to seize him by the throat, pin him to the floor and squeeze the breath out of him. He wished Mrs Bruzzese hadn't told him. It was queer to sit there knowing that this big, healthy-looking, smiling man who brimmed with life was unable to grant her the ultimate satisfaction of pregnancy, as it was disturbing to think she could choose him as a substitute.

He had no illusions about his appeal to women. He was short and no more personable than any other bloke in the bus queue. He was just a normal-looking northern chap. There were thousands like him. Women didn't preen in his presence or look twice when he passed on the street. Almost without knowing it, he'd assumed he'd find a woman by getting on in life. Women, after all, wanted a nice house, a car, holidays, frequent trips to the hairdresser; with a good job and an above average income he'd find someone. Someone who'd do. He was trying to make idle conversation with Gino but his brain was assailed by these fearsome ideas. Yes, it was true. He'd always had, somewhere in the back of his mind the notion of a woman who would do. Laura, good-looking and as sensual as a leopard in the sun was the kind of woman who was beyond him; one of those beautiful or pretty women who raised his spirits as readily as a nice tune or a sunny morning and who he'd always idly dreamed about. It was a revelation to him to discover he'd never seriously imagined such a woman might share his bed and his days.

Why had he spoken to her? Had he really been thinking of an affair? The idea now seemed a ridiculous, childish fantasy. No, it was just his chancer's way, the cheek as native to him as sap to a rubber tree. Now here he was. The situation was impossible. This was another man's wife, and Gino was obviously a charming, pleasant bloke. How could he get into bed with his wife? Wouldn't it break the poor man's heart? Yet he knew that if he'd had the chance to seduce Mrs Bruzzese without Gino suspecting, if he'd been able to win her with his cocky, backstreet ways, he'd have done it without a care.

Most men would go through life and never know the ecstasy of making love to such a physically entrancing woman. Most men made do. They accepted a woman is a woman is a woman, in the way of dirty bar-room jokes. They knew they would spend their lives listening to tin-pan-alley melodies and the exquisite harmonies of Verdi were for others. And here was music he'd never heard. If only he could accept it. He was anxious that at any moment she might tell Gino what they'd talked about. In his place, he would be mortified and enraged. Would he jump up and punch him in the mouth with his big, handsome fist?

"Well," he said, setting down his cup and saucer, "I'd better be going."

"Thanks for the lift," said Laura.

"Yes, a-thanks for a-bringing her 'ome. Very kind of-a you. Very kind."

Bert shook Gino's hand and smiled. He liked him. Already in the few minutes they'd been in one another's company was the basis of a long friendship. Bert was a great believer in first impressions; when something sprang up in his mind on first meeting someone, the image of them doing something underhand or generous, the sense of them as reliable or untrustworthy, he didn't dismiss it as a fleeting product of vagrant ideas, but clung to it and worked on it and he found that usually this automatic response proved right. Blokes he'd known in the RAF who had at once struck him as unsympathetic turned out to be selfish or crude or dishonest. On the other hand, his best pal, Jack Slotover, had impressed him immediately as a genuine and thoughtful bloke; and so it turned out, which was why Bert had kept in touch with him and wrote to him regularly now he was married, with his first child born, and working in a factory near Oxford.

Gino was the same. Bert would have liked to get to know him and in that idea he found the solution to his disturbance: if he could make a friend of the husband rather than a lover of the wife, things could stay pleasant and straightforward.

"Nice to meet you. Do you follow football? Maybe we could go to the match together one Saturday?"

Gino threw up his hands and spread his fingers.

"Football! I love it. Good-a idea. What-a you think, Laura? Good-a idea, eh?"

The rain was still splashing on the dirty pavements, as if a malevo-
lent god wanted to drive the little portion of humanity that lived in
this grimy town indoors, to give them a foretaste of what some future
disaster might feel like, to remind them they were at the mercy of
physical forces they would never control. In his chugging little car,
the valiant wipers going back and forth with the mechanical resolution of donkeys on Blackpool sands, the futile little heater humming
away and the windscreen steaming up like the windows of a café full
of drenched customers, Bert felt he'd escaped disaster. It was true
he'd rolled the dice in inviting Mrs Bruzzese, but he'd barely imagined she'd allow him a peck on the lips, let alone suggest he make
her pregnant. But was that what she was getting at? Maybe she was
just unembarrassed and was telling him about her dilemma. Maybe
he was a bit overwrought and so got the wrong idea. One thing was
sure, he needed a woman. All his thoughts had been about getting on
and he'd somehow imagined love and sex would sort themselves out;
but he realised he was going to have to think about things, to make
them happen, if for no other reason than to avoid ending up in bed
with Mrs Bruzzese, on bad terms with Gino, at odds with himself
and the father of an illegitimate child who might have a bad life by
being brought into the world in such an odd way.

It was a few days later that he crossed Elsie Craxton from the other
side of the street who he'd written to during his time in Italy and
Egypt. They'd met the day war was declared. He'd hoped for an epis-
tolary romance but the correspondence faltered, partly because of her
objections to his occasional drinking.

"Morning!" he called.

She looked a little surprised and shy but smiled and called back.
How had he failed to spot how pretty she was? He was baffled. He
puzzled over it all day like an obsessive crossword solver running an
impenetrable clue through his mind and then out of nowhere the answer came to him: she was always busy, tense and preoccupied.
There was something rejecting about her demeanour, as if she was
intent on such impossibly important private matters she couldn't possibly find time or energy for something as simple as idle conversation. She walked with quick little steps, always hurrying; he'd never
seen her stroll along the street, or pause, or look as though she was
just taking the smoky air that smelled of the iron foundry behind her

terrace. No, she was forever on the way somewhere, as if the very orbit of the earth depended on her errand.

He'd seen her with her shopping basket over her arm almost running to the Co-op or coming back laden and diligent as if from her little trove she was about to feed the five thousand. He spotted her too on a Sunday in her dark best, her Bible clutched in her leather-gloved hand trotting to Marsh Lane Methodist Chapel. He realised this inward, clenched quality was what had prevented him noticing her as a pretty, slim young woman. His instinct was to stick with his aversion but on the other hand he needed to get know young women if he was going to experience the whirl of love and the heavy satisfaction of sex; if he was going to become the married man he wanted to be, successful in his small way in this small town, suburban, accepted, a good citizen, a father, a man who'd found his place.

He criticised himself for being negative. His judgement was unfair. He'd never even spoken to her. It might simply be her manner, something utterly superficial. In private she might be quite different, voluble, expansive, charming and loving. In this little, quiet internal conflict between an instinct he felt was reliable and a modifying voice which told him to be more considered, the latter won out, but only because there was a little kick of desperation telling him if he rejected women on the sort of grounds he was refusing the girl across the street, he might spend the rest of his life waiting for the woman to come along who lit up his brain as soon as he met her. It was more difficult than friendship. There was more at stake. Friendship had always come easily but women, love, sex; this was a much more complex and perilous business, as Laura Bruzzese had made him realize.

Like many young men who make it their business to get to know a young woman, Bert was as clumsy as a drunk on an ice-rink. He stopped her in the street, which was the only space they had in common, and talked as if he'd mastered speech in the last twenty-four hours. She was polite and receptive and he was charmed by her complaisant, ready smile and friendly laughter. Their on-the-pavement conversations became regular and she would let him beguile a pleasant five minutes before she excused herself: she had a lot to do.

"You're always busy," he said. "You'd think you had more on your plate than the Prime Minister."

"Well, my mother needs a lot of looking after."

He felt his attempt at light-heartedness had been badly misjudged and apologised, but she smiled, gave a little laugh and said:

"That's all right."

He watched her cross the street and turn and wave to him on her doorstep. She really was a sweet little creature. *That's all right*. The words seemed to sum her up. She wasn't a woman to take offence or to speak ill. In the privacy of his mind he called her *that's-all-right* and in the way of exponentially growing affection and interest between the young and inexperienced, he found his ideas running away with him. They'd done no more than chat on the street but his head was full of images of church weddings, comfy nights by the fire, long kisses beneath the eiderdown. He had to force himself to restrain his expectations. A girl as pretty as that, even if she was forever cantering to the shops looking as if the stars themselves were her responsibility, could have her pick of men. He examined himself in the mirror. He wasn't ugly. He was clean and neat. He dressed nattily. But if she was one of those women who will accept only a man as good-looking as herself, he was done for.

Though he had no feeling for religion, disgusted as he was by the low, hypocritical and meaningless Catholicism of his grandparents, he went along to a fund-raising Beetle Drive at the Methodist church. The brightly-lit hall was full. The tables had been set at funny little angles to create a jaunty atmosphere. He was struck at once by the plainness of the place and the people. There was none of the oppressive ornateness of St Wilf's, no drooping-headed virgins looking as if they'd just been violated by the lord himself; no banks of candles lit by those seeking remission for sins they were prepared to admit and hoping god wouldn't notice those they kept quiet. This was the church itself. They didn't have the money to build a hall for social events. The church served the poor of the streets of cramped houses and outside toilets and got by, like they did, on a shoestring. But it was popular, even with those convinced there was no god, those who didn't know, those who didn't care, those who hoped there might be and those whose loneliness would have made them believe in the man in the moon if it had brought them company: because it was the most welcoming milieu in the grimy, harsh, little conglomeration of darned-at-the-elbows streets which tried to call itself a community. He loitered by the entrance, trying to spot his neighbour.

A woman of fifty or so wearing an apron came over to him.

"Are you all right, luv?"

"Yes," he said, "I'm just looking for someone."

"Who's that? Perhaps I can help you?"

He looked into the woman's face. He saw a kindness in her eyes and a gentleness in her features which softened him. She genuinely wanted to help him. He was a stranger but she'd approached him to help without ulterior motive. She was smiling at him as if he deserved to be smiled at. She was kinder to him than his grandparents had been. It gave him an odd feeling, as if he'd at last found home, a place where he would be accepted and looked after whatever he was.

"Well," he began, and just at that moment he spotted her coming from the kitchen, a tray of cups and saucers in her hands, hurrying as usual. "Ah, there she is. There. The girl with the tea things."

"Oh, Elsie. She's wonderful isn't she? Never stops working for the church. Such a shame about her mother."

"Yes," said Bert. "Thanks for your help."

"That's all right, luv. Nice to see you."

Bert made his way to the long trestle table where there were plates of scones and fruit cake and rows of cheap, white cups and saucers waiting to be filled at the interval.

"Hello Elsie," he said, beaming.

She looked him full in the face and he noticed the whisper of alarm in her expression.

"I hope you don't mind. Can I give you a hand with the tea things?"

"No, there's no need. I can manage. You should find yourself a table. They fill up quick."

He was struck by the appeal of her hazel eyes. One by one the charms of her young beauty were catching his attention like primroses that sway tipsily in the breeze. He wanted to stop and examine them; but the more he looked at them the less he understood why they caught his eye . He could have stood and looked at them all day without grasping the secret of their appeal. He could have stared at her for hours. She was as pretty as Rita Hayworth or Elizabeth Taylor. She was a little bit of glamour in the grey, dull, rainy streets of the smoky, industrial north-west. It seemed unlikely. It was odd that such a beautiful product of nature could spring up in such unpropitious territory as if instead of weeds, the cracked mortar of the back-alley walls gave rise to honeysuckle; a hint of the promise of beauty and happiness.

Yet at the same time she seemed to retreat from her own election: she'd been born beautiful but didn't wear her beauty with the perky pride of a snowdrop; she seemed to shy away from herself. Not that he would have wanted her arrogant or preening, but she could have worn her attractiveness with a modest, happy acceptance. It was a fact of life, after all, that some women were more attractive than others. Beauty was an accident of nature to be celebrated and there was a certain easy acceptance of attractiveness in a woman which was as appealing as the attractiveness itself. Yet Elsie didn't have it. When he watched her busily getting things ready, it was as if some force at the very centre of her, right at the point of her solar plexus was pulling her down, making her shoulders hunch a little, forcing her to be forever fussing over some little task or other. It made him want to go to her and say:

"Come on. Sit down. Stop working. Relax and let yourself open up."

In his inexperience and callowness he imagined it was something superficial, something it would be easy to massage away like taking the tension out of a muscle. He couldn't let it stand in his way, even though it troubled him, because there was too much promise in her youth; in her slim waist, in the strong movement of her slender legs, in the curve of her small breasts, in the geometry of her buttocks.

He sat at a table with three people he'd never met but they were friendly and accepting. He found the game boring and more a less a waste of time. He didn't like things that left him feeling he wasn't getting anywhere, making some progress to a destination he wasn't sure of. Yet, as the evening moved on like a slow train on Sunday, he began to realize there was an atmosphere he wasn't used to among these people; they were all of a kind. The thought came to him that maybe it was the influence of Methodism, and then the contrary idea sprang up that maybe Methodism attracted them because of the kind of people they were.

They were straight and uncomplicated. His own family was quite different. Aunty Alice was an exception, but the rest were rough, mauling, brazen, vulgar; you couldn't trust them an inch. His grandfather would have robbed a child for the price of a drink. Yet in spite of their low, cheap ways, they were full of noisy patriotism, waving the flag at any opportunity and voting Tory to keep what they called the "left-wing nowts" out of power. It was queer how these apparently opposing tendencies fought in them: on the one hand they were ugly drunk at any opportunity, slovenly, dirty, careless of simple needs and the feelings of others, and his grandfather was ready with his fists once he'd had a drink or two, relishing nothing more than throwing punches or rolling in the gutter with some other booze-giddy fool on a Saturday night; on the other they thought themselves a cut above because they bowed and grinned complaisantly at a Tory MP, genuflected before the priest and sent a card to the King at Christmas.

Somehow, there was none of that here. No-one bore that shoulder-rolling aggression that was visible in his grandfather in doing nothing more than getting up from his threadbare armchair to go to the kitchen. All these people were from the same streets. They worked in the same factories. Yet they were nothing like his family. Here they were, organising sociability and kindness as if it was the most ordinary thing in the world. It made him laugh inwardly. It was something he'd never experienced or thought of. His life had been all about making it through from one day to the next, looking for any handhold on the cliff-face of opportunity and hauling himself up with every ounce of his strength. Not that he felt any maliciousness towards others; he'd just always thought life a battle of everyone against everyone for what you could get. He liked the generous spirit that lived amongst these people as naturally as the hum of conversation. He wanted to be part of it.

At the interval he was quick to the tea table to offer Elsie a hand. As he'd expected she was all don't-bother-yourself and I'll-manage; but he was used to batting away refusals like an opener sending easy balls shaving grass to the boundary and forced his way in, standing beside her pouring tea from the fat metal pot as he said:

"Milk and sugar at the end of the table, ladies and gentleman. Help yourselves to a biscuit."

He was a charming and funny host. He loved a little bit of limelight in which he came to like a parched plant given water; if people were watching him and he could speak to attract them he was as comfortable as a lizard in the sun. He had a deep, warm voice which appealed to people even when what he said was redundant. He was aware of this and it was one of those things that lifted him from the poor tenor of his life. So he filled his role as fully as his chest filled his shirt. He'd never imagined he'd enjoy himself pouring tea at a Methodist Beetle drive, but he chatted as the steaming brown liquid streamed and splashed and every few seconds he found something to say to Elsie.

He was delighted and relieved that she smiled, laughed and agreed. He felt she'd agree with him if he said the sun was made of butter. She was so complaisant he couldn't imagine her expressing even the most blunted criticism. It was very different from his family where if you said it was a nice day someone would pick an argument. People often make decisions based on a few minutes' experience which determine their fate for decades. Bert had no idea he might be doing this. He was lost in the moment. Had he stopped to think he was possibly about to make Elsie the centre of his life for years ahead, he might have felt much less elated; but who can hold back a potentially difficult future when they are caught in a fleeting present of joy?

At the end of the evening all the men were shaking his hand and saying;

"Nice to meet you, Bert," or "Hope to see you on Sunday,"

and the ladies smiling and chirruping, "Hope you'll come again."

"Shall I walk you home?" he said to Elsie as she pulled on her black coat and tightened the belt.

Her brother was coming to meet her.

"Well, I'll come too," he said, "then you'll be doubly safe. You know what they say about Marsh Lane; even the coppers walk in twos down there."

But she insisted he shouldn't bother, she had things to clear away and she didn't want to hold him up. He wanted to brush her objections aside and hang around till she was ready but he judged it might offend her, so turned up his collar and went through the dark streets where his heels clicked on the flags and cobbles reminding him of the days when he had clogs and those when he didn't. At home he made himself a cup of strong tea and a thick wedge of toast which he layered with butter and honey and sat in the little kitchen to eat and drink. He felt something was about to begin. His life was taking a turn for the better. Elsie was obviously a reliable, hard-working girl, not one of those frivolous fribbles who bat their eyelashes, open their legs and tug a man by the groin till his mind is as mushy as tapioca pudding and humiliation his only emotion. He had the feeling he'd be all right with her and as he pushed the last corner of sweet, buttery toast into his mouth he hoped he would soon get to meet her parents, make friends with her brother and be welcomed into that mystery he'd never known: the love and support of a real family.

Whenever Elsie was hauling shopping back from the Co-op, the bags making her shoulder hunch, he would appear like the genie from the lamp, grab the handles, smile and say:

"Come on, lass, Let me take those. I need the exercise."

A PERFORMANCE

Little by little she grew used to him and his intrusiveness didn't make her blench. He even noticed a little glimmer in her eye and a shy hint of blushing when he spoke kindly to her: she was starting to find him charming. It was all he could hope for, in the first instance. Later, he intended to impress her with his hard work and ambition. She'd see he was the kind of bloke who wasn't going to stay around the poor streets. The world was opening up and he believed he could show her how they could find a way through. One of those big semis with a garden front and rear, a driveway, three or four bedrooms, fitted carpets throughout and a bathroom with a shower; that's what he wanted to offer her; and if he could lead her to that, if together they could make a life, then surely they'd stick like chewing gum to your sole.

When he was invited into her house to put down the shopping and she offered him tea, he was astonished at the tasteful, neat homeliness of the little place. They obviously didn't have much money to spare, but nothing was cheap or vulgar. There was a heavy, dark-stained chest of drawers in the living-room, two little drawers at the top and three deep drawers beneath. It was a good quality. They must have saved hard. In his own home, saving was unheard of: if you had a shilling you went to the pub. Putting money by was as exotic as head shrinking. He liked the sense of responsibility the walls of this house exuded. It created a sense of limits his life had always lacked. His grandfather lived as if the universe were too small for him. He thrashed around trying to make room for himself like a pike with a hook in its mouth and like the small-brained fish struggling against what it can't defeat, the more he thrashed, the more he refused to accept the truth of life, the more damage he did to himself. But these people were different. Their house didn't stink. It wasn't filthy. In every detail: the little bookshelf in the corner packed with volumes whose titles he bent to read – *The Mill On The Floss*, *War And Peace*, *News From Nowhere*, *Britain For The British*, *The White Peacock*; the little wooden frames showing pictures of smiling children and one of Elsie's mother and father on their wedding day; the vase of tiny white flowers whose name he didn't know on the window-ledge; the polished brass and copper on the mantelpiece; the

27

neat, clean chrome fender; the bleached net curtains and the heavy, purple ones on brass hangers carefully pulled back and tied; he could read the character of this family – serious, maybe a bit dour, restrained, frugal, sober, high-minded and morally astute. Had he come from more propitious circumstances he might have said to himself that the place lacked a little ease, a touch of humour, a hint of devil-may-care sloppiness; but having lived with chaos and suffered its constant mortification, he found the order and responsibility of this home irresistible.

"Do you take sugar?" said Elsie.

"Two please."

She swept the teaspoon though the dry granules and he noticed how she shook it as she lifted it to level off the contents.

"Heap it up," he said laughing. "I like it sweet."

"You shouldn't."

" Why not?"

"It's wasteful. And it's not good for you."

"A bit of sugar won't hurt me."

"'Appen not. But you shouldn't be greedy."

"I'm not greedy. I just like sweet tea."

"Two level spoons'll make it sweet enough."

"How do you now what's sweet enough for me?"

He hoped she'd pick up on his innuendo but she showed no sign.

"Think of the folk who have nowt," she said. "If we all take more than we need some are bound to end up without."

"And who decides how much I need?"

"I do when you're having tea in my house. Two level spoons in a cup is enough for anyone."

He laughed and shook his head but he liked her attitude. It was funny and contained no threat. A girl who thought about *folk who have nowt* when she was putting sugar in tea wasn't going to do him any harm.

"I'm sorry, we've only plain biscuits," she said.

"Plain's fine for me."

She sat opposite him on the sofa. He made himself comfortable in the armchair. The tea was sweet enough. Maybe she was right and he should cut down, but he had a craving for sweet things and had always piled four or five sugars into his drink.

"I like your house," he said.

"Do you?"

"Yes. It's very.......homely."

"It's a good little house," she said, "well built. But it's hard to keep clean. There's so much soot in the air."

"You're right. One of those big semi-detached houses over the river, that's what I'm aiming for. The air's cleaner up there, away from the factories."

"It's nice there," she said looking to the window, lost in her thoughts. "My dad used to take me walking when I was a girl. The fields and woods by the river. Then we'd climb up behind the church and come home along Church Avenue. The houses are lovely there."

"Then you should have one," he said.

She turned to him, her reverie suddenly broken, her face a little severe.

"Why should I?"

"You deserve a nice house."

"Why do I?"

"A lovely young woman like you should have a lovely house."

"I live in a perfectly nice house," she said with that iron tone of self-denial he was already getting to know. "We shouldn't envy what we don't have."

"Why not?"

"Because it makes us greedy and discontented."

"Perhaps we're right to be discontented."

"Not with material things. We should want to do good in the world not to get more for ourselves."

"Perhaps the two go together."

She looked at him from under furrowed brows.

"I don't see how."

"If a man wants to get on and do the best he can for himself then perhaps by working hard he'll do some good that benefits others."

"More likely he'll take what he can for himself and leave others to their fate."

Bert laughed and took a swig of the good, sweet tea.

"It's too hard to think about others all the time. Get on as best you can and let others do the same, that's my view."

"You're welcome to it."

He laughed again. The combination of steely moral resolve and her slender, pretty frame sparked up amusement in him. He realised he'd always taken for granted that people were cutting through the tough undergrowth of life in pursuit of a clearing for themselves, and he'd admired them for it. He'd never felt any animosity to the people at work or the blokes he shared a hut with during the war. He didn't imagine they bore him any ill-feeling either. He was perfectly well-disposed to them. If he'd won a million on the pools, he'd've given his best mates ten thousand each. If he'd heard one of his friends was down on his luck, he'd've have done what he could to help him. If his neighbour had a bad back, he'd set his fire for him. But Elsie wasn't like that; she was in the grip of a moral injunction. She took her Methodism not merely seriously but literally. She had to love her neighbour as herself and how could she do that if she put her own interest first?

He wondered if she didn't push the obligation even further than Christ and love her neighbour a little more than herself. He was about to tease her but held back, fearing he might offend her sincere moral sensibility; and though he couldn't share her orientation, though he could no more have given up pushing for himself and hoping he'd come through to material comfort than he could have renounced sweet tea or toast and honey, the idea of a woman constantly on the *qui vive* against selfishness in her own behaviour, permanently striving to set the interest of others as high as her own was irresistible. Aunty Alice had something of the same sternness, but with her it was more a question of conformism, of *not showing yourself up* as she liked to say. As for his grandmother, she was as base as her husband, never happier than when she was too drunk to know what she was doing. He'd always stopped himself thinking about her

30

sexual behaviour. It would have been too painful. As a young boy full of affection, after all, he tried to cleave to her and the thought of her giving herself to some rough bloke from one of the dockside pubs in a back alley would have shredded his heart. So he'd long blocked all thoughts of her love life. Just as he'd stopped himself thinking about his mother.

He knew almost nothing about her and no-one had ever said anything. He only had to let the idea of her leaving him with her disastrous parents rise from the pit of his brain for his heart to pound unpleasantly and humiliation begin to seep through his marrow. His mind had been formed in denial of those thoughts. From his earliest years, he'd grabbed whatever was positive, whatever gave him the possibility of feeling good about himself and he'd clung to it like baby chimp to its mother. And now here he was in this neat, clean, pleasant little home with the prettiest girl in town who was as firm in her self-denial as his grandparents were lax in their self-indulgence. He couldn't believe his luck. What it would be to have Elsie as a wife. To delight in her physical charms on the one hand and to be reassured by her titanium principles on the other. For a man like Bert, raised in muck and manipulation, the clean, clear light of her character was as beautiful as her hazel eyes, her trim waist, her delicate, white neck, her lovely even teeth and her soft, pink lips.

"What's your view?" he said putting his cup and saucer on the fresh tablecloth.

" Like I said, we come into the world to make it a better place, not to get what we can for ourselves."

"I agree," he said and smiled broadly.

She was standing by the window. How lovely she was, so slim and girlish. He could have got up and put his arms round her. Had she been one of the vulgar girls from the pubs he might have done. He might have tried his luck. But he knew she would be affronted by anything opportunistic and hasty and he was pleased he'd have to behave subtly and take things slowly.

"I'm glad you do."

"You've converted me," he said. "I'm a sinner saved."

She looked askance at him, slightly disapprovingly but with a hint of amusement at his silliness.

"Are you a sinner?"

"I'm too busy working. Doesn't the vicar tell you it's idle hands the devil makes work for?"

"He does. What's your job?"

This was the first interest she'd shown in him and he wondered if she was starting to think of him as something more than a neighbour she spoke to on the street and a strong pair of hands to help her with the shopping.

"I work in accounts at Cropper's."

"Very good," she said.

He knew at once that she thought a *white collar* job gave him a little advantage in the economic jungle and he was instantly worried she might see him as outside her sphere.

"Just a clerk," he said. "I'd earn more at Dick Kerr's."

Kerr's was the aircraft factory where thousands of men from the local streets worked. Before the war it'd been a private engineering business and though nationalised and transformed into a producer of fighter planes in the early forties, the locals still referred to it by its former name.

"Good prospects in a job like that, though."

"Might be. If I work hard. I'm studying at night school."

"Are you?"

"I'm going to qualify as an accountant."

"That sounds a fancy ambition."

"Why? I'm as bright as the next man. I can do figures. I've always been good at calculation, ever since I started school. Look at Nye Bevan, he started off in poverty but he's raised himself. That's the kind of man I admire."

She was looking at him with a new interest and he sensed he'd said the right thing. Methodism and socialism were the poles around which her life turned and though the former meant nothing to him he was at ease with the latter.

"So do I. The NHS is a godsend to my mother."

"Is she poorly?"

"Bedridden."

"That's a shame."

"It is. A cryin' shame. Worked herself till she's crippled with arthritis."

Bert wondered if it were true that hard work had crippled her. Perhaps she would have succumbed if she'd lived a life of leisure. But he wasn't going to contradict Elsie's theory.

"So who looks after her?"

"I do."

He picked up on the note of defensiveness in her voice and the challenge in her eyes. She was like a big cat prowling its territory, growling at any marauder. He smiled.

"Don't you work?"

"How can I? I've looked after her since I was thirteen. My dad took me out of school. There was no-one else. I don't resent it. You have to do what you have to do."

"Of course."

But he knew she did resent it; he knew the cast iron trapdoors of her mind could shut off an impulse she felt unworthy as easily as most people could close a cupboard and not to look after her own mother would have filled her with shame as surely as a rubbish-littered back alley fills with rats. He felt sorry for her and that was unusual because most people he met came from better circumstances than him and needed none of his pity; but Elsie shared something with him: a part of her had been denied by her family. He quickly worked it out; she must have been looking after her mother since about 1935. So she'd had that to cope with and then the war had hit her. It was terrible that she'd never known the carefree days of youth. He'd left school early too and gone into the hated mill, but at least he'd had his free hours out with his mates, kicking a ball around the back alley or running by the river to see the big ships arriving from Canada or Russia. At least he'd been allowed to work off a bit of wildness, to climb trees and fish for newts in the little pond behind Parry's Farm. At least he'd been able to wander out of the town through the woods on summer evenings, making little fires with his pals or carving his initials in the bark of a great ash. And at least the war had given him the chance to see another part of the world, to know that these grey, pinched streets, this smoky air, this treeless enclave of demeaning poverty was a tiny part of a big planet and there was a better life, a life where the sun shone and the air was good to breath and you could feel alive.

He looked at her and knew she'd given up part of herself to do her duty to her mother. Once more it made him think of his own family. When he had the flu as a child, his grandparents left him alone in the house, shivering beneath his blanket on the floor. Ever since, his chest had been bad in winter. What it would be to live with a woman who knew how to care for you? But a woman who knew how to care for you and was plain or ugly would take you only half way to happiness. In Elsie, there was the beauty and charm that sparked his desire like the hammer of a gun against gunpowder but also, beneath her toughness, the warm, gentleness of a caring nature. It was almost too good to believe.

"I'd better go and see she's all right."

"Is she upstairs?"

"Yes."

"Wouldn't it be better to have her down here?"

"Why?"

"Then you wouldn't have to be going up and down to tend to her. It must be hard, taking meals up from the kitchen and so on."

"But there's no room."

"It'd be difficult, I agree. But she must come first if she's bed-ridden."

She looked at him as if he'd just told her the secret of eternal life. Her face lost its background severity. He'd said what she wanted to hear and he knew he'd pleased her.

"Yes. It might be a good idea."

"I'd help."

"Would you?"

"I'd love to."

"I'll mention it to my dad."

"Is he at work?"

"Yes."

"What does he do?"

"He works at the power station. Cleans out the furnaces."

"I see."

"I'd better go up."

"Can I come with you?"

"To see my mother?" her eyes were wide and he wondered if he'd ruined the good impression.

"I'd like to say hello to her. We live just across the road from one another after all. She might like to meet me, seeing she can't get out."

"'Appen she would."

"I'll just pop my head in. I won't disturb her."

"She might be sleeping."

"I'll be quiet as a worm."

He followed her up the steep narrow stairs noticing her slim, strong ankles and calves. There was a tiny square of landing and two white doors next to one another. She pushed open the door to the front room with preternatural care, as if some fierce beast, a komodo dragon or a hungry panther were dozing behind it. She craned her head to look inside and he heard her say:

"Hello, mum. There's a visitor here. Bert, from across the road. He's Mrs Delafield's nephew. He's staying with her till he finds a place of his own."

There was an indiscernible mumble and Elsie beckoned with her head. The bed dominated the little room. It was a double iron bedstead, one of those sturdy items such families hung onto for decades, shaking their heads at newer flimsier products. The elderly woman was propped on two feather pillows. She turned her eyes to him with a tiny, painful move of her head. She had a strong, big-boned face, with a prominent nose and eyes dark as caverns. Her shoulders weren't covered by the bedclothes and he could see she was a big woman, broad and powerful, not at all like her svelte daughter. Her white face showed all the agony of her condition; not only the physical pain of the arthritis which made her joints as stiff as a rusted

35

hinge nor the stinging, endless irritation of the bedsores which appeared in spite of her husband's and Elsie's efforts; but the hurt too of no longer being able to look after herself and the terrible isolation of confinement to this meagre cell. Death was revealing itself through her pallor, immobility and strain. It was terrible to see a human life come to this. Yet it was obvious from the neatness, cleanliness and order of the room that everything was done to keep her comfortable. Life was a cruel business. Bert hated to see this. The thought of the poor woman lying there yet for years, the life being slowly pressed out of her like water from clothes in a wringer was too dreadful. He would have liked to close her eyes; to gently put his hand on her shoulder and tell her the suffering was over. He hoped that if ever such a thing became of him, someone would be kind enough to give him an injection and put him to sleep for ever.

"Hello," he said quietly with a smile, "I'm Bert, Elsie's friend. From across the street. Just come to say hello. If there's anything I can do..."

The old woman was looking at him from her black eyes. Her face showed no expression but she tried to give a little nod and a groan in which he believed he heard a tone of approval emerge from her throat. She switched her slow look to Elsie and back to Bert and tried once more to give a small nod. Elsie looked at Bert and indicated with the tiniest of movements that he should leave.

"Well, lovely to meet you Mrs Craxton. I'll see you again. Don't worry, Elsie, I'll let myself out."

He pulled the door closed behind him and went down the stairs thankful for his young and nimble feet. Just as he arrived in the brief hallway, the front door opened and a man in a sawdust-sprinkled overall, the sleeves of his thick check shirt rolled up to his elbows, his cap pushed back from his forehead and a pencil behind his right ear took a step in and wiped his feet on the postage-stamp doormat. Seeing Bert he smiled widely and held out his strong hand.

"Hello. Nice to meet you. Eddie."

"Bert. I live across the street."

"Aye. I've seen you comin' and goin'. You know our Elsie, don't you?"

"That's right. I just gave her a lift with the shopping."

"Good of you. Good of you. Come in and have a cup o' tea."

"I've had one. I was just leaving. I popped up to see your mother. Elsie's with her."

"Aye? Well, come in anyway. Another cup o' tea won't hurt you and I could do with someone to chat wi' for a few minutes."

There was such an easy-going generosity in the invitation, Bert couldn't refuse. He wasn't used to people wanting his company. The hurtful taunts of his street pals still rang in his inward ear. In some hidden part of himself he was still the kid who stank and others goaded because of it. There was an assumption in him that he'd have to push his way in. He wasn't the kind of man people would want as a friend. It had become part of him and didn't trouble him more than an itch. He'd found that people were willing to let him in. They took him for what he was and though he sometimes sensed he was pushing too hard, people were always willing to excuse him. People, after all, were pretty kind. At least if you put them on the spot and forced them to be.

"Been working on a house in Penwortham all day. Parched I am. That and starvin'. I could eat a scabby donkey."

"You live here, then?" said Bert.

"No. Married. I live in Hutton. Little cottage. Rented like. We'd like to move further out. April's family are market gardeners. Keep hens too. Give me the nod if you want to some eggs. But we'd like to be more in the country. Get out beyond Longton maybe. Hesketh Bank way. House wi' a bit o'land. Keep hens of our own and an orchard. Aye. I've allus fancied an orchard."

Bert experienced another of his instant likings. There was something missing from Eddie. He couldn't say what it was, but somehow he wasn't threatening. There was a naïve openness about him, as if he lived in a small tribe where everyone knew everyone and mistrust was unnecessary; as if everyone shared a set of benign values which guaranteed well-being and no-one needed to be on guard against being used. He was as sweet as a child who knows nothing of the corruption of the adult world and expects love and support from every grown-up like a cat expects to be welcomed on every lap. It was the oddest thing. It made Bert stare at him as he went about the simple task of brewing the tea, as if by looking he could penetrate the secret of his character, as if it were expressed in the sure movements of his hands or inscribed in the heavy shifting of his body around the furniture in the tiny kitchen.

"Sugar?"

"Two, please."

"You've a sweet tooth. Our Elsie'll nag you for that."

"She already has."

"Aye, well she will. She's a beggar for it."

"For what?"

"Indulgence. Aye, she takes it all straight, you see. What t'Bible says about give your money to the poor and all that. She's a beggar for all that right enough."

" I have a few sugars in my tea but I'm not rich."

"Me neither but our Elsie'd say so. There's folk starvin' in Africa. All that palaver. Aye, she's handy wi' that argument. Count your blessings. She's a strict'un. But you've got t'hand it to her, she sticks to her guns like. Never touched a drop o' drink. Cut out sugar when she heard they treat workers rough on't plantations like. Aye, she's all for that. Unions and socialism and the like."

"Where's she get it from I wonder."

"That's no wonder. Chapel and my father," he said the word so it rhymed with blather. "Aye, he's in't T and G. Worked for 'em all his life. And t'Labour Party. Mind you, 'e's had it rough all right."

"I'm a Labour man myself," said Bert, conciliatory. "We all were when we came back from the war."

"Oh aye. You'll not find a soul in Talbot Road votes Tory. They'd no more do that than they'd rob your washin'. But our Elsie's a rare 'un. She'd vote communist if she could."

Bert laughed.

"She wouldn't."

"She would 'n'all. She's stern wi' 'erself d'you see and thinks others should be't same. But we're not all made o't' same timber. I'm all for Attlee and Bevan and such, aye. But I don' think t'devil's in a pint of ale like Elsie does."

"She might grow out of it if she's given a chance to see a bit more of the world," said Bert almost thinking aloud.

"She'd not leave mi mother," said Eddie lifting his pint mug to his lips.

"No more should she," said Bert. "It's touching to see how devoted she is."

"Aye. Oh, I'll not criticize. No. You can't fault her. But she's her own life to live. Sometime or other you've got to break away. That's puzzle. Aye. So long as mi mother's in that state, Elsie'll be beside her."

Bert was tempted to say the old woman didn't look like she was long for the world, as he would have liked to open up a discussion on eu-thanasia. It was one of those ideas he thought of as modern. Progress couldn't be held back. Everything had to be thought through anew as circumstances changed. He relished those moments of flux. They were also times of opportunity. The settled order of things disturbed him as did those occasions which confirmed a life he'd never known. Christmas made him as nervy as a cornered rat. The world shrank. Everything closed as people retreated to their families. They were in warm front rooms with people who loved them, or so he thought. But he had nowhere to retreat to. His home was the public realm. When the town was busy, the streets full of strangers, the cash tills ringing, the trams clanking down the iron rails from Church St to the railway station; the pub doors open, the office girls with their handbags on their arms tripping out for a sandwich at lunchtime; the stately, cool banks taking deposits, the buses chugging out from the little station heading for Deepdale and Fulwood; that was when he came alive for in that world where all men and women were strangers he could feel at home. He had a chance of some kind of belonging and fulfilment. He could get what he needed, one way or another. But when that shut down; when the shops were locked and the lights out; when the pub doors were as firm as graves; when the streets emptied like terraces at the end of a match; when the buses sat silent as bribed witnesses in the locked garages and the tramlines curved to nowhere; when the typewriters were hooded, the telephones as quiet as Trappists, when the town might have been afflicted by the plague or the final desola-tion of proud humanity; then he was the lonely, frightened child again, dependent on grandparents who let him know he was a bur-den, whose most tender expression of love was that they didn't throw him out on the street or make him beg coppers for their beer.

"She needs some time for herself," said Bert.

"Aye, she does. Who's to tell her though? You'll no more move Elsie than you'll shift t' sun in a wheelbarra."

It was good to sit in the cosy room with a man he liked. He could have stayed and listened to him all evening. He was a working man, his pencil was still behind his ear and he didn't think to take off his cap because he was indoors, but he was as sympathetic as a warm day in May. How lucky Elsie was to have a brother like this. The idea came to him that if he was to get to know Elsie well, if they could become a couple, then Eddie would be almost his brother. It was one of those deep regrets which clung to him like a cold, wet shirt that he had neither brothers nor sisters. His mother, so he'd heard whispered by his grandparents, had children from her marriage; but he had no contact with them. It was unpleasant, this terrible loneliness of his bastardy, like a bad taste in your mouth when you're ill that nothing will swill away. It was as if he'd been thrown into a world which didn't want him and while he'd made the best of this by seeing himself as the agent of his own fate, determined to wrestle with raw circumstances, the first touch of the warmth of belonging, the sweet blessing of sharing your life with people whose biology was strongly like your own, made him wish he could relax in the comfortable bed of that curiosity called *family*.

"How long has your mother been bedridden?" said Bert.

"How long? Na then. Before t'war. Four or five year. Aye, must've been '35, about then. Never set foot outside th'ouse sin'."

"Elsie thinks hard work did for her."

"'Appen. She were never still. That's true enough. Times were 'ard you see, when mi father was wi'out work. She cleaned folks' houses. Took in washin'. That and mi father's allotment fed us in them years. Aye, it's a beggar. Depression and next we're off t't war. It's a rum life, Bert, and no mistake."

Bert was tempted to ask him about his time in the services but the gloom of all that, the knee-in-the-groin poverty of the thirties, the shipping abroad wondering if you'd ever see your home again, was starting to weigh on him. Here was Eddie, after all, a six-foot young bloke, working for his living, obviously trying hard to make something of his life; all that misery of the slump, the rise of Hitler and the slow inevitability of having to go to war to defend a system

40

which had given him nothing but loneliness, poverty, humiliation and struggle, was in the past. The world had learned its lessons. Bert, full of that youthful sense that the future can't but be good, together with the confidence that the difficulties of history will not beset the generations to come, was sure the stupidity of recent events was gone forever. There was no doubt the war had left people unwilling to contemplate armed conflict. Everyone he knew thought the NHS was a wonderful thing. There was a new world being made and he and Eddie were part of it. Wouldn't it be something if Eddie were to become his brother-in-law and they could be friends for the rest of their days? How he would relish hundreds more moments like these, good male moments, two blokes chatting together over a cup of tea. How he would love the sense of belonging, especially to a family like this; a family of principled people, good people, people you could trust and rely on.

"So you've been working in Penwortham today?"

"Aye, big house. Roof. Six valleys. Hard work right enough but a lovely house."

"That's the kind of house I'd like."

"Wouldn't we all. Solicitor. Money you and I'll never see."

"Who knows, Eddie. If we work at it and the fates are good to us."

"Aye. But a bloke like me, I could work twenty hours a day and never make what they earn. Things are set up to keep us where we belong. That's my thinkin'."

"But they're changing. We are the up and coming blokes. They can't ignore us anymore. We fought a war for them. Our votes put them in power. We're never going back to the thirties. Unemployment. Poverty. All that's in the past. No. They've got to make the system work in our favour. That's my thinking."

"Aye. 'Appen yer right, Bert. We'll do our best, eh? That's all we can do."

"It is, Eddie. We all must do our best for ourselves and one another."

In the weeks that followed, the idea of becoming part of Elsie's family began to grow in Bert's mind. There was something about her people which brought alive part of his psychology that had never been stimulated. She had two other brothers, Jimmy, a big, slow, hard-working electrician who smoked untipped Capstan full-strength and drank canals of slow stout in the rough, careless pubs by the docks because, being quiet and shy, he liked the crowd, the noise and the easy vulgarity of the *regulars*; Elsie, from her tough, unforgiving Methodism despaired of him, though she loved him with a little sister's élan and tenderness; and Henry, the *black sheep* who joined the army at seventeen and got a young woman *in trouble.* He came home to confess to his parents who told him he must *do the right thing* but he couldn't. He didn't even like the girl. His father tore a strip off him and would have liked to take the leather belt from behind the parlour door. But Henry was as obstinate as bad weather. As a boy he'd always been contrary; if his mother told him to go to the sink and wash his hands, he'd stand his ground and cry "No!" as if she was about to murder him, and this defiance riled his slow-blooded father who would slap his legs with his big, reluctant hand. He acted out of anger that grew from fear. He was afraid for his son. The world was harsh and there were as many snares for a child from the poor streets as segs on a workman's palm. To escape these conditions required discipline and Henry's refusal pointed to a tragic outcome. So the more the boy resisted the more he was disciplined and the more he was disciplined the more he resisted; but a spirited horse won't be broken, it can only be brought round by patience and gentleness and too late the parents realised their mistake.

"And who'll look after't chile if tha dunt?" asked his father.

"She will. And her mother."

"And tha'll get away scot free."

"It's not my fault alone. She were willin'"

"Tha' great lout. Willin'. Tha's t'think on't responsibility not willinness."

Henry was at home for a sullen week and Bert met him when he carried the shopping back for Elsie.

"This is our Henry," she said, "as I told you about."

"Pleased to meet you, Henry," and Bert held out his hand.

"Aye. And what's she told you."

Henry's handshake was strong. All the Craxton men had powerful hands and arms unlike Elsie who was delicate as a primrose. His face was set and his eyes looked blankly into Bert's with that animal suspicion of a man who faces an inevitable enemy.

"That you're in the forces," said Bert, "home on leave to see your mother. A good son to her. That's what she said."

Elsie turned away with the sugar and butter from the shopping in her hands.

"Owt else?"

"No," lied Bert. "Except she was glad to see you."

"Have a seat."

Bert turned the conversation to life in the forces. In truth, he was at a loss to understand how anyone would want to sign up. He found being in a uniform and subject to bizarre, arbitrary rules thoroughly uncongenial. It wasn't life. Life had to be choice. It had to be enough space to do what you want. It seemed to Bert war was possible only because men were willing to turn themselves into cattle. If they stood up like men and demanded their freedom, there would be no war. That was one of the ideas that bubbled up in his brain and which he loved to talk about: the common man could put an end to war by refusing to put on a uniform or pick up a gun. But he wasn't going to tramp tactlessly over Henry's clean carpet in muddy size tens. So he fed him questions which allowed him to open up slowly and he found that once they got talking about machines and engines Henry was animated.

Bert had little feeling for mechanical things. He preferred words or figures. Getting his hands oily on the piston rings of a motorbike or the carburettor of a Morris Minor was as about as appealing as cleaning a toilet; but he was prepared to feign interest to establish a rapport with Henry. He smiled and nodded, raised his eyebrows at those moments Henry produced a supposedly amazing fact or riveting anecdote. It took a little effort, and aware himself of the difference between how he truly felt and how he was responding, he wondered if Henry could see through him. But once he was in full flow, recounting how his motorbike spun off the road and threw him into a ditch, how he had to climb out and with the few tools in his pannier get the damaged engine working again, Bert could see that lost in his tale and thoroughly absorbed in his own interest, he didn't notice at all those little nuances of expression which might have given him away.

It was curious. Most people were the same. If you could find what really meant something to them and get them talking about it, they were oblivious to the boredom they might be inflicting. As for himself, he was aware that his fear of unpopularity, his dread of being mocked as he was as a child, his bowel-dissolving anxiety at being pushed out and turned into an unwanted outsider, made him seek out whatever made others open up to him. He could have sat for a week listening to a fishmonger explaining how to fillet cod if it were necessary to win his friendship. So he let Henry talk and at length he came round to the girl.

"Aye, she's a bitch and no mistake."

"Sounds like it."

"Led me on all right. She came after me. That's the truth. I almost wonder if she wanted to get herself pregnant."

"She wouldn't be the first."

"You're right, Bert. They're a sly breed women. There's nowt straightforward about 'em."

"Your Elsie's not roundabout though, is she?"

Henry looked at him, his face suddenly open with naivety and questioning.

"She's a pious one. You're right. She's honest as death, but there's summat about her gets on my nerves."

"Aye?"

"If there were cakes for tea on a Sunday, as a treat, she'd allus take smallest. If I reached for't biggest first, she'd start up like a blackbird on a nest o'young: 'You'd shouldn't take biggest for yourself." 'Aye,' I'd say to her, 'and what would you tek?' 'Smallest," she'd say. 'Well, shut tha gob," I'd say, 'tha's getten it."

Bert laughed though he found Henry's story vulgar and brutish. What was wrong after all in a bit of politeness? And the image of the big, hungry lad shovelling his tea with all the ceremony of a navvy shifting clay and then reaching for the best cake before anyone else had a chance made him want to dismiss Henry as a thoughtless rough.

"That's a good tale, Henry."

"Like her, do you?"

"Oh, I just give her a hand with the shopping and chat to her now and again."

"Aye, but she's a pretty lass."

"She is."

" Church has got her, though. I'd stay away from a woman like that. Too godly to be good. Are you religious?"

"Not at all. All medieval mumbo-jumbo to my way of thinking."

"Mine too. I can't put up wi' their pretending they're not human. Do yer get me? I tek biggest cake. Cause I do. I'm bloody hungry. I want biggest cake. I'm not goin' ter lie 'bout it. Aye, I'm greedy. I'll admit it. I can do wi' that. It's honest. But our Elsie, she's too bloody good to be good to yer. Though she is good to me, in her way. Do yer get me?"

"I think so."

"She's tied, to mi mother, like. Bugger. In her shoes I'd tell me father I want a life of mi own."

"You're right. But she's devoted. You can't fault her for that."

"No more would I. But I pity her. Aye, I do. Poor lass. Thirteen she was when mi mother took to her bed."

Though Bert was wary of Henry after this conversation, he found in him the same gentleness, the willingness to be generous and the absence of judgement and prejudice which seemed to characterise the family. He knew the snobbery of the working people. They didn't need more than a decent terrace and a clean door step to start setting themselves above those with less. He knew how a family like his was disdained for its lack of cleanliness and its chaotic ways; and that disdain had fallen on him, though he was innocent. He'd hoped he could shake it off but he would run into people who knew him as a child and he sensed at once from the look in their eyes and their tone of voice they judged him by what they knew of his origins. It was terrible to wonder why his grandparents were so slovenly and vicious. Having no answer made him anxious so he sought theories: he read Freud and elaborated a view of his grandfather and grandmother as neurotics, driven by unconscious conflicts; or perhaps they were borderline psychotics whose superegos had never been given a chance to develop. Having these ideas to help him was like finding refuge in a doorway beneath a thunder storm. It provided him a tiny space from which he could exclude worry and humiliation by talking to himself like a professor of psychoanalysis. He could rise above the difficulties of his life by understanding them. Small though this relief was, it was wondrous. It showed him the straight road out of the clinging, stinking swamp of his past. Knowledge was freedom. What we understand doesn't need to scare us. The more he could understand, the more he would be able to push the lacerating facts of his early life away from him, he could become a quite different person from the poor, cold, confused little Bert Lang who everyone called Pongo, knowing it hurt him, wanting to hurt him; he could become the kind of person who commanded respect. He could assume responsibility and be called Mr Lang, but above all, he could quieten the howling monsters of doubt and insecurity in his mind; he could slit their strong, foul throats and replace their mean cries with the steady and secure voice of reason.

He knew the snobbery of the working people and he knew it was absent from the Craxtons. Why were they different? It puzzled him but the puzzle wasn't enough to hold him back; who could have resisted being close to this family with its mixture of astringent principles and gentle emotions? They didn't judge him. They knew where he came from. They'd heard the tales of his grandfather's drunken fighting in the streets on Saturday nights. But they welcomed him. When he met Elsie's father, Bert felt himself in a very strange presence. He was a curiously inward man of very few words yet he needed to do nothing more than look at him and Bert could see the kindness in his eyes. He was one of those working-class men who had left school at twelve and gone into the mill. Fifty years of hard work had made him physically tough; during the Depression he'd worked as he could on the docks, hauling impossible loads of timber on his shoulders or unloading sacks that might have been filled with rocks from the greedy maw of dark holds; but it wasn't hard physical work which had marked him most severely. Into his mind was burned the cruelty of a world where fifty hours of muscle-melting effort could hardly put food on the table for his family while a mile away, in respectable, church-going Penwortham people sat down to good dinners in their three and four bedroom comfortable homes, never skimped, never strained, never knew the shrinking humiliation of being unable to afford a pair of shoes for a child using cardboard to fill the holes in their soles in winter.

Circumstances had concentrated his mind. He asked himself this question again and again; in fact, he didn't even ask it: it pulsed through his arteries with every beat of his heart. Why were people divided by property? Bert came quickly to understand that Tom Craxton would have shared his last crust of bread with a hungry man. It was very odd. Bert had never been able to twist his mind away from the need to get on, to escape, to rise. That was what you were supposed to do. It was a rule of the game. When you played football you tried to score more goals than the opposition. It was simple. And life was like that. It was a simple rule that you tried to get the best for yourself. Bert had always thought it absolutely as straightforward as knitting. He didn't want to do anyone down, anymore than he wanted to inflict pain or injury on opponents on a football field. He just wanted to win. When he played football, he wanted to walk away with the cup and in life he wanted a big house, good food, nice furniture, smart clothes, pleasant holidays, friendly nights out, a good, well-made car, a garden, meals in the best restaurants, weekends in the best hotels; it had never occurred to him that his own poverty, the alligator bite of demeaning deprivation from which he was struggling so hard to escape was a result of such desires.

He'd always laid the blame on his grandparents. They were feckless drunks who worked only to earn enough for the next pint of bitter or bottle of gin. They had no ambition, no desire to lift themselves. They lacked that tight discipline so characteristic of Elsie. He'd always thought it was no more than that. They were wretched failures whose obsessions destroyed their own chances of any remotely decent life. But Tom Craxton was a man of strict principle. He never drank. His one indulgence was tobacco, but even then if money was short he went without and even during the best of weeks restricted himself to two pipes a day. He'd worked hard all his life and yet here he was in this little house, holding things together, a wage away from a bare table. It made Bert think.

There was something missing from his view of things. It wasn't right these people should live such a restricted life; and though he couldn't turn his thinking away from the new world of possibility he believed was coming, though he couldn't rest on the rotten branch of the old order, the huddled poverty of the streets he grew up in, opportunity being closed down like a manhole cover dropping into place, life being little more than a clinging survival; he looked at Tom Craxton and thought it a tragedy he'd been denied.

Little by little, Bert became almost part of the family. He could knock on the front door and walk in and no-one blenched. The little child in him, the neglected, frozen little boy who'd learned not to cry when he was left alone in the house while his grandparents went to the pub, the back-alley tough who'd found a way to blot out the mean taunts of his playmates, came alive in the Craxton house. Even their rows made him feel at home. The territory between Elsie, Eddie and Jimmy was peaceful. They had a way of keeping space between them so any potential dispute dispersed like smoke in the wind. The three of them stayed on good terms with their father too. Though some of his ways infuriated Elsie – he would spit into the fire when his pipe made him cough which she thought disgusting, and he never poured milk into a jug or cup but drank straight from the bottle – she knew how to make some quick remark and disappear before the fuse could burn. When Henry came home, though, there was sure to be an explosion.

"Don't put your feet on't table!" Elsie would say.

"Why not? Is Queen Mother expected?"

"We've to eat off that tablecloth. We don't want stink of your socks in our nostrils."

"My socks don't stink. I wash 'em once a year."

"You think you're funny but I don't. You bring this house down with your slovenly ways."

"Do I?"

"You do."

"And what d'you know about owt? Eh? Tha's never left threshold o' this house. Tha knows nowt o't world."

"And you think you know summat. If that's what you learn in't th'army, God help t'country."

Tom Craxton, hearing the disturbance and hating friction in his household would come through and seeing at once the cause would say:

"Get tha' feet off my table, Henry."

"I'm doin' no harm, father."

And before the young man had time to look up the big, hard palm would swing and clip him swiftly across the back of his head.

"When tha's under my roof tha does as I asks."

Big as he was, Henry would never physically challenge his father. Though he hated being corrected and was humiliated at being struck, he a soldier, fully grown, a man who handled rifles and was trained to kill, he submitted to his father's authority because he knew he was in the wrong. It was his house and he could ask for good behaviour. Henry would pull on his shoes and tramp out, slamming the door like a petulant child and Elsie would go satisfied about her little domestic tasks, justified as if the Lord himself had chastised her erring brother. As for Tom, he hated these moments. Henry was like a paralysed leg he must drag through the years. Why was he so different from his other lads? Where did it come from, his defiance and ugly behaviour? It broke the old man's heart and he worried for his son's future. Bert was party to all this and loved it. It was a real family. In his own, there were no rows just fists. And he had no sister or brother he could quibble with like Elsie with Henry. It must be nice, he thought, to be so close to one of your own to be able to spar like that and still love one another.

Often, chatting to Harry Clow, because Bert liked to talk and saw no reason why work should exclude friendliness, Elsie and her family would be mentioned.

"Courtin' then, are you?" said the older man with a sly glance.

"You might say so," said Bert.

But he knew he'd given himself away. Harry was mocking him. Married with two teenage children he never spoke of his wife except disobligingly but his mouth was full of sewer water about the girls in the office.

"Get that Brenda Marsden's legs wrapped round you, you wouldn't get off for a fortnight."

Bert knew he'd had an affair with Joan Spicer, a dumpy little nineteen year-old from Greenlands estate, the huge stain of council houses two miles out of town; it was one of those post-war estates thrown up in the optimistic belief that if you give people a house with three bedrooms and a bathroom, it doesn't matter if there's no shop, no pub, no cinema, no café, no swimming pool, no park; nor does it matter who their neighbours are. If the place becomes a last resort for economic and social casualties, who cares? The council was doing its bit by providing houses. Shouldn't people be grateful? Before the turning of the decade notoriety was hanging over the eyesore like a bad smell over a rubbish dump and the Tories on the council together with the homeowners of salubrious Fulwood, Broughton and Penwortham, not to mention the wealthy with their two acre gardens in Woodplumpton or Chipping or Treales were regretting the folly of spending public money to house the feckless oiks who were never grateful for anything and scientifically proven to be beyond improvement. Joan was one of those girls given a perfunctory education because she was female and working-class who took the first job she could on leaving school and saw her future in finding a husband who could earn a bit. Because she saw finding a man as the route to happiness, she was excessively conscious of her sex and was flattered when Harry, a man with position, a salary and car ogled her and put his arm round her shoulder while she worked.

"Goes like a fuckin' bunny," Clow said to Bert. "She'd drop 'em for sixpence."

This sexually overwrought atmosphere played badly on Bert's nerves. Maybe he should be a bit more like Harry. Should he make an approach to Joan? After all, if she was willing for a married man with a bald head, a paunch and bad breath, why shouldn't she do the same for him? But his attraction to her was nothing more than the low need to overcome tension. It had a brutality to it which attracted and repelled him. Little Joan with her bulging breasts and her broad backside became his masturbatory fantasy; but when he talked to her, the brutal desire ebbed and he liked her. She was obviously intelligent. Given a chance she could make something of herself. Like him, she had the burden of a bad start in life. One lunchtime he walked with her to the *Farrier's Arms*, the little pub on the corner where the men from the dye works came for pie and chips. They sat in the snug with a plate of cheese and tomato sandwiches. Bert sipped the pale, bitter beer and thought how nice it would be to disappear for the afternoon. It was odd, this truant wish given his drive to get on; but it was true, some impulse arose in him to throw it all aside and take life as it comes. Joan lit a cigarette.

"Want one?"

"Don't smoke."

"No vices?"

"None I can tell you about."

"I'm broadminded," she laughed.

"Have to be in this life."

"Aye, especially if you live on Greenlands."

"Bit rough, eh?"

"Aye, but it's not that. Folk are all right. Nowt to do and if you come from there you're lucky to find a good job."

"You did."

"Mr Clow interviewed me," and she gave him a mischievous look.

"You shouldn't stay though, Joan. You're a bright girl."

"Oh aye, top of the form me."

"You can get on if you try."

"That what you gonna do?"

"If I can."

"I like a man with ambition."

He looked at her questioningly and she roared with laughter.

"Cropper's is too small. No scope there. I'm going to qualify as an accountant. Get myself a nice house in Broughton."

"Well, you'll need a nice wife to share it."

"I've one in mind."

"Anyone I know?"

"Doubt it."

"Engaged?"

"No."

"Just courtin'?"

"Aye."

Being asked for the second time shed a stark light on his thoughts of Elsie. There was nothing between them but friendship. They'd never been anywhere as a couple. He'd never held her hand. He realised how naïve this must seem to someone like Joan. He thought of Elsie

51

as a potential future wife, yet he'd done nothing to move the shoreline friendship out into the deep waves of passion. They were paddling with their shoes off and the warm, foamy water caressing their ankles. Yet he knew the peril of asking her to swim for her life. What he had was good. He was happy helping her home with the shopping, chatting, sitting in the kitchen with her father as he smoked his pipe and listened to the football on the radio.

Was he just trying to find a substitute family or was he really going to lift Elsie from the security of her island and show her the bigger land she would have to swim for? And if she said no? If she decided to spend her life looking after her mother and then her aging father and if her will to self-sacrifice meant that her own life never really began?

There were always girls like Joan. She wasn't unpleasant or malicious. He could have happily spent time with her. Could he even think of marrying such a girl? It might be all right. She was as easy-going as a cat. It would have been hard to imagine falling out with a girl like Joan. Yet it would have been just as hard imagining a passionate love for her. It was as if there was some extra dimension to Elsie, as if her mind included a room absent from Joan's and which he must explore. It puzzled him because Joan was appealing. She was nothing like as pretty as Elsie but she was uncomplicated. Life with a girl like her would be straightforward; but it was the lack of complexity which put him off. It was the difference between following a boot-familiar path up a friendly hillside or finding your own life-saving finger-jams on the sheer face of a slippery crag. There had to be some difficulty for it to be worth undertaking. There had to be the possibility of falling into the void, of risking everything to arrive at a summit your own way, through your own power.

Joan was looking at him as she drew on her cigarette. He wished she was the kind of girl who roused him to passion, because a packet of fags, a night out with the girls, a gin and tonic, Al Read on the radio, a song by Doris Day and a week in Filey in the summer were enough to make her happy. Something about Elsie scared him. They weren't ordinary people, her family. They were hard-up and had no airs and graces, but they were rare as Tories in the Rhondda as far as their character went. A girl like Joan would be easy to live with, but she'd just as easily get into bed with the bloke next door if it took her fancy. He knew she'd be forgiving if he got into bed with the woman next door. She'd draw on her fag and drink her gin and shrug her shoulders and that was comforting. Joan was all live and let live, but behind that there was a terrible failure; a refusal to abstract from the average and see the exceptional. The exceptional was worth fighting for. A rubbing along and getting-by marriage to a girl like Joan might be what most men settled for, but he wanted something which asked more of him and which by asking more returned more.

"What's her name?"

"Elsie."

"What's she do?"

"Looks after her mother. She's bed-ridden with arthritis."

Joan stubbed out her cigarette and blew a great cloud of grey smoke in front of her.

"I'm sorry to hear that."

"These things happen."

"They do." Joan paused. "Is there no-one else to take care of her?"

"No. Well, I think it's fallen to her because she's the youngest and a woman.

"She wants to watch it. She'll be on the shelf."

"Not if I can help it."

Joan laughed and Bert was glad he was with her. It was good to simply sit and talk with a girl like her. She was fine, even if she was having sex with Harry. She was essentially good and kind. Her vulgarity was what it was, but she wouldn't have deliberately done harm to anyone.

He stopped thinking about Joan as a possible sexual outlet; she was a friend. She deserved to be treated properly. He eliminated all thought of her as an easy conquest, though she made it clear she might well be willing. What began to take over Bert's mind was how he could make Elsie his girl-friend, how they could be *courtin'*, as folk put it.

He thought about the problem for weeks and finally decided the best was to invite her to something which would flow naturally from what had happened between them so far. One day he saw a poster. The church had a dramatic society and they were performing *Rutherford and Son.* He could ask her without asking her, almost.

"I see," he said to her when they were sitting in the kitchen having a cup of tea, "there's a play on at the church this week."

"Is there?"

"I thought it might be nice to go along."

"I'm sure it would."

"We could go on Friday."

"Who?"

"Us."

"Who's us?"

"You and me."

"Just the two of us?"

"Why not?"

"Who'll look after mi mother?"

"It's only a couple of hours."

"She can't be left alone."

"Your dad'll be here."

"He'll've worked all day."

"He only has to sit with her."

"You think that's all I do?"

"No. But for two hours or so. She might be asleep."

"She might not."

"Your dad'd cope."

"He might fall asleep himself. He often does."

"We could ask Eddie."

"Eddie?"

"He might not mind. He likes a chat to your dad."

"He's got his own family to look after."

"I know. But he might be happy to come here for the evening. He might like to do us a favour."

"I don't see why."

"You could ask him."

"I could but I won't."

"Why not?"

"I don't like to impose."

"It's not imposing. People like to be asked."

"Do they?"

"Yes. I'm sure Eddie wouldn't mind one bit."

"Well, I don't need to ask him 'cause I'm not going."

"It might be a good night."

"I'm sure it will for them as can go."

"You can go if you want."

"Some people have a proper sense of responsibility."

"It's not irresponsible to give yourself a night off now and again."

"You may not think so."

"I don't. I think life's for enjoying."

"Good for you."

"The change'd be good for you."

"I don't need a change."

"Shall I ask your dad if he doesn't mind?"

"You'll do no such thing."

But he did. A mood of devilment came over him which made him laugh at the risk. He could square it with her father then present her with the tickets.

"Elsie and me were thinking of going to see the play at church on Friday."

"Aye," said the old man, puffing.

"We don't want to impose on you, but we'd be out only a few hours."

Tom took the pipe from his mouth.

"What makes tha think tha's imposin'?"

"Elsie didn't want me to ask you."

"Aye?"

"She's very protective of her mother."

Tom looked at him from those blue eyes which seemed to hold all the hurt of the world in their watery gaze. They always seemed on the verge of tears, as if the old man were responsible for all the stupidity and cruelty of humanity. Bert wondered if he'd made a terrible blunder and spoiled relations between Elsie and her father but the old man looked away to the window, as if in physical distance he could find some salve for his hurting mind. He knocked his pipe into the ashtray balanced on the arm of his chair, took his tobacco pouch from the pocket of his blue cardigan and began to stuff the tender, aromatic strands into the little bowl.

"Tha guzz if tha wantsa. Tell our Elsie tha's my permission."

He put away the pouch, took out his sliver cigarette lighter and made the tobacco smoulder.

"Thanks, Mr Craxton."

Tom puffed and didn't look at him. Bert sat for a few minutes as the old man filled the air with smoke and then put on his glasses, took up the book from his lap and went on with the reading Bert had interrupted, as if he wasn't there. Bert realised he couldn't call Elsie's father Tom. He wondered why. He knew other blokes who used first names with their in-laws, but somehow he liked it that there was a taut little distance of age and respect between them. It was reassuring.

"I'd better be getting along," said Bert.

Tom nodded without looking at him or taking his eyes from the book. Had he offended him? As he drove to his evening class, Bert ran the little scene over in his head perturbed and bewildered by what might have been going on in Tom's mind. He settled on a comforting idea: Tom had realised Elsie was sacrificing herself to her mother's incapacity; he felt guilty; he knew she deserved her own life and he was glad Bert was going to open up possibilities for her. As he got out of his car, Mrs Bruzzese was going through the school gate, tall, slow and seductive.

The next day, Bert presented Elsie with the tickets.

"Who are these for?"

"Us."

"I've told you I can't go."

"You can."

"What are you talkin' about?"

"I asked your dad."

Bert was standing a foot away, smiling. He imagined she'd be grateful, that the notion of having the chance to live in her own right would at last settle on her mind; she would warm to him; he was the man who had broken the grip of her mother's dependency and henceforth they would be able to share time and activities together which would allow the long withheld need for autonomy to flourish, like a withering plant moved to rich ground, light and rain; they would be seen together around town and soon everyone would know they were *courtin'*; she would link her arm in his as they strode down Fishergate or Cheapside and he would be proud to have the prettiest girl in town beside him; they would go to the pictures to see Rock Hudson or Judy Garland and their poor, small town lives, held as tightly by the facts of having to earn a living and get by as a barrel by its iron bands, would take on some of the glamour of the Hollywood stars, as if the huge gulf between rich and poor, between powerful and impotent could be breached by the tawdry products of a dream industry whose very wealth and power rested on the widening of that gulf; they would go dancing at Hopkirk's Dance Hall where big bands made up of local musicians did their best to reproduce the sounds of Glenn Miller or Duke Ellington and men in smart, dark suits and shining, smoothed-soled dancing shoes swept women in elegant dresses, some of them with hooped skirts so wide they couldn't fit in any wardrobe, around the sprung floor in a charming competition of grace, poise, skill and style; they would walk hand in hand in the park, by the river, on Sunday and stop to sit on one of the little wooden, slatted green chairs to listen to the brass ensemble on the band stand, eat a cornet or a choc ice and laugh at the jaunty, inconsequential music; and coming home from a concert by the Philharmonic or the Halle to which he would take her to improve her mind, they would kiss in the back alley where the rats scuttled on bin days before entering by the front door to stand before her father and announce their engagement.

"You did what?" she said, recoiling.

"He was quite happy," he said, still smiling; but her expression, as shocked and severe as if he had tried to rape her or announced he was about to be tried for bank robbery, disturbed his heart and put him in that impossibly tight space between flight and holding your ground where so many bad decisions are made.

"I told you not to."

"I know, I know. But he didn't twitch a muscle. He gave us permission."

"Us?"

"Yes."

"Why do you keep saying us as if we belong to one another?"

"I'm not saying that."

"I told you not to ask him. What did you expect him to say? You put him in an impossible position."

"How?"

"He couldn't say no could he?"

"Why not?"

"Oh, are you so stupid?"

"We can go out. You can go out for once. You need to get away from your mother now and again."

"What do you know?"

"It's a couple of hours. Your dad is happy to…."

"You don't know what my dad's happy with. This is my family. You don't have a family. Your family are drunks and thugs. Go back to your own family and leave mine alone."

"It's just a play, Elsie. At church, after all. There's no need for…"

"Don't tell me what there's a need for. Get out of my house. You've no business, no business at all. Get out and don't come back."

She threw the tickets at him. He looked down at them on the cold, flagged floor. He wondered if he should pick them up. He'd paid for them after all. Maybe he could get his money back. Maybe he could find someone else to go with. But he looked up at her and the rejection in her demeanour, the dismissal of him, the exclusion from this house which had become his home reawakened all his feelings of being an outsider, of being forever illegitimate, the poor bastard brought into the world between the legs of a wild, irresponsible, thoughtless girl who had given herself in who knows what circumstances to who knows who, turned his feelings ugly.

At that moment the prettiness which had charmed him by its unselfconsciousness had disappeared. All he could see was her expression. She was hatred, resentment and rejection. He turned and left. He would have liked to talk to someone, but he was alone. Aunt Alice was kind in her way. But he couldn't demean himself by telling her about his aching heart. There was no-one. He was utterly alone in the world. In this town of tens of thousands of people there wasn't one he had real contact with. He had been abandoned by his mother as a baby and abandonment was his fate. He could have done some damage. He walked into town because he couldn't settle. The shops were closed and the streets were almost empty. He could have gone into a pub but he hated drink. Getting drunk was no answer. It was the stupidity and the failure of his grandparents. They let themselves down. Life asked them to live and they ran away. Was Elsie the same? Did she just run away to a different addiction? It was all too difficult. Life was impossible to understand. Even the simplest little conversation hid such complexity the best minds would be minced by it.

No, it wasn't comprehension that was missing but sympathy. Love. He said the word to himself. Who loved him? It was true. Not a soul. Who'd ever loved him? He'd come into the world unloved and he remained unloved. People who are loved understand it no more than people who aren't. All the theories under the sun made no difference. There it was. Some were lucky and were born and grew in the sunny garden of love and others like him were left to do what they could in the dark, cold back-alley of neglect.

BULL'S EYE

That night he dreamed a beautiful woman with no breasts and huge muscles in her arms and legs came at him with a fearsome knife. He woke in a sweat. He felt utterly distant from himself. He went to work and did what he had to do but it was as if someone else was adding the figures and answering the phone. In this state he went on for many days, till he woke one morning with a clear head, a quiet heart and a new resolution. He had to get on. He must make money. Lots of money. That was something he could do whether he was loved or not. He had to work harder and harder till he was rich. Then people might not love him but they would have to respect him, or at least his money. He put on his suit and went to work. That morning Joan seemed particularly desirable.

But the following evening Eddie turned up. He'd changed out of his working clothes and displayed that awkward smartness working men often have when they spruce themselves.

"We'd like you to come to tea a Sunday," he said.

"That's very nice of you."

"At mi father's like."

"I thought I was *persona non grata* there," he laughed.

"Aye, well. Our Elsie's a funny bugger. But you're invited if you fancy."

"Is it an occasion?"

"No. Get together and no more."

Bert took along a box of cakes. He assumed there'd be himself, Elsie, Eddie and his wife and Tom, so he bought six from Baxter's, reputed to be the best baker's in town. The assistant tied a red ribbon around the box and finished off with a large bow. When he handed the package to Elsie she said:

"You shouldn't have."

"I wanted to," he said.

"Wasting your money," she said and turned on her heels.

All the same, she set the cakes on her mother's best stand and put them in the middle of the little table. As they ate sliced ham with lettuce, boiled eggs and tomatoes, Bert was tempted to recount the little tale of the cakes Henry had told him, but he judged it would probably be taken badly by Elsie so the meal proceeded to the timpani of the cutlery against the plates and polite exchanges about the weather, the quality of the meat and the enduring difficulties of rationing.

"Still," said Bert, wanting to raise the tone and temperature a little, "Attlee is moving things in the right direction. Opportunities are opening up for people like us."

"It's not a matter of opportunities," said Elsie.

"What then?" said Bert.

"Equality."

"I'm all for it," said Bert taking another triangle of buttered, white bread. "Break down the class barriers and let everyone have a share of the good life."

"Aye," said Eddie, "there's much yet to be reformed."

"There is," said Bert, "but we've got the NHS and the railways, coal and steel in public ownership. That's a good start."

"Give people too much, it makes em lazy," said April, Eddie's wife.

Bert noticed Elsie blench and wondered if she was going to take off in a rant against her sister-in-law, but she merely blushed a little and went on eating.

"Got to get the balance right," said Bert. "Let business do what it does well and where it fails, well, there has to be public intervention."

"Aye, that's about it," said Eddie.

"I've heard of people going to their doctor for a toothbrush on prescription," said April. "You can't change human nature. People are greedy and selfish."

"Not all people," said Elsie.

"What d'you mean by that?" replied April.

"Them as is, allus blames others," said Elsie, falling into her broadest accent as she always did when she was roused to anger.

"You can't expect people to run businesses to see all they make taken in tax to keep folk who won't do a hand's turn," said April.

"Like me mother?" said Elsie.

"I don't say that," retorted April.

"The point is," said Bert, "human nature does change." He was thinking of something he'd read in Karl Marx and which had made an impression on his mind. Not that he thought of himself as any kind of Marxist. He was a magpie and whatever gleamed on a page, whether it was in Adam Smith, Charles Darwin, T.S.Eliot or Tom Paine, he seized on and made it his own; it was no longer part of Marx's system of thought, or Eliot's poetry, or Darwin's meticulous science, it belonged to the exciting swirl of ideas in his own mind: *A capitalist is not a capitalist because he's a commander in industry; he's a commander in industry because he's a capitalist; command in industry is an attribute of capital, just as in feudal times, command in war and a seat on the judge's bench were attributes of landed property.* He loved the logic behind such formulations. It seemed to him to shed light on a little mystery and to be such a glowing example of human intelligence that it raised his spirits and made him want to discuss it with anyone who would engage. He knew there was no point in reciting the quotation, but the idea it contained he was eager to get across. "Supposing," he said, "we'd all been born five hundred years ago. Just as we are, if that was possible. We wouldn't have the ideas we have today. We wouldn't think the same or behave the same. We'd be different people because our conditions would be different. We'd believe in the Divine Right of Kings and the ducking stool and even that the earth is the centre of the universe. So human nature does change. In fact, it never stands still. It changes every minute."

He'd expected everyone to be as excited by the idea as he was, but they went on eating as if he'd said it was slightly chillier than yesterday. No-one looked at him. No-one wanted to engage in debate.

"Some things never change," said Elsie.

"For example?" said Bert, hoping desperately she'd give him the chance to get a discussion going.

"The battle between good and evil."

"That's true enough," said Eddie.

Bert didn't like that religious view. Good and evil as absolutes

seemed to him absurd. Hitler was evil, but what did it mean? Perhaps
Elsie thought the devil had taken him over or some such nonsense;
but it seemed to Bert the explanation was more mundane. Hitler
couldn't have put his evil into practice without the power of the State
and if the State had been democratic, he could have been removed
before he got a chance. It wasn't a matter of good and evil as eternally oppositional forces, it was a question of law and politics. In any
case, when he thought of Hitler he concluded he was more of a
madman than a force of evil. A neglected and abused child, he'd
turned out badly. Wasn't that what it was about?

But he too was neglected and abused. Was he also mad and evil? He
might have been if conditions had been a bit worse. After all, he got
a chance at school, Aunt Alice took him in, he lived in a democracy
and the experience of war made him despise violence. It was all impossibly detailed. The battle of good and evil was too broad, too
sweeping. And who defined what was good or evil anyway? According to the church, sex before marriage was evil, or at least a sin, but
Bert couldn't believe that. What harm were couples doing by getting
into bed together? What kind of god got angry about that? A god of
power. A god who was useful to the powerful.

And Bert couldn't think of himself as good. He had a desire to be,
that was certain; he enjoyed behaving well; but he was made up of
too many impulses to be able to refine something he could call good
and say it was what defined him. The very idea that some people
were good and some evil disturbed and upset him. He was the kind
of bloke, after all, people were quick to hang a sign on. Were his
grandparents evil? Was it evil to leave a hungry child in a stinking
home while you went to the pub? It was evil enough. But he couldn't
think even of his grandfather as an evil man and only an evil man.
There was a good side to him. He was capable of small acts of kindness and patience. There was something wrong in him. He couldn't
control himself, but to call that evil, as though it was a force beyond
him which invaded him and meant he must be condemned seemed to
Bert impossibly cruel. He needed help. Maybe he needed a psychiatrist. Or perhaps there was a fault in his brain.

Time and again when Bert tried to think things through his intelligence quickly ran aground. There were no simple explanations. It
was all impossibly complicated. Good and evil. Bert looked at Tom
who was slowly eating ham and bread. He was a good man. Bert

would admit that. He was rare. Maybe he was the only man Bert had ever met who he'd call good without any reservation. He was taciturn, moody, grumpy and he'd leathered his sons when they were young, but all the same Bert knew he was kind, honest and would never have caused hurt if he could avoid it. And Elsie? She was sitting very upright loading little packages of salad onto her fork. He noticed how she enjoyed her food. She had a real sensual delight in eating. Did she think herself good? Did she dismiss people like his father as evil? What did she think of him? One part of him felt he was out of place and another that he wanted more than anything to belong to this family.

"Well, let's hope good wins out," he said.

"God will see to that," said Elsie.

Bert's feeling sagged. The other-worldliness of Elsie's thinking depressed him. He wanted to live. He wanted life here and now, while he was young, while the chance was before him. Yet when he looked at her, her prettiness overcame his ill-feeling. She was life. She was a beautiful young woman and no amount of tosh about god could deny that. Nature had made her thrillingly attractive and if he had to choose between eternal life and kissing those lovely lips, he'd choose the latter without pause. God was a kind of death to his mind while Elsie set his brain alight. She was a potential future. She was warmth, togetherness, happiness, laughter, belonging, security, stability. If he could win her, if he could be in bed with her, if he could marry her and make her pregnant, if they could draw close in the hard, joyous work of raising children, what would all the flummery about god matter?

"And Nye Bevan," said Bert, hoping to raise a laugh.

"Don't blaspheme," said Elsie.

"How is it all to be paid for, that's what I want to know?" said April laying her knife and fork across her plate.

"There's plenty if it's spread round reet," said Tom.

"Aye, there is," said Eddie.

Bert found something he'd read in Shakespeare creeping back into his mind.

"*Distribution should undo excess and each man have enough*," he said. "It's from *King Lear*."

No-one looked at him or made any comment. He felt as if he'd brought pork sausages to a Jewish wedding or offered a bottle of whisky to a Methodist minister.

Elsie cleared the table. They all went into the parlour and she brought through a pot of tea and the stand of cakes. Bert was beginning to feel restless. He wondered if they would sit there for hours, the conversation never getting beyond courtesies; it brought a sense of futility to his mood, the feeling he could never tolerate of things having stalled. He had to be pushing on. The overwhelming need to be making way always troubled him if he felt time was passing too idly. He could waste a few vagrant hours if he could think of the day and see it as productive, but today he'd done nothing. What he was here for was to drive forward his relationship with Elsie. Sitting on the little sofa, squashed beside April who clearly didn't think much of him, he was struck by the thought that this could go on for years. If he didn't force matters he could be sitting here in ten years time, never having even kissed Elsie, let alone discovered if her naked body was as stunning as her face, her eyes, her hands.

The teapot was empty. There was one cake left on the stand.

"Will you have it?" said Elsie to Bert.

"No, no. I'll not be greedy. One's enough."

"I'll wrap it for you. You can take it home."

"No, you keep it. Eddie, can't you eat it?"

"Not me. I'm full as a brewer's keg."

"Your aunt Alice might like it," said Elsie.

She disappeared and came back a few minutes later with the cake in a neat wrapper of greaseproof paper.

"Oh, thanks," said Bert.

There was a silence. Tom was filling his pipe. He looked over at the window.

"Bonny evenin'."

"Aye," said Eddie.

"Tha wants to get out for a walk, Elsie."

"I've kitchen to clean yet," she said.

"Eddie 'll see to it. Won't tha?"

65

"Aye. I'm accustomed," and he smiled broadly.

"I'm not goin out on me own," she protested.

"Bert'll go wi thee. Eh, Bert?" and the old man looked at him with that slow, kind gaze which made him feel at home.

"Of course." He jumped up. "Come on, Elsie. Put your cardigan on, we can go by the river. It's lovely on an evening like this."

She protested all she had to do and the needs of her mother but the others prevailed, so she pulled on her mauve cardigan with all the gravity of a woman going to the gallows and the two of them left the house alone together for the first time.

They walked through Avenham and Miller parks, open spaces close to heart of town endowed by nineteenth century philanthropists. Bert had read about how the place had been a quiet market town before the industrial revolution and the parks by the river always made him think how beautiful it must have been. The mills, the factories, the streets, the chimneys, the smoke, the dust, the filth, the soot, the clatter, the slums, all these had destroyed the gentle sweetness of the natural gift of the area. This was one of the places where the modern world was born. Money had been made here. Lots of money. But it didn't come to the people. It made him sad and angry and puzzled, but all the same he loved being by the water with a sense of openness and the feeling of possibility which seas or river always brought to him. And now he was here with Elsie. This was his chance to formalise his hopes.

She walked beside him, neat and quick. There was surprising strength in her little frame which charmed him. She chatted away in that voluble drift he'd got used to: when she was in the house she would talk and talk to her father or one of her brothers and it was all inconsequential chirping about the things she'd done or seen or what someone had said to her at church or gossip she'd picked up out shopping. He'd asked her if she liked the parks and she'd started talking about the days her dad brought her here or the times she walked out with her school friends and the occasion when a man flashed at them on the path by the belvedere and her mate Jenny who was cocky and afraid of no-one turned on him and gave him a mouthful, calling him *a dirty little wretch* and a *disgusting cockroach who should be locked up for life*. She laughed at the memory. And as they walked she talked as if to create such a stream of words he'd be unable to swim against it.

Her compulsive talking took on a new aspect now it was aimed at him. He'd always thought it was inconsequential. Now it seemed full of meaning. What she said might be trivial but the way she said it was as fatal as light. Its effort to repel attracted him. It seemed to him that behind the defensiveness of the cascade of words lay its opposite. She wanted a silent communion she was afraid of. He was afraid too but he'd grown so used to layering over his fear with an impulse to betterment, a command of the future as complete as the earth's dependence on the sun and the bravado of a backstreet kid whose sharp corners haven't been rounded by years of attention and the daily rubbing up against the love of others, that he hardly knew it.

They stood on the tram bridge watching the water spurt and bounce. They started the steep climb up to Frenchwood and it was here, with trees on either side, hidden from view, the two of them utterly isolated in the universe, he dared to slip his arm round her waist. She didn't recoil or rebuff. She walked on as if it were as natural as moonlight. Bert was lifted on the spurt of pride and amazement; her waist was unspeakably trim and the movement of her hips, as regular as a quiet heartbeat was the voice of life itself. It called to him and he wanted to make good its invitation. As they were about to emerge from the trees he stopped and turned her to him but the kiss he placed on her lips was dry and brief and she walked on quickly so he had to catch up and take her waist in his arm again. All the way home he was asking himself how he should turn this physical contact into a pledge but it wasn't till they were almost at her house that he said:

"I suppose we're courtin' now."

"We might be."

The words sent him reeling, as if he might fall through space itself and into some unknown void where everything human ceased to signify.

"I'd say we are."

"Would you?"

"We could go to the pictures."

"'Appen."

"I'll see what's on, shall I?"

"If you like."

"I'm ready for a cup of tea now."

"I'll have to see to mi mother. Goodnight."

She was gone so quickly he wanted to hammer on the door and put his contract before her. He wanted some definitive statement, as if he were a judge and could insist by the power of law. All the same, he considered the file opened and if he hadn't yet become the advocate of her heart, he was her chosen counsel and he would diligently pursue his brief.

In the months that followed there were several of these little outings: the two of them walking in the park or spending a hour together in town on Saturday afternoon; visits to the pictures to see Clark Gable or Audrey Hepburn and nights at Hopkirk's where he carried off the foxtrot as if his feet had been made for it and waltzed so well, she laughed as they sat down and said:

"I never thought you'd be such a good dancer."

"Why not?"

"I don't know. You don't look like a dancer."

"What does a dancer look like?"

"I don't know. Tall, long legs," and she laughed again.

Their physical intimacy didn't go beyond holding hands, his arm round her waist or a kiss as quick as a wren in a hedge; but Bert felt it wise to be patient. The prize he was seeking was a lifetime of love and mutual support and that was not something to risk by moving too quickly. Always at the back of his mind also was Elsie's mother: the more he thought about it, the more he felt Tom Craxton was wrong to expect his daughter to assume the burden; but what was done was done. The nexus of dependency was established and even if it seemed to him unhealthy and a barrier to Elsie's fulfilment, he had to tread carefully. Her sensibilities were as brittle as dry twigs. On the one hand, he was delighted to be part of a real family and to have the possibility of a pretty and loyal wife; on the other his back-alley desire to throw himself at life, to cast caution aside and take existence by the throat, like a rough heedless boy, made him restless and overwrought.

68

It happened that he was leaving his accountancy class on another rainy evening when Mrs Bruzzese appeared at his side.

"Fancy giving me a lift?" she said.

He looked at her and was amused by the almost neutral but slightly cheeky look on her face.

"Why not?"

"How is the car?" she said as he started the engine and got the wipers working.

"She chugs along," he said.

"Like me."

He laughed.

"I'd say you were in fine fettle. No need of a rebore yet."

As soon as the words were out he realised their ambiguity.

"A rebore?" she said "What's that?"

"The cylinders," he said. "There are four pistons in the engine and they work up and down in cylinders. That's where the fuel ignites. So they get clogged and they need reboring so the engine can run properly."

"Ah," she said. "My cylinder doesn't need reboring. It's a new piston I need."

He laughed and looked at her. She had a little mischievous smile just perceptible at the corner of her mouth.

"How's Gino? I meant to get in touch about going to the footie but I forgot."

"He's fine. He gets what he wants. I'm the one who's frustrated."

The rain was beating down on the windscreen almost as hard as the previous time he'd driven her home. He wondered if she would invite him in and if he should accept. After all, he was *courtin'* now. He ran through his head how Elsie might react. She'd probably refuse to see him again. The idea sparked off a little inward rebellion, like a child told to eat his greens who folds his arms and sulks, feeling that this defiance raises him above parental admonition. Why shouldn't he sit with her and enjoy a cup of tea and a laugh? She created a relaxed atmosphere, so different from that of Elsie's home. Everything about her was sensual. She couldn't put a biscuit in her mouth without making him think of the enticement of her lips.

"But he doesn't stand in your way," said Bert.

"No. Not exactly. Not in principle. But once the theory becomes a reality, well, I'm not so sure."

They arrived outside her charming little house and she invited him in. He sat on the sofa in the cosy living-room where the coal fire had been burning slowly for hours. She made a cup of tea.

"Gino made this cake," she said, setting the tray down "you must try it."

"What is it?" said Bert who relished desserts and exulted in that experience of being indulged which children love so much and which he'd known so little when young.

"Apple ring cake. He claims it's his mother's recipe but I don't believe him."

She cut him a succulent slice and placed it on a little white plate ringed with a silver band. He bit into it with that relish of a man who likes his appetites and sees no reason they shouldn't be satisfied. It was truly a well-made cake. He sat back comfortably. He was warm, the food filled his mouth with pleasant flavours and the promise of satiety. Mrs Bruzzese poured his tea.

He'd worked hard all day and spent two dull hours listening to tedious explanations of tax law. Now he began to relax. It was always easier, he thought, to relax in someone else's house. The same was true at Elsie's: he had no responsibility for the place; he bore no expense, he didn't need to worry about the repairs. Other people's houses were refuges from the severe demands of making a living, of staying solvent, of paying the bills, even of holding relationships together. How nice it would be to live forever in other people's houses. He experienced one of those epiphanies when the current arrangement of life seemed to him absurd and burdensome. Everyone was driven into their little corner. Everyone had their house, their mortgage or rent, their bills for gas and electricity, their rates, their shopping bills, their insurance; everyone lived separated from everyone else by high walls of petty financial responsibility. But if we could all be free of those trivial and ridiculous worries by living in one another's houses, if society were one big house where we could be freed of the irritating burdens of monetary bagatelles by sharing them; wouldn't that be something. He let the idea fill his mind like the moist cake filled his mouth and for a few seconds it was as if he really did belong to a different order and the electric buzz of the need to get on was quietened.

"Is the recipe good?" she said.

"The recipe and its execution. Delicious. You're spoiling me."

"I like to spoil my men," she said.

He threw back his head and laughed once more.

"You sound like you have dozens."

"You don't need a dozen kettles, you just need one that whistles."

"A kettle can boil water whether it whistles or not."

"Yes, but there's no point boiling water if you've no tea to brew."

He enjoyed this oblique banter and he liked Mrs Bruzzese. How different she was from Elsie and her strict, straight ways. She would no doubt have thought the Italian's wife a loose and disreputable woman whose tongue was moved by the devil. Would he mention this encounter to Elsie? No. It would be impossible. She couldn't be made to understand it was just friendliness even if Mrs Bruzzese filled her conversation with sexual whispers. There was nothing to do with a woman like Elsie but keep from her those facts she couldn't accept. It made him wonder if she really was the right woman for him; but the thought of her family, of their honest and principled ways and especially of Elsie's extraordinary beauty reassured him. He would just have to learn to be discreet. What Elsie didn't know wouldn't hurt her; he took refuge in the cliché.

Mrs Bruzzese asked him how things were and he explained he was now *courtin'*, in fact almost engaged.

"Who is your fiancée?" she asked.

"Her name is Elsie Craxton. She lives across the road from me. Looks after her disabled mother."

"Ah, poor girl. Always the girls who get burdened."

"Oh, she takes it in her stride. She's committed to her mother. She's a woman of some principle."

"Well, I would hope so. You wouldn't want to marry an empty-headed woman."

"She should get an education," he said wistfully.

"An educated woman doesn't need a husband," she said.

Bert looked at her in surprise.

"Educated women don't need to be dry spinsters," he said.

"A spinster doesn't have to be dry."

"Education is one thing, marriage another."

"Of course," she said, "but a woman who can earn her own living and make her way in the world doesn't need to depend on a man."

"But men can make their way in the world and they still want to get married."

"Of course they do. They're possessive. They want their exclusive rights."

"So do women."

"Let me tell you a secret. Women want men because they want children."

He laughed. Her ideas came from such odd angles they sparked up amusement and even though he disagreed with her, he enjoyed the little contest. It was a kind of sport. He might have been batting a ball back and forwards over a tennis net, chasing down her returns and congratulating her on her fine passing shots.

"Not all women."

"Let me tell you another secret. Women who don't have children because they can't or because they think they don't want to, end up mothering someone else's children."

"All of them."

"Every one."

Bert thought of his own mother. She was a shadowy presence in his memory. She might have been a neighbour or a distant relative who turns up at Christmas, funerals and christenings. He wondered if she'd decided to have him. He couldn't believe it. Would she have made such a choice and then abandoned him as soon as possible? Surely he was an accident? He imagined he'd been conceived in sordid circumstances. At times he let his imagination run over it. He saw his teenage mother in a dark doorway, her skirts up while his father went about his pleasure. It was curious. Why would she behave in such a way? Of course, her parents were chaotic. She'd been brought up, like him, in booze, filth, foul language, violence, petulance and neglect. Maybe she had sex with men in back alleys because any kind of contact was better than the foul coldness of her parents' love affair with drink and humiliation. Perhaps she thought by getting pregnant she would force a man to stay with her. He might not love her. But any man was almost sure to be better than her father.

Of course, she'd left Bert behind so she could start a real family. He was the outsider. He was shame made flesh. She was a Catholic after all. Like her parents she would run to confession and lie to the priest out of fear of eternity in fire. Had the priest absolved her of her sin in having him? Was he a bit of sin cast out? Was Mrs Bruzzese right: for women the whole business of men and sex was important finally only because they could have children? It was an instinct. But what kind of instinct did his mother have? It was more an instinct to degradation than to motherhood. He couldn't believe it. She wasn't driven by instinct but by culture. She'd been ruined by her parents. Her life was a mess and he was the result of it.

"It's not a very romantic view of women," he said.

"Romance is a male invention. Women are supposed to be bashful about sex. It's a myth. They're rapacious. They're murderously competitive about men because they want children. Women will stop at nothing to get a desirable man into bed."

"That's what makes them romantic. They want their men to be desirable."

"Because they want the good traits of their men to be present in their children. It's not romance, it's survival."

"What happens to the undesirable men?"

"Hardly any man is so hopeless he isn't desirable to someone. And anyway, a woman would have sex with Caliban if it was the only way to get pregnant."

"There's hope for me yet."

He laughed at his own joke. Mrs Bruzzese took a bite of her husband's delicious cake and chewed slowly. She had her legs tucked up in a homely pose on the sofa. Bert watched her as she lifted her cup, finished eating and took a few sips.

73

"I married a desirable man," she said, setting down her cup.

Bert smiled.

"He's tall, good-looking, healthy, strong, intelligent, kind and hard-working."

"You made a good choice."

"Yes. But if I'd been able to see his sperm, I wouldn't have married him."

Bert was shocked. Was she saying he didn't interest her except if he had healthy sperm? It was terrible. It was cold and calculating and he couldn't believe it. He thought she said it out of heartbreak. She wanted a child and the desperation of not being able to get pregnant had twisted her mind. But he couldn't believe she didn't admire and respect her husband.

" Imagine the boot on the other foot," he said. "If you had the defect would you think it fair for him to reject you?"

"Oh yes. But men are different. A man doesn't have children, he can feel the loss but a man doesn't carry a child or give birth. If men were told they could never play football or watch a match, they might know a thousandth of what a woman feels when she can't have a baby."

"But you can have a baby."

"I can."

"Your husband is very generous. You can have a baby and bring it up as your own."

"We can."

Bert drained his tea.

"Problem solved."

"Once I find a man."

"Pubs are full of 'em."

"Would you do it?"

Bert felt he'd been assaulted. He'd taken her hints but he'd never expected her to ask him outright. He didn't want to cause her pain but how could he accept? He was just getting things going with El-sie. It would be a terrible betrayal and if he she found out, the end.

"Me?"

"Why not you?"

"I couldn't. It wouldn't be fair to Elsie."

"She wouldn't know."

"That would be deceitful."

"Of course, but a good deceit."

"But I'd be the child's father."

"Only biologically."

"But I'd know it was mine. You can't forget that."

"Why not?"

"You can't just bring a child into the world and then abandon it."

His own sentence made him think of his mother. Had she forgotten him or was she haunted by his existence? Did she have to make an effort every day to convince herself she was justified? Or maybe it was the easiest thing in the world for her. Perhaps he represented nothing but negativity. Did she murder him in her mind or did she think of him tenderly as a mother's supposed to?

"The child will have a mother and father. A loving home. No-one could want a child more than me."

"I know. But surely there's someone else..."

"Bert," she said, "many men would like to go to bed with me. Men are men, few can resist the offer of satisfaction on a woman's body, Men pay for prostitutes who provide a cold and hurried service. That's how men are. I don't blame them. Nature gave them the impulse. It takes strength of mind to control it. You are hesitating. I knew you would. I like that."

"How did you know?"

"Because you think."

"Do I?"

"Yes."

"How do you know?"

"It's obvious. You see what I'm saying. I'd be happy to have a child who was like you."

Bert was as surprised as if she'd told him she thought he should be Prime Minister. He was so used to assuming people would think badly of him, as if the stink of his childhood was still on his clothes and everywhere he went people recognised him as the product of debased conditions. His determination to get on in life didn't convince him he was an attractive character. It was the first time anyone had said anything truly complimentary about him. Teachers had praised his capacities but he knew they despised him. Even if they felt sorry for him they were repelled. His friends in the RAF enjoyed his company but it didn't mean they admired him. At once the thought of being naked with Mrs Bruzzese became much more appealing. The thought of doing the work of a bull left him feeling diminished but the idea she liked and admired him, that she wanted his sperm because she could imagine loving a child who was like him made him feel simultaneously relaxed and excited.

"But you hardly know me," he said to conceal his delight.

"What you know of a person in five minutes usually turns out to be all you need to know of them for the next twenty years."

"I don't know how it might make me feel."

"You mean you might fall in love with me."

Once more a shock ran through him. Was she right? Would he fall for her? Would his relationship with Elsie be ruined? That was all slowness and delicacy in anticipation but this was the offer of immediate satisfaction. She was attractive in every way. Nothing about her made him turn up his nose.

"Or you with me," he said laughing.

"It's possible. But it doesn't matter. Once I'm pregnant I will love Gino again. I can imagine it's his child. It won't matter. We will have a child, Gino and me. Who cares whose sperm did the job?"

"You're very matter of fact."

"Not at all. I'm utterly passionate about having a child. It's passion that makes a woman practical."

Bert finished his tea thinking that in a few minutes he'd be in his Austin 7 driving home and laughing to himself about this bizarre encounter but Mrs Bruzzese got up, came over and bending to him so the comforting weight of her breasts was visible, paused before she took his hand.

"Come on," she said. "Let me show you."

"What?" he said.

She led him up the narrow stairs into the front bedroom which stretched across the width of the house. It was much bigger than he'd thought. She switched on a bedside lamp with an orange shade. The room was feminine. It was the kind of room he'd never known. In the middle was a big double bed with dark, wooden head and foot boards and a cream, floral bedspread. There was a walnut chest of drawers with her potions and make-up on top and a wardrobe big enough for two. The thick, off-white carpet with a delicate pattern of nodding flowers smelt new. It was the first time he'd been in a room filled with a woman's desire, sensitivity and warmth. Oddly he didn't feel like an intruder. This was the room she shared with her husband yet he felt as at home here as a child in his bedroom. This was what he had always missed. It was a place where the raw facts of intimacy, the brute fact of sex blended with the subtle tenderness and care of love. It was a place made by a woman for a man to feel welcomed and wanted; a place where all the lonely cravings of masculinity could find a refuge.

"What do you think?"

"Lovely," he said.

She moved towards him so she was only a foot distant. As if it was as ordinary as peeling potatoes, she undid the buttons of her blouse hooked it over her shoulders and let it fall. She was looking into his eyes, serious but gentle. When she slid her arms out of her black bra and dropped it to the floor as negligently as a child drops a sweet wrapper, he was overcome by this first close sight of a woman's breasts. They were big and white and the dark nipples stood erect. He'd never known that possible. She unzipped her skirt, stepped out of her underskirt and tossed her knickers towards the laundry basket. The thick black triangle of her hair at the base of her flat white stomach made his heart thud and skip. She pulled back the covers and lay on the bed swaying her bent leg so her crutch was on display. He felt stupid standing in his clothes like he was waiting for a bus.

"Come on," she said and she extended her arm, her red painted nails reaching towards him as if she wanted to weigh his balls in her hand.

He ripped at his shirt like a boy who wants to be first into the swimming pool. She looked at his cock and smiled at his nakedness.

When he climbed on top of her he was astonished at the warmth. For the first time he knew what it was like to be held close by another human being, to feel your own skin blend with theirs, to lose the limits of selfhood. He kissed her violently on the mouth as if he wanted to disappear down her throat. One of her hands was on the back of his neck the other stroked the muscles along his spine. He tangled his fingers in her hair. No thought of Elsie remained in his mind.

The next day, after work, he spotted her carrying two heavy bags along the little hundred yard stretch to her house. Quickly he ran out to meet her.

"Oh, those are heavy," he said. "How far have you carried 'em?"

"Just from't Co-op."

"You're too pretty for such heavy work."

"Don't talk daft."

"It's not daft. You are pretty."

She ignored him, as if he'd said it looked like rain again.

"You're the prettiest woman I know."

"You're the soppiest bloke I know."

He laughed but her face was closed and she went on in that slightly-bent-at-the-shoulders way as if some invisible, imponderable burden weighed on her.

"Shall we go for a walk later."

"I've a lot to do."

"I'll help you."

"I don't need your help, thank you very much."

"It's a nice evening. We should make the best of it."

"You make the best of it if you like."

He sat at the table in the kitchen as she laboured at unpacking and putting away the shopping. He knew if he tried to help she would rebuff him. He was irritated by her resistance but he felt he knew her mind better than she did. Wasn't it true, after all, that other people always know our minds better than we do? He thought of Mrs Bruzzese's compliments. The spoken one had lifted him but the compliment of intimacy had transformed him. It was true, she knew him better than he knew himself. She saw something in him he'd never imagined he possessed. It was amazing. It was utterly amazing how another person's small act of kindness could have such a huge effect. Just as the same was true of thoughtlessness or cruelty. All those years, as a child, he'd lived with people who were almost incapable of kindness. He realised his mind had been made by them. But it wasn't final. It was incredible but true: your mind could be remade by new circumstances.

He knew he'd been right all along to fight and strive for a better life. The worst thing was to give in to circumstance. It struck him that's what people did. Perhaps it was Elsie's shortcoming. She accepted. As if the brick-coloured ugliness of these little streets was meant to be. As if at the start of time it was ordained that Elsie Craxton should live a narrow life in a little terrace house in a dull town. Bert couldn't accept such an idea. He'd discovered for himself how his mind could be transformed. That was worth straining for. Circumstances existed to be subverted. It always struck him that people went along with the hard, grey, unremitting joylessness of their streets and back-alleys when with a little imagination and cheek they could transform them. Why didn't they get together and put hanging baskets by the front doors? Why didn't they plant clematis in their back yards? Why didn't they make their streets blaze with colour and life in spring and summer? In the suburbs, June, July and August were months when the gardens were rich with green life. But here the brick, concrete and asphalt endured season after season. It was as if some rule were imposed: as if some unseen authority forbade that the hard-up folk in the poor streets should have any freshness and scent in their lives; as if the pleasure of grass and flowers and hedges and the lovely softening influence of plants, bushes and trees must be reserved for people with money.

The idea maddened him. People shouldn't accept that. They should rebel into beauty, joy and happiness. What did it cost, after all? Lots of blokes smoked and drank. What they spent on fags and beer could easily make these little streets gay and jaunty. But there was some horrible spirit of submission abroad which made people accept; as if to plant a rambling rose at the door of a terrace house was an offence against creation. He could see it in Elsie. Yes, she did submit. She did live her life as if it was given that it must be lived this way. But that was only because she lacked education and experience. He could show her. He could open her up to some of the things he'd seen. It wasn't much, he knew. But he'd read a bit of poetry and philosophy and science and novels; he'd listened to Bach and Haydn and Mozart and Beethoven as well as Buddy Bolden and Louis Armstrong; he'd been to the theatre and seen Ibsen and Chekov and Sheridan and Shaw; and he'd been to Egypt and Italy and he knew the world was various and the worst thing you could do was to live as if it was uniform.

"Shall we go to the pictures at the weekend?" he said.

"Depends."

"On what?"

"If I can get away."

"You must."

"Must I?"

"Yes."

"Why?"

"For your own sake. To open up to life a bit more."

"My life's here, doin' what I have to do."

"How do you know what you have to do?"

"Don't talk soft."

"It's a hard thing to know."

"You talk nonsense. I know what I have to do."

"You must have a life other than looking after your mother."

She looked at him sharply.

"Why must I?"

"Because it would be a waste otherwise. A waste of life. You're young, pretty, intelligent. Your life should be fulfilled. It would be a crime for it not to be."

"It'd be a crime to neglect my mother."

"Aye, but you can look after her and yourself too. You don't have to be a martyr."

"I'm not a martyr. I do it because I want to."

"And because it's expected of you."

"By who?"

"Your dad. Your family."

"They've a right to expect it."

"Have they?"

"Should I abandon me own mother?"

"You've three brothers. Why should the burden fall to you?"

"Jimmy and Eddie have their own families and Henry's in the forces. I'm here."

"Yes, but you should have your own family too."

"'Appen. Someday."

"Someday is now. Don't postpone starting your life or it'll be over before it's begun."

"I don't think like you. I put my duty first."

"How do you know what your duty is?"

"I just know!" she said petulantly and seeing he'd touched the aching tooth of her uncertainty he wondered if he should stop; but at the same time he thought it was right to go on, like a man cutting glass who senses it might crack or shatter but continues with his stroke in the hope it will split along his straight line.

"Your mother's at the end of her life. You're at the start of yours. She wouldn't want you to sacrifice yourself for her, would she?"

"How do you know she's at the end of her life? She might go on for years."

She was looking at him as if he'd said they should bring her suffering to an end.

"Maybe she will but they'll be years of decline and pain and life that is hardly life at all. It's right to care for her. It's right to make sure she's as happy as she can be. But it's right to look after yourself too."

"That's a selfish idea," she said putting a blue bag of flour into the cupboard and slamming the door.

"I don't see why."

"Well I do."

"If you were in your mother's position would you want your daughter to give up her life?"

"I don't have a daughter."

"Someday you might."

"Someday I'll deal with it if I do."

"Of course you will, you're practical."

Over many weeks this theme was taken up. At the same time, Bert was hoping to be able to get into bed with Mrs Bruzzese again. Her husband wasn't always out when she got back from her night class. It would have been difficult to explain his presence on any other night. The days were sucked up in a whirl of work. He was impatient. Like all young men after their first taste of passion, he was eager to repeat it. Mrs Bruzzese was a luscious, welcoming woman. There was no harm in it. On the contrary, there was a lot of good. But almost two months after their encounter she smiled widely at him as, at the end of their class, they walked down the echoing corridor which smelt of disinfectant:

"Bullseye," she said.

"What?"

"I think I'm pregnant."

"How do you know?" the stupid question came from his disappointment, almost his despair.

She looked at him indulgently, like a mother whose son has asked some question of extraordinary naivety.

"The usual way."

"Are you sure?"

"No. But it's very likely. I'm never late."

"Well, good news."

"Very."

"Have you told Gino?"

"No. I'll get it confirmed first."

"Will you tell him it's me?"

They paused at the double doors. Now the possibility had become a fact Bert felt the weight of his action. How would Gino respond? It was all very well imagining he'd be happy, thinking she'd be able to persuade him it was all for the best, expecting him to smile and hold out his strong, warm hand to the man who had seduced his wife. But what if the reality drove him mad? What if it made him violent? What if his Italian blood rose like a river in spate and washed away all the flimsy defences of social nicety? What if he turned up at Aunt Alice's his face dark with hatred and humiliation and his fists as tight as a vice? And then the mere fact of him being in the know was a humiliation. She was going to tell him it was a matter of instrumentality. She'd needed his sperm. Now it was done. But most of all it was lost, the sweet anticipation of watching her take off her clothes, the warm joy of her skin against his, the liquefying embrace of her wet vagina.

Mrs Bruzzese sensed his trouble.

"Don't worry. It's between me and Gino now. I will handle him."

"That's good. But....."

She looked at him with gratitude, indulgence and gladness.

"What?"

"Can I give you a lift?"

"It's not raining."

"All the same."

"Thank you, but I think it's better if I catch the bus."

For the few days that followed, Bert couldn't settle. He worked furiously all day hoping he would collapse into sleep as soon as he got home; but his mind was running like a lathe. The same ideas pounded his consciousness remorselessly. His desire for Mrs Bruzzese was as sharp as a thorn and it pricked and scratched him at every turn. Somehow he'd imagined his arrangement with her would go on for months. Why hadn't it occurred to him that she might fall pregnant quickly? Had he thought that it always takes dozens or hundreds of times before the sperm do their job? No, he hadn't thought about it at all. That was his fault. He should have driven a harder bargain; but that idea repelled him; to agree to make her pregnant only if she accepted he could have sex with her as long as he wanted or needed was despicable; and what good would it be to make love to her if she didn't want him to, if she was accepting only out of desperation? No, he'd made a fool of himself. He'd allowed himself to be used. She'd got what she wanted and he was as far from the fulfilment of his needs and desires as a man adrift after a shipwreck.

He was shipwrecked. His only possibility of security and safety was Elsie. He wanted to run to her and take her in his arms. In his worst moments he wanted to confess to her, beg her forgiveness and propose. Yet he knew he must continue his slow campaign. He wanted with Elsie the warm mutual abandon he'd found with Mrs Bruzzese. He wanted to smash all the petty road blocks to her heart and her body and drive on to intimacy, love, marriage and children. He was trapped. His only chance with Elsie was to patiently wait for the right cards to come into his hands. He could no more rush to his conclusion than a poker player could determine what he would be dealt. Yet his experience with Mrs Bruzzese had taught him that the delay served no purpose. Elsie was coming to depend on him though she didn't know it. She was thinking of him as her man though she would never have had admitted it. She would have been psychotically jealous if he'd taken up with another woman, though she would never have acknowledged it. He had to find a way of opening her up to herself.

`Elsie's best friend was Maggie Nightingale. They'd grown up a few doors from one another and in the less burdened years before Mrs Craxton had been confined to bed, played happily in the streets in that joy of forgetfulness which is the bliss of friendship. Once Elsie had her mother to look after day after day, they saw one another less, but Maggie was still a great source of ease. She worked as a seamstress and Elsie envied her the simple freedom of going out of the door every morning to exert a skill and earn money.

Bert had met her once or twice when she'd come to the house while he was there. She had a boyfriend, Max, a tall, thin quiet man who sat on a straight-backed chair in the corner, his spider legs threatening to reach from one side of the room to the other. Like Bert he'd served in the RAF and sported a little officer's moustache, though coming from the working-class he'd no opportunity to learn to fly. He was one of those people who speak only when someone prods them and who let others talk, as if they have some terrible secret about their inner life they risk giving away in the most banal conversation. He was a perfect foil for the voluble Maggie but Bert wondered what made her like him. He seemed a blank. He was a postman and Bert knew he would do the job till he retired. He couldn't understand that. His own restless desire for advancement and change was so natural, the willingness to accept an allotted role and to stay in it decade after decade seemed to him a defeat.

"Maggie's getting married," Elsie said to him one day.

"That's sudden."

"Aye, well, needs must."

"Oh, I see."

"Say nowt."

"I won't blab." He paused. "Turn up for the books, though."

"Can 'appen to anyone."

Bert was about to reply that it couldn't happen to her, but stayed his tongue. All the same, it set his mind working. Maggie was a Methodist. The two of them sat side by side in the stiff-backed pews every week. Perhaps she wasn't as ice-rigid as Elsie: she took a drink now and again; but she'd been raised in the demanding doctrine and nonetheless had found her way into bed with Max-the-lamppost who could hardly have charmed her with mellifluous love-talk.

He took a bite of the scone Elsie had baked and buttered. He tried to imagine Maggie and Max naked and entwined. It was a laughable scene, but then the thought of other people's intimacy always was funny. From the outside, sex was either gross or hilarious. Like drunkenness, you had to be within it to find it charming or sweet. But what he was trying to see was how it could have happened. He couldn't help thinking Maggie must have made the running. He thought of Mrs Bruzzese and her desperate need. Perhaps Maggie had been struck by the same lightning. Maybe the storm of longing for a child had hit her and she'd seduced the silent telegraph pole whose sperm were more articulate than him.

Or perhaps it had simply been the urgent curiosity to experience intimacy, like a child who can't resist finding out what's in the bottle and takes a swig of bleach. On the other hand, could they be so much in love they couldn't bear not to know one another? He found it hard to believe any woman could long for intimacy with Max. It seemed as ridiculous as craving cold tea or flat beer. Yet at the heart of his speculation was a seed of opportunity: Elsie and Maggie had grown together, been to school together, went to church together, knew one another's families as if they were their own, lived a few doors apart; if Maggie was getting married, wasn't it time for Elsie to think of it too? And if Maggie had shown her bare backside to god himself, defying his unbreachable strictures about copulation, why should Elsie persist in her brick-wall allegiance to the Bible.

"I lay no blame," he said. "Flesh is weak."

"That's why you shouldn't give in to temptation."

"Who do you think gave in?"

She turned from her ironing and stared at him.

"What d'you mean?"

"Well," he rubbed the crumbs from his fingers, "do think Max seduced her or was she more than willing?"

"That's not for us to think about."

"Interesting though, isn't it?"

"Not to my way of thinkin'."

"And Maggie a devout Methodist."

"Anyone can stray."

"They can. Looks like they haven't strayed an inch or two from the straight and narrow but have gone roaming the hills as if they own them."

"You don't know."

"No."

"Might have been just one mistake."

"You think so?"

"You never know."

"Unlikely," and as the word fell from his mouth he thought of Mrs Bruzzese and his atrocious luck. He wished it could have taken a hundred times or a thousand but then he looked at Elsie, her busy arm pressing on the little yellow iron as it ran over her father's shirt, and was amazed at his deception. He would have liked to tell her. He wanted her to accept him as he was. But he knew how her mind was hemmed in by the barbed wire, spotlights, guns and Alsatians of chapter and verse.

"Well," he said, "in any case I suppose Christian forgiveness is called for."

She looked at him sharply again.

"Judge not that ye be not judged," she said.

He realised she needed to trump him. She knew well enough he believed in the Bible as little as his parents' drinking. Piety was hers. It was a kind of competition. She'd been raised in fear of failing to comply with the church's demands and in the promise of reward for those who stuck to them most fervently and she wanted to win the race.

It struck him it was really no different from his wanting to be top of the class. That had saved him. He sometimes wondered what would have become of him if he'd been slow. Might he have followed his grandparent's example? Might that have been the one thing he could cling to? Might he now be a sodden bar-prop looking for a fight like his granddad? The thought of it terrified him and made him realise how flimsy was fate. A chance of nature had made him intelligent and that had been the branch to break his fall. He was competitive. He was proud of his good marks at school. He wanted to get on. But Elsie was no different. She just wanted to get on in a different way. She wanted to be first in holiness. He knew she disliked it if he trod on the perfect lawn of her Christian virtue. It was a garden where only she could go. So she quoted the Bible at him as if she'd written it herself. It always troubled him how religious people did that, as if he were to quote Shakespeare with an assumption of authorship. He was acutely aware of what his scavenging mind had stolen. He knew what he'd taken from others and what was his own. It was curious how for Elsie there was no distinction between what she received and what she invented. It bothered and amused him simultaneously.

"I judge Hitler to be evil," he said, "and if I'm judged for that, too bad. But I won't condemn a man or woman for doing what comes naturally."

"It's natural when you're married."

"The problem for Adam and Eve," he said, "was they had no vicar to marry 'em."

"Don't talk daft."

"What were they to do?"

"You talk rubbish."

"What would you have done in the Garden of Eden?"

"I won't blaspheme."

"I'd've taken the advice of that snake."

She clanged the iron.

"You talk like the Devil."

"It was impossible for them. They weren't to have sex yet how could they marry? What kind of god puts two young people alone and naked in a garden and says "Now, don't touch one another." If he thought he was going to get away with that he must be a fool."

"They were supposed to resist temptation."

"But then the species would have died out. If men and women don't have sex, the world will be left to beetles."

"God would find a way."

"He gave us a way. If he made the world he made sexual reproduction."

"For married life."

"Sex must have come first."

"How can you know?"

"The church itself is less then two thousand years old," he said. "*Homo sapiens* have been around for two hundred thousand. We must have been copulating happily for a very long time before the church decided it was a problem."

The iron rang once more its note of anger and disdain.

"We don't want your fancy ideas round here."

"They aren't fancy ideas, Elsie. You just have to think."

"I'm not interested in your kind o' thinkin'."

"Well," he said, suddenly feeling daring and reckless, "if Maggie's getting married, perhaps you should be thinking about it."

She looked at him with fierce shock as if he'd said the Virgin Mary was the Devil's lover.

"I'm not in trouble and I'm not going to be."

"Can happen to anyone," he said.

He felt he'd breached a defence which had kept him from interesting territory, like a rambler who deliberately trespasses and when the landowner appears with his dog and his gun, stands his ground, smiles and comments on the beauty of the day. In the weeks that followed he kept returning to the discussion with the relish of a man who has found a dish he especially savours and goes back time and again to the same restaurant. Elsie remained stern and dismissive but he had the advantage of his desultory reading. His mind wasn't organised. He lacked that discipline of proper education which permits someone to explain the physical world step by step from neutrons and protons to television or powered flight; or to recount the development of literature from Homer to James Joyce. He hadn't built a well-designed, robust and spacious house of knowledge but a little, flimsy nest of dry sticks and dead leaves. Yet to Elsie his references to Darwin, Freud, Einstein, Marx, Shakespeare or Tolstoy seemed extraordinarily learned and in spite of herself she couldn't help admiring and being seduced by his phoney intellectualism.

Bert was one of those people who reach into the profundity and subtlety of great minds and grab snippets to parade like advertising slogans in front of the easily impressed. He couldn't have explained how the fossil record upheld the theory of evolution to a class of bright fifteen-year-olds, but he had hold of something essential in Darwin which he felt made him *modern* and *advanced*.

"Well," said Elsie, "if we evolved from monkeys why aren't monkeys turning into humans?"

"Because they're not the monkeys we evolved from," he bluffed. "They died out long ago."

But it was the matter of sex and marriage which jolted Elsie into her most frozen objections.

"You know," he said to her as they walked through the market one Saturday morning (letting him help her with the shopping was safe), "I'm beginning to think Max is a lucky man."

"Why?" she said, reaching for a cauliflower.

"Maggie's a good woman. She's kind and loyal and works hard. She'll make a good wife and mother and he hasn't had to wait till they're married to get to know her."

"Is that what you call it?" she said, putting the few coppers of change into her little brown, leather purse.

"She's the kind of woman I could marry," he said.

"Well, she's spoken for."

"There are plenty like her. Grand lasses with their feet on the ground who know how to make a man content."

She snorted.

"Is that what a woman should spend her life doing?"

"A contented husband is a good husband."

"Most men are babies."

He looked at her as she held out four just-ripening bananas. He could have lost his temper. It was one of those moments when he felt he was wasting his time and should give up; when a sprightly devil of cynicism sprang up in him, like the desire to do mischief in school-boys left unattended; he could have walked away from her and gone after vulgar women, one after another; he could have satisfied his lust in the most degraded ways. What was the sense, after all, in continuing to walk the high and perilous path in the mountain peaks when there was easy satisfaction to be had in the foothills? Elsie didn't help him in his strenuous effort. He wanted that demanding relationship of love, loyalty and eroticism which he took to be marriage's promise, but at every turn she rebuffed and disdained him and the game was starting to wear him down. He turned away and walked to the next stall where he pressed his thumb against a firm, deep red apple. He paid the stallholder and took a juicy bite.

"You shouldn't eat in public," she said.

"Why not?"

"It's vulgar."

"I am vulgar. I'm Pongo the stinky kid from the slum whose grandparents were legless every night."

She looked at him and he stared back at her with cold defiance. He saw a softening in her look. The corners of her mouth almost curled into a smile.

"Well, mind your manners, Pongo."

She went past him and reached for a lonely white and purple turnip which had fallen among carrots.

"It's out of place, like me," said Bert.

"Don't feel sorry for yourself. It doesn't become you."

"What does?"

"Same as everyone."

"What's that?"

" Self-discipline and good manners cost nowt and they save a lot of trouble."

"What trouble can I cause by eating an apple in public?"

"Set yourself standards and stick to'em. That's what keeps things from going bad ways."

"And what if no-one else does?"

"I'm not responsible for other folks' behaviour."

"No, but other folks' behaviour can be responsible for what happens to you."

He sensed a little tensing in her demeanour.

"I don't worry over what I can't alter," she said, slipping four oranges into her bag.

"Nor do I. But I'm determined to make the best of things I can."

"Good for you."

"What about you?"

"Eh?"

"Will you do the same?"

"I don't complain."

"I know you don't, but will you make the best of what you can alter?"

"In my own way."

"We don't go through life on our own."

"I'm not on my own."

"No, but you have to grow out of your family sooner or later."

She turned to him with one of those shocked looks which always

91

seized her features when the pillars of her certainty and identity were given a little knock.

"Why?"

"Life demands it. Maggie and Max are doing it."

"I don't see why."

"It's the birds and the bees, Elsie."

"I have my mother to look after. That's what comes first. The birds and the bees can do what they like."

He threw his apple core into a dustbin standing by a concrete corner. There was no argument against her virtue. She was absolutely right to take care of her mother. It was one of the things that attracted him to her. Familiar with neglect he was repelled by it like a dog that cowers from a cruel master. Yet his admiration for her devotion fought with his need for physical and emotional comfort. Time and again there came back to him the memory of Mrs Bruzzese. Did life offer anything better? It was amazing, the balm of intimacy. He wanted a future free of the dirt, violence, indulgence and dishonesty of his childhood. Like a man lost in a snowstorm in the hills who sees the lights of a village glimmering in the valley, he wanted to make his way quickly.

Elsie was his refuge. She offered the possibility of stability, security, a clean, calm and happy home; but first she had to yield. Wasn't that characteristic of women? Or wasn't it how things had to work between men and women? Didn't there have to be a mutual yielding? His mind felt weak when he tried to make it clear; but what he knew was the vulnerability of nakedness. It was odd. Sex was used in such brutal ways. He thought of the blokes in the RAF going off to brothels. What was that but just an inadequate rubbing off of tension? No, it didn't do the trick. It was like stuffing rotting vegetables in your mouth to satisfy a raging hunger rather than cooking a nourishing meal made up of delicate, contrasting flavours. Yes, you could eat like an animal in order to fill the emptiness in your belly, but it gave you indigestion and ruined your health. He'd made his decision. He wasn't going to give up even though the fear that, in the end, Elsie might throw her Bible at him and expel him like the money-lenders from the temple made him shrink; he was going to try to fulfil this ambition as resolutely as he was going to try to gain qualifications and a good job.

"You must look after your mother," he said hardly knowing where the words came from, "but I want to look after you."

She gave him another shocked look.

"I don't need looking after."

"We all need looking after."

"Not in the way you mean."

"You need that too," he said.

This time she turned to him as if she was about to strike him. Her eyes were fierce and her little frame seemed tensed to explosion, as if the energy it contained had found some way to escape its bounds and was about to unleash a storm that would split the earth down the middle.

"You don't know what I need," she thrust the cucumber she held in her hand back onto the stall and strode away towards the fish counters.

"I'm asking you to marry me," he said, walking too briskly beside her.

"You've lost your mind."

"Maybe I have. Isn't that what love's supposed to be about?"

She stopped at Harrison's. The fishmonger was a big, gaunt man with raw hands. He wore a thick jumper under his blue and white striped apron and wellingtons up to his knees. He nodded at her in his laconic way, as if anything more would cost him impossible effort.

"Elsie," he said.

"I'd like some cod."

"Aye, nice big piece or a couple?"

"One nice big piece'll do fine," she found reassurance in repeating his words. He was part of the world she knew.

The fishmonger leant forward and his great, thick fingers wriggled beneath the cold wet flesh of the fillets.

"That one do you?"

"Can you weigh it?" she said.

Bert stood silently beside her.

93

"Two and threepence," said Harrison, twisting his head to look at her, the limp fish dangling over the weighing scale.

"Fine," she said and began to ferret in her purse.

Quicker and more resolute, Bert produced a crisp, pink ten shilling note and held it out to the big stall holder who was wrapping the cod in thick, off-white paper.

"Put that away," said Elsie, "you're showin' me up."

Harrison looked from one to the other.

"Take that," said Bert authoritatively and the fishmonger took the dry money in his damp fingers.

"You've no business," she said ignoring him and heading for the bus stop.

"It's a couple of bob, what's the fuss?"

"We can pay our own way."

"I'm not saying you can't. It's a gift. From me to you. Two shilling's worth of cod. To celebrate our engagement."

"Leave me alone," she said.

"I will. Ta-ta, Elsie," and he walked off at a relaxed pace in the opposite direction feeling he'd struck the ball as well as he could and it would either rise hopelessly over the crossbar or fly safely into the net that would catch it in its bulge and let it fall gently to the ground.

SATURDAY AFTERNOON

He didn't know where he was going, but he was free. He could do what he liked for an hour or two. It was up to her now. If she definitively turned him down, he'd have to start again; but the idea didn't daunt him. It had to be done. Things had to move one way or the other. He went into *Salisbury's Record Emporium*. It was a little place tucked in between a butcher's and an electrical shop with barely room to fit a thin man on a diet between the wooden boxes. Bert liked to idle, flicking through the classical or jazz collections. He had to play his records quietly or when Aunt Alice wasn't at home. She disapproved of anything but Methodist hymns, having converted from Catholicism to the faith of her husband and dismissed even Beethoven as *that noise*.

Bert liked almost all music. Having no musical talent himself, the genius of the simplest melody seemed a miracle. He could listen to Vera Lynn and feel the tears come to his eyes but Verdi, Mozart, Beethoven, Bach, the real musicians who were not only technically expert but knew how to minutely colour and nuance their work, set his brain on fire. He'd read somewhere about *the language of modern music* and wondered how a piano or a trumpet could speak. He knew nothing of musical theory and had never picked up an instrument. School hadn't taught him even the rudiments; he didn't know how a major scale was constructed, what a time signature was, the value of a crotchet or a minim. His complete ignorance was the ground of his astonishment; like a man from a Stone Age tribe in the Amazon watching a jet plane pass above the canopy, Bert could watch a pub pianist sit down and play *Bye Bye Blackbird* or *Roll Out The Barrel* and be utterly mystified at how the fingers found the right keys and the sounds fit together so perfectly.

He longed to be able to play but his ignorance made him afraid. It wasn't that he feared making a fool of himself, but that he knew if he plucked the strings of a guitar or tried to blow a note on a clarinet, his joy in music would be sullied if he found himself instantly at a loss. So he listened and out of his listening he whistled and sang. He was one of those men who went around the house with his lips pursed chirruping *Jesu Joy Of Man's Desiring* or *Georgia On My Mind*. He whistled on the street, in his car, in the shops and at work.

95

Harry didn't like it and told him to stop.

"Don't you like music?"

"Not when I'm working."

"What kind of music do you like?"

"Glenn Miller," said Harry.

"Nothing wrong with that," said Bert. "But you should try Bach as well."

"I find classical stuff boring."

"Bach is about as boring as Lauren Bacall with her clothes off," said Bert.

"Well, I don't like that kind of thing," said Harry. "It's too serious. I like a nice song."

"Do you know Schubert?"

"No. I mean Doris Day. She's a good singer."

"She is. But you should listen to *Winterreisse*," said Bert. "No-one can write better songs than Schubert."

"That's your opinion. But don't whistle while I'm trying to work."

"Okay," said Bert. "I'll sing instead."

He was thinking about Harry's comment as he looked at a record by the *Original Dixieland Jazz Band*. He liked the loose, nailed-together feel of their music. The precision of Bach was wonderful but so was the swaying-in-the-wind style of New Orleans. Was Harry right, that it was simply a matter of opinion, of taste? Something about the idea niggled at him like a tooth about to flare into sleep-wrecking pain. He could go along with the notion so far but he couldn't believe *The Andrews Sisters* or Gene Autry were musicians worth taking seriously. The girls in their uniforms performing a silly little dance as they sang *The Boogie Woogie Bugle Boy* couldn't be thought of in the same way as Beethoven or Stravinsky; they were pap for the masses; yet if it was all a matter of opinion, lots of people preferred Gene Autry to Bartok. Bert couldn't stand the singing cowboy. Hearing *Back In The Saddle Again* made him snort with derision. Was that merely opinion? He was coming round to the view that it wasn't. Bach really was a superior musician. But why? He wished he understood enough about music to be able to explain it to himself. These ideas were going through his head when a voice said:

"Hello Bert, how you keepin'?"

and he looked up to see the friendly face of Slick Sticks Sam.

He'd met him at Hopkirk's, where he played drums from time to time with the resident band, and had visited his bed-sit in the run down streets in the centre of town. Like him, Sam was an outsider. The idea of a steady job appealed to him as much as having a bath in cat's piss; the steady life of respectability was a premature coffin; marriage was a trap, parenthood an impossible burden: you give your life to a child for twenty years after which it spits in your face and starts counting the years till you die so it can rubber-finger the notes of the petty fortune you've carefully accumulated by reducing yourself to a boss's lap-dog for forty years and skimping so diligently you don't know what the inside of a cinema looks like and you think a tram-ride along Blackpool prom exotic; women were to be enjoyed like good food and wine, and the more the better.

Bert liked him for his runt's perspective. He understood why, being a musician before anything, the life of an accountant seemed as dull as making jam with the Women's Institute. For all he knew, Sam might be an excellent percussionist. In fact, he was nothing but an amateur with blood-pressure. All the same, he represented the glamour of the *jazz life*: playing till midnight or the early hours, heading off with any willing woman; staying in bed till midday; mooching in the streets, pubs and cafes till it was time to start keeping rhythm again. Bert was pulled towards such a life like swallows towards warm climes in winter. If he'd had a modicum of musical ability he might well have been sharing a bed-sit with Sam. But he knew a life has to be built from the opportunities available; rats don't love sunlight and clean linen. Sam's phone might ring with the offer of a job in Manchester or Liverpool or Southport; he might play seven gigs one week and three the next; he might be offered work on a cruise ship where the food was lavish and the bored, rich, married women loose. Playing jazz provided those opportunities. Bert had nothing like that to take hold of.

All the same, he and Sam got along like puppies. On the one hand, Bert liked to hear Sam's tales of bohemian laxity, on the other Sam was glad to be accepted by someone whose life was essentially *square*.

"Fine, Sam. Good to see you."

They shook hands. They were men together with an idle Saturday afternoon before them. Leaving the shop beneath a sky where the white clouds were parting to reveal a bit of happy blue, like a ready girl who shifts her legs to reveal the tops of her stockings, they were set to waste a few hours in chatter, listening to Satchmo or Artie Shaw, emptying a bottle of cheap red and even getting their arms round the waists of a couple of slim, giddy girls. They went to the *Kardomah* where the coffee was milky, the waitresses perfunctory, the carpet grubby, the lighting too bright and the clientele as buttoned-up as a priest's fly.

"Playing tonight?" said Bert.

"*The Railway.*"

Close, as its name implied, to the station, *The Railway* was run by Jack Cornelius whose taste for jazz and women led him to pay for bands which left him almost out of pocket. The *Slick Sticks Quartet*, however, was always sure to attract a good crowd because they brought in Arnold Chester, the reeds man, who could play tenor, alto and soprano sax, clarinet and flute, who had spent a few years after the war as a session musician in London, had played with Howard McGhee and who might have had a career among those few lucky proponents of the genre who manage to make enough from playing not to have to join the *unçool cats* on the factory floor, in the office or the classroom, had his wife not fallen pregnant and insisted on something more secure than intermittent tooting behind some warbling populist.

"What's the band?"

"My quartet."

"Arnold Chester playing?"

"Sure."

"I'll come along."

"How are things with.....that young lass you told me about?"

"Elsie."

"Yeah, that's the chick. Elsie."

"Okay. I proposed to her."

"Christ, man! She accept?"

"I'm waiting for an answer."

"Like the guy in Dickens."

"Barkis," said Bert.

"Yeah. That cat. But marriage. That could be square."

"You've got to make things your own way, Sam. You're lucky. The women like musicians. Me, I need some security. I want a future."

"Sure, man. You've got to do what's right for you."

"How's *your* love life?"

"Same."

Bert knew what *same* meant: Sam was one of those men who take female sexuality personally, as if every pair of swaying hips, shapely calves, weighty breasts, blue or brown eyes, every set of slender fingers, every delicate wrist, trim ankle, every gentle or surprisingly husky voice, every head of thick, shining hair was a call to him; he couldn't see a good-looking woman on the street without thinking she'd put on her nail varnish or lipstick for his benefit; the merest glance from even the least attractive woman in Lancashire was enough to convince him she'd left the house only to find him and entice him into bed.

Bert found a rasher of amusement in this. It wasn't unusual, after all. The sex-starved men in the RAF gloated over femininity like misers over gold. To a man in need of comfort and satisfaction the slightest shadow of anything female was enough to make him as excited as a child at the sight of its mother after a long absence. Bert wondered if the same mad shock ran through women: did a lonely woman experience the presence of a pot-bellied, bald-headed man with a fag in one hand and a pint in the other as potential salvation? He couldn't believe it. Somehow women could deflect their impulses, as if their brains contained some absorbent material which soaked up sexual desire and the longing for unity and transformed them into control, command and enticement.

Men like Sam, and he was just the average man pushed to the extreme, were at the mercy of women because they were victims of their own desire. Maybe it was simply that women knew this; perhaps they learned that men have far less command and made use of

99

it. But then he thought of what he'd read about hysteria and it seemed that women were just as much ruled by their desires as men. What surprised him was how willing women were to get into bed with Sam. It was true he was less fussy than a tramp in a dustbin, but all the same he was able to have sex with three or four women a week without exerting himself. Nor was he a handsome man. He wasn't like Gino Bruzzese, tall, well-made, dark and imposing. Sam was a thin, nervy man, always reaching for the next cigarette or shot of whiskey and his body was replicated in his face; his nose was the shape of a yacht's sail, his lips as insignificant as cigarette papers, his cheeks as fleshless as a gnawed spare rib.

Bert found it hard to imagine any woman would be attracted to him if he didn't impose himself; but he had a way. He would approach and talk to a woman as readily as he'd hand money to a bookie's runner. Nor would he be deterred by shyness, a subtle rebuff or even a direct verbal slap. He kept going like a spawning salmon, leaping the rapids of potential rejection, finding a current he could glide into and drift along till her legs were round him. He wasn't always successful. Some women told him bluntly to disappear. Others mocked him or blew cigarette smoke in his face. But he had many more winners in bed than on the racecourse; if he broke even at the bookmaker's he was pleased, but with women he expected seventy-five percent victory.

"Seen Marj lately?"

Marjorie Kent was a nineteen year-old blonde with a Diana Dors bosom, cross-eyes and a voice that on a good night could sound like Peggy Lee with tonsillitis. She sang at Hopkirk's, in *The Black Horse, The Wheatsheaf* and some of the rougher pubs of Manchester and Liverpool, convinced she would soon be taken up by a recording company to become the Judy Garland of the north-west. Sam introduced her to singing. Contemplating the cleft between her breasts and imagining the delight of entering the cleft between her legs, he'd told her *a girl like her* if she had *any voice at all* could make a fortune in a matter of a few years with *the right contacts* and *good management*. Thrilled, flattered and palpitating at the idea of being able to leave her job as receptionist at *The Iron Trades Insurance Co*, Marj had her introduction to the bliss of intimacy in a grubby flat in the basement of a damp house on an unmade bed whose grey sheet bore the stains of a dozen previous seductions beneath a drunken man whose breath wafted the enticing odour of cheap, stale tobacco and who, in his febrile rush, didn't even bother with a *johnny*. He fell asleep on top of her and though she prodded him and called his name, was as likely to rouse as a hibernating hedgehog; she pushed him off, got dressed and going out into the crime-inviting, early morning streets, was forced to walk the two miles home, not having enough in her purse for a taxi.

"Yeah. She's still singin'."

"Think she' ll make it?"

"Man, she wails like a cat with a sore arse."

"How does she get gigs?"

"Any girl'd get gigs if she shook her tits in men's faces."

Bert laughed. What else was there to do? He felt sorry for Marj, sorry in fact for the whole ugly business of promise-the-earth seductions and ambitions as realistic as flat-earth theory. It made him want to listen to the Halle playing Bach or Haydn. It made him think of Elsie and the solid oak ideas of her family. On the one hand, he envied Sam. It would be nice to let go and live such a loose, unmade-road existence; on the other, the narrow path where every step threatened to take you over the edge into a precipice of regret, led in the end to a green, well-fenced and flourishing garden, or so it seemed.

"Sooner or later they'll get bored and she'll be back to typing."

"Typing? That's too much for Marj. She can't concentrate for more than ten seconds. Not even in bed."

Bert laughed again.

They left the café and wandered the streets among the shoppers. Bert, as usual, was glad to be amidst a reassuring throng of strangers. The town didn't provide much opportunity for a pair of would be *flâneurs*; this wasn't Baudelaire's Paris or Pushkin's St Petersburg; the centre was bounded on the south by the river; there were two main arteries, one running east to west, the other joining it from the north via two little streets of uninspiring shops at either side of the square dominated by the nineteenth century museum and library whose eternal stone bore the edifying inscription: *The riches you may here acquire abide with you always.*

The town, however, was far les interested in mental riches than the grubby pursuit of lucre and like all these places in Lancashire, built on the engineering ingenuity and psychological nullity that drove the industrial revolution, was scarred by the greed and extermination of imagination which had raised the big houses in the suburbs and thrown up slums for the likes of Bert. The two young men could walk from one end of the town centre to the other in ten minutes; there was nothing to explore; no surprises round the next corner; no gratuitous beauty to make you catch your breath; everything was known, as if the place had been created to defeat delight.

Sam wanted to place a bet so they nipped into *The Boar's Head* where in the gents a little hive buzzed with men who were handing over slips of torn paper, coins and notes to a fat, sweaty bloke in a stained, creased grey suit; a *Woodbine* burned in his crooked mouth and the smoke rising into his eyes made him squint. As they entered everyone turned, but Sam being well-known, their fear rose and fell as quickly as the price of silver and amongst the odour of urine and tobacco, by the yellow-stained urinal whose white stones were separated by curving fins whose inadequacy in protecting modesty suggested they might have been installed in conspiracy to do the opposite, the excited men handed over the money they'd earned in factories, on building sites, in offices or driving lorries in the petty expectation that luck, as predictable as the weather, would be tamed by their wishes and into their hands would fall that something for nothing of which all people dream out of weakness and neurosis and which virtually never arrives and when it does brings more misery than joy.

Sam didn't place simple bets. He explained to Bert he was *doing a Yankee*.

"What's that?"

"Four gee-gees. Eleven bets. If they all win....."

But Bert's attention had been diverted: Harry Clow had just come in, accompanied by a smaller, grey-skinned, one-wage-packet-to-another chap; they stood side by side at the urinal, Harry looking down and talking to the younger, lesser man. Bert stood by the little chatter of punters wondering if Harry would notice him, but the boss turned from the tiles, buttoned up his fly and held the door open for his mate without seeing him.

102

There was something odd that set Bert's mind wondering. Why shouldn't Harry be in the pub on a Saturday afternoon, even with the kind of bloke he usually tried to avoid? Bert tried to recall if Harry had ever spoken about *The Boar's Head* or any town centre pub. Had he ever said he went out drinking on a Saturday? Then it came to him that he'd complained about his wife who reserved Saturdays for shopping with her mother. They'd get the train to Southport or Manchester and while they were away Harry was expected to get on with gardening or do a bit of *fettling* around the house. Perhaps that was it. Maybe he nipped out for a drink to strangle the boredom. Yet it didn't seem right. Harry was a snob. He didn't mix with people he called *common* and *roughnecks*. The bloke he was with was most definitely in the first category. Sam handed his eleven shillings to the short-winded runner and they left. As they were passing through the bar, Bert noticed Harry's companion sitting on his own in one of the little rooms that led from the semi-circular bar. He touched Sam's arm.

"Sam, that bloke there, just inside the door. Don't look now but do you know him?"

Sam took a cigarette from his packet and slowly lit the end with the little blue and yellow flame from his lighter. He nodded. Bert went out into the street.

"Who is he then?"

"Peroxide Pete. His hair's not naturally that colour. Don't turn your back on him."

"One of them?"

"Bent as a nine bob note. Ain't my business what the cat does with his dick. You know him?"

"No, but he was with my boss."

"Respectable sort, eh?"

"Apparently."

"Who knows what they get up to when the curtains are closed in Penwortham."

Bert was at first a bit troubled then slightly amazed and amused and little by little, thinking of Harry's wife and children, shocked and saddened. Did his wife know? Was Harry one of those blokes who hang around in public lavatories? Bert and Sam wandered the market, stopping at the record and book stalls which, as usual, had little of interest, and as they went Bert was running over in his mind what his discovery meant. Maybe he was jumping to conclusions: a man goes for a drink with a queer, does that mean he's queer too? Yet as he ran the scene over in his head he could read in Harry's demeanour that there was something between them. Like Sam, he felt no animosity towards Harry or any inclination to moral condemnation; it was part of his mentality, though he was only just beginning to realize it, that what people do with their intimacy is their own business.

Having no religious conviction and being on the receiving end of snobbery, of that deep British hatred and mistrust of the poor which blamed those without means for their fate and saw their misery as a moral failing, Bert could never bark with the dogs of prejudice. He knew society was against him because he came from the back streets, because he was illegitimate, because he was ill-educated; society was against queers too, but that was just as ugly. Society was a vicious beast when it was roused. It struck Bert as a terrible thing that men like Harry should have to move in the shadows like vermin; that if he were found out his wife might divorce him and he could lose his job. Supposing he, with all the disadvantages of his origins had been queer into the bargain. He'd never experienced attraction to men, but he supposed it was no more outside the bounds of nature than his own strong arousal at the sight of a pretty woman.

And then there was Sam, an outsider too because of his rabbit's sexuality. It was true there was something disturbing about it, like a nightmare whose content you can't recall though your fear haunts you through the day; it was like watching a man unable to refuse the next drink and falling from the pub into the gutter and from the gutter into the grave. Yet Bert couldn't see that condemning him was any use. Something in Sam's personality, something given or something learned, drove him to pursue women like a grizzly bear pursues salmon and just as the bears guzzle and grow fat in the time of plenty, so Sam saw every woman who came his way as a kind of irresistible sustenance. It was ridiculous, but it was Sam. And the women tumbled onto his grubby bed and beneath his skinny frame like apples in an October storm. It had to be accepted; as Eddie said, we aren't all made of the same timber.

"Hey," said Sam, "look it's Joyce and Sandra".

He was pointing to a pair of giddy girls of about nineteen, arm in arm at *Bessie's Corset Stall*. One was a brunette with the broad shoulders of a swimmer and a face as handsome as Sophia Loren; the other had hair dyed black and heavily made-up eyes and wasn't nearly so naturally good-looking.

"Where do you know them from?" asked Bert.

"Hopkirk's. Pubs. They're always around. Take a look at that Joyce, man. She could be a film star."

"Yeah," said Bert, "or she could sell lipstick in Woolworths."

"Come on."

Sam approached and began to talk. He had that ability to yap about nothing and yet to convey friendliness and warmth which makes people such good company. Bert knew he couldn't compete. He liked to talk *about* something. He knew, with these two, he would have to nestle in Sam's shadow like a pillion rider who must put his trust in the driver. He smiled as he was introduced and shook the girls' hands. Joyce tilted her head like a curious sparrow and smiled at him as if he were as handsome as Montgomery Clift. Though he knew this was no more than common flirtatiousness, he couldn't help responding. Her behaviour was an axe which divided his mind as cleanly as a butcher's cleaver divides ribs; on the one hand he was wary and alert, on the other flattered and tempted and between these two was a chasm as deep as and inexplicable as outer space.

"Fancy a drink, girls?" said Sam.

"Don't mind if we do," giggled Sandra.

"If you're payin'" said Joyce.

And they snuggled against one another like a child and its mother, their arms tightly linked and roared with that silly laughter which is one of the greatest pleasures of young, carefree friendship. In the pub they asked for gin and sat close to one another on the bench seat. Sam bought the drinks and Bert tried to move things on.

"So what do you do, girls?"

"Depends who's askin'," tittered Sandra.

"I work in accounts," said Bert hoping to drag the tone a little nearer to seriousness.

"Ooo, fancy," said Joyce and the girls looked at one another and collapsed into chuckles only they could understand.

"I bet you're good with figures, then," added Sandra.

"Not bad," said Bert with a broad smile.

"I can't add up for toffee," she said, "except my vital statistics."

They tittered like little girls being tickled by their dad. It gave Bert a feeling of exclusion. He realised he had no idea how to handle himself with girls like these. He looked to the bar for assistance but Sam's back was still turned, so he feigned interest in the barmaid and the men she was serving. He tried to think of something to say, but every possibility seemed hopelessly sober as if he were a Puritan among Restoration Wits.

The girls were locked in their private world of goofy cooing which was at once provocative and insulting. They were determined not to take anything seriously; he felt he should be able to enjoy that; it was right after all to be able to be light-hearted and headed sometimes; they were in the pub; there was no reason to talk ponderously of weighty matters. Yet he couldn't bat their ball back to them. It made him feel small and awkward and he thought of the pall-bearer's atmosphere of Elsie's home and how much more congenial he found it. Compared to Elsie he was an inveterate wag; he could feel as insignificant as a grasshopper; but with these girls he felt like the Pope in a strip club; he was a dull, slow-witted Diogenes and the more they laughed the more his barrel shrank around him and he became conscious of his nakedness.

If these girls saw him without his clothes, they would hoot like drunken owls. He thought of Mrs Bruzzese and how her desperation, serious as a shipwreck, made her embrace him with tender gratitude; and that enhanced his sense of his manhood. He imagined she'd admired him naked, that the sight of his erect cock had made her heart beat till its rhythm was almost indiscernible.. But to strike up an erotic charge with these two would be like striking a match under water. They might be willing. They might jump into bed and get on with it, but it would be as inconsequential as buttering toast. He wondered if there was something to be said for that. Why shouldn't sex be an appetite like any other? Why shouldn't it be satisfied as perfunctorily as thirst by swigging a glass of water?

"Here we are girls," said Sam, "gins big enough to wash your feet in."

"Only my feet?" said Joyce.

"Get you a bathful if you like, sweetheart," said Sam "you could wallow like Cleopatra while I scrub your back."

"She didn't bath in gin," said Sandra.

"Ass's milk," said Sam, "but where am I going to find a female ass on a Saturday afternoon in this town?"

"Pasteurised will do," said Joyce and the girls tee-heed as if the gin had already done its work.

"Is your bath big enough for both of us?" said Sandra.

"What, me and you?" asked Sam.

"No, me and Joycey. We like a bath together don't we love?"

"Lesbe friends," said Sam.

"Ooo, not us," said Joyce, "we like men, don't we Sandy. They have the right equipment."

"The bigger the better."

"It's not the size of the conductor's baton," said Sam, "it's the way he waves it."

"I don't want you waving your baton in my face," said Sandra.

"Put it where it belongs," said Joyce.

"Slip it in its sheath," said Sandra.

"Nice tight fit," said Joyce.

"Long and thin, slips right in, short and thick, just the trick," said Sandra and the two of them chortled long and loud while Sam nodded in appreciation as he lit a *Woodbine* and Bert sipped his half of bitter as if it were cod liver oil.

When the girls had swallowed four gins and Sam gulped three pints while Bert had managed one and a pickled egg, Sam suggested they go back to his flat to listen to a bit of music and open a bottle of wine. Bert tried to excuse himself saying he'd arranged to meet Elsie, but Sam squeezed his arm and whispered into his ear while the girls protested sardonically: *our company not good enough for you eh? Well, we know when we're not wanted.*

Bert felt weak in going along with what he disliked but he didn't want to offend Sam and behind his reluctance was a nervous curiosity as to how things would work out. He most definitely didn't want to have sex with either of these two; he didn't want any liaison with them, but a bawdy fascination made him want to witness what would happen between them and Sam.

The flat, as always, was as chaotic as a classroom without a teacher. There was an old sofa with a floral pattern, the kind of thing that might once have looked at home in a cottage in one of the little villages of north Lancashire; it was threadbare and cluttered with an unwashed dinner plate on which egg and brown sauce had left an expressionistic pattern; three pint glasses each with the tilted dregs of drink still in the bottom; a pair of trousers which might have been cast off as they caught fire; an odd brown and yellow sock dangling morosely over the arm and a copy of *The Sporting Life*, open and crumpled as if its reader had left to avoid the police. On the bare and dusty floorboards was a square of brown carpet with ragged edges. In the corner was a dark-stained table on which sat a two-thirds empty bottle of milk, sliced white bread in its greaseproof wrapper, an empty wine bottle, two mugs and a pair of down-at-heel brogues. There was a rocking chair on which was piled Sam's clothes. An old, yellow eiderdown served as a curtain at the dirty window.

"Oh, nice," said Joyce.

"Expecting company?" said Sandra.

Without taking off their coats the girls began to tidy. Bert was amazed at how quick and handy they were. They went at the little task as if they'd come for nothing else, giggling all the while, whispering to one another and once they were concealed in the little kitchen guffawing and whooping as if they'd won the pools. Sam, a *Woodbine* burning between his lips, winked at Bert as he made effete efforts at bringing order. He'd bought two bottles of cheap French red from the landlord of *The Boar's Head* who drove to Liverpool once a week and handed over a few quid for a couple of cases to a man on the docks, no questions asked. He went into the kitchen. The girls hooted like ships coming into port and squealed like cornered mice. Bert imagined Sam squeezing their waists or pinching their behinds. The host reappeared with a wine glass, a teacup and two mugs. He grabbed the clothes from the rocking chair and threw them behind the sofa.

"Make yourself at home, Bert."

Sam pulled a little folding table from the corner. It stood two feet high and had flimsy, hinged legs. Its surface was decorated with cack-handed *maqueterie* showing a marine scene: two rocky islands in a crashing sea and seagulls wheeling in the salty wind.

"Made it myself," said Sam proudly. "What d'you think?"

The table wobbled like a drunk on a bicycle as he put down the cups and glass.

"Smashing," said Bert.

"I've always been good with my hands. My dad was a skilled man. Cabinet maker. That's why drumming comes naturally to me."

Bert smiled and nodded as Sam yanked the stubborn cork from the tight neck of the green bottle, half filled one of the mugs and handed it to him.

"Just get the bouquet of that, man. Class."

"Thanks."

Bert took a sip of the bitter wine. He'd hardly ever drunk any but he'd tasted smooth and delicate Mouton-Cadet and mature Bordeaux from which rose the fruity odour of the grape before the liquid touched your lips. This concoction burned and almost made him splutter. He supposed it had been bottled for cooking, the kind of thing a French housewife would pour liberally into the pot of *coq au vin*; but he would have rather drunk cold, stewed tea than finish what was in his mug.

"Those French cats know how to make wine, eh man?"

"They do," said Bert.

"You watch these chicks when they taste that nectar," Sam whispered, " ready and willing, man."

Bert nodded. Joyce and Sandra, who had left their coats in the kitchen, came through and sat side by side on the sofa.

"Wine, ladies?"

Sam filled the glass.

"Do we have to share?" said Joyce.

"I'm not drinking from the same glass as you," said Sandra in mock protest, "who knows whose germs I might pick up."

"Cheeky bitch," said Joyce, "I'm very particular about what I do with my mouth."

Sam handed her the glass.

"We know you are darlin'" he said. "Taste that, the best thing that ever touched your lips."

"I thought that was the bloke from Burnley with the Bentley," said Sandra.

"Depends which lips you're talking about," said Joyce taking the glass, and the lunatic laughter of the two girls rose like an Atlantic breaker before a lashing gale sweeping all inhibition and decorum under the crack of the unpainted door.

She brought the glass to her lips, took a mouthful and at once spat it over the little table.

"Oh my god, what's that?"

"That's classy French wine," said Sam.

Joyce dragged the back of her hand across her mouth.

"Clean your bath with it," she said, "it'll move those stains in seconds. Sandy, where's the gin, for Christ's sake. That's the worst thing I've ever had in my mouth."

"And that's sayin' somethin'," said Sandra reaching into her handbag for the bottle of Gordon's.

She poured generously into the teacup and the empty mug and the girls nestled beside one another like little sisters after bath-time on a Sunday night.

"Oh, that's better," said Joyce, "that's what I call a drink."

"Put some music on," said Sandra "it's like a funeral parlour in here."

Sam knelt to plug in the record player. He put on Django Reinhardt and Stephan Grappelly with the *Quintet of the Hotclub of France*. *Honeysuckle Rose* plaintively bowed by the violinist filled the little room.

"What's this rubbish?" said Joyce.

"This is Django," said Sam "the greatest jazz guitar man in the world."

110

"Well, Django can go-go," said Joyce. "Give us something we can dance to. I'm in the mood."

So Sam took off the music he loved and found a recording of Benny Goodman playing Gershwin. The first number was *I've Got Rhythm* and at the sound of the dancing clarinet the girls jumped up and began to step around the floor in imitation of what they thought was the Jitterbug.

"What are we dancing?" called Sandra.

"Who cares. Lindy Hop."

"That's not the Lindy Hop," said Sam.

"What do you know?" called Joyce.

Sandra collided with the table and sent the cups tumbling. Bert righted them and ran to the kitchen to find something to mop up the mess.

"My favourite dance is the collegiate shag," shouted Sam.

The girls howled, grabbed one another and swung around the little floor as if it were the Blackpool Tower ballroom.

"That's a dance for the bedroom," said Sandra.

Sam, a drink in his hand, was stepping along with the girls. Bert had found a dirty towel on the floor and was wiping up the spilt wine and gin. Sandra, panting, collapsed on the sofa and let her knees swing apart so that when he looked up, Bert saw her stocking tops, suspenders and knickers. He felt a little spurt of illicit and unpleasant excitement. Sam, taking his opportunity, grabbed Joyce and the two of them, pressed tight against one another like strangers on a crowded tram, staggered and clumped in a bout composed of an incompetent fox-trot, an inept waltz, a misconceived Charleston and a demented Jitterbug. Bert took the wet, stained towel into the kitchen, wrung it out and when he came back found Sam and Joyce with their mouths glued together as they swayed across the dirty carpet.

He sat in the rocking chair. Sandra swung her legs up onto the sofa and tugged down her red skirt as though concerned for her modesty. She picked up her cup, sipped and held it close like a child its teddy bear. Bert watched the tottering pair, as if interested. Joyce's arms were slung round Sam's neck like a boys' rope swung over an arching branch which bows and springs under the weight of its load. Her skirt was sliding up her legs, her blouse pulling free of the band of

111

her skirt and her breasts popping out of the buttons Sam was fumbling assiduously to unfasten. She let out a little squeal half of amusement, half of affront, as his long hands grabbed the twin moons of her backside. Bert had a nauseous feeling that he was going to hitch up her clothes to reveal her underwear, suspender belt and stocking tops. He thought for a distressing moment that in their mutual drunkenness they were about to collapse on the acrid rug and rut like heedless dogs subjecting himself and Sandra to the always ridiculous and unedifying spectacle of people doing what comes most naturally and yet always seems most unnatural; but Sam guided his afternoon love towards the open bedroom door. She kicked off her stilettos to steady herself. Bert and Sandra heard the heavy, muffled thud as they fell across the bed, followed by Joyce's laughter, squawks and shrieks and Sam's breathless grunts and groans. Bert got up and pulled the door to. It wouldn't close. He yanked on the brass handle but the frame titled one way and the door the other so the best he could do was fold *The Sporting Life* and jam it between the two edges. His hope that this would deaden the sound enough to allow him and Sandra to talk over the knocking shop cacophony was in vain.

"I think I'll make myself a cup of tea," he said. "Fancy one."

"I'll stick to the gin, thanks. My mother told me never to mix my drinks."

Dawdling in the kitchen he thought the circus might be over before he had to go back and be polite to Sandra. He wondered why he didn't just leave, but it seemed unmanly; to walk out would be interpreted as moral disagreement; he didn't want to appear supercilious or as small-minded as a net-curtain twitcher. All the same, he found the business unpleasant and boring; the time was starting to drag horribly, like the minutes to the end of a long sermon; this kind of low-level activity, drinking precious hours away, idling when something productive could be achieved, engaging in drunken copulation that could lead only to regret of one kind or another was a rusty saw-blade across the grain of his ambitions.

It was true Elsie could have benefited from a thimbleful of Joyce and Sandra's open-legged nonchalance, but it was equally true they could have been improved by a quantum of her self-discipline. It was odd. Why were girls like Joyce and Sandra so come-what-may? They were pleasant enough. He liked them. They had plenty of qualities and he imagined sooner or later they'd settle down and be good wives and mothers. Maybe they were doing nothing more than opening the doors and letting a little mischievous air circulate through the musty house of respectability and responsibility; perhaps they were only too aware of how narrow and low-roofed were their possibilities and were finding out how it felt to behave like a rabbit in the cabbage patch before propriety insisted they be confined to their hutches.

Yet while he could be tolerant, while he asked what difference it made, after all, that Joyce and Sam weren't married or even committed in any way; while he could wonder what difference, in the end, marriage made to the *act*, he was as ill-at-ease as a teetotaller in a brewery. Yes, having sex with a woman you were intending to spend your life with was as different from what Sam and Joyce were doing as Mars from the Yorkshire Dales, yet the *act*, the simple *act* was the same. He couldn't get upset about people satisfying their lust, if they chose to, any more than he could get upset about a man falling like a locust on a wrapper of fish and chips or a woman offering the gut-deity one chocolate after another.

All the same, he felt it a waste. It wasn't getting anywhere. It was as weightless as those insignificant ways people have of filling heavy time: doing crosswords or playing whist. He couldn't twist himself to those things. They seemed like ropes tying him to the empty moment as surely as the earth is held in its orbit by the sun.

He went back into the slovenly living-room. Sandra was stretched out like a corpse, her cup on her chest held by her unsure hand whose bright red nails contrasted violently with the white ceramic. He sat down with a sigh, trying to ignore the uproar from the bedroom but Joyce was one of those noisy women who rouse easily and let out great cries of immoderate pleasure at every effort of the cock perched on her trying to prove his prowess. Bert had only Mrs Bruzzese as a comparison and she was much more a delicately panting woman who sucked in air in little gasps of delight. He could hear the bed thumping and creaking. Joyce's full-lunged hoots and whines were as impossible to ignore as a wasp after your ice-cream. At a particularly loud, three-fold whoop, Sandra giggled as if her ribs were being tickled.

113

"Sounds like they're having a good time," said Bert in the hope of diminishing the embarrassment.

"She is," said Sandra and after a pause, "she always does."

Bert wondered if this was a gambit to entice him into licentious territory but he had no desire to do more than chat about the weather or the continuing privations of rationing.

"Do you have a job, Sandra," he said with a smile in his voice.

"Unfortunately."

"What do you do?"

"Packer."

"What do you pack?"

"Biscuits."

"Do you get free samples?"

"Enough to feed the Eighth Army."

"Perk of the job."

"I hate biscuits."

"Why?"

"I must have packed ten million *Morning Coffee*. The very sight of one makes me want to commit murder."

Bert laughed just they heard a clamorous wail from Joyce "Yes, yes, yes," and the dry scrape of the bed increased its clunking pace. Sandra giggled again.

"Still, you've got a job."

"Worst luck."

"There might be prospects."

"The only prospect for me is *Chocolate Digestives*."

"You never know. The world is changing, Sandra."

A brassy caterwaul of "Oh, my god, oh, my god" almost drowned him out. Sandra giggled again and as the noise from the bedroom increased, the hoarse squawk of the bedsprings beating a galloping rhythm, she was unable to bring her simper to an end, as if an electrical impulse was applied to her nerves every two seconds making her rock and emit little throaty mewls.

114

"Opportunities are opening up for women," Bert went on as a lusty ejaculation of inarticulate moans and screams filled the room. The door might have been open, the walls composed of nothing more substantial than brown paper. The din was as close to them as if they were sitting by the bed, as attentive to its occupants as parents to a sick child. Sandra's giggles were getting more frequent, like the contractions of a woman in labour.

"I'm a great believer in female emancipation," said Bert

Joyce's braying was as regular as a piston. There was barely a second between one whinny and the next; as they edged nearer together they increased in volume. Bert sipped his tea in the hope the climax would arrive any instant and in the ensuing lull he would be able to talk to Sandra as if they were sitting on the church lawn for a Sunday afternoon picnic; but the ecstatic frenzy only quickened and the pumping of the screeching, unoiled bed frame became more and more reminiscent of a mill at full production.

"They'll go through the ruddy ceiling," exclaimed Sandra.

The hooting and honking grew louder, the drones between one peak and another longer, the exclamations more urgent; she soared to a shrill falsetto like a piccolo blown altissimo; she sank to husky, sepulchral bellows, like a calving cow.

"Education, that's the key. An educated woman should be able to go as far as any man."

There came the final roar like an engine gunned to master a steep climb; the shuddering gasp of intense pleasure pounded once, twice, three times, four times.

"Christ, the bed'll be in pieces."

She went on: five, six, seven.

"You'd think it was a bloody rhino in there," said Sandra.

Bert drank his tea. Eight, nine, ten. Little by little the volume diminished. She gave a brief cackle. There was a pause followed by smoky, bouncing laughter, as if she'd just heard a joke that amused her to incapacity. Bert was relieved. He set his mug on the floor. Sandra was tapping her nails against her cup: one two three four, one two three four.

"Whereabouts do you live?" said Bert.

115

"Thinking of walking me home?"

He laughed.

"Just interested. I live with a relative of mine. That's the war for you. But Attlee'll sort it out."

"Who?"

"Clem Attlee. The Prime Minister."

"I can't be doin' with politics. It puts me to sleep."

"All the same, things are changing. The war was a terrible thing but it's brought some good. We'll never go back to the poverty of the thirties now."

Sandra wriggled herself half upright and propped her tousled head with a cushion.

"What did you do in the war?" she said.

" RAF."

"Pilot?"

"No. They wouldn't train lads like me. I worked on the ground."

"Doin' what?"

"Loading bombs. Paperwork. Whatever needed doing they told you to do it."

"Not every exciting then?"

"War isn't exciting."

"Bet it's more exciting than packing biscuits."

"Men say nothing's more exciting than being shot at, but it's a perverse excitement. It's little boys playing games. When you think about what war does to people. There's no excuse for it."

"I don't understand it, but I'm glad it's over. The blackout drove me crazy."

Sam came through in his shirt and trousers a firm *Woodbine* sticking out from his lips.

"Got a light, Sandra? Can't find mine."

"I'm surprised you've got the energy to smoke," she said swinging her legs round and picking her red handbag from the floor.

"Plenty of petrol left in the tank," said Sam. "Fancy a ride?"

She tossed a box of *Swan Vesta* to him.

"I'd have to wait an hour for your tyres to be pumped up," she said.

"Hard as rock in a minute."

"I think you've got a puncture. Better get it repaired."

"Want to check me inner tube?"

"No thanks. I'm particular. Never pick things up off the street my mother said, you don't know where they've been."

He nodded and smiled, drew on the cigarette and went back into the bedroom. Bert felt ready to leave.

"Smoke?" said Sandra.

"No."

She lit one for herself and puffed as she set her elbows on her knees, her chin in her palm, looking wistfully in front of her as if for inspiration.

"I love a cigarette," she said. "I don't know how you can live without them."

"The way I look at it," said Bert, "they cost a small fortune and do your health no good."

"My granddad smokes and he's fit as a ferret."

"There's always an exception."

"Anyway, you have to have your pleasures in life, don't you."

"Of course."

"What are they?" she said, leaning on the sofa's arm and bringing her right leg up onto the cushions.

"Mine?"

"Yours."

The question bothered him because it was true he didn't organize his life around everyday pleasures. What people thought of as pleasures – smoking, drinking, gambling- seemed to him silly indulgences. They were a kind of weakness, a compensation for being unable to rise to life's stern demands. Yet faced with someone like Sandra who could get as much pleasure from a cigarette as he might extract from making his plans for the future, he felt his life lacked something; his character lacked something.

117

Perhaps he should be more like his grandparents? But the idea was ludicrous. They'd wasted their lives. They were victims of their own debased appetites. And Sandra, what would she make of hers? Forty years of packing biscuits; a conventional marriage more endured than enjoyed; a couple of kids; a decent little terrace or a council house; retirement on a paltry pension; death from emphysema wondering what her life was all about? It seemed to Bert that things were set up somehow to ensure girls like her couldn't make the best of themselves. Yet what did that mean? He wasn't sure, but it was to do with wriggling free of what you were supposed to be, rubbing off the wool of what you were supposed to do, finding some small space in which you could discover some way of living which defied imposed definitions. What saddened him about a girl like Sandra was it looked as though the map of her life had been drawn by others and, utterly unaware of following a route laid down prior to the start of her journey, she would take a path she thought was her own and never know how she had been cheated.

Yet it was true: she was more able to go directly to her pleasures than him. What were his pleasures? Reading?Listening to music? Watching a football match?

"My greatest pleasure," he said, "is reading."

"Crickey. Your *greatest* pleasure."

"I'd say so."

"Find yourself a good woman," she said, throwing back her head and blowing a long, grey, feather of smoke into the unhealthy atmosphere.

He laughed but he wasn't sure he hadn't made a fool of himself. He thought of Mrs Bruzzese. It was true the pleasure was like no other, but so was the pleasure of reading. It wasn't possible to compare them. It was like comparing an after dinner nap with a brisk walk by the sea. Every pleasure was its own. The pleasure of sex was curious. He was only too aware he was basing his conclusions on flimsy evidence, but to go on like Sam, to have one Mrs Bruzzese after another, might keep frustration at bay but it dragged with it an inadequacy as heavy as a trailerful of bricks.

Just as you wouldn't want to sit across from someone you didn't like and eat a meal; as life would lack continuity, like a task begun and never accomplished, if you ate with a different person every day; so sex was nothing but a fleeting if intense sensation if it wasn't embedded in the delight of sharing. It was hard for him to bring it clearly into focus, but the anticipated gentle pleasures of living long with Elsie, of having children, of living beyond himself in a set of relations which demanded discipline as well as delivering fulfilment, was far more appealing than the rat-in-a-box life Sam led.

It was true he got to know lots of women. There was something to be said for seeing nineteen year-old girls naked in your bed; but in the end Sam was like the rat programmed to hit the lever to get its lump of cheese; round and round he went, one girl after another, but never anything that rose above mere rubbing off the tension. Maybe he was fond of Joyce. Maybe they could have a life together. But it was much more likely he couldn't get beyond seeing her as tasty young flesh, that he would be bored of her five minutes after the tangle, that he would rather head off to the bookies or the pub or in search of another pair of young thighs than spend an hour in her company.

"I have," he said.

"Who's she?" said Sandra and he was surprised by the hint of jealousy in her tone.

"My fiancée."

"When's the wedding? Do we get an invite?"

"As a matter of fact," he said, "I proposed this afternoon."

"Did she accept?"

"I don't know."

Sandra let out a rollicking, mocking, snigger of a laugh.

"Find yourself someone else," she said.

"It's a serious matter. I wouldn't want her not to think about it."

"While you're thinking about what to do with your life, your life goes by," she said, rocking her right knee.

There was something ugly in her provocation; something, he thought, almost evil. The afternoon had put her in a nasty mood. Maybe it was having to listen to Joyce's pleasure; maybe she was jealous; maybe she just felt left out and in that flat, couldn't-care-less mood which makes people do things they regret. She drew hard on her cigarette.

She was a young girl after all, what had made her so hard? Her cynicism frightened Bert. As always the sense of people giving in to their
whims brought his childhood to mind; the horrible fear of being left
alone; the terrible shame of seeing his drunken grandfather swing his
thick branch of an arm to catch his grandmother against the side of
her head with his knuckles so she staggered and cursed.

She was willing to have sex with him, but why? Because she just felt
the urge? As a way of passing the time? Or did she find him attractive and sympathetic? He didn't like it. It was like the poverty he
was determined to escape and the grim duty of war: things that
sprang from the vicious side of human nature and which should be
fought off with as much energy as possible.

"If you don't think about it, you waste it," he said.

"I don't see why."

"Life is a challenge," he said. "You have to rise to it to feel you're
living and to rise to it you have to know what it is."

"Really?" she said, as bored as a child in church.

"What do you want out of life?"

"Right now I could do with some more gin and a good man," she
said and he heard a hint of violence in her voice which shocked him
and made his heart race.

Joyce appeared combing her hair.

"I could've done with some ear-plugs," said Sandra.

"You two been enjoying yourselves?" said Joyce, standing before the
little mirror that hung above the table.

"He's been telling me about his pleasures," said Sandra.

"Mmm. Fancy."

"You know what he likes best?"

"Surprise me."

"A good book."

"*Fanny Hill* you mean?"

"I don't think it's fanny he favours."

"You're not one of them, are you Bert?" said Joyce turning to him.

He laughed and was immediately aware of how nervous and defensive he sounded.

"He's just asked someone to marry him," said Sandra.

"Congratulations," said Joyce smiling widely so an inadvertent observer might have thought her innocent as a daisy.

"She turned him down," blurted Sandra.

"No, she didn't," protested Bert.

"Never mind. There'll be others," said Joyce as if all the experience in the world lay behind her opinions.

"She wants time to think, that's all," said Bert.

Sandra and Joyce looked at one another. They raised their eyebrows as resignedly as women who have brought up children, suffered bereavement and known every disappointment. Sam came through rubbing Brylcreem into his black hair.

"Can I borrow your comb?"

"No. I don't want it full of all that grease."

"It's only a bit of Brylcreem."

"A bit? You could lubricate the Royal Scotsman with what's on your head."

"Got a comb?" he said to Bert.

"Sorry."

"Tyres pumped up yet?" jabbed Sandra.

"Full pressure."

"Come on, Sandy," said Joyce. "Time for us to go."

"You've had yours, I want mine."

"You been sitting here for an hour slurping gin," replied Joyce. "You should've got stuck in."

"I want some action not a bedtime story," protested Sandra tossing her head like a horse breaking free across an open field.

Joyce and Sam laughed in unison but Bert could only smile and drum his fingers on the arm of his chair.

"Got to get to the bookies," said Sam.

"Come on, Sandra. We'll be late for the pictures if we don't get going."

"What you going to see?" said Sam.

"*The Captive Heart*," said Joyce.

"Sounds romantic," said Sam.

"Well, you know me. I'm all romance at heart."

"You'll be too busy snoggin' to see the film," said Sandra.

"So will you," retorted Joyce.

"But I'm ready for a snog. You've just had fish and chips and now you're ready for egg and bacon."

"I always did have a good appetite."

Joyce and Sam chuckled. Bert got up and followed them to the door. Sandra came after him. In the street Joyce gave Sam a peck on the cheek, as if he were a faithful husband leaving for work. The girls clicked away on their stilettos.

"Comin' to the bookies?" said Sam

"No, I'll get on."

"Maybe see you in *The Railway*?"

"Maybe."

The two men shook hands and went in opposite directions.

Bert spent the evening at home. Aunty Alice had made hot pot. She always prepared it in the same bowl, deep as a canyon and wide as the Mersey. When she drove the shovel of the serving spoon through the thick crust, it was as if the fire at the centre of the earth was forcing the hot contents to the surface; steam rose over the table till a grey mist stood between them, like clouds descending quickly on Coniston; the thin gravy bubbled and oozed as if it would keep coming like the lava from Vesuvius, bury them in its scalding progress and leave them charred and encased to be discovered by the future's mystified archaeologists.

She heaped the impossibly hot delicacy onto his plate and in that mound of potatoes, steak, carrots, onions and pastry was a love he'd never known; the petty circle of his plate embraced a shy intimacy which made him long for something better. In her odd and quiet way, Aunty Alice loved him. She'd spent the afternoon making this meal for him out of devotion. No-one had ever looked after him like this. He was like a wild boy left in the woods by his parents, reared by animals, who comes to civilization and is baffled. He'd done nothing to deserve this. There was no demand for anything in return. It was gratuitous kindness. He glanced at Aunty Alice without letting her notice. She was, as always, reserved and quiet. Here she was, a poor widow in the back streets of an industrial northern town; a woman whose life was limited by the size of her meagre purse; and yet in this little house, in these unlikely circumstances was all that was needed for happiness. He lifted the food on his fork. It was tasty and filling. He knew she would be pleased to see him eat with relish. When his plate was clean she said:

"Would you like a bit more, Bert?"

"I certainly would."

He held the plate out to her and she piled it as high as before. He liked to mash the potatoes in the hot liquid, spread them on the crust and enjoy the mixed flavours and textures. As he chewed, happy in a curious way to be sitting opposite good Aunty Alice, he thought of the afternoon; what would she think of Sam and Joyce? Was she right or was she just a deluded and conformist old lady, naïve about the realities of the world? Sex was a conundrum. Sam and Joyce weren't intimate yet they'd committed the *act* of ultimate intimacy. It was odd how the act could be separated from the emotion. They were almost strangers. They knew one another no better than Bert knew people he said hello to at Hopkirk's or on the street. Could it be as simple as that? Could people rub off the tension as strangers, part from one another and feel no regret? It seemed wrong. Not in any moral sense; Bert was far too familiar with the difficulty of getting by in life to raise himself to the level of a moral judge and condemn others for what they needed to do to avoid despair; but it seemed to twist his feelings in a way he didn't like. It was true, he'd done as much with Mrs Bruzzese; but that was different; the woman was dangling by her fingertips over a cliff-face of radical disappointment; her very destiny was in question; and anyway, he liked her and felt connected to her.

No, it was the oddness that sex was an intimate act that could be stripped of its intimacy which troubled him. He wanted it not to be true. The raw physical act ought always to be wrapped in the warm blanket of intimacy and love, as modest and undemonstrative as Aunty Alice's, should always make lust veil her face. He wondered

123

about Aunty Alice's married life; had she had her nights of wild passion? It was hard to imagine, yet women were like that; it was hard to imagine the slim and delicate frame of a young woman going through the pain and effort of childbirth; most burly men would faint at the prospect. So perhaps Aunty Alice had once moaned and wailed in her ecstasy like Joyce. And he thought of Elsie. Would she too let out those unrestrained animal howls? He wanted to know, but not in the way of Sam and Joyce. He wondered if he should tell Aunty Alice he'd proposed. He looked up from his almost empty plate. She met his eyes.

"Delicious," he said.

She smiled and in the creasing of her eyes he glimpsed the fresh young woman she'd been fifty-years ago; a young woman with all the charms to make a man lose his head. He thought it better not to tell her.

Elsie went home on the bus, unpacked the shopping and began to prepare the tea. She was angry at Bert for having proposed. She felt it an intrusion she must fight off. She went about peeling potatoes, chopping carrots and browning the meat with a brisk definitiveness which gave her away. Her father watched her for a few minutes and disappeared with his pipe. She felt as if she'd been handed a burdensome secret, as if someone had confessed murder and told her where the body was buried. It pushed her to a limit of aloneness she didn't like. She wanted to tell someone but couldn't talk to her father; he was a quiet, solid presence, as reliable as dawn, but she couldn't share what troubled her most with him. She would've liked to talk to her mother but that was impossible too. Anything which disturbed the old woman might tip her towards death; Elsie was as careful with her as with the china on the mantelpiece which she dusted every day.

Of her brothers, Eddie was the one she could confide in, to an extent; but she needed to talk to a woman. Only a woman, after all, knows how it feels to be in this situation. Yet what she was looking for was not advice but relief. She wanted the weight of her experience lifted from her. It was as if Bert had corrupted her by his request. Who was she to decide if she should marry him? She knew she didn't want to marry him as certainly as she knew she wanted to be married. She wanted to be a mother and that meant the respectability of marriage;

but marriage should just happen; it should be as inevitable as rain or the phases of the moon. The idea that she had to *choose*, that she had to make marriage happen, that she should be *responsible* for marriage, enraged her to the point of madness. Marriage was a thing *out there*. It was a given like birth or death, it must be accepted and made the best of; but it wasn't *personal*. It was terrible, terrible to have to choose. She'd never imagined it would happen like this; in her dreams, marriage had arrived, like a thunderstorm or a sunny day. It was the work of forces outside her which she neither understood nor could control. She would *be married*. It was an inevitability; but to choose a husband, to be *forced* to choose was too unpleasant to bear.

Bert was to blame. He had made her responsible and she hated him for it. If he hadn't asked. If somehow marriage had crept up on them like a back street thief and one day they'd found themselves man and wife, she could have accepted it; but Bert had thrust the map and compass into her hands and told her to find her own way through life. If only she could talk to her mother. If only she could ask her point blank what she should decide. If her mother said no, then Elsie could stand in front of Bert with her chin held high, her expression firm and tell him it was out of the question; if her mother said yes, she could look up at him shyly, smile wanly and accept with all the alacrity of consenting to have a kidney removed.

Why had he asked her? She had no idea. She hadn't anticipated it for a moment. They were *courtin'*; she accepted that; but it was a silly bit of boy and girl, hand-holding, doe-eyed dalliance; she'd never imagined from this innocent paddling at the shoreline he would suddenly drag her into the deep, cold water where the breakers rose over her head and she had to struggle to breathe. She who had never learnt to swim. Yet she would have to marry. Why not Bert? Perhaps it was meant to be. Nothing happened, after all, unless God intended it. Had He brought them together? Yet Bert's background worried her. His was the most disreputable family in the area. She'd seen him when he was a little boy running barefoot to school and she'd heard the other children's cold-blooded calling: *Pon-go! Pon-go!*

She'd felt sorry for him then as she felt sorry for him now. Her own family seemed to her a fortress against the viciousness, cruelty and corruption of the world. She thought herself very lucky. Her mother's non-conformism had taught her from her earliest days to think and act for herself and her father's faith in the Trade Unions as agents of improvement for working people and the Labour Party as the means of social transformation gave her as strong a hold on secular as on heavenly salvation. This sense of her family as superior to the surrounding culture, a little island of calm and restraint in a fast-flowing river of drink, tobacco, gambling, fecklessness and improvidence tugged at her Christian conscience like a hawthorn that catches your clothes on a country walk: was she being tested?; would marrying Bert be the good Christian way to behave?; would making him part of her family give him the chance he'd never had? At the same time her pulse quickened at the thought that he didn't bring a family with him. It had always bothered her, the thought of having to pick her way through the potholes in the cracked and uneven road of an inferior family's troubles; even worse was the thought of a conventional family, one of those nose-in-the-air working-class families which prided itself on earning a little more than the average, voted Tory, touched its forelock to its betters, read the *Daily Mail*, had a picture of the King over the mantelpiece and thought the Empire a great achievement.

Bert had the advantage of no baggage. He was the outcast looking for a home. She would need to make no effort to get to know his people. There would be no question of visiting his grandparents. She would refuse to set foot in their fetid house. As for his mother, Elsie had heard all about her from her mother and father and the rumours in the neighbourhood. She and her sister had been wayward girls; complaisant almost to timidity up to the age of fourteen or fifteen, the quiet stream of their lives, dominated by the histrionic drinking of their father and the terrifying braying and violence of the home, had swelled and broken its banks so they were hanging around the pubs, out on the streets late at night, seen with one man after another and both pregnant before they were twenty.

It was said Bert's father was a sergeant at the local barracks, a hard-drinking, thuggish arrogant young man, strong and athletic who used his good-looks to seduce one fribble after another. At a loss after the birth of her child, Winnie went on chasing men, became a drunk in the family tradition and was saved only when she took up with a married butcher from Blackpool, a man thirteen years older, who left his wife and set up home with her. He'd done well out of the black market during the war. Settled in her ostensibly respectable home in

Cleveleys, with two daughters and a good income from her husband's thriving shop, she had nothing to do with Bert, the shame and confusion of her past.

Bert's isolation made him attractive to Elsie: she could draw him into her family. He would have to adjust to her ways but she wouldn't need to orientate herself to anything new. She could carry on looking after her mother. They would have to live in her father's house. She would have her brothers as protection. The fear of other people's families, a terror which had always haunted her out of a feeling that only her own family was real(if she were to shift her thoughts and feelings to meet the ways of a new family, she'd no longer be herself), had always seized her when she moved from thinking of marriage as a distant abstraction, as something that would just happen like the other events of her life, to thinking of it as a reality. There was bafflement in it. Why should she want to leave her family? Why couldn't she have babies and stay with her family? Why couldn't a husband come into the light to give her babies and then retreat to the shadows? The truth was she'd never met a man who appealed to her strongly enough to be more important than her family.

At school there'd been boys who'd showed an interest in her. Colin Standish, who always flattered her, gave her cards for her birthday, Easter and Christmas; and others who looked at her in that curious way boys did, a kind of staring, as if something had switched off in their brains and they no longer knew how to be polite. It disturbed her that she could have this effect on them. It was nothing to do with her. It wasn't something she wanted. It happened. When she asked herself why, she realised it was because she was pretty. Hadn't Colin said she was the prettiest girl in the school? But she thought that stupidly soppy. Who would want to spend time with a boy who said such soppy things as he looked into your eyes and smiled like an idiot? A man should be like her father.

Bert, of course, was anything but. In a way, she despised him. She thought his talk of *getting on* vulgar and superficial. He was impressed by money. He bought himself expensive clothes. Compared to her father's selfless belief in a better future, that was nothing but cream on a trifle. Yet the thought of a nice house, of bringing her children up in Penwortham or Broughton, of a garden for them to play in, of a nice little school and a neighbourhood away from the docks, the pubs, the Saturday night fights and the prostitutes who served the Norwegian and Russian sailors from the big boats, softened her feeling towards Bert. He did have nice blue eyes. He was quick and easy in his movements, his voice resounded like a church bell and he could sing beautifully. These notions almost made her feel romantically towards him. She could nearly see herself with her head on his shoulder, allowing her feelings to depend on him, trusting him to be honest and fair and to behave in ways that would keep her happy.

She'd seen the films: *Casablanca* and *Brief Encounter* among others. Sitting in the darkened *Empire* with Maggie she'd allowed herself to be Ilsa or Laura; she'd experienced the power of love which runs up against the bars of convention like a hawk madly straining at its tethers ; she'd known the heartbreak of having to do the right thing, to let love run away like molten gold tipped into a sewer; of course, the sweet temptation of love was soured by the bitter shame of potential adultery; what could be worse for a woman than to behave so indecently? A woman must flee such a degrading possibility or be condemned. She didn't know that *Brief Encounter* was based on Coward's play in which doubt remains about whether physical love took place, nor that Coward was prodding conventional morality in the ribs, even though he feared offending his middle-class audience. She believed it was right that for both Ilsa and Laura love should go limping like a lame dog in the shadows.

Yes, the heart could stray but the strict laws of Christian propriety must crack like a lion tamer's whip and the wild howl of desire become a defeated whimper. She didn't know either that the plot of *Casablanca* was as likely as snowdrops on Mars; that uniformed Nazi troops were never in the town, that Laszlo would have been arrested by the Vichy officials. The images on the screen were more real than reality. It was hard not to be drawn into the world beyond the world of overpowering images. It never occurred to her that the sequence had been carefully structured to play on her ideas and emotions; it never struck her that she had the right to criticize; though she might like one film and not another, it didn't strike her that she had the means to go beyond mere liking or disliking. A film was like a sermon: something delivered which you must accept. So though she found fault here and there she felt it was her duty to value what was offered. It appeared to come from some authoritative source. Such big, powerful bodies as the Church and the film industry couldn't be founded on falsehood.

So her view of womanhood was compounded of revealed Biblical wisdom and manufactured Hollywood sentimentality. Was it a woman's lot to be forever unfulfilled? Did a woman have to accept dull conformity if the satisfaction of her mind and body meant defilement and censure? A woman had to be so careful; poor Celia Johnson imagined her meetings with Trevor Howard could remain innocent; but *the Devil went round like a roaring lion*; temptation could creep up on you like the 'flu and before you had time to think, your life could be in ruins and *eternity in Hell* ensured. She would come out of the cinema in a chastened mood. A serenity came over her that she cherished. She would walk home quietly with Maggie. They exchanged a few words about the film, smiled and said goodnight; Elsie went to her bed curiously at one with the world; but in the morning the effect of the film had worn off. She got up, washed and dressed, brought a cup of tea for her mother, began tidying and cleaning the house; the pictures of the actors were still in her head; she could hear their words; but the irritating facts of daily life were diminishing their sedative effect. Her father, as usual, had missed the bowl when he'd gone to the toilet so there was urine on the flagstones; she had to get down on her knees and scrub them clean; she accepted it was her job, but his carelessness annoyed her. Why couldn't he shoot straight? Jimmy had been to visit and helped himself to bread and jam, leaving the loaf on the table, the crumbs unswept, the butter unwrapped for the flies to land on, the sticky knife across the open jar, his plate sitting beside it asking to be washed. She could've throttled him. As she ran the things under the tap, she wondered if he did it consciously; did he think to himself: "Ah, Elsie will wash those up. That's her job." The idea drove her mad.

She would do anything for her mother because she was helpless, but for a grown man to behave so negligently, to make work for someone else, was despicable. But then she asked herself if it was simply thoughtlessness or preoccupation; perhaps he didn't at all imagine she would clear up after him but was so used to the idea that men didn't wash up, he simply didn't register that he was leaving a little mess for someone to attend to; then she wondered if he meant it as a sort of compliment: he was saying that without her or some other woman to take care of him, his life would be disordered. She had no idea which of these conjectures was right, but they made no difference: whichever was the correct explanation she was still niggled by being forced to carry out the little task.

She served her father liver and onions with mashed potatoes and peas. They sat opposite one another at the little table and it struck her he was an old man; most of the time she didn't notice. He was her father: that was as absolute as death. She had the idea of him in her head so she ignored the reality; but this evening with the gentle sun hitting the opening lights of the kitchen window and showing up his face in its glow, she noticed the sagging of the skin under his chin, the deep lines that ran from his nostrils past the corners of his mouth, the slight tugging down of his left eyelid, his scalp visible through his thinning hair, the long, wiry hairs sprouting from his ears. He was no longer the father she could look up to as a continuing source of strength. He was declining. If she stayed at home much longer, she would be alone with her invalid mother and a slow, needful man, who spent most evenings asleep in the armchair and who depended on her for almost everything.

Yet the thought of leaving home was impossible. No, if she had to establish some life of her own, if youth had to assert its rights, it must be done under this roof. The thought came to her that she didn't want to have children who wouldn't know their grandmother. How long would her mother live? And what if her father took ill too? She had to have children while her parents were alive. Yet this attractive imperative entailed an unpleasant necessity: a man. Not that men were unattractive but the *necessity* was. There were lads she thought a lot of: Maurice Bairstow for example, an honest, straightforward type who worked as an electrician for a local firm and clearly had a soft spot for her; he was what she always called a *grand lad* by which she meant he exhibited the values characteristic of her family. What puzzled her, however, was why she couldn't think of a man like that as a husband. Oh, she could imagine him coming home from work, sitting down to his tea, reading the paper, lighting the fire, playing with the children; she could see him up a ladder paper-ing the ceiling or coming back from his allotment with a bagful of dirty potatoes, cabbages, peas, carrots and cauliflower; she could envisage him on the beach at Blackpool, playing one touch cricket with the children, running to the sea in his rolled-up trousers ; she could conjure up the idea of them together in the cinema or doing an admired fox-trot at Hopkirk's; she could evoke them side by side at the six o' clock service at Lune St; she could witness Christmas, Easter, evenings, mornings, weekends, shopping, eating; but the one thing she couldn't bring to life was the idea of kissing him and all that followed.

Why was it a man like Maurice left her cold? It was strange. There was something about Bert that got things going in that respect. She'd seen handsome men on the street or at Hopkirk's and even Joe Dawkins at church was better looking than most; she knew the curious thrill of seeing an out-of-the ordinary man ; it was as if the very shape of his face was enough to take you in seconds from seeing him to having his baby. Bert wasn't like them. He wasn't so handsome you could feel yourself getting moist in spite of trying not to look at him. Yet she did stir. Mostly it was his voice. Yes, when she had her back to him and he laughed in the long, deep way he had there was something in it that stole away her self-control. She knew you had to be vigilant against the Devil, yet she liked it. It was a warm, soft feeling as comforting as bed at the end of an exhausting day. Then she was surprised to find she liked the *go-getter* in him. Or was excited by it. She didn't like it as a matter of choice. A man like Maurice Bairstow would be as good fresh shrimps; but he wouldn't go anywhere. The circle of his life was tightly prescribed and though she believed God had decided everything beforehand and nothing could prevail against that, couldn't it be that He meant her to have a husband who would provide well? Wouldn't it be wrong to defy God's will? A man who could give his children a good life was something to value. And she could visualize kissing Bert. Why was that? She had no idea. She decided to talk to Maggie.

A POT OF HONEY

Above the *Booth's* food shop on the corner of Glover's Court was their café. Though it was ordinary enough and not expensive, Elsie thought of it as *posh*; it was true that middle-class ladies would have high-tea there or well-dressed couples enjoy a flimsy lunch of diminutive triangle sandwiches and salad. She and Maggie walked the brief mile into town. They sat at a table by the window so they could see the trams, buses and few cars go by. Elsie remembered the previous winter when the snow had been thick on the pavements and it seemed the thaw would never arrive. They'd sat at the same table then. How different things were. How odd it was that your feelings could change so quickly. Maggie ordered coffee and a scone. She thought of coffee as a luxury and liked to spoil herself now and then. Elsie had no taste for it so the waitress brought two pots, a scone and an Eccles cake.

"Bert proposed to me," said Elsie.

"Have you accepted?"

"I haven't seen him since."

"Oh. You turned him down?"

"No. I don't know what to do."

"Take your time. He'll not leave the country."

"You know his background, Maggie. I'm not sure I want to marry into that."

"You're marrying him, not his background," said Maggie slicing her warm, crumbling scone.

"I know, but when I think about his mother," Elsie cut her Eccles cake into quarters.

"His mother's long gone isn't she?"

"But he's her son. Blood's thicker than water," replied Elsie.

"He's not a drinker," said Maggie adding sweet, thick raspberry jam to the buttered surface.

"No, that's one thing."

"He's in a good job." Crumbs stuck to Maggie's lips. She wiped

132

them with her laundered serviette.

"Oh, yes. White collar."

"You can't blame him for his mother, can you?"

"I don't blame him. I just wonder if his family's devil's in him." She sipped her tea whose lovely flavour held her from setting the cup back in its saucer.

"You never know how folk turn out, Elsie. Look at our Stan."

Stan was Maggie's older brother, scion of their hard-working, steady family. Her father did heavy work on the railways, her mother cleaned for the posh folk in Penwortham. Methodists like Elsie's mother, there was never so much as a delinquent bottle of pale ale in the house; Maggie's father didn't know what the inside of a pub looked like, and he and his wife Molly prided themselves on being able to get by on their modest income, put a little bit by, *stand on their own two feet* and present a face of disciplined decency to the world. But Stan was a drinker from the age of fifteen.

The war held back his career, but once demobbed he rose into the first rank of imbibers, lost his job, was regularly found incapable in the gutter, thrown in a cell, and scrounged off Maggie and his age-ing, hard-pressed parents to stay alive. Elsie shuddered to hear his name mentioned. Why had he gone bad ways? She was at a loss, but she blamed *the demon drink*. It should be banned. If people couldn't get their hands on it they couldn't end up like Stan. It was terrible that people made money from serving drink to *lost souls* like him. She would have been ashamed of making a living from selling drink. She would rather clean floors on her hands and knees for five shillings a week than earn twenty pounds selling booze. At least that was honest work which did some good. If only everyone made that their creed, to do honest work that brought good into the world, she was sure tragedies like Stan's could be avoided.

"Oh, Maggie," she said, "it's terrible. How is he?" and she put her cup to her lips for the comfort of the familiar drink.

"Same as ever," said Maggie, matter-of-fact, as if she were talking about the health of her budgerigar. She added half a spoon of brown sugar to her coffee and stirred with the delicacy of a painter applying a pattern to china. The liquid turned and made little waves that rose to the rim, threatened to climb over and run in little rivers down the side but fell back and gently slowed till the surface was still as a puddle on a windless day.

Elsie looked into her friend's face. She had a pale complexion and black hair which gave her a stark and impressive look. She wasn't pretty or beautiful. Her nose was long and slightly hooked and her lips were thin. They'd known one another so long and spent so many careless hours together Elsie felt they almost belonged to one another. Yet Max had fallen in love with her. Why? It was a puzzle. And why had she fallen for Max who was ordinary as a brick? Wasn't love supposed to be out of the ordinary? Wasn't it supposed to arrive like a tornado and leave you gasping for breath and unable to stay on your feet? All the same, Maggie and Max had done it. She was tempted to ask her what it was like, but she knew it was a silly question. It was one of those things you had to do for yourself. How peculiar it was that everybody did it and yet it was always private and intensely personal. There was a danger in it. It might drag you to some extreme. You might be unable to tell anyone about it. And wouldn't even an extreme of ecstasy feel odd if you had to keep it to yourself?

"Well," said Elsie with a falling intonation, as if the world were irrevocably tragic and nothing could be done, "if your Stan can end up in the gutter, someone with Bert's background hasn't much chance." She put another quarter of the moist Lancashire delicacy into her mouth and reflected that it was too buttery. Her own recipe was better.

"It was always in him," said Maggie buttering the second half of her scone, " he was wild as a boy. You could never get to him. There was some bit of him that was cut off. He was always like that. My mother took him to the doctor. He said he'd grow out of it. I think he was born like that, Elsie. There was some bit of his mind that was as dark as the Mersey tunnel in a power cut."

Elsie was shocked by the idea. It had never occurred to her that people could be born wayward or bad. The Bible said nothing about that. Babies were born innocent. That was a belief she couldn't renounce. How could the idea of the innocence of the new-born sit with the notion that Stan was born wayward? Perhaps it was true. Was there some imperfection that made people like Stan destined for disaster from the outset? Yet why would God make imperfect babies? She knew babies born with deformities. Why would God let that happen to the innocent? It was impossible to fathom. Unless it was the work of the Devil. Why couldn't He, after all, intervene while the child was growing in the womb? Yes, that must be it. The Devil would stop at nothing. He had invaded Stan's mind when an innocent child and turned him to drink. All the same, Elsie couldn't believe it had been inevitable. If Stan had turned to God, He would have helped him. The church would have rescued him. There were plenty of good souls who would have given him support and comfort. No soul was ever lost. There was always the chance of Redemption. Even now, if Stan repented, the way to the light would be open to him.

"I feel sorry for Bert," said Elsie. "He's had it hard." She poured more tea which was now almost black. Seeing it, she could taste the bitterness which always lingered in her mouth after too strong a brew.

"Aye, it's a shame, but he seems to be making the best of things." Maggie lifted her brimful cup with the slow attentiveness of a man disabling a bomb.

"He hasn't turned out too badly considering," said Elsie picking up two stray currants from her little white plate. "But I wonder if it was meant to be, if it's my Christian duty to take pity on him."

As small shock of alarm showed itself on Maggie's face as if she'd broken a tooth against something hard in her scone.

"Pity is no basis for marriage," she said.

Elsie looked at her. She was mystified. Why shouldn't pity be a basis for marriage? Christian pity. What was wrong with a wife pitying her husband? Wasn't pity close to love? Wasn't it an expression of Christian love? She liked Bert as much as she'd liked any man, which was little. She was no more than a girl when she had to leave school and devote herself to the care of her mother. She'd had no time for boys. Bert was her first experience of *courtin'*. He was all right, in his way. She was attracted to him. He wasn't an ugly man with repulsive habits. He kept himself clean and tidy and smart. Yes, she liked him and she felt sorry for him.

Perhaps that was enough for love to grow. She wondered about Maggie's feeling for Max. She had no reason to pity him. Yet what was Christian love if not pity for those in difficult circumstances? Didn't Christ help the poor, the lepers, the sick, the lame? Isn't that what a Christian should do? Wouldn't anything else be selfish?

Wouldn't it be selfish to marry someone for your own pleasure? Was that how Maggie felt about Max? Did she enjoy being with him? And they'd *indulged*. She knew the pleasure of sex with him. Was that what made her willing to marry him? She couldn't believe it of her friend. There had to be some Christian self-sacrifice in marriage. She thought of her mother and father. Compared to her, he was a shadowy, secondary presence.

Her mother's Methodism dominated the home. Her father's socialism followed in its wake like a rowing boat bobbing behind a big ship. Was there passion between them? It was impossible to imagine. She'd always thought, without knowing it, that her mother had taken pity on her father. Why? She couldn't bring it into focus. Perhaps it was because he was a quiet man who disliked being noticed. He rested on the domestic. He wasn't a man for the pub and the crowd. He recoiled from humanity in the collective, his socialism growing out of his strong sense that no-one should compromise their personal morality in front of power. Perhaps it was this slightly exquisite sensitivity in him her mother pitied. She was different: full of the certainty of her religious convictions and ready to impose it. In any case, Elsie couldn't grasp what Maggie meant.

"What do you mean, Maggie?" she said, and looking down at her empty plate, regretted her cake and wished she had another, or a scone as delicious as Maggie's had looked.

Maggie laughed. She had an anarchistic laugh which mocked every reverence and made Elsie feel she was in the presence of someone who would never betray her.

"Oh Elsie, what does a man want from marriage? He wants to be loved. In every way. So does a woman. That's what it has to be. Mutual love, not pity of one for the other. Too much in either pan and the scales won't balance, Elsie."

Elsie felt she should understand, but it was as if she'd just been told the second degree of a major scale produces a minor chord; all the words were comprehensible but she had no idea what it meant. It seemed rude to press Maggie, but they were good friends. Who else did she have?

"And you love Max."

"Of course I do," replied Maggie with a little smile, as if telling a child she could have another biscuit; she lifted her cup and took another sip of the hot strong coffee as if it contained the secret of her passion.

"What's it like?" said Elsie dabbing the corners of her mouth with her serviette.

Maggie looked at her hard and seriously.

"You mean physically?" she said putting the cup in its saucer and scooping a few crumbs from her plate on the tip of middle finger.

"No," said Elsie blushing a little. "Not that. I mean, being in love." Her cup was empty. She tipped the pot, but it was dry.

Maggie looked at her, lowered her eyes to her plate, then looked out of the window. A *Morris Minor* was creeping along behind the bus its trafficator indicating left. The thought occurred to her it would nice to own a little car like that, to have a ride out to Blackpool or The Trough at the weekend. Perhaps, one day, she and Max would save up enough to buy one.

"You just know, Elsie," she said and she turned her brown eyes on her friend. "Like as a child you knew your parents loved you. How? You just do. If you don't know, Elsie, you're not in love with him."

The plates were empty, the tea and coffee exhausted. The two of them looked out of the window. The street was pleasantly busy. It was curious how comforting the coming and going of strangers could be. There were women carrying bags of shopping, young girls arm in arm, young men in suits smoking as they went. Elsie noticed a lad hurrying to keep up with his father, a rough-looking man with a strong stride. She recognised him as one of the men she'd seen coming out of the pubs on Marsh Lane on a Saturday afternoon. The boy was skipping and hopping along beside him but the man refused to slow his pace or look at him. What a shame, she felt. Why were people cruel to their children? The God who was slow to chide and swift to bless was her model of a parent.

"Look," cried Maggie. "Isn't that him?" She'd got out of her seat and was waving as if she'd spotted her long lost mother.

"Who?" said Elsie still on her chair.

"Bert."

Elsie jumped up. As she put her face close to the window, she saw him. He'd noticed them and was smiling and waving.

"He's coming up," said Maggie.

"Heaven help us," said Elsie falling back into her seat as if gravity had grabbed her by the hips.

"Have I done the wrong thing?"

"No, no," said Elsie. "It'll be fine."

Maggie put her hand over Elsie's.

"You can introduce me properly. You know, I've hardly ever done more than say hello to him on the street."

The touch of Maggie's hand was surprising. Physical contact was avoided in her family. Her mother had an abhorrence of what she called *soppiness*. More than once, out in public with her as a child, Elsie had heard her say with disdain about a couple walking arm in arm or hand in hand: "Frightened of losing one another!" She couldn't recall ever seeing her mother and father touch one another, nor did she have any memory of being cuddled by her mother. Sitting on her father's knee to look at a book she remembered. Thinking of it, nestling against the warmth of him with a coal fire cracking and flaring in the grate, she could still smell the reassuring tobacco on his clothes, and though he wasn't demonstrative, he would let her curl up on him, rest her head on his chest and go to sleep.

She'd never seen her mother touch her brothers either. Her love was expressed in keeping their clothes cleaned and ironed and in placing big plates of good food in front of them; yet her declarations of maternal affection were frequent and fulsome: "One thing you can't give your children too much of is love," she would say, or if some ill-fate touched the life of a child she knew: "If it were one of mine I'd be heartbroken." So the gentle warmth of Maggie's touch opened up some part of her, like a flower closed against the night which spreads its bloom in the morning sun. It seemed very odd to Elsie that friendship and kindness could be expressed in such a direct way. She and Maggie had linked arms often enough a girls, but that was more chirpiness and the devil-may-care *joie de vivre* of youth than any subtle indication of generous feeling.

Bert appeared smiling at the top of the stairs. He was wearing a blue sports jacket and matching trousers. He looked fresh as an April meadow, clean-shaven, his hair neatly combed back from his forehead. As Elsie turned to look at him she thought, for the first time, that he was a man women might notice. She realised she'd never seen him in this kind of setting before: he'd been to her home, they'd gone to events at church together, to the cinema, strolling in the park; but even on their trips to the cinema they'd walked into town, bought their tickets, sat in the dark together and walked home, as if the rest of the world didn't exist. Suddenly, this seemed public. The café was crowded. There were plenty of women; in pairs, with their husbands or boyfriends, even a few with their children. It struck her Bert might be attractive to a young woman looking for a husband and seeing him stride towards them across the maroon carpet the big smile still on his face like a child about to receive his present from Santa Claus, she felt a twinge of jealousy.

It was odd and she didn't like it. It clanged with her view of herself as a loving Christian. He didn't belong to her. She had no claim on him any more than he had on her. Yet, she felt he should be mindful of her feelings. He shouldn't behave in a way which might attract the attention of other women. He was young, strong, confident, well-presented. The life in him made her wince. He seemed to be calling to her, like a siren to a returning sailor, and she felt she should leave what was familiar to her and go to meet him in whatever the un-known territory of love of a man was like; yet at the same time she resented that he could evoke new feelings in her. Who was he, after all? Just Pongo, the unwashed boy from the pig-sty home. He should be grateful she allowed him into her life, but he paced the room as if he could walk on water. She didn't like it. The very way he held himself was something she wanted to correct. Her father's more re-served, contained demeanour was congenial. Her brothers were the same. There was no look-at-me-here-I-am in their carriage.

There was something too present in Bert's presence, like the yapping of a fox-terrier faced with a muscular bulldog. The men in her own family were the opposite; like whales they swam in the social ocean with huge calm which contained a power without need to impress. The odd thought came to her that she would need to reform Bert out of his too ostentatious ways. She recoiled slightly from it. Did it mean she was already thinking of him as a husband? A week ago he'd proposed and now she was locked into the definition of pro-posed-to-woman. She found it very disturbing. If she were to turn him down, would other proposals arrive? Suppose they didn't. Oh, men were interested enough in her, but there was no guarantee. And would a proposal come from anyone more to her liking ? How much longer could she wait? The war had interrupted the flow of life. Those were years when, under normal conditions, she might have been getting to know boys, *courtin'* a few, moving from whimsicality to seriousness; but none of that had been possible. She had her mother to look after.

Once war was declared, young men disappeared like bees in a July downpour. All those *grand lads* she knew were in uniform. It was an emotional interregnum which made the needs all the more urgent. Wasn't that why Maggie had ended up *in trouble*? The pain and restraint of war pushed people towards a healthy nonchalance. *Que sera, sera.* Shouldn't life embrace that come-what-may attitude? But the war had made that impossible. Every detail of life must contribute towards the *war effort*. You couldn't throw away a crust of stale bread without feeling you were letting the country down. Your life wasn't your own. If you were going to have a life you had surrender it to the *effort*. This was life and death. If the Nazis hadn't been defeated, life might have been no more than slavery. Yet it was a terrible wager. She felt, in some vital way, she'd stopped living for six years. Had the war never happened she might be married with a child by now. It made her, like it made lots of young women, impatient. And here was Bert, looking like a man on the way somewhere. He had created a difficulty, but at the same time he had lifted her out of isolation and the possibility of spinsterhood.

Being a proposed-to-woman conferred a certain status after all. Elsie had been raised to care little for what others thought. Behaving well towards others, always considering their interests and feelings, went hand in hand with the courage to refuse to bark with the dogs of common wisdom. From her earliest years her father had told her: "Never mind what others do, tha thinks for thaself" She couldn't but understand, like a child told every day to wash her hands before meals. Though he had no religious belief, he was strongly attracted to the individual conscience of non-conformism. Sitting in church singing hymns or listening to a sermon seemed to him a waste of time; the practical business of getting people decent wages, improving their housing, making sure they had a doctor when they were ill and a school for their children, made much more sense. But what he'd always admired in his mother's Methodist faith was its powerful insistence on making your own agreement with existence. To work out a personal morality without the intervention of a priest; to be able to correct your own misbehaviour without sitting in a box making false confessions to a loveless man in a frock; to have to find, somewhere in your own mind, in spite of all its weaknesses and the forces assailing it, the strength to face the world armed only with your moral convictions, even if the rest of the world disagreed with you; that was worth pursuing and sat well with his commitment to democracy and equality.

Yet she knew the difference between being seen as a woman *on the shelf* and a woman soon to be married. There was a prejudice against spinsters. What was wrong with Miss Bates, the woman who lived alone at number 17? She'd heard the question asked. It wasn't natural. As far as anyone knew, there'd been no man in her life. There was no story of failed love, a broken engagement or the loss of her man in the war. No-one could believe she chose to be single. Her mongrel seemed her only company. She had a job in a confectioner's, went to church on Sunday morning, but apart from that appeared never to venture out. People said it was strange. Children were warned to stay away from her. Elsie herself had moments of suspicion. A woman on her own attracted disdain like a jumble sale attracted punters. So in spite of herself Elsie enjoyed her new status as a proposed-to-woman.

She didn't know that when hard choices have to be made the mind rationalizes difficulties like a conflagration burns oxygen and though what is left may appear as beyond combustion as water, it is in fact as volatile as petrol. In Bert's final three paces she was going to decide to marry him. She had no idea she was making such a decision, but her mind was already well advanced in the process of setting the objections aside in pursuit of what it saw as advantage, like a woman who applies for a low-grade, demeaning job and when she's appointed thinks only of the benefit of a regular wage and two weeks holiday. In the full light of her consciousness she still saw Bert as pretentious, too pushy, too impressed by money and lacking principle; but her conscious mind was a flimsy, balsa-wood road block against the advancing tanks of unacknowledged need and desire, and she had no more chance of doing what she thought than a bee giving up seeking nectar.

"Hello, ladies," he said.

"Hello," said Elsie with a nervous little laugh.

"Hello, Bert," said Maggie. "Were your ears burning?"

"You were saying nice things about me were you, Elsie?"

"I was telling the truth."

"Even better."

"It's nice to meet you anyway," said Maggie, "We've only ever given one another the time of day."

"Nice to meet you too. And congratulations."

Maggie laughed in her unbridled way.

"Most folk commiserate."

"They're fools," said Bert. "Bringing a child into the world is always something to celebrate."

"Bringing it into the world is the easy bit," said Elsie.

She was thinking of Bert's family and spoke before she could stop herself. A niggle of irritation at his breezy declaration impelled her.

"You're right," said Bert. "You and Max've got your work cut out now, Maggie."

"Yes, but it's good work," she said.

Elsie realised her barb had missed. She wanted to start a little argument with Bert. She didn't know why, but somehow she felt more alive in an argument. She knew where she was.

"Does it make you broody, Elsie?" said Bert turning to her with that broad smile she found too willing to please.

"Not me," she said, "I've enough on my plate."

But he'd hit his mark. It was true, Maggie's pregnancy did prey on her mind. They'd grown up together and without thinking about it she'd assumed they would marry and have children at the same time. People didn't move away from Elsie's little corner; it was part of the culture of working people that they stayed put and made the best of things. Even Bert, who'd been shipped out to Egypt in demeaning conditions and hadn't sniffed the dirty air of north-west England for six years, didn't think of escaping. There were little villages in the Cotswolds unscarred by the acid of industrialism; there were places in Berkshire and Surrey where you could almost forget factories existed; there were corners of Oxfordshire where you never heard the hooter at five or saw hordes of men jumping on their bikes, their snap-bags across their backs; and even in Lancashire some people lived as if electricity came from a distant planet; Bert would take to the lanes in his car, as if the countryside belonged to him, but what struck him quickly wasn't a sense of freedom, but amazement at the big houses and the huge swathes of land. He would drive through Woodplumpton which was no more than three miles from the town centre, past Beacon Fell and out to Chipping and Whitewell. Why were people so cramped in the town? Why did people talk about Britain being overcrowded? It puzzled him. There were thousands of acres of unused land; and the difference between his grandparents' tiny house, or Elsie's, or Aunty Alice's, and the places out here, houses that could house four families, tightened his muscles and brought a constriction to his chest.

Five miles out of town it was a different world. Something was wrong. He'd grown up in streets where there wasn't a tree or a blade of grass; you didn't see a butterfly or hear a blackbird. Why wasn't the town full of greenery? Why wasn't there space and fresh air? Bricks and concrete and tarmac rubbed harshly against the mind. He would've liked to live in a big house with an acre of field behind it for his children to play. Why hadn't he grown in a better place? Why not a little house surrounded by green, with a rambling rose over the door, a bit of garden, the chance to breathe? He couldn't understand it. The towns had grown out of industrialism, that was simple. People had to live near the factories. But surely it couldn't have been intended that they should live in such soiling conditions; surely everyone wanted children to live and grow with gentleness and ease and what would make them healthy and happy.

He couldn't believe that it had been deliberately arranged that most folk should be shoved into towns where there was barely room to breathe. There was enough space to give everyone a garden and an orchard. Yes, they were Tory voters in these spots, but he couldn't believe they were so mean-spirited they wanted to keep the land and fresh air for themselves. It didn't make sense. All the same, Bert didn't think of shifting to another part of the country because to do so needed money. His most far-gone ambition was to be able to live in the suburbs; a house with three bedrooms and ten square yards of garden was, for him, an exorbitant aspiration. He didn't know that in

Oxfordshire, Berkshire, Kent, Surrey, in Cheshire and even in the salubrious nooks of Lancashire, there were people who disdained his ambitions, who mocked his desire for betterment, who thought of him as an *oik*, a *ruffian*, a *guttersnipe*, a *Yahoo*, a brute who should stay where he belonged; who feared the rise of his kind as a contagion and would do whatever they must to keep him *in his place*. He believed in the promise of democracy and he had faith that everyone would play by the rules. Had he known the truth, he might never have found the will to make his attempt.

So Elsie expected to live and die in the same tiny area, among the same people; why then shouldn't a friendship begun at the age of four last a lifetime? The breaking of bonds which is the first principle of ambition, the notion that no affectionate connection can be more valuable than advancement, the sense that all relationships are ulterior and once their purpose has been served, they should be cast aside like a broken plate; none of those things had formed in Elsie's sensibility.

She had been given no chance to be ambitious. Her well-being rested on a few dependable relationships. Among her small circle of friends, Maggie was the most congenial and loyal. She no more imagined she would replace her than she thought she would replace her father. What better way to keep friendship secure than for lives to follow the same trajectory? Maggie's life was changing in the most radical way. To become a mother was the most transformative experience a woman could know. If Elsie did the same it would bring them ever closer. They would look after one another's children. It would be almost as if the youngsters had two mothers. They would be in and out of one another's doors. They would play and go to school together. Like Elsie and Maggie they would be lifelong friends; and this self-renewing circle, never severed by the sharp blade of go-getting was what seemed worthwhile to Elsie. She could see no sense in ambition unless it served the ends of love, stability, friendship and happiness.

"Everything in its time," said Maggie. "Don't put the cradle before the wedding ring."

Bert laughed.

"That's a good way to put it. Am I invited to the wedding?"

Elsie was stunned by his cheek.

"Elsie is. She can bring who she likes."

"Well," said Bert looking the discomfited Elsie full in the face, "will I do?"

"You might."

"If you scrub up well," said Maggie.

"Aren't I always well turned out?"

"So you should be," said Elsie, "you've no-one to care for but yourself."

Maggie lowered her eyes, thinking the remark too barbed.

"Not by choice," said Bert, smiling at Elsie.

He had a record wrapped in brown paper which he'd carefully placed on the table.

"What've you been buying?" asked Maggie.

"Duke Ellington."

"I don't know much about that stuff."

"You're not missin' much," said Elsie.

"Oh, I don't know," said Maggie. "I like a good tune. I just don't understand music."

"Me neither," said Bert, "but I like big bands, especially Ellington."

"Can I have a look?" said Maggie.

"Why not?"

Elsie tutted half-audibly and gave her head a brief shake like a dog bothered by a fly. Bert carefully pulled away the sellotape and removed the album. He'd bought it second hand from a stall on the market. The records were stacked in cardboard boxes and it was delightful to idle away an hour using his middle finger to flick them forward one after another. He'd been tempted by Dizzy Gillespie and Charlie Parker's *Town Hall* but felt their music ran away with him; Ellington was safer territory, and given that he had to listen either when Aunty Alice was out or quietly enough for her not to overhear, seemed more in keeping with his situation. He liked Gillespie and Parker but it was music that could make a fool of you. There was something of the entertainer about Ellington; like Sinatra, he wanted to please and be popular; but Gillespie and Parker played what they liked and if you couldn't follow, you were left behind. It appealed to the unformed intellectual in him. There was something healthy about people who weren't trying to sell a product. He admired people who pursued the truth wherever it led. He felt slightly ashamed of having chosen Ellington, as if he'd been offered a taste of caviar and had stuck with fish and chips. He handed the record to Maggie. On the cover was a picture of Ellington at his brown grand piano, a white, halo-like line around him; in the background was a tall, American building; the title was caught in three ovals of the appropriate colours, and across the side of the piano was the legend: *a Duke Ellington tone parallel to the American negro*; towards the bottom right was a green and yellow RCA Victor logo, the famous dog with its snout in the speaker and in small blue letters across the foot the words: *as played by the composer and his famous Orchestra at his Carnegie Hall concerts.*

"What's a tone parallel?" said Maggie.

"I don't know," said Bert.

"What did you buy it for then?" said Elsie.

"I read that it's like classical music," said Bert. "Like a symphony."

"I don't know anything about symphonies," said Maggie.

"I like almost all music," said Bert. "Anyone playing an instrument and I'll stop to listen."

"Give me a good Charles Wesley hymn any day," said Elsie.

"Yes," said Bert. "I like hymns too. A church choir brings tears to my eyes."

"Well, it looks interesting anyway," said Maggie and then reflectively added, looking at the picture of Ellington and raising her eyebrows slightly, "The American negro."

"Jazz is a black music," said Bert.

"Well," said Maggie, "they've done well."

"A disgrace," said Elsie, "the way they were treated."

"You're right," said Bert.

The waitress arrived. She was a dumpy, bustling woman in NHS glasses. Her breasts lay across her chest like an eiderdown pillow, swelling the black dress of her uniform. Bert noticed how fat and

146

short her fingers were.

"Do you want anything?" he asked but the women declined.

He ordered a pot of tea with toast. The waitress, who had tiny drops of sweat on her brow, waddled away and Bert watched her quick but unattractive movement. It made him think how lucky he was to be sitting next to the remarkably pretty, slim Elsie.

"Not that we're any better," said Elsie. "Liverpool was built on the slave trade."

"Terrible," said Maggie.

"Things are changing though," asserted Bert. "We'll never go back to that kind of thing."

"Not changing fast enough if you ask me," said Elsie.

"Not long ago, blacks were slaves," said Bert. "Now Ellington is a world famous musician. That's progress."

"One black man who can play the piano isn't much good," said Elsie.

"It says something though," said Maggie.

"There's still plenty to reform," said Bert "but the worst is behind us."

"Let's hope so," said Elsie. "We've a lot to make amends for."

"Empire's a thing of the past," said Bert.

"The Empire should never've been," said Elsie. "The folk they murdered and stole from. No better than criminals."

"You're right," said Bert, "I was reading about it. Piracy was how it got going."

Elsie shook her head.

"I suppose they knew no better in those days," said Maggie.

"People can always know better," said Elsie. "They find excuses that's all."

"We can't alter the past," said Bert.

"More's the pity," said Elsie.

"Well," said Bert, "if you could alter it, what would you change?"

Elsie felt suddenly under pressure. What was he asking her? She knew well enough what she despised and rejected. It was easy for her to say there should have been no Empire, that taking other people's countries, making them slaves, sending them to fight in wars, treating them as animals because of the colour of their skin, robbing, slaughtering, starving, murdering were shameful ways to behave and forever Britain would bear the guilt of its violent and greedy past. Hadn't her father said to her, when she came home from school having been taught to be proud of the red on the map of the world, that it was something to hang your head about? Hadn't he told her about the concentration camps in the Boer War, the horrible starving to death of women and children to put pressure on the soldiers? Wasn't she secure in this one big truth: that the British had behaved like savages in bringing what they called civilization to what they called savages?

And couldn't she always put the facts into reverse and argue that we would have fought anyone who tried to colonize our country, whether or not they claimed to be bringing a better way of life? Yes, she could do all that and she was sure of her ground. It was a moral patch. She could be surrounded by oceans of learning, but her feet wouldn't get wet; it was the essential moral recklessness of Empire she rejected and no-one could convince her that a better future could be won through violence, murder and domination. Yet what Bert was asking required detail. Was he trying to put her on the spot? Did he want to make her look stupid. He was smiling at her in his charming, defenceless way. Was that just to conceal his nasty motivation?

She felt small in her lack of education. Did Bert know the facts? He was one for a book and hadn't he just said he'd been reading about it? She wished she was as familiar with the facts as with Methodist hymns. It was one thing to have your moral position, it was another to be able to quote names, dates, battles, figures. She'd always disdained that kind of learning if it wasn't tied to powerful moral conviction. Didn't her mother say the world was full of clever Devils? Churchill himself was an educated man who wrote volume upon volume, but she loathed him for a cheap war-monger and a snob. She was delighted when he lost in '45. She believed that his kind, the public-school boys, marinated in arrogance with no idea of how life was lived by most people, should never be in power again. Surely now people would have the common sense to stick with Labour. Churchill might be a passing hero, but in the long run he would be seen for what he was; it was his kind that made Hitler possible. Didn't he just carry on what the British had done all over the world? Hadn't her father told her about Stanley killing black people as if they were monkeys? How was that any better than Nazism?

But what was Bert doing? Was he going to humiliate her by showing she didn't know the facts of history? The thought of it made her retreat more completely into the territory of her moral certainty. She might lack school learning but the church had formed her moral discrimination like running forms an athlete's calves. She had nothing to fear if she admitted what she didn't know and remained behind the iron shield of what she did.

"There'd've been no Empire," she said. "We'd've stayed at home and made things right here, and what we could do to help other folk we'd have done in the proper way, not for our own advantage."

"I agree," said Bert.

The waitress appeared and placed the white pot and the rest of the things on the table. Bert thanked her and began at once to butter his toast. Elsie noticed how thickly he spread. It injured her sense of necessary frugality. There was an animal greed in it which made her intestines shrink. Was he like that in all his appetites?

"I wonder if they can get me some honey?" he said, twisting round in his chair. The waitress was approaching a table, in her plump hands a silver tray overcrowded with a teapot, cups, saucers, a milk jug, a little plate of cakes and a glass of water.

"Excuse me, miss!" he called. "Waitress!"

Elsie felt a shock in her stomach. Fancy shouting at the girl like that, as if he were royalty and she a skivvy. She turned to see the girl nod and smile as she bent to place the items in front of the customers, a couple dressed as if for the Sunday service, an old woman in a black dress whose hand shook with Parkinson's and a boy of twelve or so dressed in a short-trousered suit, his brilliantined hair brushed tight to his head so the straight parting showed the white strip of his scalp. Her tray emptied she bustled over to Bert. She was one of those ungainly women who seem to strain even to walk across a floor. Elsie felt sorry for her. It was wrong she should be *run off her feet*. They should employ more staff. She blamed Bert for imposing on her.

"Can I help you, sir?"

149

Sir? It was ridiculous. This was Pongo, the boy from the backstreets who went barefoot to school and stank like overdue fish. Why should she treat him as superior just because he was a customer? Elsie despised all that deference which she saw as nothing but bowing to money. Why couldn't a waitress and a customer be equals? She was as good as him any day. It was her view that customers should be polite to those who serve them. What did this poor lass earn after all? And here she was, shamed by the sweat on her brow, having to treat Bert as if he was someone special, as if he wasn't just one of God's commonplace creatures like her.

"Could you get me a pot of honey?" he said looking up at her with a slightly pained expression. In his voice Elsie heard something she didn't like; it was an odd, wheedling tone which struck her as cowardly and a little manipulative; why couldn't he be straight? Why couldn't he just ask the girl instead of making himself appear simultaneously needful and entitled?

"I'm afraid we don't serve honey, sir."

"But you sell honey in the shop."

"Yes, sir, but we don't serve it up here in the café."

"Well, that's ridiculous," he said. "A little pot of honey, is that too much to ask?"

"I'll speak to the manager about it, sir."

"Don't worry, love," interjected Elsie, "he'll have the jam."

She reached for the small, white pot of the heaped strawberry and clunked it down in front of Bert. The waitress hesitated a moment and turned away. Bert was about to call her back but Elsie objected:

"Leave the lass alone, she's running from pillar to post as it is without having to fuss about your honey."

"I only want some honey."

"They don't serve it."

"They should."

"Why should they?"

"They've got shelves full of it downstairs. What's so hard about filling a few pots?"

"They just don't serve it, that's all. Eat the jam."

"It's good jam," said Maggie. "It's their own."

"I prefer honey," said Bert, "it's very good for you."

"There's fruit in the jam," said Elsie.

"And lots of sugar too," said Bert.

"You pile it in your tea," she said.

"I don't see what's wrong with asking for what I want, Elsie. I'm paying for it."

"That's not the point. Putting people to trouble to suit your whims is bad behaviour even if you are paying them."

"Well, I don't agree," he said sliding the knife loaded with jam across his cooling toast.

He cut the slice diagonally into two triangles, lifted one of them by the corner between his index and thumb and took a bite. Elsie noticed his fingers which weren't at all like those of her brothers. Not that they were weak, but they moved differently. They weren't practical fingers. It was true of the way Bert moved in general. It was attractive enough but you could tell he wasn't made for hard physical work or the simple business of making. Her brothers had a way of moving which suggested command of physical things; as if they had some instinct for joining wood, laying bricks or shaping stone; but you could tell just by watching Bert that if you put a saw and hammer in his hands he wouldn't be able to build a roof like Eddie.

It was odd because he had a delicacy in his movement which should have meant he was adept, but in fact he was clumsy. She remembered when he tried to put a nail in the wall in their kitchen so she could hang a picture she'd bought at the Methodist jumble sale and it bent, he hit his thumb and her father had to do it. Yet she would have granted without demur that Bert was more intelligent than her father. How funny to be intelligent yet not to be able to use a hammer. Her thinking ran aground as she tried to work it out. It wasn't hard, after all, to make a little table like the one Eddie had made for the front room. She was sure if she'd been shown, she could do it herself; and Bert could do things that needed real intelligence. It troubled her.

When you started thinking about the world, you could run out of answers in seconds. It made her retreat to the certainties of Methodism. There at least was revealed truth. She rose on it like Christ himself ascending to Heaven. All the learning in books, all the cleverness

151

was nothing compared to that over-riding truth and what you couldn't explain just had to be accepted as God's will. The horrible, melting sense of being unable to answer even simple questions gave way to absolute certainty and confidence; Bert had the fingers the Good Lord had given him and that was that.

He was chewing heartily on the toast, like a man who might never see food again, when the manager emerged at the top of the stairs. He was tall, balding, with long arms and heavy legs. His face was concentrated in his long, thin nose which was so prominent it seemed to lead him forward, like a dog sniffing out a bitch on heat. His black suit, white shirt and expensive shoes were the uniform of authority and importance. His long stride reminded Elsie of a giraffe; he looked like some creature who should reach up with his little mouth and pull low hanging fruit from trees.

"Sorry to disturb you, sir. I believe you wanted to speak to me."

"Mmm," said Bert wiping the heavy, white serviette across his mouth and continuing to chew. "Mmm," he nodded and pointed to the white pot whose Everest of jam had been decapitated. "I just wanted," he said as he swallowed, "some honey, for my toast."

"I see," said the manager clasping his hands as if he'd just received some small piece of intensely happy news. "We don't normally serve it. Most people prefer jam, you see. And our scones are very popular. Jam and cream go naturally with them. But of course, a pot of honey is no trouble. Would you like clear or set?"

"Do you have *Gales* clear?"

"Of course, sir."

"That'll do fine. And another round of toast, please."

"Of course, sir. On us."

He strode away and Bert sat back and smiled as if he'd just been awarded the Nobel Prize for Physics.

"You see," he said, turning to Elsie, "people are only too glad to provide what you want if you just ask."

"You've probably got that poor lass in trouble," said Elsie.

"Nonsense."

"How do you know? He might have torn a strip off her for not doing it herself."

"Well, she has to do what she's paid for," said Bert.

"And the rest," said Elsie.

"No harm in asking," said Maggie.

"Exactly," said Bert.

"She'll get the blame for them having to give you free toast. You should've said you'd pay."

"It's keeping the customer happy, Elsie. That's what business is about."

"Is it?"

"He was very obliging," said Maggie.

"It's about making money out of running folk like that waitress ragged," said Elsie. "I've seen how my dad has had to near kill himself to put food on the table."

"Well," said Maggie, "I think I should be going. Max'll be expecting me."

"He's not the only one expecting," said Bert and threw back his head and laughed as if his attempt at a witticism was irresistibly funny.

When Maggie had gone, Elsie was aware of the weight of being alone with Bert. The very act of sitting at the café table with him was a declaration. It wasn't possible to be in public with a man without a horde of dwarves running to surround you; the dwarf of respectability, the dwarf of propriety; the dwarf of accusation; the dwarf of expectation; the dwarf of licentiousness. The petty tribe of them assembled round the table and she felt as if all eyes were concentrated on her, as if people at other tables were looking at them and drawing inevitable conclusions; they were a couple; they were man and wife; they were lovers; they were *adulterers*. Supposing someone had noticed she wasn't wearing a wedding ring? Would they assume she was loose? But then, lots of young men and women *walked out together* without there being anything sexual involved.

She suddenly became aware of Bert as a man. It was as if the Devil had ferreted his way into her head and made her think of his body. The image of him naked came into her mind. She'd never seen a grown man naked. She didn't know what his private parts looked like. She'd seen her brothers stripped to the waist or wearing shorts in hot weather. She knew what a man's arms and chest and back and legs and feet were like; but what was a man uncovered like? Maggie had seen Max. She had touched him and he'd come inside her. What was it all like to lie back and open your legs and have a man put his hard thing into you? And then what? Once he was in there what did you do? It made her mouth curl into a little sneer. She felt invaded. She didn't want any of these ideas in her head. They were dark and belonged in places haunted by night, they were not daytime sunny thoughts and she didn't like them. Yet Bert was a man and if she was to catch up with Maggie, if she was to have a child of the same age, if they were to remain close by watching them grow, if their friendship was going to last till they were old, their children married with children of their own, she couldn't delay. And who else had asked her? Who else would?

There arose in her imagination an idea at once vague and powerful, like a wave seen far out at sea, nothing more than a white tip on the surging, heaving mass, which once it curls to crash on the beach can lift you off your feet, send you swirling in the middle of a gripping chaos of slapping, thumping water, salt and seaweed; surely this business of love between a man and woman, this attraction that led to nakedness and conjunction, surely this was a churning force of pure emotion; surely it had the means to purify the muddy puddles of her disdain and dislike; surely once they were man and wife this love that everyone made so much of and which she herself almost experienced would overwhelm all other feeling; this good thing called love would kill off all other, lesser emotions and a bliss of togetherness would salve the painful sense of separation, of being unable to bridge the gap between herself and the attitudes and habits she deplored in him.

Had she known that mere physical arousal, even of the most intense kind, has no power to effect a change in feeling rooted in the perception of fundamental differences of ideas and values and that romantic love is, no less than friendship, dependent on mutual kindness, tolerance, discretion and gentleness, she would have recoiled into the cold nave of her principles and waited for a Methodist with socialist leanings to come and find her, and if he never arrived would have gone to her grave as untouched as Elizabeth I.

He twisted the knife to catch a thick smear of the viscous honey and as she watched him spread it thickly into the corners of his three-sided bits of toast, she wondered what it would be like to watch him do the same every morning; to sit opposite him at the breakfast table or to fuss around bringing tea and milk while he sat indulging his taste for the sweet, sticky near-liquid; a horrible sense of fate came over her. She knew she would hate him for his indulgence, yet she knew she had to give in. Give in to what? Was it the Devil finding his way into her mind? The slow warming, like the earth after winter, invisible, barely noticeable, which rose from her belly, made her feel at the mercy of an external force. Nothing in the sermons and hymns of the Methodist church had prepared her for this. Nothing her mother had said. Nothing her parents had ever hinted at. The bare facts of reproduction which she'd read about when she was thirteen in a serious and antiseptic booklet her mother passed to her, had nothing to do with her confusion. Yet perhaps it was God's will. Just as Maggie's pregnancy, which seemed to defy the church's strictures, must have been part of his plan. He works in mysterious ways. Perhaps he was goading Maggie. Perhaps he thought her behindhand; it was time to marry and bring children into the world.

When Elsie thought of children, the oppressive darkness of sex, the grim thought of having to stitch her life to Bert's foreign flesh, began to clear and the uninterrupted sunny view of the way ahead shone invitingly. Yes, children. She must have children and children were innocent. They'd read Dickens to her at school. She knew the innocence of Tiny Tim and Oliver Twist. She would be their mother and they would love her with that unconditional love only mothers know. Bert would be their father. He would work and bring home the money. But in the home he would be a shadowy presence. She would preside. The home was the woman's arena. Let men strut and do what they like in the world of making and money. It all came back to the home. Bringing children into the world was the primary fact. Without that, there was no life. And she could give birth. Yes, that was the answer. However unpleasant or ambiguous the business of letting Bert inside her, the outcome would be children and the children would be hers.

It seemed to her as she let the half-conscious thought of motherhood flood her brain that she could marry almost any man in order to become a mother. Bert had the great advantage of being almost an orphan. He was illegitimate. A bastard, as people with vulgar tongues said. She could nestle at the heart of her family and he would have to find whatever space he could. She would have her children. She would bind them to her and send him out into the world. Her own ideas of doing something beyond the home had come to nothing. She'd once thought she'd like to be a tailoress and had pictured herself cutting carefully round paper patterns with the big shears, stitching invisible seams in wedding dresses with trains as long as a nave. Then later she'd thought what an adventure it would be to go to sea and imagined she'd join the WRENS. She stood on deck in her smart blue uniform to be inspected by the commanding officer. Her back was straight. Her shoulders tight. Her chin lifted. The smell of the salt and the sound of the waves slopping against the iron sides of the great ship were symbols of freedom. But her mother's illness and her father's assumptions had confined her. She'd come to think of work as a lesser thing. It was the home that mattered; and what greater potency could there be than forming a child? No power in the world was more absolute than that of a mother. She would be forever mother to her children. It was a fact as unchanging as God. Men could seek whatever power they might, but it was paltry compared to the power of motherhood. And what was the love between a man and a woman compared to the love between mother and child?

Did Maggie love Max as irrevocably as she loved her mother? It was true she didn't always get on with her; she found her sometimes too intrusive, but all the same she was bound to her as if their ankles were joined by steel bolts. That was the power of motherhood: even if your children didn't like you, if they grew up to disagree with you like Henry set his face against their mother's religion, they were still indefeasibly yours. Motherhood was as irresistible as gravity. It didn't cross her mind that if she had children by Bert they would be like him. She'd never heard the names Darwin and Mendel. If she'd been asked why children look like their parents she would have said because God wanted them to. Without thinking about it, she imagined their similarities to him would be superficial. Her own attachment to her mother was so placental she couldn't imagine her children being drawn to their father like iron to a magnet. She didn't know how like her own father she was. She had no idea how much she had inherited from him nor that the things she despised in Bert were as likely to be replicated in her children as his blue eyes and round head.

"Mmm. That honey's good," said Bert dusting the crumbs from his fingertips. "And just for you I'll thank the waitress before we leave, and even give her a tip."

"Don't give her a tip for me," she said.

Bert laughed. Her strict behaviour attracted and softened him.

"Why not?"

"I don't believe in it."

"It's a sign of gratitude, and it gives her a bit extra."

"Folk should be paid properly. If they get tips, bosses'll say they don't need to up their wages. Then they're left depending on an income they can't be sure of."

"You're right," he said, "they should be paid properly but they should get tips too. Best of both worlds."

"Aye, but it doesn't work that way. Bosses are crafty. Any way they can cut wages they'll do it."

"Are they that bad?"

"What I know is how hard my dad and our lads have to work and how little they've earned."

"That might not be the fault of the bosses. It might just be economic reality."

"That's fancy talk."

Bert laughed again.

"What d'you mean, fancy talk?"

"The kind of talk folk use when they want to get away wi summat. What's honest can be said straight."

"I'm sure it can, but some things are complicated."

"There's nowt complicated about lining your pockets from other folks' work."

"Well, Keynes might disagree."

"Who's he when he's at home?"

"An economist."

"He'll be on the side of the bosses then."

"You might be right."

She looked at him. He was fixing her eyes and smiling. There was no doubt he had charm and though he wasn't as handsome as Cary

Grant, not one of those rare men you catch a glimpse of on the street and who set your heart beating just by seeing their face, he was young and full of life, his eyes were as blue as a summer sky, and the simple beauty of youth was enough to transfix her for a second. It was in that second, barely without knowing it, she made her mind up. Bert would do; but she wasn't going to let him know, not for a while yet. She could start planning her future because she had her fish on the hook and could reel him in as soon as she was ready. He might think himself free to explore the oceans but as soon as she tugged on the line and began to wind the reel he would be as confined as a tadpole in a jam jar.

Men were such weaklings; and what was it that overcame them after all? She didn't want to think about it but she knew it was true. Women weren't fools for that but a man was as pliable as a child in a sweet shop if he was offered it. It gave her a queer feeling. She couldn't reconcile that bit of herself, that private, hidden thing with the rest of her. Yet men would climb over ten-foot barbed gates to get to it. There was something about that she didn't like. It gave too much place to mere physicality, and a shameful bit of physicality at that. All the same, she was prepared to use what she had to get what she wanted; not Bert, not for himself, but children. He was the means and as the only means that had asked her, he would have to pass muster. All her disdain and dislike dipped out of sight like a rat down a drain.

Bert finished his toast and tea. He looked very pleased with himself, as if he'd just papered the front room ceiling and the joins were invisible. She found it peculiar he could exude such pride when all he'd done was eat a bit of bread and honey and drink a pot of tea someone else had made for him.

"Shall we go?" he said.

Once they were in the busy street she wondered if she should take his arm. Many women did it. It seemed respectable; but she remembered her mother's displeasure. Still, she liked walking beside him. People would look at her and know she had a man. She'd taken the first step to being a *lady*. In Elsie's mind to be a lady was to be married, looking after a family, sober, hard-working, clean, reliable; the worst thing a woman could be was disreputable. To be slovenly, drunken, loose, unstable was a fate that must be fought against relentlessly. Bert was the kind of man anyone on the street would look at and admire. He was well-groomed, his clothes were expensive and neat, he walked with pride and energy; he looked like a man going somewhere and beside him she must look like a woman with a future.

There were possibilities after all. Though she was dismissive of Bert's *go-getting*, the thought of a nice house for her children appealed to her. If he made his way, they could move to Penwortham or Fulwood. They could live in one of those houses Eddie helped build; a big semi with a garden back and front and a bay window with leaded lights. Her carefree children would play in the garden on long summer evenings while she was busy in the kitchen or sitting reading the local paper in the living-room. She would go to the nearby local shops with her bag hooked over her arm and chat to neighbours as if living among solicitors, civil servants, engineers, building society managers and small business people was as natural to her as sleeping. Her children would go to the round-the-corner school. They would have fields to run around on and though she would never push them, believing it cruel and evil to force children to live out their parents' ambitions, she would be glad if they quietly did well and she could read their reports with a little surge of pride. But most of all she wanted them to go to church. It would have to be Methodist or at least non-conformist. The pomp and snobbery of the Church of England was as uncongenial to her as the policies of the Tories.

She would get up early on Sunday, rouse them, have their breakfast on the table by nine. She would insist they had a bath and if she had a son who was as recalcitrant as Henry she would scrub him with the loofa herself, making sure he was spotless behind the ears. She would dress them in their best clothes which they would wear only on Sundays or for christenings, weddings and funerals. She would brush their hair until it shone like the brightest star and dressed in her good, navy blue suit, the one she'd bought from *Speights* for a sum that still made her blush, her face made up, her hair combed for a full ten minutes, her little blue and white hat secured with the hatpin she always thought of as a potential weapon in case of assault, she would take them by the hand, sit them in the straight and demanding pew, hand them their hymn books and preside beside them, stern as an Arctic winter and self-contained as a clam. Her children would come to be known for their piety. It would be said of them they had faith to move mountains. Would they make their way in the world? Did it matter so long as they were good? She would be their mother. She must save their souls not fuss over their worldly success.

"Where do you want to go now?" said Bert.

His words brought her back to herself.

"I don't know," she said. "Home I suppose."

Everything seemed strange. Her father smoking his pipe in the kitchen, the steep stairs to her mother's room, the well-brushed back yard, even her own bed which had always seemed a refuge. She was no longer fixed here. She'd made a decision. No-one else knew. It was the first real decision of her life and it cut her off irrevocably from what she had been before. She was going to be a married woman. She would have a home of her own. Of course, she would still have to look after her mother so they would have to be close by; but it felt as if fate had put its arm round her shoulder. She was a woman and a woman's responsibilities would soon fall to her. She'd be a mother. Maybe not long after Maggie. She went on for weeks in this transformed state without taking any action; but one Sunday afternoon she went for a walk in the park with Bert. She'd been waiting for him to ask her if she'd thought things over but he said nothing. Instead he talked about himself:

"I think I might set myself up in business."

"I thought you wanted to be an accountant?"

"I do. I'll qualify. But I want to work for myself."

"As an accountant?"

"No."

"Why not?"

"It's a good business but staid. I fancy something a bit more exciting."

"Exciting?"

"You know, something people enjoy. People use accountants because they have to. I fancy doing something people choose to do. A restaurant, a café...somewhere people are enjoying themselves."

"You'd be better off sticking with accountancy."

"I'll always have it as a string to my bow."

"It's steady and respectable."

"And conservative. All the accountants I know are Tories."

"Are they?"

"The world of money is a Tory world."

"That's true enough," she said.

It was one of the few times she'd agreed with him. Sometimes she grudgingly admitted he might have a point but hardly ever did she meet him in a way which he felt confirming.

"Spend too much time among them, I might become a Tory myself."

"I hope you've more sense," she said, some of the customary scolding tone returning.

"I have. The only sensible thing to do with money is spend it. Spread it around so everyone can spend it. The Tories put it into too few hands. Too much gets taken out of the economy. But give everyone a good income and security so they spend, then things move and that's good for businesses. That'll be good for me. If I can get something off the ground. Things are moving in the right way. People'll have more leisure. More money. That's the opportunity."

Elsie had always thought of business as something other people did, but the idea of Bert working for himself and making a go of it appealed to her. She put aside her reservations about opportunism. There was no argument against hard work and if he made a good living from his own efforts, that was fair; and it might provide a good life for her children. She wouldn't be involved. It was his affair. Let him get on with it.

"Well, good luck to you," she said turning away to look at the river.

AGREEMENT

It was growing dusk. They walked over the tram bridge and between the trees of the old tram road. The chill across her shoulders made her shiver and without thinking she took his arm and pulled herself close to him. He looked down at her for a second and then walked on. She was pleased with that. It seemed manly and appropriate; but at the same time she was astonished at herself. She seemed to be watching herself, as if it wasn't really Elsie Craxton arm in arm with Bert Lang. When they reached the end of the unmade road and he turned, drew her to him and began to kiss her mouth she was astonished at how he ceased to be Bert and became a mere sensual warmth. She allowed him to carry on. When he drew away he looked into her eyes and smiled. She felt unsure and awkward. This was what it was all about then. It was nice enough, being kissed; but it didn't melt her negative feelings. Perhaps that only came with the full thing, going *the whole way*, as people said. He kissed her again and as they made their way back, they stopped two or three times. Each time she was aware of that point at which he stopped being Bert and became a sensual presence. It shocked her because, in a way, he could be any man. Was it true that the physical satisfaction of sex was something you could have with any man? It rocked her belief that physical desire was contained by romantic love, respect and fidelity.

Her experience, this tiny, chaste experience of a few kisses had taught her the opposite. It was a terrible, terrible discovery. Kissing didn't dissolve her feelings. It didn't bring love like the gentle calm after a raging fever; it didn't settle the turmoil of wanting and not wanting. Still, she had in reserve the idea that once they were married and shared a bed, once they met in nakedness and he did what a man had to do, some transformation was bound to follow. They were back on the park in full view of the few people walking their dogs. She wouldn't let him kiss her again but she allowed him a peck when they reached her front door.

She went to bed in disappointment. A horrible idea had come to her: there was no reason under the sun a woman should marry a particular man. As far as the business of breeding went, we were no different from dogs. Any mongrel would do for a bitch on heat. A kiss was a

162

physical matter. It was nice because it was warm lips against warm lips. But supposing you were blindfolded and told it was your husband kissing you when in fact it was any man off the street; you might tell the difference but would it be any less nice? As a kiss, just a kiss, without any of the ideas, hopes, dependencies and mutualities which surround it, it was merely physical sensation. Was it true of going *the whole way*? Was one man as good as another as far as the physical sensation goes? In her mind there were now three Berts: the physical creature whose lips were attractive; the husband who would give her children and marital happiness; and Pongo, the neglected boy from one of the worst families in the town, the fighting-upwards, full-of-himself little go-getter who lacked the English oak principles she loved in her father.

As she lay awake she wondered if she should bring it all to an end. Surely some other man would come along? Some grand lad with his feet on the ground. Yet, when she thought again of the men at church, Brian Rowley or Maurice Villiers she found their straight-forward, working men's ways less attractive than Bert's determination to climb his peak. What would life with Brian be? Oh, he'd work in the factory and turn over his wage packet; they'd afford a nice little terrace; he'd be kind enough and he wasn't the type of man women go after; but he couldn't provide that little thrill of rising in the social scale Bert offered. She came back to the idea of children and doing the best for them. When she saw herself as a mother in the nice home Bert's striving could provide, all the doubts receded. It was worth everything to attain that. And what if it was true that sex could be divorced from romantic feeling as easily as the skin peeled from an orange? She would be saved from degradation by motherhood.

The kissing became frequent. She grew so used to it she was no longer surprised by the moment of transformation; but then Bert began to become more pressing and unleashed; he forced his tongue in her mouth which at first she thought disgusting; he pushed his lips hard against hers; and then his hand rose from her waist and rested on her breast.

"Don't do that."

"Why not?"

"That has to wait till we're married."

"Why?" he said without acknowledging she'd just accepted.

"Because it's what a man and wife do."

"Who says?"

"The Bible."

"It didn't stop Maggie."

"I dare say."

"You don't think she's a sinner, do you?"

"I don't judge her. That's for God."

"Is she any worse in God's eyes because she makes love to Max?"

"God'll forgive her if she repents."

" Well, we can repent."

"You can't repent before you sin."

"Why not?"

"It's not sincere."

"If I offend God I'll apologise sincerely."

"You have to be sorry for what you've done."

"Do you think Maggie's sorry?"

"I don't think she wanted to get pregnant."

"No, but is she sorry she sleeps with Max?"

"I think she wishes she'd waited till they were married."

"Aye, but she couldn't. We're not kids, Elsie. We're grown men and women. Six years of our lives were taken from us fighting Hitler. I didn't want to fight him. You didn't want the blackout. Politicians drove us into that. Had it not been for the war, we might be married and settled by now. You might be a mother."

"We can't think for ever about what might have been."

"Why shouldn't we live our lives? We're only here once. Anyway, my view is couples should know all about one another before they marry. Marrying in ignorance is a Victorian idea."

In spite of herself she liked what he said. It was true, the dark life of the last century into which her parents had been born was a bad thing. Perhaps he was right that couples should know one another. It seemed modern. It recognised her as a woman. She felt he was giving her a chance and a choice; and then she would find out if what went on between a man and a woman in bed could change the way you feel in some elemental way. She was caught between God who watched her every minute, knew every intimate thought, and would condemn her to Hell for eternity if she sinned, and the idea of her right to know a man before she married him. Could God disapprove of that? She wasn't doing it solely for her pleasure. She was thinking of her children. For their sake the marriage had to be right.

"We can live our lives, but we get married first. I don't want to be in Maggie's position."

"There's no need for that, if we're careful."

And so it went on till it didn't seem so bad to her that he should rest his hand on her breast as he kissed her; but his frustration at not being able to go *the whole way* bothered her; on the one hand he should be able to wait, on the other she wondered if she was being unfair.

"We should be married by now," he would say. "It's the war that's ruined everything. It's stopped us growing up."

It was flattering to have a man want her so much. It was a kind of attention she'd never had; and he was right, the war had made a mess of everything; even now they were going to find it hard to get a place to live. It was a cramped life they lived in every way. It was hard to come from the bottom like they did and to make a life for yourself. Even the straightforward things like getting married and having a home were tough. She began to see him more and more as a way out of her back-alley life. It wasn't wrong, after all, to want a few flowers and some grass to soften things. It was wrong they had to live as they did when two miles away there were folk in houses big enough for three families with gardens you could play the cup final in.

And Bert was a socialist. He wanted prosperity for everyone and wasn't one of those mean-minded Tories who preened at having tuppence a week more than the neighbours. She told herself he wasn't as bad as she'd thought him. She reproached herself for having judged him which was an unchristian thing to do. Everybody has their faults. She had her own. Poor Bert had to put up with not having a family of his own. It must be hard for him to have to adjust to her ways; and her family was so special. Her father was known as Red Tom for his unflinching socialism. He told his sons never to do *foreigners*.

"That's someone else's work. You're tekkin't food frae another family's table. Folk want jobs doin' they pay't reet price, above board and honest."

It was common among tradesman to take work after hours, cash-in-hand, no questions asked so there was bewilderment and admiration for the Craxtons who refused it. Bert himself had laughed when Elsie had told him.

"But if people want to work in their own time for a bit extra, what's wrong with that?"

"What's wrong with it is simple: it's folk wantin't job done wi'out payin't price. It puts folk outta work. Proper contracts, proper pay, tax paid. That's th'honest way."

"You Craxtons are a breed on your own."

"'Appen we are, but we can hold our heads up."

Over time, Bert absorbed Tom Craxton's values. He was puzzled by him but he grew fond of him. What it would be to have a father like that. He could no more be dishonest or manipulative than the sun could turn to ice. Bert wondered if he was born like that or if something in his background had instilled it. Elsie witnessed this slow transformation in Bert; he was drawn into her family's culture as inexorably as a man sucked down into the quicksands of Morecambe Bay. She'd won. She could marry him and stay within her family. He was learning. When she first met him he was a Labour man but he favoured business. Slowly he was coming to see business was the problem. For the Craxton's, the idea of working for your own enrichment without a care for others was base. Working hard for prosperity was a fine thing; but what was prosperity for? Wanting to be rich was also wanting others to be poor. It was a matter of arithmetic. Tom Craxton disdained a show of wealth as much as he despised drunkenness and men who hit women. It was low behaviour.

Elsie repeated what she'd heard her father say: when a man or woman works they should own what they produce. So she softened her feelings towards Bert. It wasn't that he was no longer annoying in wanting to get on and impress, nor that she didn't find him insensitive; but he'd moved a long way in her direction and for that she admired him. He was a sow's ear, after all, and would never be a silk purse. It was a shame. It was a shame he didn't earn enough to buy a house. Cropper's paid him as little as they could. It was a shame they couldn't live a wider, more relaxed life. It was a shame the rats still ran in the back alley and now and again one fled from the coal shelter when she drove the shovel under the black heap.

They were seldom alone in her house and she didn't often visit his bedsit, but one evening he invited her to listen to a new record: Bizet's *Carmen* which he played over and over in wonder at the melodies, the energy and the melting sensuality of the heroine. It was pleasant sitting in the almost threadbare armchair while the black disk spun on the turntable and the stylus bobbed like a fisherman's float. Elsie was attracted by anything *higher*. Classical music was obviously edifying. She wanted to like it. Bert sat opposite her in the straight-backed chair. His face was touched by rapture. She assumed a little smile of approbation; but the truth was the music didn't quite reach her. She couldn't feel it belonged to her and even the rousing voices and the lovely tunes couldn't make her feel at home.

It clearly ran through Bert's veins like alcohol, but intoxication was foreign to Elsie. The music that meant something to her was hymns and they garnered their significance from Methodism. What was all this singing and orchestration about? Even though she began to sense there was something in it, something too big for her yet to understand and which it might be worth working at, there was a stronger urge to remain with what she knew. She had no idea whether *The day though gavest Lord has ended* was a better tune than Bizet's, but she knew it meant more to her. If she headed off into this unexplored territory, how far would she stray from the righteous path that sustained her? Who was to say whether Bizet was a Methodist? A musician could be evil. Being able to write tunes didn't make you virtuous. Hadn't her mother quoted to her, *Why should the Devil have all the good tunes*? Who had said that? She couldn't remember but she knew there was plenty of music in league with the Devil. Virtue came first. Her adherence to God and the Methodist church made it impossible to give in to the music. It might turn out to be as corrupting as alcohol or lust.

Yet she didn't want to be rude to Bert. At least he wasn't asking her to listen to low-level jazz that came out of who knows where: bars, or strip clubs or brothels. At least this was respectable music. Yet was it? She knew nothing of Bizet and her ignorance frightened her. She wanted to be where she belonged, in a pew with a hymn book in her hand and the organist playing the opening bars of *Onward Chris-*

tian soldiers.

"What do you think?" said Bert as the arm lifted and clunked into its resting place and the turntable stopped abruptly .

"It's very nice," she said, "very nice," and she gave a little nervous laugh as if she had to excuse her own liking.

"I'd like to see it performed," he said. "Carmen is such a sensual woman."

"I don't know about that," she said, "but I liked some of the tunes."

"It's a tragic story."

Elsie felt suddenly undermined. Story? She hadn't realised the songs were telling a story. She searched for something to anchor her and thought of Rogers and Hammerstein. Perhaps it was the same kind of thing.

"It didn't sound tragic," she said.

"Passion. Don Jose loves Carmen and will kill her before he will let another man have her."

"That's not right in the head," she said losing the complaisant expression she'd held throughout the music.

"It can drive people mad, Elsie."

"What can?"

"Love."

"They should learn to control themselves."

He laughed.

"If only we could."

He made her a cup of tea and sipped at a small glass of red.

"That's a bit extravagant," she said.

"I won it. In a raffle at work. I only drink a little glass now and again. On special occasions."

She'd stood up to look out of the window. It would have been nice to be able to see something green. To Elsie, the countryside was a pure place. It was the earth as God had made it while the cities and towns were what men had made and as mankind was wicked town and cities were places full of evil. She had no idea how the landscape had been transformed by human action and would have been astonished to learn that fields bounded by hedges weren't part of the natural topography. In her imagination the farmland of Lancashire was as primordial as the Garden of Eden. Her ideal would have been to live in a little village where people were simple, uncomplicated and virtuous.

Before the war, when she was just a lass of thirteen or fourteen, she'd gone walking in the Lake District with Maggie, Joan Curzon and Polly Garrick; her uncle Vic was her example. She did her first walk with him and was smitten. It seemed to her the beauty of the Lakes, the great, heaped weight of the hills looming right and left as you sat in the train carriage heading north with the smell of the burning coal in your nostrils, was all the proof anyone could need of God's power and wonder. Her own environment of streets, bricks, concrete and tarmac was as alien to her deepest self as sunbathing to an Eskimo. She was at one remove from what she should be. There was a genuine life which must include grass, streams, hills, copses, birds, flowers and kindly, uncorrupted people somewhere before, beyond or after the tainted life of the town.

Bert stood behind her and laid his hands on her shoulders. He kissed her neck. There was something almost forbidden about that. He'd kissed only her lips before. Now they were alone in a private place as if they were man and wife and he was bowing his head to kiss a curiously sensitive spot on her neck. She put her cup down and turned to him. She was happier with him kissing her lips. It was more legitimate. His hand rested on her breast as usual. It had become as ordinary as white sliced bread. She no longer wondered if she should allow it; but when he began to unbutton her blouse, she stopped him.

"What's the matter?"

"I've told you, that's for when we're married."

"Can you wait that long?"

"It doesn't need to be too long."

"If we're to have a place of our own it might be."

"We can live at our house."

"There's hardly any room."

"You can always make do if you try."

"I want something better than making do."

169

"If wishes were horses beggars would ride."

"I'm not a beggar."

"I should think not."

He stroked her breast through her blouse and her bra. She let him. He looked into her eyes. It was romantic, like in the films. There ought to be music playing. They ought to be the centre of things like Cary Grant or Vivien Leigh. She felt she was entering that world of romantic fulfilment she had seen so often at the pictures. Yet at the same time she felt strangely distant from it. He was stroking her breast but it might not have been hers. It was almost as if it were a thing separate from her. He undid her top button.

"Don't do that," she said.

But he carried on. The next two were undone. Her bra was becoming visible. She began to feel louche. It was odd how it overcame her. Looking down and seeing her own blouse falling open and her underwear peeping out made her feel as if she was no longer Elsie Craxton. She had the power to tempt Bert. She could arouse him. Probably she could satisfy him. It was queer. It was a potency she'd never anticipated. It took her by surprise and made her feel she was losing control. She put her hand on his.

"You've got nice breasts," he said.

She liked the compliment but at the same time it was suspect. What if she didn't have nice breasts? What if they were big and ugly? Or too small to be appetising? Would he still say they were nice? Was it just a ploy to get his hands on them?

"Just be satisfied looking at them," she said.

"If I can touch them through your blouse why not in the flesh?"

It was a tricky question. There was nothing in the Bible about petting. His argument was logical. She'd let him touch her breasts after all. What was the difference? Nakedness. In fact, he hadn't touched her breasts. It was as if he'd listened to a symphony outside the concert hall. The difference was elemental. If he touched her flesh it would no longer be hers. Those people who touch you in your most intimate places in an intimate way have forever a special connection to you. A part of you belongs forever to them. If she allowed him to touch her uncovered breast she was handing herself over to him in a fundamental way. She was expecting him to be the custodian of her feelings. He pushed his hand inside her blouse and caressed her bra. What was the difference? He was still light years from her flesh. He was fondling a factory-made garment some woman had run up on a machine in Sheffield or Barnsley on a Friday afternoon. What was intimate about that? But suddenly his hand moved as quickly and deftly as a water vole and was inside her bra. She felt her nipple instantaneously stiffen as she wriggled free.

"Bert!"

"Where's the harm, we're practically man and wife."

She buttoned her blouse.

"Practically? You either are or you aren't."

"Well, let's get married as soon as we can."

"All right."

" The register office will be quickest."

"I'm not having that!"

"Why not?"

"It's not in the eyes of God."

"If he made the universe surely he can get along to the register office one Saturday morning?"

"Don't blaspheme."

"Well, how long will it take if we have a church wedding."

"You'll have to find out."

"Me?"

"You're the one in a hurry."

For the next few weeks she was obsessed by his hand in her bra.

What troubled her was that she liked it. It was like the taste of a delicious new food; she wanted to taste it again and make it part of her diet. What surprised her was the response of her nipple. She'd never imagined her body could betray her so slyly. What did it mean? She reasoned it must be God's will. We are what we are because He wants us to be that way. If her nipples sprang up hard at the first touch of a man's fingers than it must be to serve God's purposes; and what could they be other than bringing children into the world and taking care of them? It was hard to connect the two because at the exact moment of her nipple's erection, all she was aware of was the pleasure. Yet it must be that God made her capable of the pleasure so she would do His will. Then an awful thought came to her; if it was His will, why not fulfil it? Why wait to be married? If God had wanted her to be married before she experienced sexual pleasure, He could have arranged it. What would be simpler for God than to switch sexual pleasure on only once people were married? Yet the truth was, if she'd been thinking only of the pleasure, she would have let Bert carry on. It was terrible but she couldn't deny it.

Now she knew how Maggie had *got into trouble*. Perhaps Max had slipped his hand inside her bra, her nipple had sprung to attention like a private before a sergeant major and she'd given in and *gone the whole way*. And what was the pleasure of *going the whole way* if the merest touch of her nipple could be so exciting? There was also the question of shutting off the tap once the bathroom was flooded; could she now deny him what he'd had? She was happy to let him feel her through her bra, so she couldn't now object to that without losing face; and if he were to take a liberty and shove his hand inside again what would she do? The terrible fact was she wasn't prepared to *finish with him*. That would have been the only certain way to halt his progress. She'd made her choice and she wasn't going back on it. Maggie was already ahead of her in the race to start a family; if she finished with Bert, it could be months before she met another man, years; Maggie's first child might be starting school and she could still be a virgin. She wondered if it might not be best to let him fondle her flesh. After all, they were going to be married as soon as they could arrange it.

Was it so bad? In perhaps just a few months they'd be naked next to one another in bed every night. Was it too sinful to permit a little taste of the full meal? Was sin absolute? Was it as bad to let Bert feel her nipple as to have sex with him? No. There had to be a difference; if all sin was of equal weight it would be as bad to let Bert put his hand inside her bra as to be a prostitute and that was ridiculous. God wouldn't be so stupid. And wasn't it true that a petty sin committed in pursuit of a greater good was no sin at all? In this way she almost persuaded herself that to give him free access to her breasts while her bra remained fastened might be admissible but what she didn't admit to herself was that she was eager to explore the little pleasure she'd known; she had no sense of sinfulness at the moment of excitement. On the contrary, it was like a little bit of blue peeping through a sky of grey cloud. Had it not been for the retrospective intervention of religious doctrine, she would have thrown off her clothes and *gone the whole way* with the alacrity of a child running to the slide on her favourite park. She couldn't admit to herself that sensual pleasure could be more powerful than religious injunction and she had no idea how quickly her paltry clay dam of resistance would be swept away by the flood of desire.

The Sunday after the hand-in-the-bra crisis, Eddie and April came to tea. Elsie wasn't prepared for anything unusual but Eddie made the announcement that April was *expecting*. It threw her so badly she had to go into the kitchen and pretend to be busy. She was overjoyed at the thought of being an aunty but at the same time she was disturbed by the thought of Eddie and April's intimacy. At her age he was married. Had they been trying for a child for two years? It bothered her because she didn't believe April would make as good a mother as her. She'd look after her children well enough but she didn't have Elsie's sense of the need to bind your children to you. She was one of those women who would have her children in bed by seven whether they were tired or not. Elsie would let her children sit with her on the sofa in the evenings till they nodded off. They would listen to the radio or she would let them colour or do a jigsaw. She wanted them close to her. To put them upstairs in their lonely bedroom while they were still wide awake was an act of cruelty; it was a rejection. She remembered how it had been done to her and how she hated it. Her mother was as strict for regularity as a surgeon for cleanliness. Those hours she'd spent as a little child listening to the voices of her parents downstairs and wishing she could join them, that she could snuggle on her mother's knee and fall asleep with the warmth of her breast against her cheek and the beating of her heart in her ear, made her resolute to treat her children differently.

So the news troubled her because together with the fact of Maggie's condition, it made her feel she was being left behind. She was as pleasant and kind as she could be to April.

"Have you thought of names?"

"Keep 'em simple," said Eddie.

"Plenty of time yet," said April.

The thought of it played badly on Elsie's nerves. She couldn't think of her brother as a lover. Yet, no doubt he must have kissed April as Bert kissed her. No doubt he slipped his hand inside her bra and her nipple became as stiff as the button in a telephone box; but thinking of her brother in that way was impossible. He was too familiar, too much a part of her. The point about Bert was otherness. He was a stranger. How odd it was that intimacy required strangeness. It made her feel once more that there was something ungodly about sex; yet she couldn't reject it. She couldn't be a nun. She had to have children. So she had to believe that the muddle and mystery of sex were God's intention. She was overcome by a desire to announce that she and Bert were engaged but everyone would ask about the ring and the embarrassment would be mortifying. She tried to find a way of hinting at it, but all the words she thought of seemed wrong.

She looked at April as she cut up her ham and ate her tomato. It was so simple. Getting pregnant was as ordinary as buttering bread. Yet here she was, a woman who wanted nothing in life so powerfully as to be a mother, outpaced by her best friend and her sister-in-law. An odd idea went through her head: that Eddie should have told her. Told her what? That he was having sex with April? That they were trying for a child? She realised it wasn't something a brother should say to a sister, yet the idea had sprung into her head. As if it was a betrayal of the family to go ahead and make your wife pregnant without saying a word. It puzzled her. She belonged to her family, yet the whole business of sex and motherhood meant betraying it.

Was she supposed to love Bert more than she loved her mother and father? She wasn't even sure she loved him at all. She was softening in her feelings because she wanted children, because he'd proposed, because he was charming; but was that love? It wasn't at all like the indissoluble attachment she felt to her tribe. And then another shocking idea rushed into her head: why did she have to marry outside her family to have children? Why wasn't it possible to have children within your own family? It was such a vile idea she couldn't believe her own mind. The Devil must have planted it there. Marriage was God's way. It was His answer to the problem of bringing children into the world. Within her family, relations were pure. Sex was a sin, but what redeemed it was motherhood. Better to marry than to burn. That was God's way. Sex was the work of the Devil yet God had

174

turned it to his advantage; but there could never be the purity between man and wife that existed between her and her mother.

Finally, out of her confusion, arose the idea that Bert was a means to an end. She was utterly justified in marrying him because of her motivation. She would be a good wife because what mattered was to be a mother. She would cook and clean and be dutiful. That was God's will. It set right the pitching vessel of sex. It gave her precedence. That was how it should be. A woman reproduced. A man merely aided the process. A woman's power, she reflected for the thousandth time, was in her capacity to bring new life into the world. It was queer that God made the means sinful but we mustn't question; everything He did was mysterious. Yet she was sure she'd worked it out; there among the boiled ham, the sliced white bread and margarine, the cups and saucers, the cakes and biscuits, she had solved the insoluble riddle.

A calm of supreme confidence came over her. She knew God's mind. She would get pregnant as soon as she could. She was shocked by her own resolution. Was she thinking of having sex with Bert before they married? But did it matter? She knew what God wanted. Her own desires and His tallied precisely. She knew He wanted her to be a mother, and could it be right that April and Maggie should become mothers before her? Perhaps it was a sign. Was God goading her? At any rate, she knew what she had to do. She no longer felt unsure about Bert. God had decided he should be the father of her children. No doubt he was giving him a chance. God was good and poor Bert had started badly in life; God was letting him into her family so he might find the right path ; and much more, God was allowing him to have her for a wife and the mother of her children. It was elevating to know she was chosen. It swept away all doubt and insecurity. She went into the kitchen with a pile of plates and began her work at the sink. Yes, she must be a mother as soon as possible. She would be an example to April and Maggie. She knew neither of them could be as good a mother as her. God needed her to have children so they could learn from her. She dried her hands and went back to the table. Everything was calm and sure.

"Well," she said, "it'll be lovely to have a little baby in the family."

They went on eating their cakes and drinking their tea but all Elsie could think of was the certain bliss of motherhood.

The following Wednesday it rained all day. A grey, spoil-sport sky pressed down on everything and the rain fell with an insistence as steady as toothache. In the evening, Bert appeared in his raincoat with a big, black umbrella; the kind businessmen carry, clearly expensive and durable. She thought it outlandish. There were cheaper umbrellas that did the job perfectly well. He invited her to his bedsit so she pulled on her coat and tied a scarf under her chin.

"Come on, get under," he said pushing up the tight, black canopy as soon as they were in the street.

She was reluctant but he put his arm round her waist and pulled her to him. The rain blew into their faces. Bert tried to position the umbrella as a shield but the wind grabbed it like a thief seizing a purse and turned it inside out. He struggled to get it back into shape as she stood by, the cold drops lashing her cheeks.

"Oh, put it down," she said, "the wind's too strong."

He did, and taking his arm they cantered along the wet flags, the water splashing up into her shoes and soaking her nylons and toes. In the short distance to his door they were sopping. Upstairs he yanked off his coat and threw it over the table then took a towel to his head. It was curiously intimate watching him rub and seeing his hair ruffled as if after a night in bed.

"My feet are soaking," he said, pulling off his shoes and socks.

She was aware this was the first time she'd seen his bare feet. They were small and neat. Her bothers had big feet. Harry's were particularly ugly. His toes sprouted little absurd tufts of black hair and his neglect meant his nails were thick and curled; but Bert's feet were well-tended. They were almost cute, like the feet of a child.

"Take your shoes off," he said "I'll plug the fire in."

He had one of those little two-bar electric fires which send out heat at ankle level, burn your legs and hardly warm the room at all. He plugged it in and sat beside it combing his hair back from his forehead.

"Sit down," he said. "Take your wet things off."

She took off her scarf and coat and hung them behind the door. Sitting opposite him she was glad of the glow of the fire but regretted the rumbustious heat of the coal fire at home, stacked high with the black jewels, cracking and spitting and making the room warm enough to be comfortable in her nightgown.

"Take off your shoes. I'll put some newspaper in them to dry them a bit."

"No, they'll be fine," she said with a little laugh.

"Aren't your feet wet?"

"Only a bit."

"You'll catch a cold."

"I'll not melt," she said.

"I'll get a bowl of hot water. You can warm them up."

Before she could object he was gone. He came back with a steaming, round, plastic, green bowl and a towel. He put the bowl on the little brown rug in front of her and the towel over the arm of her chair. She pushed off each shoe with the toes of the other foot.

"I need to take my nylons off," she said.

He stood by the rug and smiled down at her. Without thinking what she was doing she hitched her skirt enough to let her unclip her suspender belt and rolled the stocking down her leg; then she crossed her other leg over her knee and did the same.

"Here," he said, "I'll hang them up."

He took the stockings, went into the kitchen and came back with a little wooden maiden which he unfolded and set up in front of the valiant heater

"Not too close," she said.

She put her feet in the bowl and sat back. It truly was comfortable after the soggy chill of her drenched shoes.

"Cup of tea?" he said.

"Yes, please."

It was curious to see her nylons hanging there as if this was her home. She wondered what her father and mother would think. It wasn't *ladylike* to take your nylons off in a man's room when you weren't even engaged. What did it mean *ladylike?* It was what her mother had always said and she vaguely sensed she might know what it implied; but for the moment, sitting with her feet in the water, her legs bare and Bert having seen her take off her stockings she didn't feel at all *ladylike*.

She felt as if she wasn't really herself. She'd given him a glimpse of her intimacy. No man outside her family had ever seen her exposed thighs, not since she was a heedless, innocent girl doing headstands against the front wall. This wasn't how the Elsie Craxton who sat in a restricting pew, the thick, black hymn-book in her hands was supposed to behave; but how was that Elsie ever going to be become a mother? Another disturbing idea seeped into her mind like foul water from a flooded sewer oozing under a door: how had her mother behaved towards her father? Had she tempted him? Had she let him see enticing bits of her hidden flesh? Or had they undressed in the dark and never seen the flesh that came together under the blankets? Was that the right way to have sex, under a shroud of darkness which hid its shamefulness? Yet she'd been to the cinema. She'd seen Greta Garbo, prone and available being kissed by John Gilbert in *Flesh and the Devil*; Jean Harlow in a clinch with Clark Gable in *Hold Your Man*, leaning back as he loomed to kiss her, a smug, crooked smile on his lips; she watched Jayne Russell in *The Outlaw* use her extraordinary sensuality to drive men wild, and the poster of her on the straw, her blouse pulled tight across her breasts, her legs tantalizingly apart, the pistol in her hand seeming to stand for something else, haunted her imagination for weeks. Was that how it had to be? Part of her believed the act should be done as quickly as possible, with a minimum of contact and in total darkness. It was a matter of getting the seed to the egg, nothing more. Surely to linger over pleasure would draw down God's wrath? But what if the pleasure was the means to pregnancy? She'd heard it rumoured, in that gutter-level way that sexual ignorance is transmitted, that the longer sex lasted the more likely you were to get pregnant. She had no means of knowing if it was true but she thought it might be. All the truth she knew was revealed; but the Bible didn't shed any light on biology.

She'd never been taught thoroughly about the mechanism of impregnation. What happened? What were her insides like? She knew the egg was in there, in her womb or somewhere near, in a tube; she knew the sperm swam up to it and the two became one. Maybe it was true then that if the man was inside you longer the sperm had a better chance. Perhaps they couldn't escape and had to swim to the egg. She'd heard it said too, by vulgar girls when she was a teenager, that the longer a man's penis the better the chance of pregnancy. Suppose

Bert had a short penis. Would that mean she wouldn't get pregnant? She knew the stories of couples who tried and failed. Was that because the man was too short or the sex didn't go on long enough?

Bert arrived with the tea.

"This'll warm us up."

He gulped a mouthful from his cup. She noticed once more how he relished it. There was a kind of greed in everything he did. As if he wanted to devour the world. It was the opposite of her father's reserve: he drank his tea as if it might be his last, as if he'd had to work to the last ounce of his energy to get it.

Bert was wearing a chunky, green pullover and a pair of slacks. They made him look at once smart and homely. He had a way of wearing clothes well. Everything seemed to suit him. Poor Henry could put on the most expensive suit and still look as if he was about to lay bricks; he had no grace in his form. For a few seconds she almost felt Bert would be a good husband and father: he would come home from work and hang his suit in the wardrobe; he would put on his sweater and slacks and play with the children in the garden or the living-room while she made the tea; they would eat together around a neat table in the dining-room; she would put on a clean tablecloth every day; there would be wholesome, well-cooked food, a main course and a dessert; she would make rice pudding or apple crumble and her children would clamour for seconds; after tea they would put on their pyjamas, clean their teeth and sit on the sofa listening to the radio or reading; when they fell asleep, Bert would carry them up; before she went to bed she would pop her head round the door to make sure they were all right; she would slip on a nice nightdress and get into bed with Bert.

A terrible thought struck her: would they have sex every night? Would Bert expect it? Would he think of sex as he thought of his honey and toast for breakfast or his after-dinner mug of tea? Once she had three or four children, why would she want sex? To do it for the mere pleasure was sinful. Yet, if she did it for Bert, that was also to do it for her children and that wouldn't be sinful; but if Bert was doing it just for the pleasure, she would be married to a sinful man. Could it be right to have sex with a sinful man even if you did it for the good of children?

Once more the thought of her mother and father sneaked past the sentries in her mind like a murderer slinking in the shadows: did they go on having sex once their children were born? She couldn't imagine her mother enjoying the affectionate embrace of a man. The idea of her mother and father *kissing and canoodling* in some fond way like lovelorn adolescents was as offensive as it was ridiculous. Her mother was all effort. She was work made flesh. Work was what God wanted us to do. It was a means to salvation for *the Devil makes work for idle hands*. Wasn't physical affection between a man and a woman a sort of idleness? What was its purpose? To have sex to produce children was a kind of work. It was effort with a goal. But what was the goal of holding hands, or kissing and caressing if no children were wanted? It was mere pleasure. It was two people thinking only of the pleasure they could give one another and that was as sinful as drunkenness or sloth. No, there must surely come a point at which a man and wife leave one another alone. They've had their family. The task is done. They must now pull themselves up straight and get on with the work of raising children and forget about sex.

"Are your feet warming up?" said Bert.

"Yes, thank-you. It's much better."

He knelt down facing her, looking at her toes in the water.

"What pretty feet you have," he said.

"Feet aren't pretty."

"Yours are."

"Don't be soppy. Feet are for walking on."

"Eyes are for seeing but they're beautiful too."

It stopped her as if she'd been hit by a twelve foot wave. It was true. Maggie had beautiful eyes; and Eddie. She'd always thought they were the most lovely, gentle blue and when he smiled and the creases appeared before his mouth curled upwards, she'd always too had a warm sense of belonging and security because of the kindness they expressed. Without a word, Bert took her feet in his hands and set them on the towel. He patted them dry then began to press his thumbs into her soles, moving rhythmically.

"What're you doing?" she said, but she was surprised that although she wanted to sound disapproving her voice betrayed an invitation. It was as if she was spoken through. There was a hint of helpless pleasure in her tone. The sternness she wanted to evoke was running away from her like a rat from a swung shovel. She was astonished at the flushing of her cheeks. They began to burn and she wondered if she was starting to look ridiculous. She was taken aback at the pleasure which ran through her but most of all at how excited she became *between her legs*. She tried to press her knees together in the hope it would cut off some of the excitation; but the shocks of pleasure ran up her calves as if he was applying electricity to her skin. She knew she was growing wet *down there*. Her nipples were growing hard too. She couldn't understand it. Her feet? How could her feet do this to her? She'd never associated her feet with an excitement that could take you out of yourself.

"That's enough," she said.

"Don't you like it?"

"It's very nice but you should stop now."

He let go of her foot and looked up at her with a smile.

"Are my nylons dry?" she said.

He felt them with his finger then pressed the toes against his cheek.

"Still a bit damp," he said, sitting opposite her.

She drank her tea for the sake of something to do. The curious and awful thing was that she would have liked him to caress her feet again. She tried not to look him in the eyes. She began to talk, though she had no real idea of what she was saying. She said whatever passed through her mind without filtering or adjustment. It was as if Bert wasn't there and she was merely mouthing her thoughts to thin air as they arose:

"Well, when I got home I'd lost it. I thought, dear Heaven, has someone pinched it? But I'd only been in't Co-op and there was no-one else in there except Mr Orrit and you know him. He's simple but he's harmless. Or anyway I think he is. He wouldn't harm a fly to my way of thinking. And it was in me pocket. He couldn't have got it out of me pocket without me feelin' it. I know pickpockets can. They're sly. Oh, yes. They're quick all right. They know what they're doin'. That's why me mother allus said 'Keep your hand on your purse when you're in a crowd.' That's how they work. In crowds. Someone nudges you, you think nowt of it, next thing you know your purse is gone. It happened to Alice Webster. Aye, on't pot fair. You see, she was distracted. Listening t't patter. They're smart you see. I wouldn't put it past 'em to have folk in't crowd. You know? Crafty as a cartload o'monkeys. Anyway, she lost her purse. Two pounds and her house keys. Well, that's the worry. Money is money, we know that. You can replace that, but someone's got your house keys…. Well, I said to her 'Was your address in't purse, Alice?" But she didn't know. That's what she's like. Lackadaisical. I said to her 'Alice you should allus have your name in your purse. Most folk are honest." Anyway, she went t't police but it never were handed in. I said to her 'Change t'locks, Alice.' But you can't tell her. Ockered. That's what she is. I warned her. Anyway, she were burgled all right. I said 'What did I tell you, Alice?' But that's the way't world is. It'sad. Aye, it is. Most folk are honest but there's allus a few that spoils it. Anyway, I looked everywhere. I thought, did I leave it on't counter, but I couldn't remember putting it down. I would've sworn it were in me pocket when I left. I only bought a loaf and some sugar. I paid wi half a crown. I remember that. So I must've had change. Now where would I put it but in me purse? But could I find it. Dear Lord! I thought well there's nowt for it I shull have to go back. 'Appen I'd dropped it. Easily done. It could have fallen out of me pocket but I've good deep pockets in that coat. It's good quality. I got it from't Co-op. I like a good deep pocket for that very reason. Anyway, I went back but it were gettin' dark you see, and I was looking at ground all't way there when who should I bump into but….."

She could tell Bert wasn't following her story but she was comfortable. So long as she could keep the stream of words between them there was a kind of safety. Now and again she turned her eyes on his and she was struck by how blue they were. He was almost handsome. She could see him as Clark Gable or Robert Mitchum. She could lie, delicious and attainable as he kissed her and betrayed his inability to resist her. She could be Jane Russell in the hay.

She was aware of a distant but inordinate desire to take off her clothes. Bert was charmed by her feet. She had a power over him. It was true she was attracted by his eyes and his smile and the quick, neat way he moved; but she could take it or leave it. If he'd taken his clothes off she would have thought of it as a threat; she also knew she would find him worthy of disdain or laughter. It was true of her brothers; a man's body wasn't made to attract like a woman's. Though she'd never seen *it* or *them*; though manhood dangling or standing to attention was something she still needed to discover, she'd been struck by the ridiculousness of her brothers' exposed flesh. Perhaps that was because they were her brothers, but she thought of men in general. Their faces were the best things about them. A man's eyes could be enticing, his smile could throw you off balance, his voice could be winning, but his naked body? Was that something she could drool over like Bert bewitched by her feet? A man's body could mean pleasure and the pleasure could lead to children, but she couldn't swoon at the sight of Bert's instep.

Herself naked would have been an invitation he couldn't resist. It was astonishing, the power her body had over him. How odd that men could be so deprived of their self-control by the mere sight of female flesh. She went on talking but beneath the flow there swirled a vortex of confusion: she was aware of the memory of pleasure in her feet; she wanted to keep Bert at bay but at the same time to attract him as surely as Joan Crawford drew a man's gaze; she disdained much about him but wanted to marry him because the most urgent need in her was to have a baby. Without knowing it, as she threw back her head and laughed at a funny part of her own tale, she let her knees fall apart. When she glanced at Bert, with one of those split second glances in which women absorb all they need to decide if a man is attractive, she saw his eyes intent on her legs and the little smile of slow-fuse delight on his lips. He came over to her and put his hands on her knees.

"What d'you think *you're* doin'," she said.

He gave a little laugh and kissed her just above the knee. She was caught between finding it charming and exciting and thinking it soppy and foolish; but before she could say any more he slipped both his hands up her thighs so they rested right next to her crutch. She pushed them away urgently and straightened her skirt. He got up and seated himself on the chair arm, bending his head to kiss her. She couldn't object. It had become customary. Nor could she brush his hand away from her bra, but when he began to unbutton her blouse, she restrained him.

"You have lovely breasts," he said.

"No I don't."

"From my point of view you do."

"Your point of view is too impatient."

183

"We're as near as damn it married."

"Well then, you can wait a short time."

"Why should we wait?"

"Why shouldn't we?"

"We should go into marriage with our eyes open."

"What d'you mean by that?"

"We should know what we're letting ourselves in for."

"You mean once you'd had your way you might change your mind?"

"No. You might change yours."

"Why should I?"

"Perhaps you'll find it's not what you thought it should be."

"Why should I think about that?"

"Why shouldn't you? It's important between a man and a woman and marriage is a long journey."

He kissed her again and as the warmth of his mouth was on hers, she reflected that he was right; it made sense to her down-to-earth non-conformism and her straightforward socialism; to go into marriage blind was daft. Why did the Bible say sex before marriage was wrong? Surely to stop people treating it frivolously; wasn't it an injunction to make people serious? It wasn't as if she and Bert were silly youngsters. They'd made their decision. She'd made her decision. Her protestant mind, formed in the belief that every individual must decide for themselves, smelted in decisions worked out in absolute loneliness and against the entire world if necessary, almost pushed her to the point of being able to reject doctrine.

If it wasn't possible to argue with God, it was possible to interpret what he meant. He wanted them to take the business seriously, and above all to take on their responsibility for bringing children into the world. Bert's hand was on her bra. A legitimate act. God himself would be relaxed about it; but with the deftness of an inveterate shoplifter, he slipped it inside, his palm pressed against her nipple. For a few seconds it merely rested there, inert as a big cat waiting to pounce. Her will to make him remove it deserted her. Not that she was taking the easy route; but she couldn't see any longer how it was sinful for her to press on to motherhood. She'd asked herself a thousand times if Maggie had sacrificed her immortal soul for a passing earthly pleasure and every time she'd been unable to believe it. Wasn't God *slow to chide and swift to bless*? Her version of The Almighty was based on her father; he might be grumpy and strict, but beneath the bluster was a soft heart. Her father would seldom condemn anyone, least of all for a common failing. God would look down on her and smile when he peered into her heart and knew it was to fulfil his purpose she was willing to let Bert's hand stay inside her bra.

Bert began to caress her, as best he could given his hand was trapped between the wire of her bra and the softness of her breast. Her nipple was taut. It was queer that it could feel so big. In a way she wouldn't have thought possible, he flipped the cup up so her breast was fully exposed. Should she stop him? Why? It was exciting. They were nearly married. She wasn't pursuing her own selfish pleasure. The struggle to remain untouched had to be worth it; there had to be something to be gained from it. She couldn't believe it any longer. The great gain was to have a child. Bert pulled his lips from her mouth and in an instant was sucking on her nipple. Her hands were on his head. How strange. Why did he want to suck her like a baby? She'd never imagined such a thing would be part of a man's sexual repertoire; but then, she'd never really imagined at all what it might be like.

The mechanics were straightforward but the accoutrements a mystery. Eating fish and chips out of newspaper would give you sustenance, but a five course meal at the *Bull and Royal*, with silver service waiters hovering and being as obsequious as Uriah Heep, unexpected delicacies and a protocol you had to master as you carried it out, was something quite different. Both led to the same essential end but one was direct and uncluttered, the other a self-conscious ritual.

How had Bert learned to suck on a breast? Did it come to him naturally? Had he read about it? Had he done it before? Perhaps during the war, in Italy or Egypt, he'd had the opportunity. Had he sucked the breasts of foreign women? She imagined a sultry, subtle-hipped, dark-eyed African beauty; a seductive Cleopatra with breasts as generous as the Nile; a woman whose long, black hair reached to her buttocks and who, not having been raised a Methodist, had no scruples about using all her charms. Had Bert caressed the breasts of such a woman? Or maybe a fiery-spirited Roman, as beautiful as

Sophia Loren, accustomed to having her bottom pinched in the streets by hot-blooded Italian men; a woman made restless by the implacable summer sun of her native city, fecund as an olive grove, sweet as an orange plucked in her own garden, juicy as the grapes grown in Calabrian vineyards, pursued by many men, loved by many and always ready for a new adventure.

She became convinced this couldn't be the first breast he'd had in his mouth. Both her breasts were naked. He sucked one and caressed the other. Was this the behaviour of an experienced man? What if it was? The war had been hard on everyone. Who could blame a man for taking comfort? Perhaps her own brothers had done the same. Surely what mattered was that he was now committed to her. They were a couple. They were going to make their life together, here in the cobble and flagstone streets of north-west England; they were going to build a little oasis of gentleness amidst the harsh facts of factories, and money-grubbing and the unedifying struggle between those with nothing and those with a bit more.

She was a mere lass of seventeen when the war broke out. It had taken those years from her when she should have been happy and care-free, when the shape of her future should have begun to emerge; it had been hard. The restriction had worn her down. The worry had eaten at her flesh and spirit; but she'd come through. In spite of all the death, misery and privation, here they were. Life asserted itself in the face of human stupidity and cruelty. She wanted to let go for once and let life have its rights. God and her pleasure became one. In her mind's eye she saw Him; he was looking down on her benignly. He was nodding. Her arousal was God's arousal. He'd given her this surprising body so His will should be carried out. God was sucking her breast. God was caressing her. God would make her pregnant. Bert was doing God's will. God was acting through him.

When he took his mouth from her breast lifted up her skirt and pulled down her knickers, she was convinced that as in the impregnation of the virgin, the Holy Spirit was about to enter her womb; but it was definitely Bert's finger that slipped inside her. She didn't know any longer where she ended and he began. It was odd. He was kissing her mouth again. The limits of her self had been breached. She was no longer contained within her own body. There was a new element to her and it required another person to bring it to life. It must be God finding his way into her body. God and Bert became blurred in her

186

mind as her pleasure grew. What was Bert doing? How did he know to do that? He seemed to have some instinct for her sensitive spots.

She let out little cries which embarrassed her. Supposing Bert's aunty could hear her. Imagine the shame. Yet it seemed now that what was happening had to happen. It had to run its course. Bert lifted her to the floor and on the rug he spread her legs and came inside her. There was an instant of pain amid the intense pleasure and then he was working away in a manner that surprised her more than ever. She'd thought that *going the whole way* would be a gentle, careful, tender thing like a romantic kiss in the films; but this was like hard, physical work. Bert might have been carrying a hod of bricks or sawing timber for a roof. He was grunting. She could feel the slightly chilly sweat on the back of his neck. He was as intent as a cyclist climbing a one in three. On he went, back and forth like a machine. It made her think of the mill and the clanking, shifting looms she'd seen when her uncle had taken her one day to show her what the work was like. She heard the impossible, inhuman din. She couldn't hold back her own cries. She was moving with him in spite of herself, as if a little motor had been turned on in her hips. There was no relenting. His lips were on her neck. She was astonished to find how pleasurable the touch was. She wrapped her arms around him and wondered how long it would go on. It was like one of those rides at Blackpool Pleasure Beach; you clung on and hoped it would be all right and with every dip the butterflies became more agitated and your anticipation of the next descent more acute. How long had he been going? She was losing the sense of time passing. There was a concentration of intense pleasure between her legs which seemed to draw the whole world into its petty orbit. Her existence was limited by its grip. It was almost terrifying, this loss of her customary sense of identity. Her eyes were closed. She was in the dark. All was dark except for this white flare of pleasure. It was an alien force. It subverted every conscious idea, every ounce of will; and Bert kept going, as regular as a metronome. How queer it was, the aloneness of her pleasure and the togetherness of its source.

Bert's shirt was stuck to his wet back. Surely aunty Alice could hear them. What was she doing? She was half naked on the rug in a bedsit having sex with a man who might have had sex with loose Egyptian or Italian women. Was that any way for a good Methodist to behave? She wanted it to stop but she was powerless against her own wish because she wanted it to go on too. Surely it would end soon. She was growing more and more tense and felt she must soon shudder in a pitch of release. Was that what was supposed to happen? She'd never thought about it. The very words that described it had never meant anything to her. She'd expelled them to the far corners of her mind. What she'd thought of was the mere mechanism of delivery; yet this was no uncomplicated instrumentality; it was a thing in itself; it was remote from her idea of sex as a necessary but unfortunate means of becoming a mother.

She was aware of her own clothes becoming damp. She felt a little tear of sweat creep from her brow onto her cheek. Then all at once, while her tension was still about to break like a thread stretched too far, Bert speeded up and in an instant, arched and let out a groan of a higher pitch and she felt the spurting between her legs. He collapsed on her like a weak ceiling under the weight of a flood. She felt the tension in her limbs recede, disappointingly. It was like reading three hundred pages of a novel and finding the last ten had been ripped out. How odd. Was that how it was meant to be? Bert had his satisfaction. The job was done. Would she now be pregnant? Had it lasted long enough? Was his penis as long as it should be? She didn't know what to do or say.

Now her pleasure was rushing away like a river over a weir, she became fully aware of how sweaty she was. Her clothes were crumpled. It was undignified and not in the least bit *ladylike*. She wanted to push Bert off, sort herself out, comb her hair, march home and have a bath but she felt it would be rude and cruel. He was a weight upon her, as if he no longer had the strength to lift himself. He was like a baby. He depended upon her. Yet she had only come close to her satisfaction and still couldn't imagine what it would be like. Bert. Who was he? She felt strangely alone. Why Bert? Why not any other man? Her own thought shocked her. Yet it was true, what they'd done didn't require them to be Bert and Elsie; it required only the bare facts of nakedness and arousal and the butcher's shop reality of flesh.

She knew in the minutes he was on top of her, his breathing slowing little by little, she didn't like him. She was attracted to him as a man. She wanted children. He'd proposed. He had a job and could provide. Yet she didn't like him. She tried to think of a man she did like. There were lads she thought well of; hard-working, reliable, cheery, uncomplicated blokes. Yes, she had a good opinion of them; but did she like them? Not in the sense she was searching for. The truth was, she didn't like any man she could think of, in that sense. Why not? Didn't Maggie like Max? But that was different. Maggie didn't have the same need as her. Need for what? She was at a loss to know but there was some need in her that was answered only when she was in church, only when she felt herself capable of sacrifice for something beyond herself, a need not touched by whatever Bert could offer.

He stirred and raised himself. His kissed her on the lips and smiled. She felt his shrunken penis pull out of her.

"You all right?"

"I'm a bit uncomfortable."

He stood up and she caught her first glimpse. Was it big enough? How could she know? It wasn't like buying pork chops or cod fillets; she had nothing to compare it to. She quickly made herself respectable. She took her comb from her bag and stood in front of the little mirror on the mantelpiece. He came up behind her and kissed her neck.

"Let me comb my hair," she said.

She didn't feel at all romantically about him. It was as if she'd been purged. She was   woman. She knew what Maggie knew. Maybe she would soon be pregnant like April.

"I'll make another brew," he said.

"I need to go home."

"Right away?"

"I need a bath. I'm sticky."

"Have one here."

She looked at him as if he'd suggested she should climb on the roof and mend the slates.

"How will you heat the water?" she said.

"Oh, there's a boiler. It's an efficient little thing. Just turn on the tap and out it comes. I'll show you."

She followed him to the bathroom. The fat, white boiler sat on the wall at the head end.

"Look," and he turned on the tap so the steaming water was soon gurgling and splashing onto the yellowing enamel. "I'll get a towel. There's soap."

"I don't know."

"I'll leave you to it. I'll have the tea ready when you've finished."

He went out leaving her watching the bath fill and the steam billow. She stood still for a few moments thinking how odd it was to be here. His hand appeared holding a big, white towel. She took it and closed the door. When she took off her clothes she had an impulse to go and stand in front of him. Why? She had no idea. She would have been happy for him to do it all again. She was naked and alone but there was something of Bert inside her. She put her palm on her belly. Was her little child soon to start growing in there? The idea excited and frightened her. She must get married as soon as possible. She must be a respectable woman. That she didn't like Bert was insignificant. He was her means to respectability and motherhood; and he was kind enough. It was good of him to offer her the bathroom. He wasn't a bad man. He might be a reasonable enough father. But that wasn't too important. So long as he could earn the money to let her be a mother she would be happy.

She turned on the cold tap. When she sat down in the water she was glad. She would go to church on Sunday and hold her head high. She hadn't sinned; she'd worked out what God wanted and done the right thing. Soon she would be a mother and she would love her little child as Christ loved us all. She lay back and drenched her hair. She was a woman. Her true life was about to begin.

Bert had the tea ready. He was very solicitous. It struck her he was changed. He was like a little boy around his mother; full of that simple joy and unlimited affection typical of young lads in their relation to the women who brought them into the world. She found it almost intrusive. She didn't experience more affection towards him. She felt anxious, or at least, that she ought to feel anxious. She was now, in the eyes of the world, a fallen woman, though in her own she was justified; but what existed between herself and God was unknown to the rest of humanity. Judged by the bald rules, she was a sinner; but her non-conformism had taught her to attend only to the judgement of her own conscience. She made her own agreement with God and she knew precisely what He wanted her to do. She hoped she would be pregnant. She was trying to work out, as she lifted the green mug to her lips, when she was due. Surely if God wanted her to be a mother, if it was His will she shouldn't be outstripped by Maggie and April, he would make her pregnant as soon as He could. It occurred to her he could have provided a virgin birth but if her child was to be a second Jesus, surely He would have chosen a better father than Bert? And why should God repeat himself? He'd sent *his only begotten son* once and the world had rejected him. Why should he give humanity a second chance?

The tea was strong and refreshing. Bert was attentive and made it just as she required, without too much milk and after steeping the leaves for exactly three minutes.

"Was the bath all right?"

"Yes, thank-you."

"It's a good boiler that one. The water's nice and hot."

"What if I'm pregnant?"

"It doesn't happen that fast. You've time to finish your tea."

"Don't be stupid. If I turn out to be."

"Then you'll have a baby."

"Folk'll talk."

"They'd talk if next door's cat had kittens."

"It's all right for you."

"I'd be happy to be a father."

"It's the woman who gets the blame."

"There is no blame."

"You may say so."

"I do say so."

"We'd better be married soon."

"Sooner the better."

"I don't want to go down the aisle with a rounded belly."

"You're not pregnant yet."

"You should've used something."

"I will."

"It's not responsible."

"You're right."

She wasn't going to admit to Bert she hoped she'd be pregnant. If she was, she'd be able to use it against him. Forever, he would be the reckless one who'd got them off to a bad start. Nor did she relish his assumption they would now be regular lovers. In truth, she liked the idea. She wanted to get used to it and to find out what it was like for it to be as much a part of normal life as breakfast or shopping; but she was aware of her potential for power over him. Sex was something she had and he wanted. It was important to have a hold over a husband. Her mother had always dominated the house like a shadow cast by a huge tree. Her father occupied the space she granted him. Yet she feared Bert would want to be *master in his own home*. She'd heard her mother use the phrase with disdain as she sympathised with women whose husbands went to the pub every night, or expected to come and go as they wished. There was nothing more despicable. She needed as many means as possible to keep Bert where she wanted him. Not that she could imagine spending much time with him. She would be busy cooking, cleaning, washing, ironing, looking after the children; all the same, she would expect him to be at home, to submit to her will.

"We shall have to live at me dad's."

"We might afford a little place."

"And who'll look after me mother?"

"You've three brothers."

"They've jobs to think about."

"You could get a job."

"Don't talk daft."

"Why not?"

"You know very well. And if I'm to have a child.."

"You might not."

"I will when we're married."

"We could wait a year or two."

"A year or two? I'd be nearly thirty."

"That's not old."

"It's too old to have your first."

Bert finished the last of his tea with that uninhibited enjoyment which bothered her.

"Anyway, Elsie," he said coming over to her and putting his arm round her shoulders, "we're man and wife now, in every way that matters."

"Not till we're married in the eyes of God."

"If he was bothered he'd have sent a fireball by now."

"You'll burn in Hell for your blasphemy."

"Well, we'll be there together."

She stood up abruptly. He was laughing. She walked out slamming the door. He came down the stairs still laughing.

"Elsie! It was a joke."

"It wasn't funny."

He was walking beside her. She didn't look at him. Her eyes were fixed on the pavement and her shoulders were pushing forward as if the air itself was a weight she must move. She was striding with those quick, short, steps that propelled her by an energy her slight frame didn't look capable of. He was hurrying beside her, like a child pursuing an absconding mother, looking at her closed face, laughing and explaining it was just a silly quip; he was in a light-hearted mood; he hadn't meant anything by it.

But she felt she *should* be angry. Was she genuinely in a temper? She had no idea. She was behaving as she thought she ought to; and by closing him out and making him chase after her and plead, she was consolidating her power. The more he ran along beside her, the more she felt the dislocation between her feeling and her behaviour. It was an odd emptiness that made her wonder why she was being petulant; but at the same time she liked it. The important matter between a man and a woman, of course, was that he should know his place. She had to be sure of her power. He was still beside her. She was a few yards from her front door. Suddenly, he dropped back and when she glanced slyly, she saw him crossing the road, his hands in his pockets; his couldn't-care-less-demeanour, the attitude of so many working men who understand intuitively from an early age they're running up an ever-accelerating escalator and whatever they do, can never get any further, sent a shock of panic through her.

She pushed the door and went inside. As always, there was plenty to busy herself with. She felt clean and fresh from her bath. How nice it would be to have a bathroom like at Aunty Alice's. She caught herself; she was almost thinking of the old woman as one of her family. She wondered how she'd afforded to have it fitted. None of the neighbours had a bathroom, though there was talk of the Council being about to build a little street of houses that would have them. What it would be to live in Penwortham or Fulwood in a house with three bedrooms and a bathroom; she felt her desire was verging on greed and envy; but wasn't Clem Attlee trying build a better world for people like her? Wasn't it time the poor folk who worked hard got their share? Wasn't Nye Bevan setting up a National Health Service so ordinary people would be looked after? That wasn't greed, it was justice; and wasn't it justice too if her children should grow up in a house with a bathroom, if they should never have to fill a cold, metal overgrown bucket with a kettle and take a bath in the kitchen?

As she searched for something to clean, she was aware she'd taken a step which made her partly a stranger in this house. Nothing she'd ever done had been hidden from her parents. Now she had a secret. She had *a life of her own*. It was an odd, uncomfortable feeling. Part of her wished it wasn't true. Why did she have to change? Why did growing up entail such dislocation and difficulty? Above all, why did it mean having to leave behind your own flesh and blood, people who were like you in fundamental ways, to take up with someone who was completely other. It was queer and unsettling.

In bed, she began to worry about Bert. He'd come back. She'd hooked him. He didn't have the power to leave. Yet he knew her now. What if he was comparing her to other women? What if he'd *gone the whole way* in Egypt and Italy? What right did she have to know? But she was going to be his wife; man and wife were one flesh. It was his duty to tell her. She would ask him. She would put the question as directly as a punch in the guts. She had to. It was her right; and his reaction would tell her the truth. If he was lying, she would know. He would give himself away.

She fell asleep wondering when she would see him again and in her dreams hordes of veiled, exotic women with huge breasts and tiny waists danced in vibrant silks before soldiers with burnt skins, short-back-and-sides and ugly knees visible beneath their khaki shorts; she sat in a pew her huge naked belly visible to all as the vicar delivered a sermon on *the sins of the flesh* and the need to resist temptation; and in the maternity ward she was surrounded by a dozen midwives who scowled and commanded as one baby after another appeared between her legs and before she could see or hold it, was wrapped and hurried away.

SUGAR

The next day, it was hard to look into her father's face. She tended to her mother as dutifully as ever, but she was no longer just her mother's daughter. She was separate. It had never occurred to her there were experiences which drove you to a point of aloneness which made them impossible to share. She'd always been able to talk, in her falling-downstairs way, about anything. Now there was something which mustn't be said. Why not? Why couldn't she tell her mother what she'd done? Was it that the old woman would be upset? Or because it was a sin? Did she fear her response? Yet even if she and Bert were married it would be impossible to talk about. It was simply true that the bond was broken; the old assumption of absolute openness was no more. She'd created a part of herself which existed apart from the people she loved most in the world and try as she might she couldn't find it natural.

Yet it had to be done. God knew what He was doing, even if Elsie felt that life was too much of a strain. Nothing she'd read in the Bible, heard at Sunday School or from the pulpit had prepared her for this. The sunny land of goodness where the lion and lamb lay side by side and where all conflict and disagreement was as unknown as whiskey in Chapel, now had its back alleys, its dark streets where the mortar was falling from the walls and the odour of moss and cat's urine mixed with the damp of midnight rain to make you turn up your collar and hurry home to safety and light.

At dinner-time, Jimmy arrived. He was working on a house nearby and popped in to eat his *butties*. Starting a half-past seven, by midday he was ravenous. In his canvas bag which smelled of solder and putty was a big square of sandwiches folded in brown greaseproof paper. He bit into the thick white bread his wife had sliced from the fresh loaf at six and while he chewed and read *The Daily Herald*, slurped the hot, sweet tea Elsie had made him from a pint mug.

"You shouldn't eat and drink at the same time," she said.

"Why not?"

"It's bad for your digestion."

"How'd you know?"

"It's common knowledge."

"'Appen too common."

"You shouldn't read while you're eating either."

"An' when shall I get to read't paper else?"

"Your bad habits will come back to haunt you, our Jimmy."

"Aye, well I've my bad habits and you've yours."

She felt a quick electric current in her abdomen. Did he know? How could he? Was it somehow given away? Could it be read in your face if you'd had sex before marriage? She corrected her reaction at once: she was overwrought; she was thinking about it so she imagined others were; there was no possibility of him knowing; but the persuasion of her rational mind couldn't settle the trouble of her visceral fear. It was as if her tripes could think; as if in her intestine was a little, primitive brain, incapable of the fine and subtle judgements of her thinking mind but intense in its response to every stimulus.

Like the woodworm that silently devours, millimetre by millimetre, the beams beneath the floor so the first you know of their presence is the boards collapsing under your weight; or the malicious dry rot drawing the moisture from your roof joists by infinitesimal degrees while you sleep confidently or eat at your dining table as if nothing could ever undermine your house, till one day the slates fall in and you discover every inch of your home is infested; this primitive consciousness worked away, in the glaring light of the midday sun, in the blackness of a starless night, constantly weakening the foundations of everything you thought secure.

She looked over his shoulder. He was reading about the strikes following the attempt on Togliatti's life. She'd never heard of the Italian. How odd it was that such things went on all over the world while she did the shopping and washed up. She gleaned he was leader of the Communist Party. The strikes seemed to augur the possibility of something new. It was exciting and stirred her as much as a Wesley hymn or a stern sermon.

"They're right to go on strike too," she said.

"Are they?"

"Aye. Shooting their leader. You can bet the Americans were behind it somehow."

"Russians'll be pulling some strings too."

"I dare say."

"Dare yer?"

"I'd vote communist myself if I could."

"Aye, you're daft enough."

"What's daft about it?"

"They don't like Methodists in Russia."

"I'm not talkin' about Russia."

"What are yer talkin' about?"

"Here. Where we've democracy and free speech."

"Aye, well 'appen if yer voted communist we wouldn't 'ave."

"Don't talk soft."

"Yer free to join't Communist Party any road."

She felt badly undermined. She had no intention. Her declaration had been one of those expressions of the absolute which always quickly left her feeling empty and adrift; yet she couldn't keep herself from them. If socialism was right, why not *go the whole way*? The shining absolute of equality was as irresistible as the glory of God. She would have been happy with it. She wasn't a hypocrite. She could have lived in complete equality and relished it. She was devoid of the commonplace ignorance which makes people believe their self-interest is served only if someone else's is injured. She was convinced without knowing it that her best interest was advanced only by defending the best interests of others. Her ignorance lay elsewhere; she didn't know the corruption that lies an inch from purity; that the difference between goodness and evil is not the distance of the sun from the earth, but like a fresh, wholesome steak left uncovered in a warm place which turns, in mere hours, into rotting, stinking putridity, covered with the vomit of a thousand flies.

Jimmy turned the page. There was a picture of Nye Bevan and an article about the implementation of the Health Act.

"No need to," she said. "I'll vote for Attlee. Bevan's got right idea."

"'Appen he has."

"You'll not argue against a Health Service wi' our mother the way she is."

"I'll not," he said looking up at her, "but I'll argue against you."

"You just do it to be awkward," she said.

"'Appen I do."

She went into the kitchen. She was annoyed and upset she hadn't been able to make contact with him. He wasn't usually in such a mood. Henry could be relied on to be sharp as a thorn and quick to sting as a drunken wasp; but Jimmy was usually more taciturn, like her father, and willing to let her talk. What had got into his blood? Perhaps it was thoughtless of her to criticize him when he'd been working hard all morning.

She was contrite. He was one of her big brothers and she should be able to rely on him; but there was something askew in their relationship. What was it? She felt as if he was guilty and was trying to hide it; as if somehow the blame was hers. She searched her memory for a reason but nothing came to her. She knew that, in a way, Jimmy was her mother's favourite. He was like her. All three of her sons were as strong as bears, but Jimmy had her frame; her broad shoulders and big hands. Elsie recalled her telling that when he was a little child she'd noticed how well he could handle scissors and a screwdriver. She saw her own skill with a needle in him. And he was like her in temperament: lugubrious and touchy. He was her first son and in the two years between his birth and the arrival of her second she'd built a special bond which couldn't be replicated.

Elsie rebelled at the thought. How unjust the first born should have a privilege denied those who followed. She, the fourth, was almost an afterthought. She knew well enough in the families of ten or twelve of her grandma's generation, the younger ones were virtually left to the care of their brothers and sisters. Didn't Mrs Mannion, who had ten, forget or confuse their names? She experienced a prick of resentment against Jimmy. She looked after her mother. It was always the daughters who took the burden. Why should he still be privileged? It was an established fact. She'd come last and she couldn't help wondering if she'd been wanted. It made her swear fervently to herself all her children would be planned, wanted and equally loved. Even now the mysterious events which led to the creation of a child might be happening inside her. Would she want her child any less because she wasn't married? The idea was foul. It stank like a blocked drain.

Jimmy finished his lunch and cleared up.

"Back to it," he said.

"Say hello to Jessie for me."

"Aye," he glanced at her and she noticed a cold defensiveness in his eyes.

He turned and left. Watching his strong bulk swing around the big table and disappear through the door frame which seemed hardly tall and wide enough to let him pass, she was struck by how odd it was that such a strapping healthy man could be gnawed by some secret unhappiness. What was it? Something was wrong with Jessie. She knew he wouldn't tell her. He was as close as her father who would say nothing if he was diagnosed with cancer. At once she understood his truculent mood. Was Jessie ill? Was it serious? She wanted to run after him, grab his arm and make him tell but she knew he would shake her off and tell her she was a fool. She sat down at the table.

The idea came to her that Jimmy's marriage wasn't working. She knew it happened. Yet she had no idea what it meant. How did a marriage turn sour? It baffled her. Man and wife were impelled to get along. It was like taking a job: you did what you had to do as best you could. What was this mystery of marriage going wrong? She knew about families like Bert's; but that was the drink. Nothing could prevail against the diligent alcohol worship of his mother and father. Jimmy enjoyed his hours in the pub too, but he was never drunk. He wasn't a sloven who lived in filth. He was clean and neat. His modest little terrace in one of those poor but decent parts of the town where people strove to make the best of inadequacy was beautifully decorated.

No, it wasn't drunkenness that was to blame. She strained her imagination but she couldn't fathom it. What could go wrong? She thought all marriages were like her parents', or at least should be. It didn't occur to her that within the genus *marriage* are many species. The idea that every marriage was as individual as the people in it would have shocked her. Marriage, like God, was an absolute. Just as she couldn't imagine the mind of an atheist, so she couldn't grasp the infinite variety of marriages. There had to be one form to which everyone adhered. It had to be as plain as a Bible's cover and strict as an elementary school mistress.

So how could things be wrong between Jimmy and Jessie? Perhaps it was because they had no children. Had they been trying? Was she unable? Or was he lacking? Her feeling was dragged down in the terrible vortex of possibilities. This was her brother. This was her family. Henry had brought shame on them through his thoughtless behaviour. She was mortified. Was there more pain to come?

She fretted all day which got in the way of her work. She was so distracted she forgot to scrub the front step, a neglect which when she realised made her heart accelerate. When her father came home from work, slow, tired and dirty, seating himself heavily at the table as if his limbs were cast iron, she couldn't contain herself. She put his meal in front of him. He ate in his usual slow way, as if he would be chastised for showing too much eagerness. She hovered; went into the kitchen; came back.

"Our Jimmy was here," she said.

"Aye?"

"There's something wrong with Jessie."

"I know."

She stood opposite him in wonder. He knew? Why hadn't he said something? She felt left out. This was her family yet there was a secret being kept from her. How long had he known? It shouldn't be allowed in families. Everything should be told to everyone. Jimmy was her big brother. It wasn't right.

"What is it?" she said

"Bad wi' 'er nerves."

"'Er nerves?"

"Aye."

"What's brought that on?"

Her father shook his head. She looked out of the window onto the narrow little yard. The phrase played in her head like an unforgettable melody. What did it mean? Bad with her nerves. She'd heard it before. It was said of Mrs Kitchen before she was taken into Whittingham. But she went mad and threw herself under a lorry. Surely Jessie couldn't be like that. It was true she was nervous. She seemed to be apologising for herself a lot of the time but she couldn't be mad. It was puzzling. Bad with her nerves. What were nerves? How did they get bad? Was it just doing too much and getting exhausted? Jessie worked in the light bulb factory. They'd promoted her to supervisor though she didn't want it. The same had happened when she worked in the mill. She was clever, quick and conscientious so they always spotted her and picked her out for promotion. She'd left the mill because she didn't like having to do the bosses' dirty work. She refused to tell girls off or report them if they broke too many threads. She repaired, got the loom working again and left with a smile. She didn't want to supervise, she just wanted a job.

Jimmy earned fair money so long as the work was steady and what she brought in paid for a few extras: a new carpet or a week in Blackpool in July. But wherever she worked her ability was spotted. She'd left school at thirteen but she was a reader and what she liked most was science. She kept it quiet because she didn't want people to think she was a big-head; but she went to the library every week and borrowed books about physics and chemistry. Reading them was like coming home. It was as if she was discovering something she'd always known and even the maths which sometimes baffled her she could find her way through with enough time and effort. Jimmy would pick up her notebook filled with calculations and say:

"What's this all about?"

She would take it gently from his hands and put it in her apron pocket.

"Oh, it's nothing. Just little puzzles to keep me occupied."

Was that it? Did being a supervisor play on her nerves? Elsie could understand that. She wouldn't like it either. Having to report people to the boss would have been as uncongenial as being forced to attend Catholic Mass. There was a loyalty to your own people which came before wanting to get ahead. Let everyone move ahead together. Let everyone work for the common good and everyone benefit. That she understood; but joining forces with the bosses to get more work out of lasses who were working themselves hard eight hours a day for a wage that couldn't keep a family of sparrows, that would have made Elsie *bad with her nerves* too.

"Is it work?" she said.

"'Appen."

"What else could it be?"

Her father said nothing. He went on eating. It annoyed her badly. Why wouldn't he open up?

"Has she been to the doctor?" she asked.

"Aye."

"What does he say?"

"She's bad wi' her nerves."

"But what does that mean?"

"How should I know?" he said pushing away his plate. "Am I a blasted doctor?" and he went in his clumping way as quickly he could from the room and she heard his fateful tread on the stairs.

Why had her simple question hit the mains? There was something behind it she couldn't fathom and it bothered her to her marrow. It was as if there was a secret known to everyone in the family except her. She went about her little tasks with her usual diligence, as if the fate of the universe depended on the fender being polished and the handkerchiefs ironed; but her intentness wasn't happy. She couldn't find herself in any job. It was as if someone else pegged the washing on the line and wiped the windows; all objects seemed to move away from her. Their familiarity became strange. She wanted to talk to someone. Who? Who would be able to offer some kind of answer?

The idea of Bert came into her head. He was a fool in many ways but he read books and knew about modern ideas. He'd once talked to her about the *unconscious*, which she thought all mumbo-jumbo; but he knew about such things. He read the papers and picked up on what was causing a stir. Maybe if she asked him he would have some idea. Even if she thought what he said ridiculous, it might give her a clue.

Poor Jessie. Poor Jimmy. She couldn't bear the thought of their lives going wrong. It always seemed to her disaster was an inch away. The slump had hit when she was a girl of eleven and her father had been thrown out of work. She'd lived with the grim day to day prospect of poverty becoming destitution. The one thing they had was a roof over their heads because her mother and father had squeezed their domestic budget like a wash-leather to pay off their mortgage in ten years. They couldn't be thrown out on the street but they could go hungry. As it was, only her father's allotment ensured they always had potatoes and onions and sometimes blackcurrants and raspberries. There wasn't always coal. Her father gathered twigs and branches from the woods by river. Her clothes were patched and darned.

Not long after her father had found steady work, war was declared. Her brothers were conscripted. They might never come home. She lived a hedgehog's hike from an aircraft factory. Would the Germans bomb it? Would their house, the only security they had in the world be destroyed? She had lived so long with terrible uncertainty, her brain had adjusted to it. She believed disaster as likely as rain with the readiness of a medieval priest believing the earth is the centre of the universe; and because she was sure calamity was at hand, she was vigilant in trying to hold it at bay. She felt it her responsibility. Any act of carelessness filled her with guilt: she let a pan of milk boil over and would try to find someone or something to blame other than herself.

Her mind had been formed in the possibility of imminent catastrophe and she couldn't prevent herself feeling responsible. In the midst of the blackout, lying in bed in terror of an air-raid warning, she'd wondered what she'd done to make the war happen. Was God punishing her for some sin she denied in herself? Had her thoughts been unchristian? Or was Hitler the Devil's handyman? But surely God could overwhelm the Devil; He wouldn't let innocent people suffer. She didn't know guilt can be experienced by the most innocent while the most guilty hide behind an efficient denial of their fault. Nor was she aware of the deluding effect of power. She fretted for a few hours before pulling on her coat and rushing to Bert's.

"Hello, this is a nice surprise."

His smile almost made her feel at home with him. He did have a charming way of welcoming her. She sat in the armchair by the fire and was glad of the warmth. He brought her a mug of tea and sat opposite. He was dressed in a chunky, maroon sweater of the kind he often wore. It suited him. He looked relaxed and nearly handsome. She realised with a jolt he might be thinking she'd come round to make love. She blushed. She wanted to tell him. She wanted to blurt out: "Don't think I've come here to do it again. I want to talk." But she knew it would sound wrong. He began to talk about what he'd been doing at work and how Mr Clow was getting on his nerves, but she wasn't listening. She didn't want to know anything about his work. It was nothing to do with her.

"Our Jimmy's wife is bad wi' 'er nerves," she said.

"What?"

"Jessie. Our Jimmy's wife. She's bad wi' 'er nerves. He was round today. She's been t't doctor. Aye, bad wi' 'er nerves he says."

"She should see somebody."

See somebody? What did he mean? She'd seen the doctor. Who else was there? The priest? Jessie was a Catholic. It couldn't be helped. That was how she'd been brought up. In Elsie's mind there were two people to consult if you were in difficulty: the doctor for athlete's foot and the vicar for fungus of the soul. She was unaware of anyone else you might see. She looked at Bert with wide eyes. He smiled and drank his tea. She was intrigued by what she thought of as his education. Her father was a reader, but he didn't have Bert's squirrel-after-nuts eagerness. He read Dickens and Kingsley, Robert Blatchford and the Fabians, but he found Thomas Hardy a little too modern and wouldn't go near Lawrence because of his *messing in filth*.

Bert, on the other hand, was always looking for what was new, as if some discovery was about to be made that would transform humanity. Her father's brother had his little library too, but like her father he read a lot that came from the century in which he was born. He was very serious in his devotion to George Eliot and unlike her father had all Hardy's novels neatly stacked. She remembered he'd once said to her: "He's a good writer but he goes on too much about sexual relations." The warning had put her off and she'd never opened *The Return of the Native* or *Tess of the D'Urbervilles*.

"Who?" she said.

"A psychiatrist."

The suggestion seemed utterly exotic. How did you get to see a psychiatrist? And weren't they for people who were mad? Jessie wasn't mad, she was just bad with her nerves. Women were often bad with their nerves. It was a woman's thing. It might be to do with her periods. Surely seeing a psychiatrist was a far-fetched idea.

"What could 'e do?" she said.

"Or a psychoanalyst," said Bert. "They can talk you through it, bring out all the repressed ideas."

The what? It was queer he knew such things. Repressed ideas? Her mind struggled with it. Nothing in the Bible, any sermon, what she'd been taught in fear in her strict and punishing classrooms or her father's socialism gave her the means to make sense of it. She drank her tea and tried to look as if she wasn't at a loss.

"What d'you mean?" she said at length.

"It's Freud," he said. "Ideas you can't cope with get pushed out of your conscious mind, but they don't disappear; they stay in the unconscious and though you don't know it they affect the way you think and behave. A lot of it is to do with sex, of course."

"That's ridiculous," she said, putting her empty mug down firmly.

He threw back his head and laughed.

"Does sound a bit barmy when you first hear about it."

"What's that to do with Jessie's nerves?"

"Well, it's about conflict, isn't it?"

"Who with?"

"Herself."

"How can you have conflict with yourself?"

"In your mind. A conflict of ideas."

"You wouldn't disagree with you own ideas."

He laughed again.

"You're right. It's not that. You see, Freud believes in the Oedipus complex. Little boys want to make love to their mothers so they want to murder their fathers. That's the conflict. If they get stuck in it, when they grow up they go after women who are like their mothers and they have problems with sex and affection."

She couldn't believe what she was hearing. It seemed like ideas plucked out of the air. Little boys wanted to make love to their mothers? It almost made her physically sick. The innocence of childhood was part of her Christian inheritance, reinforced by Dickens. The thought that a child could think about sex was vile; and that a little boy could want sex with his mother was the idea of an evil mind. It was evil, evil, evil. And did Bert believe it? Did he think if they had a son he would want to make love to her? She could have jumped up and beaten him around the head with her fists. She'd come to him hoping he would have something to say about Jessie's nerves and he starts talking evil filth. How could she marry a man who believed in such things? That's what you get for being the child of drunkards. She should never have had anything to do with him. To think she'd lost her virginity to such a monster.

"I've never 'eard such rubbish," she said, getting up.

"Where you going?"

"I'm not staying 'ere to listen to that filth."

"It's only ideas."

"The ideas of the Devil."

He laughed. She looked at him with murder in her eyes.

"Sit down," he said. "It's just something I read. I don't know if it's right."

"Right? How can you 'ave any doubt? It's evil. Sex with children. He should be locked up who wrote that."

"He's dead."

"And good riddance."

"You need to read it to understand it."

"You think I'd read such muck?"

"How d'you know it's muck if you won't read it?"

"Anyone who talks about sex with children is wicked."

She was pulling on her coat. He put his hand on her arm to stop her.

"Don't you touch me."

"What's the matter?"

"Your 'ead is full of wicked filth."

"For Christ's sake, Elsie."

"Don't mek it worse by blasphemin'."

"I was just explaining what's in Freud. There's no need to take it personally."

"And do you believe that rubbish?"

"It's not a question of believing it. It's just a theory. It might be right or wrong. Or bits of it might be right."

"How can anythin' be right that thinks children want sex?"

"That's not what he says. It's about what goes on in our minds even though we don't know it."

"Rubbish."

"It may be rubbish, but you asked me."

"I asked you about Jessie's nerves."

"That's right. Maybe there's something wrong in the marriage."

She couldn't believe what he was saying. Something wrong in the marriage? What could be wrong? He was insulting her brother. Him, Pongo, the boy from the stinky, boozy family. What right did he think he had to talk about her brother in that way? She stared at him as if by looking she might be able to see into the cesspit of his mind. He was smiling as if it was a joke. He was rubbing his hands together in that funny way he had. She was stunned by her own stupidity. How had she believed he could come to anything? She'd given him a chance. She was welcoming him into her family; but it was hopeless. She came to talk to him about her sister-in-law and all he could do was spout malicious slanders on the innocence of children. If she'd had a Bible in her hands she would have clouted him with it.

"What do you know about our Jimmy's marriage?"

"Nothing." He held out his arms, palms upturned, like a cheeky, backstreet Buddha expressing bewilderment at the state of creation.

She turned and was gone like a shoplifter evading store detectives. He went down the stairs but she hurried across the street and into her house. She put herself quickly to bed but couldn't sleep. The idea kept coming back to her. What had he called it? Complex something or other. Little boys lusting after their mothers. The more she turned the image of a child climbing on his naked mother over in her mind, like an archaeologist turning a mysterious coin, the more she began to feel sick, till at last her disgust overcame her and she had to fly down the stairs and out into the cold back yard in her bare feet to be sick in the toilet.

She swilled her mouth with water in the kitchen. Back in bed and shivering she tried to think of something else. The words of Jesus came into her mind: *Suffer little children to come unto me.* She pictured him, tall and calm, his face tanned from the Jerusalem sun, his beard and hair the same shade of brown as her own, crouching in his robes to enfold children in his arms and say comforting and kind things to them. As she began to grow warm and sleep crept up on her in its thief's way, she saw herself stepping forward to be taken up by Jesus. He lifted her and carried her, his sandals dragging in the parched dust. He had beautiful blue eyes and his voice was soft and caressing. She lay her head on his shoulder and was at home. Nothing could harm her. She fell asleep as they drifted up into the clouds and God himself became visible, huge, white-bearded, seated on a throne of mist surrounded by angels waiting to take her on his knee and kiss her with the innocence of a father kissing his new-born daughter.

In spite of her resolve to have no more to do with Bert, she found the tension of keeping up resistance unpleasant. She was also worried she might be pregnant, ashamed she'd given herself to a man who was no better than a child molester and fretful about Jimmy and Jessie. When was her period due? She checked the calendar and the date was branded on her mind. What could she do but carry on and wait? She became ever more diligent in her minute household tasks. Every day she climbed the step ladders to wipe the lampshades. As she smoothed away the dust that had barely had time to settle, she thought of the days when she went to bed with a candle. There was no doubt electricity was better. The change had happened so fast: first the gas lights with the fragile mantles, the steady hum of the jet and the odour of burning. She thought it marvellous to have two little brackets on the wall of the living room and to watch her father open the valve and light the flame with a little, harmless explosion; but when a house in Good St was blasted because of a leak, the mother and a child dead in the rubble, every time her father lit the spill, she cowered and put her hands over her ears.

Then in no time the house was wired and every room had a brass switch. It was a great improvement yet she regretted the days of the candle. It was charming to carry the long, white column of wax, your finger curled through the hook of the holder, watching the yellow flame totter if you didn't keep your hand quite still. In her mind there grew an association between technical improvements and loss of innocence; it was true: the years of her maturation had seen a rush of advances. Yet for Elsie it was as if the development of the light bulb was responsible for her loss of bliss. It made her yearn for nature. Wasn't nature pure after all? Wasn't it *God's* nature? Even as she relished the ease and comfort of electric lights, she wished she lived in the simplicity of nature where problems like Bert and Jessie's nerves would surely be impossible. She was up the steps in the kitchen when Henry appeared.

"What you doin' 'ome?" she said.

"It's my 'ome as much as yours."

"I dare say. But I don't come and go like a commercial traveller."

"No, you don't fight wars either."

She was blistered by the accusation. Like her father, she thought war an abomination. She was strongly drawn to the pacifist movement. Yet, at the same time, the forces might have given her a chance. She could have left home, seen a bit of the world, learnt a trade. She was full of resentment that her lout of a brother had been given a chance denied to her.

"No more do I want to."

"Aye, but someone had to stop Hitler."

"He should've been stopped before he re-armed."

"Hark at you. You'll be Prime Minister afore long."

The sparring that was their common way of getting along didn't mean she wasn't glad to see him. She had a special fondness for him because she thought of him as a *lost sheep*. He annoyed her and she despaired of his refusal to go to church or take religion seriously; she thought his behaviour with women a frank disgrace; but he was her brother and she knew he wasn't bad. He was a big baby. He needed looking after. Somehow while Jimmy and Eddie had managed to find enough comfort in the heart of the family to grow up untroubled, Henry had never nestled. It was as if he was fighting the world; he seemed to be in pursuit of something he'd never found in the family and she felt, in spite of their inability to show warmth and tenderness, she ought to help him.

She made him a sandwich and a cup of tea. He sat at the table reading a magazine about motorbikes. It infuriated her. Why was he always thinking about machines? An engine, a car, a train, a tractor a plane: these were Bert's fascination. Anything which moved or flew. Anything with an engine or wheels. But people he had no feel for. She was in the room with him tidying and dusting but it was as if she didn't exist. She felt like flicking her duster under his nose. He chewed and drank and read so she clunked and clattered as much as she could; but it made no difference.

When she could contain herself no longer she said:

"Our Jimmy was 'ere t'other day?"

"Was he?"

"Jessie's bad wi' her nerves."

"I know."

"'Ow?"

"Our Jimmy wrote to me."

"Wrote to you?"

"Aye."

He looked up. His brown, defiant eyes stared straight into hers. His long, raw-featured face which might have been chiselled by a vengeful drunk, bore a hint of nastiness.

"Why would 'e do that?"

"Folk write letters tha knows. Nowt in't Bible agin it."

She felt left out and alone. He'd never written to her. She realised that was foolish because he lived a mile and a half away, but all the same this *secret correspondence* ignited her easily-inflamed jealousy. Jimmy had told Henry about Jessie but had said nothing to her. She felt as if the locks on the family home had been changed and she was outside in the cold. She wanted to ask to see the letter. She wanted to wave it under Jimmy's nose and say: "Why didn't you tell me?"

"Don't talk stupid."

"Ask him, he'll send thee a postcard."

Henry always lapsed into his deepest vernacular when he wanted to offend her.

"And what did he tell you?" she said before she could stop herself.

He looked hard at her again.

"Jessie's bad wi' her nerves, as tha says."

"And what does that mean exactly."

211

He chewed the last of his sandwich as his unflinching gaze burnt her eyes.

"Thas sure tha wants to know?"

"Why shouldn't I?"

"Aye, why shouldn't yer." He paused and drew his big, rough hand across his mouth. "Problem is," he went on, "Jessie dunt think she's married."

"What?"

"Bein' a Catholic like and Jimmy insistin' on a Registry Office do. She thinks she bin livin' in sin and it's turned her mind."

"Who says so?"

"Doctor. He says she needs to see one of them head doctors. Sort her mind out like. In't meantime she'll not be gettin' pregnant."

"How d'you know?"

She knew at once she'd made a mistake.

"Kettle dunt get full if tha dunt put it under't tap."

She stared at him in disbelief. A whirling blade might have torn her brain to shreds. Her heart pounded as if it was about to break out of her chest. Jimmy and Jessie weren't having sex and he'd told Henry? How could he tell such a thing to his brother? Poor Jessie. Did she know? And how long had it been going on? Living in sin? She had sinned too. Would it turn *her* mind? If she didn't now marry Bert would it play on her nerves till she fell apart? It had been done. She was no longer pure. The terrible irrevocability of it weighed on her. Yet why did it turn Jessie's mind that she didn't feel married? She couldn't grasp it. What Bert had said to her came rushing in. The confusion was dizzying. If the house had suddenly lifted off and flown into the clouds she wouldn't have been surprised.

"Well," she said, "if she doesn't feel married she needs to get married."

"Who to?"

"You great lump. Jimmy should swallow his pride and marry her in church."

"'Appen you're reet. I dunno. 'Appen it's gone too far."

She went into the kitchen. She was as agitated as a wasp's nest. The practical solution forced itself on her mind. In spite of what she believed about herself; that she was devout and spiritual, that her mind belonged elsewhere, that the great abstractions of Christianity: The Holy Spirit, Life After Death, The Virgin Birth, all those ethereal concepts which slipped from your grasp as soon as you felt you had some hold on them, were the truth; in fact she was practical as a nail. Had she been brought up without religion, her mind would have focussed intently on immediate problems and she would have sought out, like a hawk its prey, the most direct and sensible resolution.

It seemed obvious that if Jessie was troubled because she thought she should have married in a Catholic church, then the ceremony should do the trick. She wanted to march round to Jimmy's and tell him. Was he refusing a Catholic wedding? The fool. Yet at the same time as her practical mind lasered in on the answer, she was adrift in trying to understand why Jessie's nerves should be so bad. She thought of sex with Bert. How had she convinced herself it was right? She traced her thoughts back: she wanted children. Having children was the will of God. Nothing could be wrong if you were carrying out His will. Her doubts wilted. She felt secure, tall and strong in her conviction. She wasn't married but God understood. He put doing His will above obeying man-made laws. A marriage licence was a human invention. It couldn't come near the importance of God's desires.

Why couldn't Jessie feel like that? Surely she wanted children. The image of Jimmy, the great, heavy-limbed, bear-handed, unsophisticated lummock on top of little Jessie, her legs open as he grunted and sweated, appeared in her head. She turned on the tap, ran the dishcloth under it and wrung it out in her straining, delicate fists. It was disgusting. It wasn't at all like Rita Hayworth or Ingrid Bergman at the pictures. She couldn't imagine Jimmy being romantically seductive like Robert Mitchum. She could only picture him going obscenely after his pleasure, in the way he devoured a sandwich as if he were about to starve or swigged a bottle of pale ale after a day's work.

Poor Jessie. Yet why couldn't she rise above the vile physicality? Why couldn't she escape the skinned fact of vulgar male desire, the animal grunting and sweating by allowing it all to evaporate into the lovely steam of impending motherhood? She was sure it had something to do with Catholicism. Wasn't it all fluff, the robes and the incense and the humiliating business of having to sit in a little box and tell a priest your sins? She blenched from it into the stern non-conformist insistence that no-one can make your agreement with God for you. In the silence and isolation of your own mind you must work it out for yourself. The idea of expecting a priest to forgive your sins made her nauseous. Wasn't that to tell people they could sin with impunity? All they had to do was convince the priest, say a few Hail Marys and they were forgiven. She hated the idea. She knew Methodism was right. You had to fight with your own demons and defeat them. The Devil found his way into everyone's mind. You had to watch for him and build defences a mile high and ten miles thick. Wasn't that Jessie's problem? She couldn't work it out for herself. She needed a priest. She needed confession. No wonder her nerves were bad. Elsie wished she could convert her to Methodism.

That evening she went round to Jimmy's. Jessie opened the door to her. Jimmy was in the pub. The tiny vestibule opened into the small front room where a coal fire was burning. The room was cosy and neat. There was a small settee pushed against the wall and two arm-chairs either side of the hearth. On the mantelpiece was a picture of Jimmy and Jessie on their wedding day, he tall and awkward in his grey suit, she small and self-effacing, smiling shyly, looking at the camera from under her downcast brows and holding a sweet little bouquet.

How nice it must be to have a home of your own. How Elsie wished she was set up in a little house like this; a place she could be mistress of. She would keep it as clean, bright and welcoming as Jessie did. She would have her wedding photo on the mantelpiece too. The one thing missing was children. Elsie would have pictures of hers on the wall. She would welcome visitors into her friendly living-room and serve them tea, biscuits and cake from her little trolley.

"Jimmy's out for a drink," said Jessie.

She was a little woman, dark and slender but with a way of trying to conceal herself in all her movements, as if she thought herself too conspicuous. Elsie noticed she had a book open on the arm of the chair. She caught the title before Jessie closed it and put it back on the shelf: *The ABC of Relativity*. What was Relativity? How strange that Jessie whose nerves were bad could read such a thing.

"Shall I make a cup o'tea?"

214

"No, I'm not stoppin', luv. I just popped in to see how you were."

"Oh, you must stop for a cup o' tea, Elsie. Sit down, luv. Tek your coat off."

"Aye, well I'll just stop a minute or two."

"Grand. Sit by't fire where it's warm, luv. I'll not be long."

Elsie put her coat over the back of the chair and sat down. She wished Jimmy was there. It was him she wanted to talk to. She wanted to say to him: "You mun marry Jessie in church if that's what's troublin' her." She wanted to bully him. Why had he insisted on the Registry Office? Pig-headedness. She'd shaken her head at him when he refused to go to chapel as a lad of fourteen. He preferred the pub and a pint to a good sermon. She feared for his immortal soul. She knew well enough that her father had no feel for religion; and Jimmy had cleaved more to his father than his mother. He stuck close to his socialism, though it was a second-hand version, not the hard-won, pure gold of his father's conviction. Elsie knew how to speak to Jimmy. She blamed him. She thought he needed a good talking to. But what would she say to Jessie?

She was blameless. She'd gone along with Jimmy's wishes and now she was in a state. She put others before herself. She hid her talents. She demanded nothing. Jimmy spent his money on beer while she barely went anywhere but work. She should stand up for herself a bit more. Elsie, having three older brothers, knew how to do that. She knew how to use her elbows and her tongue to get listened to; but Jessie was meek as a kitten. Elsie felt a quiet outrage at Jimmy: if only he knew what a good, sweet wife he had. If only he knew how to cherish her and make her feel loved.

She could hear Jessie in the kitchen. She wanted to go through. When was the last time she was here? She'd been in the kitchen only once. Had they changed anything? It seemed right she should be at home in her brother's house; yet she didn't feel she could turn up when she liked. It was odd how your brother could become a stranger; or *like* a stranger.

She wished she and Jessie could be good friends, like she was with Maggie. Wouldn't that be *natural*? Wasn't it *natural* a sister should be the close pal of her brother's wife? Then she could come to Jimmy's like she went to Maggie's. Yet a negative thought struck her: once Maggie was married and in her own house would she become like a stranger there too? How odd these changes were. It puzzled and disappointed her. Wasn't a brother a brother after all? Wasn't that absolute? Surely a sister had more connection to a brother than a wife to a husband. It was possible Jessie and Jimmy might never have met. It was only because Jimmy did some rewiring in her factory they got to know one another. Wasn't that a mere accident? How could a life-long relationship be founded on accident? Wasn't the same true of Bert? If he hadn't moved in with aunty Alice she'd never have known him; she'd have had sex with someone else. Could it be intimacy was the result of such flimsy connection? It all seemed wrong somehow.

Blood is thicker than water; the cliché entered her mind from some unknown door and reassured her. It was God's way. The disturbing business of taking up with a stranger, having your emotions thrown into chaos, engaging in animal passion; it was all part of God's plan and though to a human mind it seemed uncertain, dirty and dangerous, it was only necessary to remember God *worked in mysterious ways* to be able to accept it.

Jessie brought the teapot, went back for the cups and saucers and made another trip for the milk and sugar. Didn't she have a tray? Elsie almost wanted to say to her: "Dear heaven, Jessie, you're back and forth like a bookie's runner;" but she restrained herself, not being under her own roof and given Jessie's condition.

"You don't have sugar, do you luv?"

"No, said Jessie thinking that she might follow up with an explanation that it was a matter of principle, the workers on the sugar plantations being badly exploited; and also because it was bad for your teeth and your health in general; but she blenched from what might seem like a little sermon because of the friendliness of the setting and the comfort of the fire and the surroundings.

"I remember. Not like Jimmy. He's a real sweet tooth."

"He needs tekin' in hand."

She noticed at once how Jessie shrank from the rebuke. Should she retract it? Should she explain she didn't mean Jessie was at fault but rather she was thinking of her own family; her father in particular who had indulged Jimmy's liking for sweets, cakes and puddings on the grounds he needed the energy? Yet the explanation might seem false; it might convince Jessie she did mean to criticize her. Elsie felt ashamed. Why had she spoken so directly and abruptly? It was as if something spoke through her. She no more intended to insult Jessie than to burn her house down; yet when she spoke, her words often came out wrong. She wanted to say something gentle, calm and friendly, but it emerged from her mouth like a pulpit injunction.

"Oh, I've forgotten t'biscuits," said Jessie in a little flurry of panic.

"No, no. Not for me, luv. I'm not one for biscuits and cakes."

"Well, will y'ave somethin'? I could toast a bit o' bread. I've some lovely jam I bought at church fete."

"No, sit down, luv. A cup o'tea's grand. I'm parched all right."

They sat opposite one another both hunched forward in the armchairs, as if to lean back comfortably would have set off a bomb. Elsie felt an urgent need to ask Jessie unceremoniously about her *nerves*. She wondered if her sister-in-law had twigged the reason for her visit. As she looked into her face whose eyes were fixed on the tea-cup and the spoon she was rotating, it struck her she wore a permanent hint of a smile, as if constantly amused by some secret thought.

She looked intelligent. Why was that? Jimmy didn't look intelligent. You didn't expect him to open his mouth and say anything surprising; but there was something about Jessie's face which suggested she could explain difficult things. Or was that simply because Elsie knew she was clever? It bothered her a little that her sister-in-law was brighter. Yet at the same time, Elsie felt she was her superior ; she was more devout, she understood the mind of God. That was more important than anything you could find in a book.

"Are you sure you won't 'ave a biscuit?" said Jessie

"No thanks, Jessie. I try not to eat between meals."

Once again she had a little frisson of self-consciousness: was she being too self-righteous? Would Jessie think she was criticising her? It took away Elsie's confidence and made her wonder why her tongue was a blade which cut those she wanted to caress.

"Anyway," she went on, "how are you, luv?"

"I'm all right," said Jessie lowering her eyes.

Elsie saw the little, modest smile on her lips. What a sweet thing she was. She wouldn't demand the hand of a stranger if she were falling under a train. She realised for the first time why Jimmy had married her: she would be attentive to him, he would be well looked after, but more importantly, she would never object to him doing what he liked; he could go to the pub every night leaving her in the house alone and she would be as pleasant as sunshine in May.

"Jimmy said you're under t'doctor."

She felt intrusive, but it was the way in her family, or at least her mother's way. Her father could be abrupt too but mostly he was taciturn and reserved. Her mother, on the other hand, had always spoken like God himself, as if she had an absolute right to say whatever she fancied and other people's sensitivities were no more to be taken notice of than a child's whim.

Elsie had grown in the belief her mother was a good woman; she was a Methodist; she didn't touch alcohol; she worked like salmon swimming to spawn. So her iron-bar, dig-in-the-solar-plexus way of speaking to people seemed right. Frequently, Elsie found herself adrift when conversation was an exchange of trivialities; she wanted always to assert some eternal truth, to enunciate some moral principle. Chatting for the sake of chatting seemed alien and frivolous.

"Well," said Jessie her eyes still lowered, "I've 'ad a bit of trouble wi' me nerves."

The confession brought a rush of warm feeling. Elsie wanted to cradle her. The poor, poor thing. She would have liked to stay with her and be as available as air. She wanted to be sunlight to bring her warmth and health.

"Oh dear, Jessie. What do you think's brought that on, luv?"

"I don't rightly know."

"Has doctor nothing to say?"

"He has his ideas."

She looked up and met Elsie's gaze. It was hard to imagine she was suffering; she seemed so calm and quiet. Elsie thought mental pain must be accompanied by cries as haunting as a wolf's howl in the desert, by the agitation of a pike on a hook; she had no idea that despair as vicious as a circular saw's teeth can lurk behind the most serene demeanour.

"What are they?"

"I don't like to talk about it."

Jessie spoke so quietly and gently Elsie couldn't take her rebuttal seriously. She was a soul in difficulty. Wasn't it Elsie's Christian duty to help her; and didn't she know just how? She wanted to wag her finger at her like an impatient schoolmistress and tell her what to do.

"I know, luv. It's 'ard. Aye, life's hard, Jessie. But I'm family. Who can you turn to if not your family. Eh, luv? Our Henry says Jimmy's written to 'im."

Elsie saw the flash of alarm that appeared and disappeared in Jessie's eyes as quickly as a mousetrap breaking a neck. She wondered if she'd said a terrible thing. Would it cause a row? Yet she couldn't feel she wasn't justified. She wanted to help. She knew the answer. She had to tell Jessie to get married in a Catholic church. She knew it would work.

" Has 'e?"

"So our Henry says."

"Well, that's their business. They're brothers."

"Aye. He says it's summat to do wi' not getting' married in church."

Jessie's eyes sprang alive like an engine at the jolting of the starting handle. She was staring.

"Does 'e?"

"Is that it, luv?"

Jessie stared for a few more seconds. She picked up her cup and drank.

"Well, Elsie, you know more than I thought you would." She put her cup down. "More than you should, 'appen. But that's what t'doctor says."

"What d'you think?"

"I don't know."

"Do you feel you're not properly married as our Henry says?"

"Yes. I do. In a way. I thought I was doin' right by Jimmy. I didn't think it'd bother me, but it has. And then t' Father…."

She tailed away and looked down at her feet.

"Aye, what's that?"

Jessie rubbed the cotton of her skirt between her finger and thumb. Her face took on that look of great preoccupation which puzzled Elsie.

" The priest has been 'ere every week since we were wed. He says in't th'eyes o'God I'm not married and me sin'll send me t'Ell. It preys on me mind and me and Jimmy don't get along as we should."

"How's that?"

Jessie looked up. Her eyes had lost their fixity. She looked long into Elsie's face as if the mere looking should tell Elsie something. Elsie could only return her gaze and hope she would speak. At length, Jessie smiled.

"Another cup, Elsie."

"No thanks, luv. I musn't stay too long."

"It was good of you to call in. I'm allus glad to see you."

"Well, I was sorry to hear you weren't well,luv. But I say Jessie, if not being married in church is t'problem, why not do it?"

"Aye, but there's Jimmy to think about."

"Jimmy?"

"Catholic church means nowt to 'im."

"Methodist church neither. He gets it from me dad. Pig-headed. I've told 'im. I've told 'im till I'm blue in't face. Any road, you don't want to fret about that, Jessie. He'll tek no 'arm so long as 'e's a pint of beer in his 'and."

" 'Appen your right, but if I force 'im to it, things might not be right after."

"What things?"

"Things that go on between a man and wife."

Elsie sat still. She understood at once. How could it be? She had no idea. Into her head came the memory of her one time with Bert. Surely if Jessie told herself it was to produce children and that was doing God's will, there couldn't be any difficulty.

"Don't bother about our Jimmy," she said, "the great lump. Tell 'im he has to. I'll tell 'im if you like."

"No, Elsie. We'll see. But I sometimes wonder…"

"What?"

"I wonder if t'priest is right. I wonder if I shouldn't leave t'church."

"Nay, Jessie. You don't want to be doin' that. Think of Heaven."

"Aye, well anyway. We'll see."

"Get yourself married, luv. I know I wouldn't be happy with a Registry Office. Marriage has to be before God."

"Aye, will Bert marry in chapel?"

Elsie was shocked to the tips of her toes. How had the idea got into Jessie's head? Had Jimmy put it there? What was she to say? She wanted to unleash a volley of abuse: "'im. I wouldn't give 'im a crust if 'e were starvin'. No better than a child molester. It's his family o' course. Drunken, Godless lot. And Tories in t't bargain. God 'elp us. You can't blame 'im I suppose, but he's turned out bad. What can y'expect wi' a grandfather who fights in't street on a Saturday neet? Marry 'im? I wouldn't touch him wi' disinfected rubber gloves, Jessie. Thought of 'im meks me sick to me stomach….." But she had to keep her disdain to herself. What would Jessie think of her if she knew? She'd look a fool all right to have taken up with such a man. Oh, it was terrible the way men could behave towards women.

"I don't know about that, Jessie, I'm sure I don't."

She was pulling on her coat. She was sorry to leave the cheery room and the feminine confidences. She liked Jessie in spite of her cleverness and her shy, quiet ways. She could have had a good friendship with her, she thought.

Out in the street they said their goodbyes, Elsie reiterating her advice. As she walked home she wondered about Jessie's *nerves*. Was it the Devil? Perhaps he'd found a way into her mind because she hadn't been married in church. You couldn't be too careful. If God had sanctified the ceremony, He would have made sure the Devil couldn't find a way in. He would have given His blessing to all parts of the marriage, including that sweaty, dirty business of letting a man between your legs. He knew what he was doing. If children had to be conceived that way, it was because He knew it was for the best. He could have arranged it any way He liked of course. He organised the virgin birth. If He wanted to, he could provide *her* with a virgin birth. No, he didn't take the easy way. He wanted to make life hard so He could see who deserved to go to Heaven. *Not forever by still waters would we ask our way to be, but the steep and rugged highway may we tread rejoicingly.* The words appeared in her head, sung by the chapel choir. Yes, she was glad to take the steep and rugged path. She thought of her hikes in the Lakes. The hard push up Skiddaw, her thighs tight as bolts, the sweat running down her face and back like little streams down the mountainside. Yes, it was hard work but when you sat at the summit, drank your water and ate your sandwich, wasn't it worth every step? Isn't that what the hymn meant?

It was people like Bert's family who wanted *life by the still waters.* It was because they were too soft to take the rugged path they ended up in bad ways. Jessie had left a small opening and the Devil had rushed in. Now he occupied part of her mind. Of course he wanted to make her nerves bad. He would enjoy ruining her marriage and seeing her collapse; but she was to blame, at least a little. She should have insisted. What was Jimmy after all but a big, clumping, beer-swilling, football-watching electrician?

He'd turned his back on God but that was his business. If his soul was to burn in Hell, well, it couldn't be helped. He was her brother. She wanted him with her in Heaven. Perhaps God would forgive him. He was a good lad after all. He'd do anything for anybody. Like her father he had a *heart of gold* beneath his slapped-on, foundation-mortar exterior. She wiped away a tear. It was terrible to think of Jimmy spending eternity burning in Hell. Would her father and Henry be there too? And Eddie? No, he did go to church now and then and God would never condemn a soul if there was a blink of a chance of salvation.

Her mind struggled with the terrible burden of eternal salvation and earthly health. She wished she knew what went on in Jessie's mind, for no matter how she tried to envision the Devil installed in her thoughts like a drinker on his favourite stool by the bar, it couldn't convince her she understood. The one thing she was sure of was that to appear before God as a couple, to ask Him to marry them, to let Him condone all that marriage entailed (even *that*) was the way to drive out the Devil and to be able to live in peace.

When she got home Bert was there. She almost launched herself at him. She could have scratched out his eyes and spat in his face.

"It's your dad," he said.

"What?"

"He's not so good."

"Where is he?"

Bert twitched his head towards the kitchen. She went through to find her father sitting on a wooden chair, a cup of water in his hands.

"Dear Heaven! What's the matter now?"

"I found him in the street," said Bert. "He'd collapsed a few yards from the door."

She bent to look at him and the smell of alcohol caught her attentive, disapproving nostrils.

" Dad, you've been drinkin'!"

The old man shook his head.

"I can smell it," said Elsie, turning to Bert for confirmation.

"I don't think it's drink," said Bert.

"You'd swear black's white," she said, ready for a fight. " I can smell it I tell you."

"You can smell his breath," said Bert. "You can smell something like alcohol but it isn't drink."

"How do you know, clever clogs?"

He looked at her impassively.

"I've smelt enough booze in my time."

"Well, what is it then?"

"I'm not a doctor but I think he needs one."

"Doctor! You think we're payin' for that when all he needs is to sober up?"

"Elsie," said Bert, " you don't have to pay any more. And your dad isn't a drinker. He's as likely been drinking as you've been backing horses. When did you last see him have a drink? He's ill, Elsie. If you don't get a doctor I will."

"Aye, and if there is a cost you'll pay."

"Yes, I will, but there won't be."

He was gone. Suddenly, alone with her pale and faltering father, her confidence dropped from her like a man through a trapdoor. Not drink? Then what could it be? She knelt in front of him.

"Tell me t'truth, dad. Have you bin drinkin'?"

"Hell as like," he muttered.

She stood up. She believed him but she doubted him. Perhaps he was so drunk he couldn't even remember having a drink. She was faced with a fact she couldn't explain and as always, if the facts didn't meet her ideas, it was the facts that must bend. If she could smell alcohol, it must be drink. Yet she knew Bert was right. Her father wasn't a drinker. There wasn't so much as a bottle of brown ale in the house and he never went into pubs because he lacked that hearty, all-blokes-together, spirit that animated most of them. Nothing appealed to him less than a rowdy crowd of drunks or the braggart enunciations of ignorance lubricated by booze.

He was truly a domestic creature. He was happy at home with a book or listening to the radio. He'd always fretted about his children when they were out of the house. His peace and happiness had been when they were all together in the warmth and safety of the home. Men in crowds attracted him for two purposes: politics and football. He'd stood with thousands at rallies to hear Keir Hardie and the comradeship had made his eyes water; he'd been packed tight in the crowd watching Finney, unable to get his hands in his pockets, and the shared partisanship and delight had given him a sense of belonging; but in the pub what joined men was drink and in drink they could be violent, stupid, thoughtless, vulgar, vile or maudlin.

She knew he wouldn't have been there. The area was notorious. Sailors often wandered looking for whiskey, women and a fight. Hadn't Jimmy come home one night his face swollen, his nose broken, his eyes closed up, one of his teeth missing, his clothes covered in blood after a beating by Scandinavian seamen in *The Mitre*? Yet still she clung to the explanation. The odour couldn't be deceiving her. There was one explanation only in her head: the smell of drink on a man meant he'd been drinking. Why should she look any further? Yet she couldn't believe it of her father. All the same it must be true. Somehow, somewhere he'd been drinking.

"Do you want some water?" she said.

"Aye," he muttered. "I've a thirst on me."

She stood by him as he drank. He held out the cup for more, emptied it in one go and held it out again. Why was he so thirsty? Wasn't that what drink did to you? Hadn't she seen Henry at the tap in the morning when he'd had too much the night before? All the evidence was on her side. It was terrible to think her sober father would drink himself into such a state but it was true. Thank God her mother wasn't able to see him. Where was Bert? Had he gone for the doctor? The fool. Wasn't that him all over? Was he going to bring him only to hear him say her father was drunk? The embarrassment. If only he could keep his nose out of things. What did he think he knew? Telling her she didn't know the smell of drink when it was in her nostrils.

"I'm not feelin' reet," said her father, "I'd best get to bed."

But when he tried to get up from the chair he swayed and fell back.

"That's what drink does for you," she said sharply.

His head was tilted back, his eyes were closed and he made no reply. If only one of the lads was home to carry him to bed. Perhaps if Bert came back the two of them could manage him. She stood by him ashamed and mystified to see her own father no better than a drunkard in the street. She was thinking perhaps she should contrive a makeshift bed on the kitchen floor when she heard the door and Bert appeared with Doctor Sheridan.

He was a little man, somewhat reminiscent of a pig in the features of his round face, his hunched, broad shoulders and his short legs. He wore the heavy, dark coat which seemed to shroud him in all weathers. He was panting from the effort of rushing along the street to keep up with Bert's haste.

"Hello doctor," said Elsie. "My father's drunk. That's all it is."

The unceremonious professional looked at her fleetingly from over his gold- rimmed glasses then bent to the patient. He sniffed his breath, took his pulse, lifted his eyelids, sounded his chest, stood up and said:

"Diabetes. He'll have to go to hospital before he falls into a coma."

Bert followed him out of the kitchen saying to Elsie:

"I'll see to it. Stay with your dad."

Diabetes? What was that? She'd heard of it and knew it had something to do with sugar; but her dad didn't have a sweet tooth. He hardly ever ate so much as a biscuit. Sugar diabetes. Isn't that what people called it? Didn't that mean it was caused by eating too much sugar? What else could it mean? And why did her dad's breath smell of beer? She felt like running after Doctor Sheridan and saying: "Did you smell his breath? I'm right aren't I?" How could he tell it was sugar diabetes just by taking his pulse and putting his stethoscope to his chest? Yet surely he must know his job. Perhaps they were both right: her father had sugar diabetes and had been drinking. Perhaps he'd been drinking because he didn't feel well. That might make a bit of sense. Yes, that must be the explanation. She felt sorry for having thought badly of him. If he was suffering and had taken a drink to try to make him feel better she could sympathise; but it was stupid. The thing to do was tell someone. That was her father's trouble: he kept things to himself; and now look where he was, drunk and laid low with diabetes.

The ambulance arrived. Her father was lifted onto a stretcher.

"Are you going with him?" said Bert.

"I've got to stay with me mother."

"Then I'll go."

"You?"

Bert looked at her. His face was very still and serious.

"I'll see if I can find of way of letting Eddie and Jimmy know. I'll stay with him till someone arrives."

She stood back. Why should he go with her father? She wouldn't go to hospital with his grandfather, not if he was twenty minutes from death. They carried her father out and the chugging ambulance growled along the street. She went up and sat by her sleeping mother but her agitation got the better of her. She tripped down to the kitchen and began cleaning. She scrubbed and polished everything. Down on her knees with a stiff brush in her hand looking for any lurking bit of muck on the stones and working till her biceps ached, she felt this was where she belonged. It was odd how the low and menial appealed to her. It was the opposite of her religious fervour. In church with a hymn book in her hand or her head bent in prayer she felt she ascended to the right hand of God. She was not only anyone's equal, she was their superior. She was as confident of her piety as Einstein of his capacity in Physics. If the whole of life was lived in church, as she wished it could be, she would have suffered no sense of inferiority; but out in the world she was a child of the backstreets.

Her mind had been formed in deprivation, an environment as unnatural as luxury. Just as those born into wealth know intuitively they are superior; just as every experience plays upon their minds to confirm their election; just as they grow in the assumption that all which is best should be theirs and that no hardship, difficulty or inconvenience should befall them; so the children of the poor know from their earliest days the good things aren't for them; they will have to struggle for every advance; those above them will defend their property and their status to the death; and even those who fight against the briars and nettles of imposed degradation to win huge wealth, power and esteem, never fully leave behind the doubt about their worth so their Rolls Royces, private jets and islands can't obliterate the painful humiliation of having been told, by the bricks of their houses, by the holes in their shoes, by the poor food on their plates, by their darned elbows, by their grim yards and back alleys, by their treeless streets, by their grassless schools, by the smoke from the factories, by the overalls of their fathers and the chapped hands of their mothers, by the overdue rent, by the absence of travel, by the rarity of a visit to the cinema or the swimming baths, by their hand-me-down skirts and trousers, by the rats in the rafters, by their *scruffy* accents, by their cold bedrooms and their outside toilets, by the once-a-week bath, by the never-wasted crust, by the throat-grasping fear of doctors' bills and funeral expenses, by the killing shift and the too-short break, by the scrimping day-before-pay-day, by the one good suit in the wardrobe, by the threadbare towels and the worn-out carpets, they are unworthy, their place is not secure and they are marked as irrevocably as low-life as they are by genetic inheritance.

She felt she must fulfil this destiny of inferiority. Down on her knees no-one could accuse her. She was where fate had placed her. When she'd finished in the kitchen she began in the living-room and when she'd hunted down every atom of dust there, she polished the hallway and afterwards punished the doorstep till it was sore. She went on till she was exhausted and when she sat down at the kitchen table to rest, without knowing why, she put her head in her hands and cried.

The next day she visited her father. Bert arrived five minutes after her. She didn't want to look at him or talk to him but he'd brought grapes and a copy of *The Daily Herald* which softened her pumice-stone resolve. Her father was alert and comfortable. He said he'd been given insulin.

"What?" she said.

"It regulates blood sugar," said Bert.

"Does it?"

"Yes. It's produced by the pancreas."

"The what?" she said looking at him as if he'd begun speaking Persian.

"It's a small organ in your abdomen. Your dad's got diabetes because his pancreas doesn't produce enough insulin."

She wanted to know more but she was affronted to receive instruction from Bert.

"How do you know?" she said, as if she might quote Deuteronomy to disprove him.

"I went to the library to look it up."

"Well, you might have looked it up wrong."

"It's reliable science, Elsie. That's why your dad's looking better. He'll have to inject insulin for the rest of his life."

She was astounded. Inject insulin? Himself? Could her father do such a thing? He wasn't a doctor. Where would he inject himself? In the arm? Questions wanted to fly from her like spoors from a blown dandelion, but she couldn't let herself go. She wanted to gain some edge over Bert.

"Well, why did his breath smell of beer?" she challenged.

"As far as I get it," said Bert, "it's because he can't get energy from sugar so his body burns fat. That's why he's lost weight. It's called ketoacidosis. It produces something called ketones and they give your breath the sweet smell."

She looked at him in horror. Keto what? Why didn't she know these things? Why was there nothing in the Bible about keto-what's-its-name? She believed she knew everything it was important to know and book-learning was superficial and barely relevant; yet here was Bert explaining in a way which sent her mind spinning what had happened to her father.

It was strange and mystical. She tried to summon up what a ketone might be, but her mind was blank. While she could picture God as vividly as a tree, ketone was just a word, a sound which attached itself to nothing. How did they know such things existed? Had they seen them? How? And what was insulin? She said the word over and over to herself but no image appeared. Was it a liquid? And if it was made in the pancreas as Bert claimed, what happened to it then? Why couldn't her father get energy from sugar? She'd always thought sugar was bad for you. Should she start eating more to get energy? But wasn't it sugar that caused diabetes?

She felt very small and weak in the face of these confusing facts. She wanted to assert that God would look after everything, that if her father had diabetes it must be God's will; but even she couldn't accept her father's suffering as part of God's plan.

"He's never 'ad a sweet tooth," she said. "'Appen that's 'is problem. If 'ed eaten more sugar perhaps 'ed've got all th'energy he needed."

"I don't think so," said Bert. "Anyway, we shouldn't talk about him as if he isn't here."

Tom was reading the paper and took no notice.

"'E doesn't mind, do you dad?"

The old man went on reading as if no-one had spoken to him.

"Anyway," said Bert with a laugh, "at least you know now he's not a secret drinker."

Elsie bridled a little and turned away her face. It was a horrible gut-twisting feeling to know she'd accused her father and had been absolutely convinced of her rightness, only to find she was utterly wrong. She wanted to find a way out. She couldn't let the miserable humiliation of knowing her way of thinking, not just this one fault, but her whole way of making sense of the world was mistaken, take hold and spread through her. She didn't know that it was only by being wrong and admitting it, she had any chance of being even partially right. She'd been raised in the certainty of revealed truth and the confidence and delight it gave her had formed her mind.

The superficiality and spuriousness of those qualities weren't something she could admit. It would have sent the flimsy plane of her existence into a tail-spin; she would have had to work fiercely and against all she had been taught to stay in the sky. She was at one of those moments of desperation when the choice we make determines the significance of our lives; one of those instants of terrible isolation when we have to choose alone, when fear and despair chew at our innards like beavers at logs, when the desire for a simple and comforting answer can lead us down a path whose destination must be pusillanimity and failure in one of life's elemental tests.

"Well, I were reet," she said, falling into her most basic vernacular, "'e did stink o' booze."

"Not from drinking beer though," said Bert smiling and trying to lighten the tone.

"It might 'a' bin. You dint know. You dint know any better 'n' me. I were reet at time."

"Yes," said Bert, "you were right his breath had an unusual odour."

"'N' suppose 'e 'ad bin drinkin'," she said.

"He hadn't."

"Aye, but if 'e 'ad. I were't one who were doin' reet."

"In a way. I suppose so," said Bert.

She felt she'd done enough. It was true. Bert didn't know all the stuff about keto-what-you-may-call-it and burning fat and so on the day before. No. She'd been right. His breath did smell of drink and in the circumstances, what was the right thing to do? Any sensible person would have done the same. Even a doctor. Sheridan knew her father, after all. He'd treated him for years. A doctor who didn't know him might have drawn the same conclusion as her. You had to use your common sense. That's what she'd done. All this book learning might be all right for doctors and the like, but it was common sense that mattered in life. Look at Buck Ruxton. He was a doctor and an evil man. What did book learning do for him? No, she was right by her lights and that's what mattered. Of course, now she knew a little bit about ketones and all that she could change her mind. She could find out more. Doctor Sheridan would have to explain it to her because she would have to look after her father.

That was two parents on her hands. Yes, it was going to be hard. Her father would depend on her even more now; and what good were her brothers? They had their own lives. It fell to the daughter to take on these responsibilities. Yes, she'd been right. She'd been responsible.

230

Her father's breath smelt odd and what explanation could there have been but drink? It was all well and good for Bert to run to the library and look it up, but not everything could be found in books. No. Doctors might know about diabetes but what did they know about the immortal soul? And which was more important, the body or the spirit? She wanted her father to get better. Death was a terrible thing for those left behind; but the salvation of his soul, in which she was an expert, was much more important than treating his ailment.

The ward sister was strict. She clanged the bell for the end of visiting and they had to leave. Elsie disliked seeing her father in the bed as she disappeared. She had a sickly fear something might happen to him. Who could look after him better than her? She turned to look at him. He was still reading the paper. She wished she could stay with him and make him a good mug of tea. She went down the wide stairs with Bert beside her.

"He'll be all right," he said. "They know how to look after him in here."

" 'E'd be better at 'ome."

"They'll soon have him right. They'll have to work out the right level of insulin and a balanced diet."

"Diet?"

"It's important for diabetics to get the right amounts of carbohydrate and so on to keep their blood sugar under control."

Carbo what? She wanted to tell Bert he didn't know what he was talking about but at the same time she wanted to know if what he said was right. The odour of the hospital filled her nostrils and lodged in the back of her throat. It was clean but impersonal. She liked the *idea* of the hospital but the reality of it made her shrink. It was true that thanks to Nye Bevan her father had a bed and the treatment he needed. She didn't need to worry about fees. This great social enterprise of health care was the finest boon people like her had ever known. There was huge wealth in this hospital. Think of all the hospitals in the country. It was enormous wealth; and it was for people like her. Her father was a working man who'd strained his muscles day and night for decades. All he owned was a little house and a bit of modest furniture. Yet the unthinkable wealth of a hospital was at his disposal. It gave her the sense the hospital was hers. It *was* hers, as it was everybody's; and that sense of ownership was so much better than the mean-spirited clinging to a bit of personal property.

Yet at the same time the power of this collective wealth seemed to loom over her. It seemed almost an alien force. It was a force for good, but what was her place in it? If, like her father, she fell ill she would be looked after. The great impersonal machine of the health service would get her back on her feet and send her home to her personal life. There was no argument against that when compared to the bad days of the thirties. Yet she wanted to be out of the place. She wanted her father back home as soon as possible. The hospital was there for bad times. It was a facility no-one should want to need but everyone should want to be available. How strange it was. It was like the church. Its power over her was huge; and just like a hospital was necessary when your body failed, so the church was needed when your soul was in danger. Yet she loved the church just as she loved the NHS. She loved them because without them she was weak, alone, vulnerable and poor.

It was queer. Her greatest wish was independence but it was impossible to be independent on your own. The vast impersonality of the NHS was necessary to ensure her personal independence. Her poor father was a unique individual lost in the echoing cave of this system; they didn't know him like she did; they couldn't be aware of his habits, bad and good; they had no inkling of the little comforts which brought him peace. Yet all that personal knowledge was impotent to cure him; it was the understanding which existed quite apart from him as an individual which would bring him back to health.

All the things Bert talked about, if they were true, were true despite her father. Had her father not fallen ill, she would never have heard about or been interested in keto-thingy or carbo-knobs-on. Yet they would have existed all the same. Other people would have become diabetic and been admitted to hospital. Diabetes was what it was whether her father suffered from it or didn't. How odd. If only it were true that we lived as individuals, free from the need of great social institutions to guarantee our personal lives. Yet she knew as surely as she needed to breathe to stay alive that she needed the NHS, her father needed it, everyone needed it, and it was a great good.

They were outside. The fresh air struck her as good as a glass of cold water for a raging thirst.

232

"Well, I suppose they'll tell us all about that," she said.

"They'll have to."

"Why do they call it sugar diabetes?" she said.

"Because of blood sugar levels."

"I thought it was because you get it from eating too much sugar."

"Not in your dad's case," he said. "It's complicated. The way insulin works. If you get overweight it can make a difference."

"He isn't overweight."

She was heading towards the road to wait at the bus stop.

"I've got my car," he said.

"Eh?"

"My little car. It's over here. I'll give you a lift."

BABIES

Eddie had a van but she'd never ridden in it and Henry of course was mad about motor bikes. He was always taking engines to bits and salvaging parts from one machine to put on another. He'd once arrived home on a rhino of a bike with a side-car and offered to take her for a ride round the country lanes of Longridge and Chipping but it seemed a perilous and reckless possibility, especially with Henry who loved speed as much as flirtatious women. No-one in the street had a car. She thought of them as luxuries available to folk in Penwortham, Fulwood or posh places like St Annes. She knew Bert had a car, but she thought he kept it for special trips.

"I'll be fine on't bus."

"Don't be daft. I'm driving home. No need to waste the bus fare. Come on."

She shook her head as if she was being asked to worship the Devil, but she followed him to where the dumpy, grey vehicle was parked. In spite of its age, the leather of the seats smelt new. She felt pretentious sitting with her knees tucked under the little wooden dashboard. People like her weren't supposed to ride in cars. Yet at the same time she thought how nice it would be to have one; how grand to be able to go where you like; how smashing to be able to drive to Blackpool on a sunny Sunday or up to Windermere in the summer to catch the ferry to Hawkshead.

Bert set the engine running. It coughed like a pipe-smoker. He clunked it into reverse and they shot back at alarming speed. He forced it into first. They pulled away. She was pushed back into her seat. They swung out onto the empty road. The engine whined like a spoilt child. Bert hunched close to the steering wheel. The whirr of the pistons rose towards falsetto; he yanked the gear stick; the growl seemed to come from the tarmac itself. They sped through the traffic lights. He grabbed at the wheel; they flew into a right turn. In such a small car, the speed seemed impossible. She wanted to tell him to slow down but it was his car. Surely he knew how to drive? He braked behind a coal lorry drawn by a horse. She was thrown forward and braced her arm against the fascia. When she got out at her front door, she felt as if she'd been on the big dipper. She vowed never to ride in his car again.

"Fancy a brew?" he said with a big smile.

"I've got to see to me mother."

"Well, nip round when you've seen to her. I'll have the kettle on."

She went indoors determined not to accept. Her mother needed changing and washing. She looked at Elsie with her big, almost expressionless eyes. It was terrible to see her helplessness. Elsie threaded one arm out of her white cotton nightgown, then the other. She worked it gently over the old woman's head. Her big, awkward nakedness was an embarrassment Elsie had got used to.

It was odd to see her own mother like this, but she had to put aside her squeamishness and get on with it. With a flannel and warm water she bathed her mother's white and painful body from her forehead to her toes. She'd dirtied herself slightly as she often did and the passing stench was remotely putrid. How long had she been there waiting to be cleaned? Elsie felt guilty but she had to visit her father. It wasn't possible to be beside her mother without a break. The bathing was long and slow. The agony of movement had become so great, the invalid could no longer turn over. Elsie had to exert all the force of her slender arms, push up with the meagre power of her little thighs, strain the muscles in her pretty back to shift the inert woman from her left side to her right.

She sweated and ached at the work. The customary thought occurred to her: if she weren't here to do this, who would? The lads couldn't see their mother naked. Her father was too old. How humiliating for her mother to have a stranger do it. Yet she thought of her father. Wasn't he being treated by strangers? Why not her mother? Why shouldn't the NHS provide for her too? Why shouldn't trained nurses who knew how to lift properly be able to see to her? She experienced a moment of rebellion against the fate which forced her to this solitary work for which she was ill-suited. If at least she had some help. Two of them could turn her mother much more easily; but no, she must do it all alone; she must struggle and fear tipping her out of the bed; she must feel her back stiffen like a corpse and must ask herself how much longer she could keep going. What would happen to her now her father was ill? She could envisage no end. Her mother might live another ten years. Another fifteen. Life didn't ebb away in the face of debasing debility. Hadn't the doctor said that despite her arthritis her organs were in good health? Her heart might hold out for fifteen years. Her father might live another twenty. Was this what God intended for her? She might be well into her forties before she was free of the burden of her parents.

She was stung by her selfishness. How could she think of them as a burden? If God wanted her to look after them she should accept it gratefully. She would be rewarded for it. She would have her place in Heaven. She would have priority over the lads. What did they do? They had their lives to live it was true; but nothing stood in the way of them helping a bit more. No, it fell to the daughter. That was God's way. All the same she felt upset and tears accumulating. She would like a life. She would like to be carefree, to go out into the world and make something of herself. She felt trapped, reduced, diminished and into her head came the idea of a saviour; someone kind and strong who could lift her from this circle of drudgery.

She wanted to cry for the waste of her own young life. Her youth was already gone. The war had devoured it; and now what she'd hoped might be relief turned out to be penny-pinching, rationing and parental illness. She wanted to cry out like Jesus himself: "Oh Lord, why hast thou forsaken me?" She thought of Maggie. She could confide in her. Maggie would support her. Yet she was bringing new life into the world. She would have a husband and a child. Once, Elsie had thought of Maggie as her friend before she was anything else. She was her parents' daughter, but their friendship seemed to exceed that. Now, Maggie would be a wife and mother first and a friend after. As Elsie tucked her mother in it struck her with a blow that almost made her fall to the floor how alone she was. Her fate was hers alone. Wasn't that true of Maggie too? And the lads? Wasn't it true of everyone? Yet Maggie had a happy fate. At least much happier than hers. Her fate was lonely. It destroyed her. She looked at her mother who had evaporated into sleep after the effort of the bathing and wished she truly wanted to be beside her. It was what she must do. Yet she couldn't deny the young woman in her which rebelled. She would have liked to walk out of the door and never return. She was pretty. She could work hard. She was good with her hands. Surely the world held promise for her.

She left the room quickly closing the door with that preternatural quietness that had become as natural as blinking. Her heart was punishing her. Was it the Devil making it beat so fast and heavily? She became extraordinarily aware of her own heartbeat. It seemed to pulse against life. She asked herself why her heart was beating. Why did she continue to live? The question frightened her so, finally she seized her coat and sped from the house as soon as she heard the door open. It was Eddie.

"Eh? What's th'hurry?"

"She's sleeping. I've just washed 'er."

Without looking into his face she ran to the only refuge she had. It was terrible. She would have fled to anyone else if she thought she'd be welcome; but the truth was the truth. She despised Bert but he held a promise. He was interested in her as a young woman. He could make her a mother. She screwed all her doubts into a tiny ball and let it fall into the gutter. There was only this certainty: the boundaries of her life were narrowly set and within them no-one other than Bert offered her anything other than dutiful service to the manifold needs of her parents. Let what must happen happen. She wouldn't resist it. She was dangling from a frayed rope over a pit of quicksand and only Bert could give her the little push which could bring her feet to firm ground.

Aunty Alice answered the door.

"Hello. Is Bert in?"

"Of course, luv. Go on up. How's your mother."

"Grand," said Elsie as she mounted the steps as if God himself were in the bedsit above.

She knocked timidly. He opened the door and smiled widely.

"Come in."

She went inside and sat down without being asked.

"I'm just brewing. Are you ready for a cup?"

"I don't mind."

"Take your coat off. Make yourself at home. Are you warm enough?"

"Don't fuss. I shall be fine."

He went into the kitchen and she heard him whistling. It was a tune she recognised but she couldn't find the title. She listened. His whistling was tuneful and gay. It was full of that carefree, get-on-with-life attitude he seemed to exude. He broke off and began to sing: *Night and day, you are the one*....The words came back to her. She hoped he'd carry on but he switched back to whistling. He had a good singing voice. It was full and rose and fell in a hypnotic way. It made her think of Sinatra.

She wrenched herself away from the idea. Was she really comparing Bert to Sinatra? She must be going soft in the brain. Not that she was a *fan* of the slick tenor: she much preferred Paul Robeson. When she listened to him she could think of his socialism; and he had known the pain of racism. What was Sinatra, after all, but a cheap crowd-pleaser? In truth, she liked his voice, but the pleasure of his singing was undermined by her knowledge of the world he inhabited; the corrupt and cheap arena of *show business*. She despised it. If you had the gift from God of a good voice, you should use it honourably. To take it into the market place and sell it for the highest price, to sing in night-clubs where gamblers and prostitutes looked for easy, dirty money, to let yourself be used by a *business*, was disgusting. Bert, of course, loved the music of that universe. Sinatra and Tony Bennett, big bands and screeching saxophonists; but that was only to be expected given his upbringing.

He came through with the teapot, milk and cups, went back and reappeared with a little plate piled with brown toast. He set it down on the low coffee table and she saw how he had lavished butter and honey.

"Fancy a piece?"

"No, thanks."

"It's warm. The honey's from *Booths*. Delicious."

"You put too much butter on," she said.

"I'll make you some more."

"I don't mean that. It's wasteful and extravagant."

He laughed and she was puzzled. Why did he find being reprimanded amusing?

"I am extravagant," he said. "I live like a millionaire in my little room."

"You talk daft."

"I am daft. The world's daft."

She watched him as he bit into the thickly sliced bread. She knew the price of a loaf and wondered he could spare the coppers for brown. She didn't like it. A good white loaf was straightforward; and she bought margarine because it saved that little bit on the shopping bill. As for honey, she found it too sweet. Jam was better. You could taste the fruit and the jars she filled from the blackcurrants her father grew on his allotment lasted a year. But that was Bert: brown bread with best butter and thick honey; slacks and a thick knit sweater; Frank Sinatra and trips to the Hallé. It was all for show.

He poured her tea. She tasted it and was pleased. The whole of her experience could be contained in the brown circle of a cup of *99 tea*, well-brewed and with a dash of milk.

"How's your mum?"

"Oh, she's all right. I had to give her a bed bath. She's heavy. It's all I can do to move her."

"You should've asked me."

She looked at him in horror. Bert helping her with her mother, seeing her naked? What was he thinking of? She felt it a terrible intrusion. His family was his and hers was hers. Yet at the same time she was shocked by his generosity. Would he really be willing to help her? Wouldn't he mind the mess and the indignity?

"How could I?" she said.

"Why not?"

"It wouldn't be right. My mother wi' not a stitch."

"We could manage that. You could cover her while I help to move her. In any case, it wouldn't bother me. Better than straining. You could injure yourself."

"One of our lads should 'elp be rights," she said.

"Won't they?"

"Never offer. Leave it to me. It's a daughter's job."

"I don't see why. She's their mother as much as yours."

She didn't like the idea. Though she rebelled against the burden of responsibility, at the same time she thought it a kind of privilege. She was closer to her mother than the lads. She was her child more than they were. A lad didn't belong to his family the way a daughter did.

She thought of it as eternally true that women belonged in the home and that the bond between a mother and daughter was stronger than the one between mother and son or father and son. Men were made to go out into the world and bring home money. It was a kind of expulsion; and though she bitterly hated the rough and dangerous work her father had to do, for men in general she closed her mind to that. Whether work was dull, demeaning, exhausting, men had to get on with it. Women inhabited the home like squirrels the forest; it was their habitat and the power they exercised there was absolute. What did Bert mean? She was constantly troubled by his ideas. If you'd told him the Bible was the word of God he'd have questioned it.

"'Appen they are," she said, "but a daughter's a daughter."

"The world's changing, Elsie. We'll have a woman Prime Minister before we shuffle off this mortal coil."

"I don't think so."

"Why not?"

"Because women have children to look after, that's why," she said, a note of irritation in her voice

He laughed again.

"There'll be nurseries for that."

"Heaven 'elp us," she said. "I'd not put my children in a nursery."

"It's good for them. They play with other kids, get lots of stimulation. And it lets women go out to work. That's good for the economy. Look how they had to work during the war."

"Oh, I'll grant you that. Aye. They 'ad to. But peacetime's different."

"The peace has been changed by the war. We are the masters now, Elsie." He laughed. "I'm all for the emancipation of women. The idea they belong in the home should stay in the last century. Anyway, it's just what the Nazis said: children, church and home, all that rubbish. Women belong in society just like men. Men are husbands and fathers but it doesn't stop them being Prime Ministers and coal miners."

What he said struck her like a rip tide in deep water. It dragged her away from her familiar shore. Children, church and home? Weren't those exactly what she believed in? Did that make her some kind of

Nazi? For a few moments she sank into humiliation, confusion and despair, but her anger soon lifted her mood and swept away her doubts. Given longer to take root, the questions might have changed her thinking; had she learned a little bit about the origins of Nazi ideology and the purposes to which its view of gender were put, she might have started to shape a new vision of the life of women and especially of herself; but as usual, the rebellion of her convictions did good and bad work simultaneously: on the one hand it dismissed the notion that she had anything in common with a gang of racist goons, on the other it brought her back to the safety of her customary convictions which bobbed on the gentle waters of the sheltered cove of her denials like a child's yacht on a paddling pool.

Yet, though she resisted what he said, it had a strong appeal for her, like a dessert we know is bad for us, a rich queen of puddings or a meringue covered in cream, but which we can't resist because of a passing whim for something sweet. Just as we can be misled by our taste buds, so she felt she was being dragged by a desire which arose in some less tangible part of her than her tongue.

She wanted to live. She wanted to know what it was like to work. She imagined the camaraderie of her workmates. How wonderful it would be to arrive at the factory every day to meet lasses she got along with as well as Maggie. How delightful to spend the day in chat and banter as they worked at their machines. How charming to sit together at the canteen table exchanging stories about their men and their families. How comforting to walk arm in arm out of the factory gate with a friend you loved and trusted. How liberating to get your wage packet on a Thursday or Friday, to count the notes and coins and know you'd earned them, they were yours by right and you could do what you wanted with them. How confidence-making to have your own machine to look after, to be responsible for what you produced. The world of work beckoned to her with unlimited prom- ise and no pain or hardship, like a practised whore beckons to the aching heart and body of a shy young man who has never kissed a girl or held her hand; like him she didn't know that what is most sweetly tempting often turns out to be most bitterly disappointing.

"Say what you like," she said, "but someone's got to look after t'children and nurseries aren't like bein' wi' someone who loves yer."

"Of course not," said Bert, rousing to the possibility of a discussion, which always animated him, "but you don't need to be with people who love you all day long. Children go to school. The teachers aren't required to love them, just give them an education. So long as they know they're loved, they'll thrive."

Of course he would say that. Elsie knew how unloved Bert had been. It was the source of her superiority. She could always trump him with the fact of her family; her intense closeness to her mother; her *heart-of-gold* father who, like Coniston Old Man was always there, unmoving, unchanging. She knew too how he relished his *success* at school. He kept his reports and had shown her the comments about *Composition* and *Arithmetic*. She felt it vulgar to boast and having been too paralysed by fear to learn much in the face of teachers who would thwack children round the head or rap their tender knuckles with a hard ruler, she resented his pride in having mastered the poor basics of his back-street-boy's instruction.

Yes, for him school had been an escape from a home of filth, neglect, drink and poverty. Of course he'd say you didn't need to spend all day with people you loved; but Elsie saw no reason why you shouldn't; and surely it was better to be at school with people you loved or at work with people you loved rather than in the cold world of relations that served some purpose other than themselves. She feared and hated that iciness. There must be love at the heart of everything. Even the mills whose looms rattled woodenly singing their night-and-day, one-note, one-bar, chant of make-more-money, make-more-money; even the factories whose chimneys coughed profit-profit-profit, lung-wrecking smoke into the grey northern sky; even they should be places full of love. What was it all for otherwise? What was all this rush and effort and spine-snapping work about if not to provide for happiness? And who could be happy without love? Was Bert happy? She couldn't believe it. He had his satisfactions and his interests, but he didn't know what it was to nestle in the warmth of a love which was offered without demand or condition. Perhaps she could show him. Perhaps she could spare a little bit of the love she knew in her family and perhaps in time he would soften.

She found she'd risen above the terrible doubts that made her question her very existence. It was a queer, twisted feeling which made her want to be with Bert and be far from him. There was promise in what he said. It rang with the same pleasing peal as the words of

Clem Attlee or Nye Bevan. There was a world behind her that was dark and fearful. Her parents had lived in terror of the workhouse. When as a child she walked along Watling St Rd holding her father's hand and saw the huge, prison-like building where the poor had once been incarcerated as if their poverty was a crime, she shrank into herself in chilly apprehension. Her grandmother gave birth to twelve children; three of them died of diphtheria. Two of her cousins died of tuberculosis before the age of ten.

The era from which she had emerged was vicious, cruel, dishonest; people like her, people from the back streets without education, money or influence could be crushed and no-one cared. The law turned away its face. Betty Middleton lost a hand in a loom and the factory sacked her. She got not a penny. The bodies and souls of the poor were as instrumental as cogs and shuttles. Yet there was a glimmer of sunshine ahead. The unions were fighting for safer conditions and better pay; the NHS would wipe out the diseases that grabbed little children from their nursing mother's arms; Labour would build houses with bathrooms; schools would become gentler and give all children an education until fifteen. Didn't what Bert said fit with this? Wasn't he right when he argued women should be set free from their enslavement to the home, the sink and the cooker? Wasn't he a good man? She squirmed at her own thought. Bert, a good man? She couldn't think of him as anything but *fallen*. His circumstances had never given him a chance. How could a man be good when he grew up among submission to drink, violence and slovenliness?

She was moved by Christian compassion. It was her duty to help him to salvation. Yet she didn't know that pity turns back on itself and becomes resentment and hatred if its object refuses to respond; she had no inkling that her desire to reform Bert through the superiority of Christian love was as hopeless as the effort to make a scorpion give up its sting; she was unaware that the human mind can't be scrubbed clean like a dirty kitchen floor or ironed crisp like a starched shirt; she didn't know that tragedy is as common as bad breath, that we make our terrible mistakes out of ignorance, fear, greed, arrogance and stupidity and they play out in miserable consequences for centuries; she didn't realize if she was to accept Bert she must take him as he was and no amount of emollient Christian love would make him what she thought of as a good man.

243

He sat on the edge of the chair and put his arm round her. When she looked up she saw his wide smile and in his blue eyes what she took to be kindness. It was terrible to be at once susceptible to his masculinity and convinced of his inadequacy. Yet as he bent to kiss her there was nothing she could do but close her eyes and enjoy it.

She got out of bed and rose on her toes to lift her dress from the hook on the back of the door. He said:

"You are incredibly beautiful."

She turned with dress in her hand to see him propped up on the pillows, his hands behind his head, the broad smile on his lips. She was embarrassed by her nakedness and quickly took her bra from the chair.

"You talk daft," she said.

"I don't. You could be a film star. You're as beautiful as Rita Hayworth or Great Garbo."

She looked at him in dismay, as if he'd said she could be President of the United States.

"They're not just beautiful, they can act."

He laughed and she looked at him in puzzlement.

"No they can't. Well, not in any special way. You could act if you were trained. You're intelligent enough."

She blushed. She liked the flattery but at the same time she wanted to run away. Was she beautiful? Few had ever paid her such compliments. It wasn't the way in her family. Her mother had always said, "I don't make a fuss." She'd never been praised by her parents. Her father had never taken her on his knee and told her she was the best little girl in the world. All that, she thought of as soppy. Love in her family was unspoken. It was as if to express the emotion was to dissolve it. Her father could stand at the graveside of a relative or friend and not shed a tear. Did he cry in private? She didn't know. Public displays of emotion were to be avoided; that was what she'd learnt.

Then how did she know her father loved her? It was a mystery. He was there. He did what was right. She knew, without knowing how she knew, he felt deeply for her and would sacrifice for her. Was that true of Bert? He looked at her bottom as she reached for her dress. He looked at her breasts as she turned to him. He'd parted her legs and smiled in bed. Was that love? Wasn't it more like the relish with which he ate toast and honey? Wasn't it appetite? Yet she couldn't help feeling coyly pleased by it. She was young. It was nice to know a man found her bottom beautiful. It was exciting to see him fix his eyes on her breasts. It was almost transporting to see him kneeling between her legs, his erection pointing to his belly button and twitching with desire. Yet it was hard to bring together this physical love, if that was what it was, and the silent, reserved emotion of her family.

"It's all nonsense. Film stars and Hollywood," she said.

"I wish you could stay the night."

"You must be mad."

"Why?"

"What d'yer think me father would say?"

"We're adults. We can make our own choices."

"Not choices like that."

"Why not?"

"Living like man and wife? It's disgusting."

He laughed.

"What's disgusting about it? It's practical, that's all."

"It's immoral."

"Is what we've just done immoral?"

"It is in a way."

"What way?"

"You know very well."

"I don't. I don't know at all."

"Well, you should."

He laughed again. She didn't like it that he found her rebukes amusing. She thought of herself as *strict and particular*. She imagined people must respond to her moral chain-mail as she responded to a sermon or the ten commandments. It would have been impossible for her to laugh at them. That would have been sacrilege. So Bert's laughter left her at a loss. She had no idea that he could intuit the gentle, easy-going young woman concealed within her self-conscious attitudes; she didn't know that ten thousand command-

ments and a million Bibles tell us less about someone than the most
fleeting facial expression; and she was entirely unaware that what
made Bert laugh was the gap between her assumed strictures and the
reality of what he perceived as her sweet and tolerant nature.

A few days later her father came home. He had his needles, syringe,
little phials of insulin and a bottle of surgical spirits. Every morning
he had to inject himself in the thigh. She was amazed. It seemed impossible that his flesh could take three hundred and sixty five needles
a year; and how many thousands of injections over the remainder of
his life? More incredible still was the mystery of how it worked.
How did they make this liquid? What did it do when it got into his
body? All she could do was be grateful for the wonder of it. Her
father was no longer sick. He could live as normally as his neighbours. It almost made her believe that medicine could work greater
miracles than religion.

She read the diet sheet carefully. It was important he should have the
right balance of proteins and carbohydrates. How did they know?
Her mind was blank. She'd never been in a laboratory or looked
down a microscope. She had no idea what bacteria looked like nor
did she know the structure of an element or the difference between
an element and a compound. Did doctors get knowledge the way
vicars got it? Did they read a definitive book like the Bible? Yet the
Bible was the word of God; whose word was medicine? Was it mere
man-made wisdom? All her religious fervour rebelled against the
notion that anything humankind had made or discovered could equal
the Truth of God. Yet, it had to be faced; the doctors and the NHS
had saved her father.

As the weeks went by and she got used to adjusting her cooking to
her father's needs, she settled into the assurance that it was all God's
will. To try to understand it was human pride. The doctors knew
what they knew because God wanted them to, because He revealed it
to them. Why did God create diabetes? It was a mystery. We must
accept it. Everything worked for the ultimate good and though to us a
disease like her father's looked cruel and senseless, it must have its
place. The relief of his being able to work and live more or less as
before overcame all her confusions. She weighed carefully the potatoes, meat and cheese. She was indispensable to her father's health
and she accepted what she must do.

But then her period was late.

It sometimes happened. If she hadn't had sex with Bert it would have bothered her no more than an itch on her nose; but the terrible thought rose in her mind like bread dough left on the hearth. How long should she wait? A few days? But then what? Wait a little more? Should she do like Maggie and get confirmation before she confronted Bert? A wayward little thought insinuated itself into her mind: hadn't she had sex with him because she wanted children? Wasn't that the only justification? Well, why not then tell him she was certain? Why not present him with the fact and force him to marry her? It was true he was willing enough to marry her anyway, but this gave her power. She could be as much in control as her mother before the head and footboards became the frontiers of her world. And if she convinced herself, if she believed she must be pregnant, then she too was forced. Whatever reservations she had about Bert, she would have to submit to the facts.

The submissions appealed to her. Like everyone, the freedom to choose terrified her. The most resolute advocates of free will are always the most fervent priests of submission; for the truth is, the dizzying lightness of genuine choice and the knowledge that the smallest of misjudgements can lead to the greatest cataclysms, sends us all scurrying like timid rabbits for the cosy burrow of received certainty. She quickly convinced herself she *was* pregnant. It must be so. She'd never been this late. She ran to Bert.

"Shouldn't you have a test?"

"I don't need a test."

"How can you be sure?"

"A woman knows."

"Well, then," he said, "we'll have to get married."

She'd hoped he'd put up a fight. In the films, things were more melodramatic. Women had to get hysterical to make men do what they wanted. She was disappointed she didn't get her moment to rail and bully and insist while he squirmed and tried to avoid his fate. He talked as if it was as ordinary as catching a bus. She wanted it to be tragic: the two of them, shamefaced, pale and drawn standing before her father breaking the atrocious news; Bert resisting buying his wedding suit and finding a best man; she having to browbeat him;

the long silences between them as they sank into their allotted and appalling destiny. All that seemed more in keeping with what she'd seen at the cinema. But Bert was as down-to-earth and practical as a plumber fixing a ball cock. It almost drove her to tell him she wasn't sure, that they could wait and see; but she'd made her choice, she'd done what she'd done and to retreat would be humiliating.

"It's not as simple as that," she said, hoping the sense of being at the centre of her own tragedy would emerge.

"Why not?"

"People have to be told. Imagine the shame."

"I'm not ashamed," he said. "I'm proud. I'm happy. I'm going to be a dad. I don't care tuppence what people think."

Her moment of potential fainting grandeur had passed. Bert was hopeless. He wouldn't wring his hands or pace the floor; he wouldn't bite his nails and turn pale; he wouldn't go to her father like a truant boy to the Headmaster. He had no shame because he had no religion. He had no values except those of the gutter. He was as resourceful as a rat and just as self-possessed. She who was paralysed by her adherence to the over-arching doctrines of her faith, needed to come alive in the tear-filled distress of collapsing virtue. She needed to go on her knees for forgiveness; but Bert didn't need to be forgiven by anyone. He had nothing to be forgiven for. He took becoming a father before marriage as if it were no more than drinking a cup of strong tea.

"Well, you might think different when you've to tell me dad."

He laughed.

"Your dad is as soft-hearted as a milk-maid."

"Don't yer think he'll be angry? I'm his daughter. Think what you've done to me."

"What have I done?"

"You've ruined me."

"Don't be ridiculous, Elsie. Queen Victoria's been dead a long time. You're not ruined because your pregnant. Do you think Maggie's ruined? She's just going to have a baby. What matters is it's looked after."

"Like you I suppose."

She glanced at him and saw the jab had hurt him. She'd found a way behind that apparently impenetrable cockiness, that take-life-as-it-comes-and-enjoy-it attitude which clashed so fundamentally with her need to refer even pegging out the washing to Christian eschatology. She was glad. She was justified. He talked about looking after the child but how could he know what that meant. *She* would look after it. His business wasn't in the home; let him work and bring home the money. The child would be hers. She would take it to the centre of her family; it would be closer to her father than to him; Eddie, Jimmy and even Henry would mean more to it than Bert ever could; she would keep it away from the vile influence of his low relatives.

"Not at all," he said with a hint of defeat in his voice which she relished, "I'll make a good home for my child. Clean and happy."

"We'll live at me dad's," she said definitively.

"Till we can afford a place of our own."

"So long as my mother needs me. And me dad too, now he's diabetic."

"I don't mind. I agree, the young should take care of the old."

He wasn't going to resist. She was desperately disappointed. Where was the soaring heartbreak that could make her the heroine of her own film? Why didn't dramatic music strike up in the background or inky clouds come heavily to blot out the sun of their young lives? How could it be that this shattering fact of her illegitimate pregnancy was as insignificant as a blackbird landing on the coal-shed roof? The silence of the furniture seemed an insult. She looked around. Bert's flat was just as it had been before she made her declaration. Through the window she could see the dirty sheet of the oppressive sky and the roofs of houses. The chimneys were as stable as yesterday. A small triangle of birds rose up like a kite caught by warm air. How could it be true what was happening to her was ordinary? Hadn't God implanted the child in her womb?

In her flatness and confusion she forgot she wasn't sure of her pregnancy. It had become a fact because it was convenient to her it should be. She sat down. So this was it. Bert would tell her father they were getting married because she was pregnant as matter-of-factly as if he were telling the result of Saturday's match. If only her mother weren't lost to her; if only she still commanded the house with her brisk dusting, cleaning and tidying; if only Bert had to face her, tall and angular, her chin raised in the pride of her Methodist conviction. Then it would be a different matter. Then there'd be a scene. She'd tell him he'd only himself to blame, that impatience brings downfall as surely as filth bring disease; that he should be ashamed of himself but at least he was doing the right thing; that he'd better change his ways and no longer expect the roof to be put on before the bricks are laid; and the sorry hand of regret would weigh down on the household; the universe would never be the same; the most distant star would experience some disturbance in its orbit; God himself would be perturbed.

She arranged for Bert to come and talk to her father.

"I've some good news, " he said. "Elsie and me are engaged."

"Champion," said the old man.

"And even more good news: she's going to have a baby."

"Aye." Tom looked at him from over his reading glasses, his pipe still in his mouth. "Then tha'd best be sharp."

She could have hit both of them. Yet she had to accept. The arrangements were put in train. There was a hurry. The ceremony would take place as soon as possible after the reading of the banns.

Three days after speaking to Bert, her period began.

"Well," he said, "as soon as we're married we can try for a child."

She was sorry she couldn't go to Maggie and tell her their first born wouldn't be far apart. Still, if she got pregnant quickly they would still be conjoined in motherhood; but she wouldn't have an illegitimate pregnancy to look back on. It would have given her something to talk about. She imagined herself in middle-age talking on the street to one of the neighbours about some young lass who'd *got herself in trouble*, saying: "Well, I had to get married. Aye, I did. It can happen to the best of us." She consoled herself with the thought she would soon be Mrs Lang. She'd have a ring on her finger. People would know she was *a married woman* with all that implied of respectability and adulthood. Yet in some remote corner of her mind, a rodent doubt gnawed: wouldn't Bert want to be *master in his own home*? The phrase came into her head without her having any sense of its origin. It terrified her. It mustn't happen. She could be *a married woman* and still her mother's daughter. She could have a husband without having to climb out onto the thin branch of being a wife. She saw no reason why it wouldn't work.

They were married on a bright day in April. Two months later the doctor confirmed she was pregnant.

Their little bedroom looked out on the yard. Bert stood knotting his tie reflecting on their physically cramped conditions. In a way, he missed Aunty Alice's. He had his own space there; here, everything was shared. There was nowhere for him to sit and play his records. There was no bathroom. He missed that very much. A civilised society must allow everyone a bathroom. The idea sent his thoughts back to Egypt. He'd seen atrocious poverty in Cairo. Yes, it was bad enough here; but that was something different. Tom Craxton was poor by British standards, but he was rich compared to the poor of the Middle East. He had a warm, dry house, good furniture and food on the table every day. Without knowing why he began to think about the Redskins. They didn't have bathrooms. Did that make them unhappy? He'd read somewhere they lived for ten or twelve thousand years in North America before white men arrived. Ten thousand years without bathrooms. There was something odd about the way his thoughts were taking him. Surely the Redskins must have been content with their life if they didn't change it for ten thousand years? Or maybe they wanted to but didn't know how; maybe if they'd hit on the technology they would have built factories, buses, ships, aircraft, weapons, houses, sewers, trams; maybe they'd have discovered radio waves or invented the telephone; maybe they'd have had bathrooms. But he couldn't believe it. The notion was set in his brain as fixedly as kerbstones set in concrete that the Redksins lived a life of primeval happiness. Why was that? Why didn't they long for a bathroom like he did?

"Yer gonna be late."

He turned to see Elsie who had just squeezed into the room. She was always out of bed first. Little by little it had dawned on him it was a matter of principle so one morning he pulled the covers back at half past five, but before his feet touched the lino, she was up and yanking on her dressing-gown. It puzzled and annoyed him. He concluded it was because she was in her own home and she wanted always to make him know he was a visitor; for him to get up first would be a kind of declaration that it was as much his home as hers. He was unaware of how this hurt him; he rose above it as he'd learned all his life to fight out of humiliation like a baby turtle struggling to get back to the sea. Yet in spite of his ignorance it had its effect: it worked away in him as inevitably and quietly as cells dividing.

"Harry Clow was telling me a cousin of his has a flat to let."

"What's that to do with me?"

"Two bedrooms and a bathroom. We could have a room for the baby."

"And who'd see to me mother?" she looked at him, her hazel eyes accusing him of stupidity as if he'd said the sun orbited the earth.

"It's in Bairstow Street. It's only ten minutes from here. We could call in every day."

"Call in!" she tutted and shook her head as she straightened the bed.

"Be nice to have a bathroom when the baby's born."

"Be nice to have rump steak twice a week. If wishes were horses...."

He looked at her busy little frame. It was nice she wasn't idle and feckless; his mother's slovenliness made him admire the effort to keep things clean and in order; but there was something driven about Elsie's activity which disturbed him. He thought everything should be done in a spirit of pleasure or fun. There was nothing he had to do he couldn't enjoy; even the most routine matters of accountancy had an element of interest, if you approached them in the right way. Yet work seemed to weigh on Elsie. It was as if she lived beneath it like a wood louse beneath a stone, but worse, because some creatures love the dark; they seek out damp, unlit places like we love light and warmth; that's where they belong and if they can experience some rudimentary form of contentment, they find it there. Elsie, on the other hand, laboured under a burden that drove her out of her natural habitat, as if a worm were forced to live in a dry box under a bright light.

It seemed to Bert that to enjoy what you have to do was as ordinary as sleeping. He could enjoy shaving. Yes, it was a chore, but if you worked up the lather with the brush in a vigorous way and watched it turn thick and creamy; if you applied it lavishly to your cheeks and chin and sang as the blade eased through it, slicing at the short, hard whiskers; well, it was bit of fun and you could splash your face with the hot water, rub your skin with the fresh towel and rejoice in a smooth face to address the day with. Why couldn't Elsie enjoy the simple business of tidying the bedclothes? Why couldn't it be a game?

"In any case, why don't we go and have a look at it?"

"Because I have to stay here and that's that."

She was gone.

Being married and living in his father-in-law's house had significantly increased life' s little irritations for Bert. Yet he rose above them; there was a future ahead and it was going to be better. All the same, he had to admit he hadn't expected, so soon into his marriage, the constant abrasiveness of his wife. He told himself it was hard for her: the adjustment to a new way of life, the dependence of her parents and then the hormonal chaos of pregnancy; he didn't know that being an outcast from birth, being an unwanted, illegitimate child no-one wished to be responsible for or to love, being neglected and having to fend for himself even as a toddler, had made him expect rejection and had closed his mind to it.

To be accepted in Tom Craxton's home was a privilege to Bert. Tom was a good man and Bert knew it. Good men were rare. The world was full of men who did what they had to, but they would cut off your ears and fry them if it was demanded of them. Good men were those who would defy what was demanded of them if they knew it to be wrong and they were as rare as snowdrops in July.

This sense of acceptance layered over the disappointment already building in him that his wife was not loving, warm and welcoming. He felt he had a family and a good one. No-one could point to him now and say he stank; no-one could make his intestines melt by reminding him his mother had abandoned him and his grandmother would have sold him for a bottle of gin. Tom Craxton was his father. He had got into the habit of calling him dad. In the early days it had been respectful Mr Craxton; then once or twice, Tom; but since the marriage it had seemed natural to imitate Elsie.

And he had brothers. When he spoke of Jimmy, Eddie and Henry he would say: "I was talking to my brother the other day..." or "I'm going on the match with my brother on Saturday." When he walked down Deepdale Road among the crowd of supporters, his thermos of coffee in his overcoat pocket, his cap pulled down tight, his blue and white scarf tucked inside his lapels, he was proud to have Eddie beside him. People knew him. The Craxtons had a reputation. Elsie's father was known as *Red Tom*. Even those who disdained his politics couldn't question his principles. No-one had a bad word to say about them. Not even Henry. They were straight, fair people. You could trust them. Bert wasn't the same man when stood with Eddie on the *Town End* as the rattles clacked and Finney ran down the wing. The boy he'd once been was fully left behind when they were back home, sitting at the kitchen table eating a steaming corned beef hash and telling Tom about the game.

He was driving to work. The tightness in his chest brought on by Elsie's sharpness had eased as he enjoyed changing gear and making his way though the town. It was coming to life. He loved the beginning of the day. The evening made him anxious. People leaving the streets and heading home always brought an empty, lonely feeling; but the men and women hurrying to work; the buses pulling in to let high-heeled secretaries and mackintoshed bank clerks jump off the rear platform raised his spirits. He was pulling away from the traffic lights on Church St when he spotted Laura Bruzzese. He was about to sound his horn but a sudden confusion came over him. It didn't often happen. His custom was to act on every inspiration. Yet the thought hit him that he was married. Why should that make a difference? She was part of his life. He'd made her pregnant, for God's sake; he couldn't just drive on without acknowledging her. Yet in seconds he'd pulled away and she was gone. When he parked up he was thinking he should tell Elsie. It wasn't right to have secrets. Yet he knew it would be perilous. There would be a row. She'd probably tell her brothers; and Maggie. Perhaps he should keep it to himself. It happened when he was single. They weren't committed to one another then. He did it out of the best of motives. What would it matter if Elsie didn't know?

That morning she'd arranged to meet Maggie and her little boy. He was a few weeks old and they'd named him Arthur. Elsie and Bert had gone to the christening. It seemed to Elsie the fault of pregnancy before marriage was wiped away by the ceremony. How could God be angry at a new born baby? How could a baby be guilty? And if the child was innocent didn't that exonerate the parents? Weren't they now committed to nurturing the innocence of their baby? Didn't that free them from condemnation? She'd heard of the doctrine of Original Sin but it meant no more to her than the photoelectric effect.

It was impossible to impute fault to this sweet little bundle. He was asleep. Maggie had left the pram downstairs so he was nestled in her arms.

"Want to take him a bit?"

Elsie nursed his tiny weight against her. He might have been her own. She didn't know the intense love she felt for this helpless mite was what she felt was missing from her own life. Her parents had cared for her, of course. She was proud of their fortitude in the face of necessity. They were stern reliable people; but her mother wasn't warm. Physical expressions of emotion disturbed her. She rocked the sleeping boy, looking into his slightly squashed face. A voice spoke to her. She looked up to see a dark woman, tall and elegant, smiling at her.

"How old is he?" she said.

"Oh, he isn't mine," she said.

The woman turned to Maggie.

"Five weeks," she said.

"Ah, what a beautiful little boy. My own is two months. And what is he called?"

"Arthur," said Maggie. "What about yours?"

"Alberto," said the stranger. "My husband is Italian. Ciao."

"Everybody loves a baby," said Maggie.

"They do."

"You wonder how folk could harm a little child like this," said Elsie, a note of tragedy in her voice.

She looked into Maggie's face but her eyes were averted. She felt ill-at-ease. Had she said something wrong? She would have enjoyed pursuing her thought ; she relished nothing more then invoking the evil of others; it granted her that sense of virtue which was so difficult to maintain and which was the essence of her life. Derived from Christian eschatology, it meant self-sacrifice and a constant assertion of the needs of others; yet she had no inkling that self-conscious virtue is the shortest route to evil; she imagined, in her childish naivety, that all self-interest is wicked and didn't realize that the celibacy of priests breeds paedophiles like rotting meat bacteria, and the respectability of dogmatic moralists, more degeneracy than brothels. If she'd been told that the most virtuous people are usually those who care least for their own virtue she would have been shocked to the ends of her nerves.

When the newspapers reported viciousness or corruption, she was quick to seize the opportunity; how wicked people were; how they lacked Christian virtue; her view of herself as virtuous required absolutely that the world be rank and had evil disappeared, she would have been as bereft as a captain without a ship.

"Have you got over the morning sickness?" said Maggie.

"Yes, I've got used to it. It's not so bad now. Not every mornin'."

"That's good," said Maggie, and after a pause. "Me and Max are going to look at a house."

Elsie was taken aback. A house? How they could they afford that? And what was wrong with living with her mother? They'd two bedrooms and for two couples and a baby, that would do.

"Aye," she said, "where's that?"

"Balderstone Road."

"What, by't river?"

"That's it."

"Those are big 'ouses, Maggie. It'll not be cheap. Mind you, they're well built. Aye, our Eddie's worked on 'em. They're good 'ouses right enough."

"Rentin'," said Maggie. "We couldn't afford to buy. "

"It's dead money, Maggie."

She saw her friend turn away. The slight disturbance she felt didn't deter her. She went on to explain, as if Maggie didn't understand, that you can pay out hundreds and still not own. Better to save and be patient. Her own parents had bought and fought hard to pay off the mortgage quickly. She loved to tell that story. She would tell it over and over to the same people, as if it was a message that must be repeated and repeated like a muezzin's call to prayer and as if those who heard it could never understand it unless it were told as often as a carefree boy must be admonished to wash his neck.

Beneath her insistent telling their lurked an unacknowledged jealousy and uncertainty. Should she and Bert think of renting? He'd love to, of course. A big house by the river would suit him perfectly, for the time being. Almost without knowing it, Elsie felt what Maggie was doing was a betrayal. They should advance through life together. Why should Maggie suddenly decide living at home was no good? Was she suggesting what she and Bert were doing was wrong? Of course, she didn't have a crippled mother to care for. No, that made all the difference. All well and good to go off and rent a place of your own if your parents were fit and well as Maggie's were. So be it. Their destinies were different. All the same, she wished intensely something would get in the way and Maggie would have to stay at her mother's.

"You're right," said Maggie, "but it won't be for long. We'll save. And Max's uncle says he'll help us out. He's a butcher you know. Opened a shop in Fulwood and it's done well. He might be able to lend us a few hundred."

"Well, it's a good start," said Elsie, wishing someone would make the same sort of offer to her.

"We could wait," said Maggie, "I suppose. It's no way to start your married life though, livin' with your mum and dad."

What did she mean? It seemed to Elsie there was no better way. If she had a thousand pounds in the bank and could have bought a nice house in Penwortham, she'd have wanted her mother and father with her. Was it Max? Was he putting his foot down? She feared poor.

"Bert'd want to be master in his own 'ome. That's trouble." she said. "I don't want 'im rulin't roost and while we're at me dad's he has to fall in wi' me dad's ways."

Maggie smiled indulgently.

"I don't think it's right Max can't have space for himself. We're cramped. He likes to listen t't radio but he has to switch it off if me mother wants peace or me dad's asleep in't chair. I think you need a home of your own when you're married."

"'Appen," said Elsie looking down at the sleeping child.

A home of your own? Why did the idea frighten her? Her parents, after all, had left their parents and set up by themselves; yet though she didn't walk the same floorboards, her grandmother was ever present, as were her cousins, aunts and uncles. Her mother had invoked them as if the past from which they came was the only reality. Her father, on the other hand, rarely spoke of his family. What she knew she squeezed from him by the curious and uninhibited questioning of childhood; but he gave up his secrets as parsimoniously as a cactus delivers water. She knew her grandfather had come to Lancashire from The Isle of Man; that his father was a farmer who'd wrecked his life through drink; that her granddad taught himself to read and write and made fiery speeches to crowds of working men and women; but it was her mother's family who loomed over her emotional landscape like dinosaurs over the ancient earth.

Wasn't it true that though she was married, her mother belonged to her childhood family? How could a husband ever replace a mother? A mother was as absolute as light. A husband was someone you chose, or worse, someone who came along and you made the best of. Had she chosen Bert? In a way, but only because no-one else had asked her. He was far from her idea of what a husband should be. Yet even that puppet in her head, that reliable, decent, good man who at the same time was charming and attractive and able to induce those melting feelings which even Bert could ellicit; even he could never compete with her mother. She wondered how Maggie felt about Max; did she really *prefer* him to her mother? Surely not? Wasn't she just being polite and generous ? Or maybe he really did bully her. She had the child to think about now and if he turned sullen and unpleasant if she wouldn't bend to his will like a sapling in a gale, perhaps she was forced to give in.

Elsie was as unable to imagine that the feeling for a man, for a stranger after all, could rival the steel hoops of submission that bound her to her mother, as a medieval peasant to think of exercising democratic rights. Marriage was a necessity, but not one to celebrate. Its essential purpose was to produce children and its secondary benefit respectability; but it wasn't an *absolute*. Chance had thrown her and Bert together. If his Aunty Alice had lived a mile away, they might never have met. The contingency terrified her. Everything of real value had to be as undeniable as God. What connection was there on earth which imitated the relationship to Him if not that between mother and child, and in particular mother and *daughter*; but it wasn't the same.

Boys were made not to fit their mothers as neatly as a key fits a lock. A daughter and a mother held the combinations to one another's feelings. It was exclusive. A woman had a right to respond with maximum resistance to a man who tried to pry her apart from her mother. Did Maggie love Max as she loved her mother? The idea was inconceivable. Did she love Bert? In a way she did; she felt a certain stirring for him and now she was married to him he was *hers*; she would have unleashed the murderousness of Medea against him if he'd betrayed her. He belonged to her now. He had to work to keep her. He had to provide for their child. There was also the other business. Yes, she had to be a wife. It was as expected of her as keeping the house clean or making meals for her father. In truth, she didn't mind it, too much. She got some pleasure from it. She even had that little storm of uncontrollable tension and release which she took to be what they called *climax*.

Bert was her only lover so they were incontrovertibly bound. That was that. Yet what was all that compared to the fixity of her belonging to her mother. On the other hand the thought of Bert's family troubled and disgusted her. Would she have been able to live with his mother or grandmother or grandfather? They were vile people. No. It was the woman's family who must be kept close. The man had a different role. It was natural for men to be cut loose. They had to go out into the world and make money. It was to be expected they would be less tied. Bert was as unconnected as a cat. Let him prowl, so long as he did so in her interests. What did she care about his work? That wasn't her business. God had made it that way. She looked up and Maggie smiled. It was good to have a friend. She trusted Maggie and knew she could depend on her. Yet she wondered about her and Max. It was odd. Did Maggie really want to be away from her mother? Did she really feel living alone with Max and her baby was best?

"Let's hope yours is as peaceful, Elsie."

"Yes. He's a good little thing isn't he?"

"He is. He sleeps and feeds and barely cries. I never thought I'd be so lucky."

"Well, they're all different aren't they?"

Arthur opened his eyes and looking into them she thought she saw recognition. She smiled. The baby stared back at her with that blank fixity of a pristine brain. It seemed to her his looking was knowing; surely he was making sense of her. Did he know she was his mother's friend? It wasn't possible, yet she wondered what he did know. She smiled and cooed and touched his cheeks. He turned his head to one side.

"I think he wants feeding," she said.

"He will. I'll take him in the Ladies a minute."

"Shall I come with you?"

"No. I'll leave my bag. I'll not be long."

Left alone, Elsie finished her tea and quickly surveyed the other customers in those split-second glances women are so adept at. In the far corner she noticed a man who seemed to be watching her. She carefully refused to return his gaze but when a waitress passed between them she took the opportunity to flick her eyes in his direction, her head lowered to prevent him noticing. Yes, he was definitely looking at her. She became uncomfortable. Men had a way of looking which was as hard as their erections. It was intrusive and threatening. She wondered if he was some kind of pervert; or perhaps he thought she was touting for custom being on her own. Yet *Booth's* café wasn't that kind of place; and in broad daylight. That was the sort of thing the French got up to, so she'd heard. It didn't go on in a respectable place like this; and how could he mistake her for a woman of the streets? She was dressed modestly and surely he'd seen her holding the baby?

What was the matter with him? That was men of course. Most of them couldn't see a woman carrying her shopping home without taking it as a provocation. She raised her left hand to smooth her hair in the hope he'd notice her wedding ring; but when she made another of those barely noticeable speed-of-light glances, he was still staring straight at her. Part of her wanted to stride over to him and whip him with insulting language, but it wasn't *ladylike*. The best thing was to ignore him. Men like that couldn't stand not to get a response. All the same, she wished Jimmy or Eddie were with her. She would've liked to see one of her brothers stand over him and ask him what he thought he was about. Of course, Henry would have been the most likely to invite him outside, but Elsie blenched from the thought of the poor chap collapsing under the fierce assault of his fists.

She hoped Maggie wouldn't be long. She'd point him out to her and Maggie would turn in her chair to look at him. That would embarrass him all right. She looked away. The light from the windows was grey and disappointing. It was one of those days which seem never to begin, when the sun seems to be running out of energy and the clouds might be a thousand miles thick; one of those days on which it was impossible to imagine a blue sky and bright sunshine. She could see the stone of the Harris Library, solid and reassuring. Never having left her home town, having no conception of the scale of The British Museum or the Louvre, this provincial monument seemed to her the greatest tribute to learning and imagination; it embraced the seriousness she'd grown up with and which protected her from the frivolity and cheapness which troubled her. She became abruptly aware of someone approaching. She turned her head and he was there.

"Hello, Elsie. Remember me?"

She looked up at him in bewilderment. He was no more familiar to her than an Eskimo or a pygmy.

"No," she said, "I don't."

"Warwick Dornan."

"Warwick?"

"Yes. Remember me now?"

"Dear Heaven, you've changed."

"You haven't, Elsie," he said. "You're as pretty as ever. Mind if I sit down a moment?"

"Well, my friend'll be back ..."

"Yes, I saw her go. Maggie isn't it?"

"That's right."

"You two were like sisters."

"We're good friends. We allus 'ave been."

He sat down and staring intensely into his face while his eyes weren't on hers, she could bring into focus the features of the boy who used to sit behind her at school. He'd been a skinny, whippet of a lad who had a cold all winter and whose thin hands and legs reminded her of an old man. She couldn't believe he'd grown into this robust, fit looking devil. He'd a little moustache which sat thick and black over his thin mouth, his hair was neatly combed back from his forehead and from the sleeves of his navy blue suit protruded clean, white shirt cuffs held by gold links.

"I knew it was you as soon as I saw you," he said.

"Did you?"

"Oh yes. You were the prettiest girl in school and I'd say you're now the prettiest woman in town."

Elsie had no idea how to graciously accept such compliments. They embarrassed and disturbed her. Nothing in her religious upbringing had taught her that to be praised by a man was a simple pleasure a woman had every right to enjoy; it seemed almost sinful. What distance was there, after all, between a man telling her she was pretty and him trying to seduce her? She had one of those minds which move too quickly from possibility to realisation; her ideas ran on in spite of her and she imagined that by charmingly accepting his flattery she would be inviting him into her bed. So she turned away, gave a nervous laugh and played with her wedding ring.

"I didn't know you were married."

"Oh yes," she said "I've been married a while."

"Whose the lucky man?"

"Bert Lang."

She saw the tiny movement of surprise in his face. At once she felt ashamed. Warwick, of course, knew Bert when he was a barefoot, scruffy, smelly, neglected kid mocked and derided by his classmates. He knew his drunken, disreputable family which was viewed with derision by the working-class folk who strove to do their best in spite of poverty; people who would never let their front door step look neglected and whose children, though they might get nothing but bread and dripping for tea, were sent out washed behind the ears and with clean underwear. She experienced a horrible emptiness opening inside her as she realised Warwick was thinking she'd made a mistake in marrying Bert. She almost wanted to blurt out that she'd married him out of Christian pity, but she looked down at her empty cup which was as deep as the Cheddar Gorge and as chilly as the caves at Ingleton.

"What's he doing now?"

"Accountancy. 'E's training to be an accountant. 'As exams to take and all that."

"Well, I heard he was a bright lad."

"Yes, 'e's a brain on 'im. I can't deny it."

"How did you get to know him? He was Catholic wasn't he? Went to St Wilf's."

"Aye, but he came to live with his aunty who's across t'road from me mother's. That's how we got to know one another, though I recalled 'im. 'Is family were well known."

"Oh, yes, they were infamous."

She didn't like the implication. It had never occurred to her that the world would judge her choice of husband. She believed her motivation was Christian. *Judge not that ye be not judged.* She would have been surprised if she could have been shown how much she did judge. The horrible thought came to her that she was now forever associated with the low behaviour of Bert's family. She'd thought that by marrying a *lost soul* she would attain a position of unassailable superiority; but now she felt she had to swim against a tide of knowingness, pity and wariness.

Warwick knew about Bert's family, as did many people who had little to do with him; the notoriety of degradation penetrates the folk memory as resolutely as the fame of great achievement. She thought she'd done something private but she was suddenly aware of the public aspect of her marriage. What was Warwick thinking? Was he feeling sorry for her? Did he think she'd made a mistake? She felt he represented a stable and honest world which was ranged against her and which she couldn't get access to.

Why hadn't she married someone like him? She glanced at his cuffs. He was obviously careful of his cleanliness and appearance. His clothes suggested he was doing well. Why hadn't she married a man from a good home? Why was she the wife of the illegitimate son of a notoriously *loose* woman? Why had the sickness of alcoholism, debt, fecklessness and violence settled itself on her heart and mind?

"Yer can't judge 'im by 'is family," she said. "'E's not like them."

"No, no," said Warwick with a gentle shake of the head, "I don't judge him at all. I think he's made a good choice. I wish I was in his shoes."

She pushed herself back in her chair and stared into his eyes. What way was that to talk to a married woman? The image came swiftly into her mind of Warwick walking beside her as she went home from school; he often joined in her games in the yard; he called her name

263

as she went through the school gate. Had he harboured feelings for her during all those years? She'd never suspected it.

How strange that someone could be thinking of you in *that* way and you had no idea. It seemed almost like an invasion; as if a little bit of her life belonged to him. Yet she hadn't thought about him for years. She'd never had the least affection for him. How queer. It made her think there might be other grown men who were little boys alongside her in Cross St Methodist School who had secretly liked her. How many? How come she'd never known? She had an unnerving sense that something had passed her by. No-one had proposed to her but Bert and now here she was facing a man who was saying he wished he was married to her. Why hadn't she met him years ago? Why hadn't he turned up at Hopkirk's or bumped into her in the street? Was it just chance? Chance? Could chance decide how your life worked out? The idea was as alien to her as the notion that the earth would one day cease to orbit the sun. No. God determined everything. What happened had to happen. For some reason she had to marry Bert. Yet why did God want Warwick to meet her today? Why did He want him to tell her he would like to be married to her? Was Warwick trying to seduce her? Was he suggesting she should have an *affair?*

"I'm expectin'," she said.

"Congratulations. That's good news."

Surely that would stop him. If he was thinking about making a proposition, that would show him he should forget it. Yet beneath her confusion and outrage, there stirred a tiny gladness: she had something about her which had made her stay on Warwick's mind for years; and even though she was married, he was being suggestive; he was talking in the way that worked up a woman's feelings; she was learning something about herself she'd never realised: that she had a power of influence that required no effort. She'd always believed she must *work* to have an effect; yet it seemed she simply had to *be*, and men were moved by her. She didn't let the feeling into her conscious mind; she wasn't going to take hold of it and work it through; she wasn't going to transform her view of herself. It was all nonsense. Yet it was curious how she would have liked to remain in Warwick's company; how, in spite of herself, she would have liked to hear him say he wished he was married to her.

"Are you wed?" she said although she'd noticed he wore no ring.

"No, Elsie. I shall have to hurry up. But I'm starting a new life. I'm emigrating to Canada."

"Whatever for?"

"Opportunity. It's a big country. A newer country. I'm a qualified engineer. I've got a job out there in an aircraft factory. Good money. I think I can make a grand life for myself there, Elsie. Big house. Good standard of living. All I need's a woman to come with me."

He gave a little smile but she couldn't return it. Was he inviting her? He must be mad. She was a married woman. She was expecting a child. Yet he was looking at her with the sweet little smile on his lips as if he'd just asked her to go egg rolling on Avenham Park on Easter Monday. How could he look so innocent when he was making such criminal suggestions? She almost wanted to slap his face. Canada? Where was Canada? She knew it was near America but her memory of the map was shaky. What was so special about Canada? It seemed a wild notion to travel to the other side of the world, to leave behind everything familiar. Yet at the same time it caught her own life in all its restriction as simply as a photograph catches a facial expression you are unaware of wearing.

Opportunity. A big house. A grand life. These vague promises tugged at unfulfilled desires. How she would have loved to see the world; how beautiful it would be to have no overbearing responsibilities and to be able to test yourself against life's great challenges; she could leave behind forever the grim, grey streets of her home town; she could visit pretty little places like Grasmere or Hawkshead where the corruption of industry and the vicious pursuit of money hadn't penetrated; there must be, she imagined, thousands of such towns and villages in the world; there her soul could find peace and her heart fulfilment; close to nature and among simple, honest people she could at last be herself; there was humiliation in the very pavements she walked; it was shameful to put the key in her front door lock; it was as if she was being watched and judged and who could not feel small and wretched knowing they were poor in a country of much wealth? Who could not feel less than human to be without even a blade of grass within half a mile of their home?

She'd walked the hills of the Lake District and been amazed. Something evil had made the towns; the factories, the workhouses, the

265

slums, all those dark tenancies which were part of her parents' past and which haunted her childhood were the work of the Devil; when she stood on the summit of Skiddaw her cheeks warm from the ascent, her legs strong, the tender April wind in her hair she knew God had made this beautiful place, as he had made the world beautiful; God wanted us to live in beauty and peace but the Devil had sown greed and discord in the world and the vile, filthy towns and cities with their pubs full of drunks, their violence, their prostitutes, their bosses who worked their *hands* half to death, their children going hungry to school and being beaten for the least misdemeanour, were the Devil's pride.

She saw herself on a ship in the middle of God's ocean; she would travel to lands where the sun shone all year round; she would meet dark-skinned, gentle people who lived still in peace with nature; she would write letters to her father telling of the wonders she'd seen and of the free and happy life which was possible away from the stinking corruption of the town.

"I'm sure you'll meet one out there," she said.

"I'm sure I might, but I'll be lucky to find one as pretty as you."

Why did he keep talking about her looks? She could have slapped his face. Was that all he could think about? Did he want a wife just to look at and admire like a nice painting or a lovely vase? Didn't he want a wife who would cook and clean and keep a tidy house? A wife who would be a good mother to his children? He was half smiling at her and she could see a watery glint in his eyes as if he might start crying.

"Here comes Maggie," she said.

He stood up but Maggie pulled over an unoccupied chair.

"No, no," she said, "sit down."

"I don't want to intrude," he said.

Elsie could have rebuked him; didn't he think it was an intrusion to come and introduce himself after all these years and then to start complimenting her? He was as intrusive as a rat in a larder.

"Remember me?" he said.

"No, I'm afraid I don't," said Maggie casting a glance at her friend.

"Warwick Dornan," said Elsie, "from Cross St."

266

"Warwick," said Maggie, "I'd never've known. My, you've altered right enough."

"I have."

" 'E's emigratin'. Canada." said Elsie as if she were announcing he'd just been sentenced to ten years in Strangeways.

"Oh, that's lucky. I've thought of that meself. Canada or Australia."

"There are opportunities," he said.

"I know," said Maggie.

"There's opportunities 'ere," said Elsie.

Warwick smiled.

" I'd love to go," said Maggie, "somewhere you could make a fresh start."

"There's nowt wrong wi' Lancashire," said Elsie. "There's far worse places to live."

"And what'll you do out there?" said Maggie.

"'E's an engineer," said Elsie, "got a job building aeroplanes."

"Good luck to you," said Maggie.

"It's a big decision," he said. "I doubt I'll ever come back. Pity is I'm going alone."

He looked at Elsie. Maggie had the baby on her shoulder and was rubbing and patting his back.

" 'Appen better that way," she said. "Set up your family out there."

"You might be right, Maggie. Anyway, nice to meet you both. You never know, we might meet again someday."

He shook their hands, they wished him well and he was gone.

Elsie was tense with desire to tell Maggie what he'd said but she thought it might seem like boasting. Outside, Maggie lay the child in his pram and the friends parted with a smile and a promise to get together soon. Elsie went home and busied herself. Yet all her activity wouldn't hold down her thoughts; the image of Warwick kept coming into her mind.

He wasn't a handsome man, but he was tall, strong and healthy. He was a Methodist. She scrubbed and cleaned and tidied. She prepared meat and vegetables and put a casserole in the oven; but when at last, thirsty, tired and hungry she sat down with a cup of tea and a biscuit, she thought of the days in school when Warwick had sat behind her; she let the idea grow that through the years when his existence had ceased to register with her, he'd been thinking of her. How had they managed not to bump into one another? He must have been away during the war. How strange to think of his affection for her enduring through his time in the forces and still to be alive now. She could be his wife. She could be going to Canada.

Yet she couldn't. She had her mother. Would Warwick be good enough to let her mother and father join them? Could they all live in a big house and have a better life. The thought brought her to her feet and made her sweep the kitchen floor for the third time. She was a married woman. She'd chosen Bert, or at least ended up with him and that was that. She decided to clean the windows and got out her little step ladder; but a horrible feeling wouldn't leave her alone: had there been opportunities she'd never been aware of? Were there good, decent lads from steady families like Warwick who were in love with her? In love? It couldn't be. Just because she was pretty. Was it true she had some devilish power over men in her eyes, her waist, her hips? She polished furiously till all the panes gleamed; but when she went upstairs to her mother, she stood in the little bedroom looking towards the window and the grimy, northern light, wondering in which direction was Canada.

THE MIND DOCTOR

Bert found himself excited at having glimpsed Laura Bruzzese. He was overcome by a powerful desire to see her. He was the father of her child; and he liked her. He found himself full of joy at the idea of sitting in her little house, drinking tea and admiring her thick, black hair, and the heavy suggestiveness of her limbs. Yet at the same time he shrank from the idea: she was a married woman; if he turned up, would it spread trouble between her and her husband? He was surprised to find he'd let his name slip from his memory. He liked him. It was remiss of him not to get in touch and invite him to a match; but it was difficult to be on ordinary, friendly terms with a bloke when you'd been to bed with his wife. Perhaps the poor man had been devastated by Laura's pregnancy; maybe he would find it hard to make contact with the child. That train of thought made Bert reflect on his own relationship with his mother. It was territory he normally stayed away from; it quickly bogged him down in a sense of hurt, lack and inadequacy.

The image came into his head of his mother walking away; he saw himself, a scruffy, near-wild little boy amidst the bare neglect of his poor home and his mother, dressed in black, walking along the flagstones by the little terrace houses with small, resolute steps and never a look over her shoulder. If he allowed himself to linger over these pictures, his feelings collapsed. He'd had to form a mind without a mother. As for a father, all he could see was a uniform. A sergeant at Fulwood Barracks. He knew no more than that. A uniform and an absence where the face should be. Not having a father was bad but not nearly so bad as having a mother who walked out.

In her disappearance she defined his status; he was unwanted in the world. His well-being depended on his grandparents. He'd tried to love them; in fact he did. How queer it was that he could think of them as hopeless, feckless, neglectful, ruined people, that if he pushed his ideas far enough he could even see them as evil, and yet he loved them. As an abandoned little boy he'd cleaved to them; he tried to climb on his grandmother's knee but she would be drunk and petulant; he would follow his grandfather around the house till the old man became irritated and lashed out with his thick hand, catching the boy across the back of the head and sending him with a few quick, hot tears back to his corner by the fire.

That was one thing: there was always a fire in winter. Those flaming coals had become almost a substitute family. At least they warmed him and were predictable. And now there was a child in the world who shared a bit of his illegitimacy. At least it had a mother, a good mother, a mother who wanted the child more than anything. He stopped in his work and tried to imagine how it might have been to have a loving mother; to be lifted up and cuddled and spoken to gently; to be put to bed with a smile and a kiss; to have someone you could run to in excitement to spill out all those inordinately inconsequential details of insignificant actions which are so fabulously important to children.

Nothing came. The feelings that attached to those ideas had never been awoken in him and now it was too late. Just as, if he'd never heard language he would be capable of no more than grunts, so as he'd missed the love a child needs, his repertoire of feeling lacked essential music. As his thoughts began to touch on these ideas, he forced himself away. He thought of seeing Laura again, and out of nowhere came into his head the blissful notion of getting into bed with her. His last memory of Elsie was of her sharp words; how lovely to be able to sink into the accepting, gentle flesh and mind of the gorgeous Laura.

As soon as work was over he drove towards her house. It would be wrong to park up outside so he left the car a few streets away. Why shouldn't he be taking a walk in this part of town? He could pass it off as innocent if he needed to. He went slowly down nearby streets. They were pleasant enough. The houses had small front gardens and most people tried to keep them pretty. It struck him how people would always do their best to make things attractive and comfortable if given a chance; yet not his family. What perversity was it in them that made them destroy all their best chances?

After half an hour of idling, hoping in a vague way that Laura might pass by, he decided to be bold and knock on her door. What was the worst that could happen? She might turn him away. It was worth the risk. He turned the corner and there was Gino with the baby on his shoulder at the front gate. Bert experienced a moment's panic and thought he should turn on his heels, but the Italian waved at him and called. He was smiling. He was walking towards him. He was amazed.

"Ciao. Isa nice to see you. Come on an 'ave a drink with us. Laura is in ze 'ouse."

Bert shook his hand and walked beside him. The baby was content and comfortable. He looked at the little round head with its sparse dark hair and was stunned to think he had given it life. Did it look like him? He couldn't tell. Babies looked more or less the same. He glanced to see if he could discern his own features. When they reached the gate, Laura was on the doorstep.

"Bert. What a surprise? What are you doing in this neck of the woods?"

"I was just passing and thought I'd call. "

"Oh, you did the right thing. Come in. Gino will make some coffee."

Gino handed the baby to its mother.

"Whatta you think, Bert? My son 'e look like me?"

Bert turned to Gino and saw his big, happy, almost silly smile. He was as thrilled with his new baby as a boy with a bike a Christmas.

"Yes," said Bert, "I'm sure he does look like you."

"Of course he does," said Laura. "Just like his daddy. We waited a long time but Gino did the trick in the end."

The Italian laughed and put his arm on Bert's shoulder.

" Is true. Like a footballer who score in the last minute, eh Bert?"

Bert laughed with him but for a nano-second caught Laura's serious glance.

The living-room was as cosy and welcoming as he remembered. Simply sitting in the armchair opposite Laura who tucked her feet beneath her on the sofa and cradled the baby in the crook of her arm made him feel at home in the world. It was a feeling akin to being welcomed into Elsie's house: the discovery of something that had always been missing. He became aware of a congenial atmosphere; at home there was a constant threat of sharpness; Elsie seemed to have some power within her that pushed him away, some petulant impulse to brittleness. It puzzled and troubled him endlessly and he didn't know that his outsider's need for acceptance had tricked him: he'd treated her defensiveness like a man treats a rash that doesn't itch or sting, hoping it will go away; and just as the apparently in-nocuous eruption spreads inexorably, covers his body and turns out

271

to be the deceptive messenger of serious illness, so her ostensibly superficial resistance turned out to be a fatal incapacity, a blank in her emotional make-up as fundamental as his own, and his daily pain was to try to ignore it, to make allowances for it, to rise above it, to try to mend it.

Here, however, the walls gave off acceptance and love. What a pity he hadn't met someone like Laura when she was single. He needed a home like this to come to after the working day. He needed to be able to shut his front door on the pettiness of Harry Clow, the tension of having to suspend an essential part of his personality during the hours in the office. He'd come to realise Elsie didn't grant him the full status of a husband; he was a visitor in her father's house; he was unable to relax and be fully himself, without any thought of ulterior purposes, of pleasing the boss and ensuring his advancement. It was mortifying that he felt more accepted by Laura and Gino than by his own wife; yet he didn't let the hurt flood his mind. He'd grown so used to living in tight emotional and psychological spaces he was as resourceful as a dung beetle.

"So, what do you think of your son?" Laura whispered to him.

Bert laughed in that bring-on-the-end-of-the-world way he had.

"He's a smasher."

"Want to hold him?"

Bert took the little lad and laid him on his knees. He rocked his thighs gently and began goo-goo talk. He was astonished to see small signs of response in the baby's face; he'd always thought tiny ones incapable of any connection or communication; but the little chap was definitely alert to the sounds. His eyes looked at the ceiling, at the light, and then made contact with Bert's. It was uncanny, the feeling of recognition it engendered. This was his son. Was there some identity between them, some ingrained similarity which both of them recognised without knowing it? He let the child grip his thumbs and moved his hands from side to side. His little legs kicked and he smiled. His own son.

He thought of the child growing in Elsie. Soon he would have another child. Without realising, he assumed it would be a boy. He would play with the child like this every day. He would be a point of security and certainty for him. The two of them would do things together. He saw himself striding down Deepdale Road, the little lad's hand in his; he imagined hoisting him on his shoulders to let him see the game; he dreamed of them plunging together in the big pool at Saul Street and swimming strong lengths of crawl. In the idea of a new life was the possibility of the rectification of all that had gone wrong in his. The boy was kicking hard now so Bert took his feet and made his legs cycle; the child cooed and smiled.

"Think he looks like Gino?" Laura whispered.

Bert shook his head.

"Gino does," she said barely audibly.

"He looks like you," said Bert.

"He has your eyes," she mouthed.

Gino appeared with the coffee.

"Hey, 'e like you," he said to Bert. "Sometime 'e cry when a stranger take 'im, eh Laura?"

"Yes. Bert is a natural," she said as she reached for her mug.

"Well," he said, "I soon will be."

"Really?" said Laura.

"Elsie's expecting."

"I didn't even know you'd got married."

"No, it all happened pretty quickly."

"Congratulations," said Gino shaking his hand, "I atell you bein' a father, is best feelin' in world."

"I can imagine," said Bert.

They were full of questions about Elsie and his life with her. He put the best sheen on everything but the more he spoke the more he became aware of what he was refusing to say: there was a part of him, the hurt, vulnerable part, unformed, primitive, importunate, unable to find its way into expression through the ordinary game of conversation, which wanted to cry out; he wanted to tell them of Elsie's crushing insistencies; how he found it hard to get close to her; how she tried to make him a stranger in her home; he wanted to tell how hard he had striven to love her, to make them twine and cling together like a clematis that tangles itself round a rose; he wanted to hang his head and confess how confused he felt and how a dread of something ahead he couldn't control and which threatened even his compromised happiness, haunted his dreams; but he could no more do so than he could tell Gino he wasn't a father. So he talked on and on over his emptiness and it was only when he felt he'd stayed long enough, had said goodbye, promised to bring Elsie to see them and was walking back to his car, that he felt utterly alone; Laura and Gino were good people, they were his friends and he could visit them any time, but it was impossible to tell them what lay at the centre of him; it was impossible to tell anybody, most of all Elsie. She was his wife but she didn't want to know. She had her ambition: to be a wife and mother. He knew well enough she consigned him to his limited role of earning. He turned the corner and saw his car. A horrible desire seized him not to go home and the idea sprang into his head of looking up Slick Sticks Sam. *There* was someone he didn't need to tell; they occupied the same hinterland. They were forever outsiders.

He turned the ignition. The little engine whined. He drove home and parked in front of Tom Craxton's house.

Jimmy and Jessie were at the kitchen table with Elsie.

"Nice to see you," said Bert with a big smile.

He was genuinely glad there were visitors. Inviting people or being called on, even if it was only Jimmy and Jessie (people he had little in common with) always altered the atmosphere, and there was nothing worse, to his way of thinking, than living day after day in the confines of the same unchanging relationships. One of his ambitions was to have a home he could make open house. How good it would be to invite round a couple of people from work, even the uncongenial Harry Clow; or some of the blokes he went on the football with or even used to enjoy a kick around amongst when he was a lad. Company was transforming. It was pleasant to have strangers in your house. In that, he wasn't at all like his father-in-law who was as likely to invite people into his living-room as to join the Tory Party. For Tom, the home was a kind of refuge and he shrank from the easy sociability that gave Bert a sense of relief.

"Aye," said Jimmy, " 'ow yer doin'?"

"You're late," said Elsie.

"Bit of work to catch up on," said Bert.

"Jimmy and Jessie are stayin' for tea."

"Good," said Bert, "have you killed the fatted calf?"

"Bangers and mash," said Elsie, getting up and going to the kitchen.

Bert sat down noticing that Jessie seemed at once lacking élan and agitated. There was an apology in her presence. The big, heavy Jimmy, strong and physically imposing sat opposite her and didn't look at her. No doubt it was the old business of Jessie's *nerves*. Yet what did that mean? What were nerves anyway? He had a vague idea of how they transmitted messages from the brain and he pictured them like the wires in a complex circuit; but he had no real understanding and he found it hard to make the common term *bad with nerves* mean anything. It was one of those things people said almost as a form of reassurance, as if by giving a name to something they had eliminated its mystery. Yet for him, the opposite was true. What was the matter with Jessie? Sitting between the two of them it seemed obvious: they weren't getting along. For whatever reason, there was a stiffness between them and nothing wore away at your happiness more than having to spend your time in the company of someone who made you uncomfortable. Bad with her nerves? Maybe she just needed to get out of Jimmy's way.

"So, what you reading, Jessie?" he said to her.

"Oh, nothin' much."

"She's allus 'er nose in a book," said Jimmy.

Bert laughed.

"So she should. I like reading too, though I can't read the clever stuff you like."

"I just have a few interests," she said, turning her handkerchief in her hands.

"Elsie was telling me you were reading about science."

"Yes."

"I can't fathom it entirely."

"Greek to me," said Jimmy.

Elsie came through with two steaming plates piled high with creamy mash next to which lay two well cooked, crescent sausages as if they were trying to hide and avoid being eaten.

"We're just talking about science," said Bert.

"That's nowt to do wi' me," said Elsie. "I'll stick to Methodism."

She brought her own food and Bert's and sat down. Bert doused his sausages in HP sauce.

"D'yer 'ave to use so much?" said Elsie.

"I like it," said Bert, "it perks up the taste."

"Yer can't taste sausages wi' all that on."

Bert accepted the rebuke because to argue was wearying and no matter how he tried he wouldn't get Elsie to see the funny side. The meal progressed in silence. The clicking of the cutlery against the plates made Bert want to laugh out loud. An odd feeling of disconnection overcame him. Who were these people? What was he doing amongst them? He could have stood up and without a word left the house never to return. It was a defeating sentiment. Above all he wanted to feel there was a place he belonged and people he belonged to so irrevocably he could no more leave them than shed his skin; but he might have been in a restaurant with people he'd never met before.

He felt as lonely and inauthentic as when he'd signed up for the RAF. He'd made the best of the war because that was all there was to be done, but the whole business was stupid and humiliating. Who would want to spend their life fighting except a drunken, deluded fool like his grandfather? Yet he'd chosen to be here and now he felt it was no more his destiny than Cairo was the capital of Sweden. He was first to clear his plate.

"Delicious," he said, "what's for pudding."

"Don't be cheeky," said Elsie.

"I'm not being cheeky," he said, "I'm complimenting you. You're a good cook as well as a good wife."

"If you were a good husband you wouldn't talk so daft."

Jessie and Jimmy diligently ate their food as if commanded by some whimsical dictator. Bert suppressed his anger. He could have unleashed his worst invective against Elsie. Why couldn't she laugh? Why couldn't she take a joke as a joke? He was glad when Tom appeared and spoke to Jimmy. He turned to Jessie whose plate was half full.

"I'm just reading Virginia Woolf," he said. "Do you like her."

"A bit," said Jessie.

"I can't get into it," he said. "The characters seem frozen."

"Maybe because she perceived them through her own depression," she said and turned to him.

It was the first time he'd sat close to her and looked into her eyes. He was suddenly aware of loneliness in their expression. He smiled and nodded.

"Yes, depression must be a terrible thing."

She cut the end of a sausage, loaded a little mound of potato and lifted it to her mouth.

When Bert and Elsie were alone in the bedroom, speaking in the hushed voices they always had to use, he said:

"Jessie doesn't seem too good."

"She'll be aw right."

"She seems in a bad way to me."

"What d'you know?"

"Just what anybody knows. You can see when someone's suffering."

"She's just bad wi' 'er nerves, that's all."

"What does that mean?"

"Don't be s'awkward. It means she's bad wi' 'er nerves."

"That's just something folk say, Elsie. They don't know what they mean. Bad with her nerves? It isn't a medical condition. Something's not right between her and Jimmy I'd say."

"No-one's askin' yer to say owt."

"I'm only saying. Why be so touchy?"

"I'm not touchy. Yer've no business poking yer nose into me family's affairs."

"Christ, Elsie."

"Don't tek t' Lord's name in vain."

"I didn't mention the Lord."

"Don't split 'airs either."

"She's my sister-in-law. I'd say she's depressed. Why shouldn't I be worried about that?"

"She's not depressed, she's bad wi' 'er nerves."

"Whatever name you give it she's in a bad way. She could barely eat."

"She'll mend. She's seein' someone."

"Who?"

He looked at her. She was all but naked with her night dress in her hand. He was astonished at his own luck, being married to this extraordinarily pretty, shapely woman. Her belly was bulging slightly and he thought at once of his son. He wanted to tell her. Yet he knew deceit was necessary. He didn't like it. He was what he was and he wanted to tell her. She was his wife after all. Why shouldn't she know. He'd done Laura a favour. She and Gino were happy. The child was loved. What was wrong with that? Yet he knew it would drive Elsie into a madness of rage. She would revile him. She would tell her family. She would probably kick him out. All the same, how beautiful she was, and her beauty alone was enough to enchant him because he'd never known love and so had never learned that what someone looks like is far less important than what goes on in their minds. The power of physical attraction, so overwhelming yet so superficial, finds itself superseded by deeper needs in the minds of almost everyone because beauty is rare and love must settle for plainness or even ugliness; but for Bert, who'd never had those deeper needs responded to, it flooded his mind irresistibly.

"A psychiatrist."

"What does he say?"

"It's a woman."

"Well, what does she say?"

"She won't have sex as she thinks she's not married," said Elsie petulantly and raising her voice a little. "She thinks she's sinned, like we did, and it's turned her mind."

"She think's she not married?"

"Aye, because our Jimmy insisted on't Register Office. Priest's been to see 'er time and agin and towd 'er in God's eyes she's no better than a prostitute."

Bert's Catholic past came back to him; his grandparents' demeaning fawning before the Father, the leather strap across his own hands for the slightest fault at school; his rebellion against being a choirboy after Father Carrigan touched his backside. He threw back his head and laughed the mocking laughter of the knowing abused.

"The evil bugger," he said.

"Don't use language."

"Language? He should be bloody horsewhipped."

"'E's tryin' to save 'er soul."

"He's driving her to madness, Elsie. It's nothing but evil to put such ideas in someone's head. If I were in Jimmy's place I'd give him a mouthful."

"Aye, well you're not."

"Somebody should. Priests. They're a wicked bunch."

" 'E's a man o' God. 'E has to do what Bible tells him."

"If the Bible tells priests to bully women and make them feel guilty about going to bed with their husbands it should be torn to shreds."

She tensed and drew back.

"Don't you say such a thing in my 'ouse."

"I live 'ere too."

"Aye, but it's my 'ouse."

"She'll drive Jimmy to other women. That'll be a good day's work for the priest, eh?"

"Our Jimmy wouldn't."

"Wouldn't he Elsie? He's a man. You can't deny a man, make him feel small and not expect him to rebel."

"Not everyone thinks sex is as important as you do."

"Don't they? And would you have that if it wasn't for sex," he reached out and touched her abdomen.

She pulled away. He saw fear and incomprehension in her eyes.

" 'Avin' a baby is one thing, sex for pleasure is another."

"Nature made it pleasurable so we'd have babies."

"Not nature, God."

"Fine, God. He knew what he was doing when he gave us cocks and cunts."

She gasped.

"Don't you use language like that in my 'ouse. I'll tell me father."

"Your father's heard it. He's worked on the docks."

He turned away, weary of the futility.

"Any road, they're to marry in church. Psychiatrist thinks that'll fix it."

Bert pulled on his pyjamas without replying. It was a mystery. That a ceremony which to him was as empty as a politician's promise could transform Jessie's feelings seemed bizarre. Why was it the church had the power to control her mind? How had the priest managed to rob her of her volition. It seemed to him he was immune from such influence; part of his outsider's mentality was that he could fly in the face of convention. It was incredible that Jessie, an intelligent woman, could be so subject to religious mumbo-jumbo she could be incapable of a proper relationship with her husband.

The idea crushed his feelings. His mind was full of questions. He wished he understood it; he wished it was visible, like the figures in book-keeping. It frightened him that he knew so little of how the mind worked, which meant he knew so little of how his own mind worked. Jessie would go to church, and though Jimmy no more believed in God than fairies, the nuptial mass with its Latin incantations no-one understood, the incense that was nothing more than sanctified *eau de cologne*, would settle her troubled mind and whatever went on between her and Jimmy in the bedroom would begin again. Bert found it hard to imagine a tender passion between his brother and sister-in-law. Jimmy struck him as too unceremonious. He was one of those men who went directly at everything. He had little sense of flourish and embellishment. He wore conventional, unimaginative clothes and his idea of being smart was to put on a dark suit, a white shirt with a plain tie, his long, brown raincoat and his flat cap. He would never, like Bert, have enjoyed the rococo ostentation of a flowery cravat. He'd've thought it pretentious and effeminate.

Yet it was exactly that transgression which appealed to Bert. Just as he enjoyed flying in the face of the assumption that a man must like his beer; that a bloke who wasn't comfortable washing his gullet with cheap ale was someone to be suspicious of; so he relished challenging the narrow conventions of provincialism through a little super-added bohemianism and cosmopolitanism. Nevertheless, the idea that Jessie had been frozen in her sexuality because of the insinuations of a dark-frocked confession-hearer enraged and troubled him. He realised how much he hated priests. The Catholic Church had frightened him as a child. It had humiliated him. It held his hopeless grandparents in thrall. When he'd needed help, generosity, security and a smile, the church had terrified him with its vicious recipe of purgatory and perdition.

He recalled his confessions; sitting in the dark box thinking of something to say that wasn't too bad but all the same bad enough to require absolution. It was nothing but abuse to do such a thing to child; and of course the psychological abuse was accompanied by the physical. Didn't all the boys know about Carrigan? Didn't they call him Carrigan the cassock lifter? It was all too ridiculous and corrupt; and the heart of it was worship of a deity no-one had any evidence of. He slid into bed and pulled the chilly covers around him. Elsie turned out the light. In the silence and darkness he felt irrevocably alone. He existed in a tiny space like an insect. That was what people granted him. It'd always been so. Would it always be so? Well, what if it was? What if this little edge of bed was all that was granted him; what if he was unwelcome on the earth. He had as much right to be here as those whose entrance was legitimate. He would live out his life in the way that suited him, whatever priests and Elsie thought.

He found himself imagining Laura and Gino together. He saw the Italian's cheerful, innocent smile. He pictured them in bed with the child between them. He wished he was in bed with Laura, and his son. Soon he and Elsie would be parents. What would it be like? A fear sprang to life in him that she would want the child for herself; she would try to exclude him. Don't you do that in my house; don't you say that it my house. He was contemptuous of her for speaking to him in that way. Well, he wouldn't let it happen. He would be a good father. He would be kind to his child and would raise him to be confident and happy. He would see to his education. He didn't want him to leave school ignorant like he'd done. No, she wouldn't stop him. No-one would stop him. He would take on without demur his responsibilities as a father. The thought excited and lifted him. He could make amends for all the cruel failings of his own upbringing. What greater opportunity did life offer than parenthood? He would seize it. If it meant rowing with Elsie, he was ready for that.

He fell asleep in the early hours and dreamed of a priest who beat his hands till they bled, took off his cassock and revealed the body of a young, sleek woman. Her black pubic hair contrasted with the white flesh of her belly and her firm, full breasts attracted his mouth; but when he sucked the nipple, it disintegrated in his mouth and he found himself cast to the ground by a skinny, smelly hag who glugged gin from the bottle, pissed on the floor and farted in his face. He woke as the horrifying images were evaporating. Elsie was already out of bed. He went down to the kitchen to shave. She was busy with breakfast and washing-up and didn't speak to him. He got himself ready and called to her as he went out:

"'Bye, Elsie."

She didn't reply.

The following Saturday, he met Slick Sticks Sam. It was curious how much of a relief it was to sit opposite this wayward, chaotic, harmless fool. Did he really think him a fool? In a sympathetic way, he did. Yet Slick lived out his life as he had to; a steady job, a wife, a house in the suburbs, two kids and a fortnight in Skegness in July would have destroyed him. He needed his petty *jazz life* routines; drifting home along Main Sprit Weind at two in the morning, sucking on his last Woodbine, falling into bed without a wash or cleaning his teeth; getting up at midday and going to the pub for his breakfast; these were as necessary to him as church on Sunday morning to Elsie. The last thing Bert wanted to do was judge him. It wasn't as if he harmed anybody; he played the drums, chased women, smoked, drank, backed horses, lived in something approaching squalor, but he wouldn't knowingly wrong anyone and if Bert had asked him for ten bob he'd have lent it him if it was his last.

He wasn't like Bert's grandfather. He was vicious and enjoyed harming people. Where did that come from? How did he get satisfaction from damaging other people? Bert did judge his grandparents; he thought them despicable because their degradation brought pain, especially to him; but though Slick was superficially like them, he was in fact quite different. He was almost a saint. Saint Slick. The notion went through Bert's head and amused him. Why was he saint? Bert puzzled a few moments as he drank his strong coffee. Wasn't it because he wasn't a hypocrite? Had anyone accused him of drunkenness, slovenliness, licentiousness, he'd have readily admitted to them; he had nothing of that unpleasant and depressing attempt to pass themselves off as better than they are which Bert thought typical of the middle-classes, and even the *respectable* working-class. He was a kindly, easy-going, generous, drunken, self-indulgent, woman-hungry, bookie rat. Elsie would've condemned him. She would have quoted the Bible to show how unacceptable his behaviour; but Bert liked him. He was comfortable in his company. He accepted Slick for what he was and Slick accepted him. That was the best of life. There was something horrible and wearying about the business of having to keep up with a set of standards you didn't believe in; not that Bert wanted to imitate Slick at all; he simply wanted not to have to live according to a false and empty self-aggrandizement.

"How's things?" said Bert.

"Somethin' on my mind."

"Lost too much at the bookies?"

"Woman trouble."

"Nothing new."

"Joyce is in the same condition as your missus."

"Oh, Christ."

"Gotta sort something out," said Sam.

"She doesn't want to have it?"

"Naw, man. What life would that be for a kid?"

"Better be careful."

"Sure. Careful but quick."

"You know, it's dangerous Sam. Women die. You need to get a doctor who knows what he's doing."

"Yeah, I'll go to Harley St, Bert."

"I'll help you out. I can lend you a few quid."

"I can sort out the money."

"You don't want some woman who's in it for the loot and uses knitting needles. You need someone qualified."

"This is against the law, Bert."

"I know, but there are doctors who take the risk. I'll see what I can find out."

"From who?"

"I don't know. I'll think about and ask around."

"It's a bugger."

"It's life, Sam."

"Too much life."

They left the café because Sam wanted a drink. Bert preferred the atmosphere of cafes; there were women there, on their own or with children; blokes came in to read the paper. Pubs were male places, a woman on her own was for sale; and the sickening memory of his lonely hours at home while his grandparents drank in *The Railway* or *The Theatre* made pubs uncongenial. They were associated with violence and stupidity. Still, they went to the *Black Horse* and no sooner were they through the door than Bert spotted Harry Clow chatting to a young bloke at the bar. Bert put his hand on Sam's shoulder.

"Look, Harry Clow. Who's that he's with?"

"Johnny Speed. Likes dressing up in women's clothes."

"Nip in here," said Bert. "I don't want Harry to spot me."

He went into one of the little rooms off the bar while Sam bought himself a pint and Bert an orange juice. Standing by the fireplace he could cock his head and catch Harry in his line of vision while at the same time keeping himself concealed.

The young bloke was slim and blonde with a thin face reminiscent of a vole. Harry put his arm around his shoulders as he raised his glass. It was one of those condescending gestures older, pub-familiar men make to the not yet initiated young; as if years of standing in smoky snugs tipping beer into their bulging stomachs amounted to some sort of achievement whose secrets should be conveyed to the innocent.

Bert's strongest desire was to approach Harry and to make clear he knew what was going on; yet he stayed where he was. The scene disgusted him; not because Clow was homosexual; Bert had no wish to condemn anyone for seeking their fulfilment; but because of his hypocrisy. Yes, it was illegal; and he understood that Clow wanted a wife and children for security; but all the same it sickened him that he could pass himself off for something he wasn't. The thought came

284

to him of how different things would be if a man like Clow could be honest. Yet how could he ever tell his wife? Surely she'd divorce him. So should men like him never marry? Suppose he liked women as much as men; what was wrong with that? What was wrong with finding a wife who would understand and accept? He asked himself if he'd accept Elsie having sex with other men. He wouldn't. So was he just a hypocrite too? Or was it a matter of making your own arrangements? Why not? Why should there be a norm everyone was supposed to follow when people were so various?

"Oh, that's smooth," said Sam sipping his pint.

"Cheers," said Bert. "So who's this Johnny Speed, then."

"Just a kid. Knocks around with older blokes. Fancies himself as a singer."

"Any good?"

"He's not Tony Bennett. He gets by belting out numbers in noisy pubs. No-one can hear him."

"He looks about sixteen."

"Yeah. Not much more. Eighteen or so I guess."

"What's he get from a bloke like Harry Clow?"

"Abuse probably."

"You think so?"

"Pretty likely."

"We should stop it."

"What you gonna do, Bert, tell the police?"

"No, tell Harry to leave the kid alone."

"And if the kid doesn't want to be left alone?"

"He's too young to know what he's doing."

"Kid's a mess, Bert. His mother killed herself. Dad's a nasty piece of work. Used to beat her up."

"That's terrible."

"It is."

"And Harry's taking advantage."

"He's not the only one."

"I think I'll have a word with him."

"Leave it be. There's nothing we can do."

"There's always something we can do, Sam. I'll just go and say hello."

Bert wriggled between the drinkers, approached Harry from behind and put his hand on his shoulder. Turning to him, Harry tried to smile and appear unconcerned.

"Bert. I thought you were tee-total?"

"I am. Great orange juice they serve in here. Nice to meet you," and he held out his hand to Speed.

The lad shook it and Bert was struck by the softness of his slender fingers. It was a hand that had never done any work, as tender as a child's and light as a girl's.

"This is my nephew," said Harry. "Johnny."

"Yes," said Bert, "I believe you do a bit of singing?"

"Yeah," said the youngster.

"I'm with Slick Sticks Sam."

The boy nodded.

"Oh yeah, I've heard him play lots of times."

"He's says you're a good singer," said Bert.

"That's nice."

Bert looked Harry full in the face. The older man's expression had turned ugly. He lowered his chin and looked from under his brows, like a bull about to charge.

"You never told me you had a nephew who could sing, Harry."

The boss poured his beer into his mouth.

"I didn't think you'd be interested. I thought you preferred Beethoven."

"Oh, I'm a mug for a good tune. I can listen to a Sally Army Band if they're energetic."

"Well, you'll have to come and listen to Johnny sometime. I'll let you know when he's on."

"That'd be grand," said Bert. "You know what you need, Johnny. A manager."

"I'll look after that side of things," said Harry.

"Better to have someone in the business. I can introduce you to Sam. He'll look after you."

"Doesn't need looking after," said Harry. "He'll be all right with me. Come on. Better get you home."

"Live nearby, Johnny?" said Bert.

"He lives with my sister. His mother. Don't you Johnny?"

Before the boy could construct an answer Bert said:

"That's funny because Sam told me Johnny's dad's a widower."

Harry buttoned his coat. He didn't look at Bert. Johnny looked from one to the other.

"Come on, Johnny. Time to go."

Bert held his hand out once more. When the lad clasped it Bert held onto him.

"Need any help, you come to me and Sam. We'll look after you."

Harry took his friend by the arm and led him out.

"So?" said Sam.

"Says he's his nephew."

Sam scoffed. He finished his drink.

"Fancy another?"

"No, there's only so much orange juice a man can drink in an afternoon."

"Yeah," said Sam, "and only so much beer. About two gallons."

They sat side by side in the little room, the leaded window behind them admitting the noises from the street. A petty coal fire burnt in the hearth and on the walls were black and white photos of scenes from the town over the past decades: men in clogs, overalls and caps leading great dray horses over the cobbles; kids playing whip and top on the pavement in front of their terraces.

It was homely and friendly and Bert felt it odd that this apparently simple, charming scene should be associated with Harry Clow's secret. It bothered him that he was preying on a young man. Sam might be right: the singer was a willing participant, but that wasn't the point; adults had a responsibility towards younger people. Bert knew Harry Clow: he would use anyone for his own ends. The skinny blonde was just a means to his illicit satisfactions. It made Bert think of his own childhood, of what went on where no-one could see; he knew the terrible loneliness of being frightened, neglected and needful while the world went about its purblind business; and he knew the cold force of power, the church with its self-advertising virtue concealing the vilest sins.

Wasn't Johnny in the same place? Wasn't he a frightened, lonely kid who needed someone who wouldn't exploit his weakness. Bert had no idea that the sexual instinct, trapped and trammelled by constraining social forms, can sweep away the scruples of the most self-disciplined; that robbed of our need for warmth and closeness we can easily become monsters of controlling greed who can see nothing but our own immediate desires.

How strange everything was: Sam had made Joyce pregnant and she wanted rid of it; Jessie had been terrified out of intimacy by the suggestions of a medieval-minded priest; Henry was the father of a child he had nothing to with; he was father of a child another man thought was his; Harry Clow was deceiving his wife with young men and Elsie who was soon to be the mother of his second child hardly spoke to him. Yet in spite of the terrible confusion of it all, he felt cheerful. Just as he had during the war. There'd been times when the German bombers came close and they could have been blown to chunks of raw bleeding meat; yet his pleasure in simple things never left him. Life, even in the face of the uncompromising evil of Hitler, was inexhaustibly interesting.

"How's Elsie?" said Sam.

"Prickly."

They looked at one another and laughed.

Bert decided to walk home. He didn't get around on foot much anymore; *why walk when you can ride*, had become his motto. He was one of those men who saw the car as a great symbol of progress and source of freedom. He was lucky enough to own one. His hopes coalesced around the notion of steadily improving models; it was a simple mental and emotional shorthand: the better the car, the better your life. If he'd been asked to offer a view of himself at fifty, a big house and an expensive car would have been the first things to enter his mind. It didn't occur to him that a big house could contain an unhappy family or an expensive car take a man back and forth to a job which drove him to self-hatred.

The promise of the moment was material improvement and it seemed to bring every other advantage in its train. He passed an advertising hoarding twelve feet tall; it bore the image of a sophisticated, good-looking man lighting a cigarette and the rubric *You're never alone with a Strand*. Though he had no desire to smoke, the advert appealed to him. He could be sophisticated. It was easy; you just had to wear the right clothes and assume the right pose. It required no effort. Sophistication was for sale. If he did well and earned enough, he could buy the trappings of a superior mind. Without knowing it, Bert associated wealth not merely with intelligence but with all the most demanding qualities: honesty, modesty, loyalty, trustworthiness, generosity, diligence, tolerance, patience, love itself; he had no inkling of the straitened inner life necessary to uphold these values. The dream of increasing national wealth to furnish increasing income to permit people to buy a better life, attributed to money the power to embody all human strengths and Bert saw no reason why a higher salary shouldn't entail a better mind.

The town was grey. There was no doubt it was forbidding. He thought of the light of Italy and the heat of Egypt. Why hadn't he been born in Rome or Naples? Yet, if he'd been born poor, his life might have been worse. Attlee was going to improve things and bit by bit the greyness would lift. Even towns like this, spewed onto the earth in the great rush of money-making in the early days of the industrial revolution; transformed into smoky, noisy, cramped, joyless cotton machines which sucked workers in, adult and child alike, crushed them body and spirit for a few bob a week so the fortunes of the mill owners could grow like a virulent tuberculosis; even these places he believed would become beautiful and sunny; healthy, proud towns where children would grow strong and energetic and where men like him could transform themselves.

He passed the corner shop with the *Hovis* advert painted on its gable end. He loved brown bread; and wasn't it healthy? A thick slice of *Hovis* lavishly painted with butter and spread with rich honey, wasn't that mouth -watering and lovely? Didn't it represent the future? Men like him, born in the thinnest of circumstances could taste the true

289

sweetness of life; yet it wasn't men *like* him; it was *him*. The misfortune of his early years was behind him. Henceforth it was *Hovis* and honey, Austins and Hillmans, big houses in the suburbs, good schools for his children, free hospitals; even the thought of Elsie's thorns couldn't strangle his ever newborn optimism and he turned the key with a smile on his face, as if the little house were a palace and he a king.

JUDITH

In the evening he and Elsie went to the *Ritz*. As usual she was nervous about leaving her mother, but Tom gave a gruff assurance he'd be fine; he liked to settle in his armchair with his pipe and listen to the radio. In truth, he was glad if Elsie and Bert went out and he could have the house to himself. It irritated him that Elsie thought she was the only one who could take care of his wife. So Bert was glad he had his father-in-law's support for a few hours out. He put on a clean shirt and changed his tie, pressed his trousers and brushed his best overcoat.

"We're not meetin't Queen," said Elsie.

"I wouldn't get dressed up for her," said Bert. "I would to meet Nye Bevan."

"We'll be in't dark any road," she said. "Folk won't see yer."

"That's not the point. I like to be smart. It makes me feel good."

They took the bus to the little station on Lancaster Road and walked down Church Street past the notorious *Red Lion* where the prostitutes hung around in the shadows of the alleyway, opposite the Parish Church, long and imposing looking down in apparent equanimity on this trivial Gomorrah. Bert was very proud to have Elsie on his arm. In those few hundred yards of public show, the married man with the pretty woman belonging to him, the man smartly dressed and with the strong stride of a resolute amateur footballer, felt all the shame of his past fall away. It was as remote as the smell that gained him his childhood nickname. He was clean. His shirt was newly laundered and ironed. He thought himself as *chic* as the Italians he'd seen in the cafes of Rome. That poor, neglected little boy was no more. He had definitively escaped his past.

They went into the foyer of the little cinema. Bert bought the tickets from the good-looking girl in the kiosk. He smiled at her and she made a coy little face which gave his heart a boost. They made their way up the two red-carpeted, wide steps and Bert was about to hand the ticket to the usherette when a voice said:

"Pongo! How are you mate?"

Bert turned. His face had collapsed into dismay and defensiveness.

291

Before him was a tall, gangly, raw-handed man in a suit whose trousers were too short and sleeves too tight. Bert looked into his face. The long nose, the prominent chin, the thick brows, the little brown eyes and the smile that showed pink gums and tobacco-stained teeth brought no glimmer of recollection. The stranger held out his hand. Bert shook it but was unable to smile.

"Remember me? Stan Tyrer."

"Stan?" said Bert. "I remember the name."

"I lived in Good St. Number seven. We were in't same class."

"Yes, yes," said Bert. "Nice to see you anyway."

"This your missus?"

"Yes, Elsie. This is Stan. Seems we were at school together."

"Evenin' Elsie. Well, you're a smart one now, Bert. What you doin' with yourself?"

"Accountancy."

"Crickey. White collar, eh? I'm on't trowel. Murphy's. Money's all right. This is my missus. Mavis, this is Bert I was at school with."

A dumpy, bustling woman in glasses, searching for something in her red handbag came to join them.

"Pleased to meet you," she said without looking at either Bert or Elsie.

"What you lost?" said Stan

"Mi fags," she said. "I'm sure I had 'em on't bus."

"You did," said her husband. "You lit up. Twice."

"We'd better get in," said Bert, "don't want to miss the start."

"Don't worry," said Sam, "there'll be a trailer and Pathe news."

But Bert hurried Elsie away. The usherette shone the torch to show to them their seats on the third row. Bert had once thought sitting at the back in the cinema the pinnacle of romance but now he liked to be near the front; he felt it mature and sophisticated. He tried to regain his previous mood but the knee in the groin from Stan had left him badly disconcerted. He found himself worrying that people might have heard. He looked over his shoulder to make sure Stan wasn't coming to join them. He folded and refolded his blue ticket till Elsie in annoyance put her hand over his to stop him. He found himself thinking: that was the problem of living in a small town where you grew up; there was always someone who knew your past and if it was as full of humiliation as his, there was always the chance it would hit you like a brick on the back of the head thrown by one of those people who like to ruin others' lives. Maybe he should move away. Could he persuade Elsie to move to Manchester? A city provided anonymity. Not to belong was essential for Bert because the past he belonged to would have made a scorpion blush. He had to create a new belonging and it must be in denial of everything he'd been.

He turned to look at Elsie. She was eye-defeatingly pretty but she too was part of his past. Would she ever forget what he'd been? Would she be able to see him as the new Bert who wore smart clothes, took a bath every day and worked in a respectable profession? Lost in these thought he didn't notice what was on the screen till the *feature* began.

As soon as Elsie heard the accents, saw the posh circumstances of the characters and the first woman on the screen smoking, she knew she wasn't going to like it; but Bert relished the peek into the lives of the metropolitan wealthy and sophisticated; what it would be to live in such a flat in London, to answer the big white phone to important people and to tell the cook what time to have dinner ready. When Margaret Leighton appeared playing the disillusioned and dangerous Leonora Vail, Elsie knew at once where things were going; a story of adultery among the rich; at its heart a woman disappointed in love who was intent on using her sex to get a silly, self-regarding revenge. It wasn't something to elicit her sympathy. All the same her interest quickened when Noel Coward, playing the sophisticated psychiatrist Christian Faber, was shown talking to his patients. He was referred to as an *alienist*. The word rang through her consciousness; what did it mean? An alien was a foreigner or an imagined invader from another planet. So why was a psychiatrist called an *alienist*? And how did it work, this business of talking to people about their lunacies?

She thought of Jessie. Is this what happened to her? Coward was asking a patient to speak the word that troubled him; he scribbled on a pad; when he made the man look at it there was nothing there; the client protested; the psychiatrist insisted it was only a word. Was it true that a mere word could drive someone mad? She wished the film could concentrate there, that it could reveal the mystery of how people could be ruined by their own ideas, of how poor Jessie could become a quaking shadow because of what the priest had said to her.

Yet it was quickly passed over and she experienced a rapid mental blankness; the film was dragging her where she didn't want to go; into the foolish world of people with too much money and too little discipline. The cynical, self-entrapped manner of Leonora made her angry; she was the kind of woman who needed to be brought up short; those kind of people always get away with their casual insults and hurtfulness because everyone makes allowances for them and enjoys the superficial amusement their consistent intrusiveness and wilting self-pity evokes. She would give her short shrift.

What a fool Barbara, Faber's wife, was to invite her into her life; from the first it was obvious she was a marriage-wrecker, one of those people who can't live with the idea of other people's contentment but must wilfully shatter it because of their own petty grudges. There came, however, a reference to the Bible: a quotation from *Deuteronomy* Faber needed in his lecture:. .. *smite you with madnesss, blindness and astonishment of heart*...Elsie found herself sitting upright. Was Leonora to be punished by God? Was she to go blind and mad and find her heart astonished? Elsie relished the possibility the film would invoke the Bible against Leonora's louche and selfish ways.

Bert, on the other hand, found Leonora attractive. Not that Margaret Leighton was a particularly beautiful woman; Elsie was unquestionably more attractive; but the free-floating sexuality Leonora exuded, the iconoclastic battering down of every barrier which stood between her and her regressive whims, stirred his too easily aroused desires.

He could respond to a woman of that kind; yes, he could sort her out all right, have raging sex with her after which she'd light a *Peter Stuyvesant, cool as a mountain stream*, as the adverts said, and engage in empty, cynical chit-chat while she lay naked and accessible on the expensive bed linen. Yes, he was the kind of red-blooded man to give her what she wanted, no strings, no marriage, no in-laws, no babies; yes, what a lovely dream it was to imagine such a woman offering herself to him just as Leonora was going to offer herself. When Faber, delivering his lecture, paused as he spotted her in the audience, Bert's heart jumped like a badly-firing engine.

What a bitch. Turning up at the lecture delivered by her friend's husband. What a manipulative cynical bitch. Yet though he could see how despicable her behaviour, all he could think of was the easy sex it proposed; he saw her with her legs open, the cigarette between her fingers, watching him as he threw off his clothes. Yes, he could give it to her all right; she could keep the burning filter-tipped where it was; when he'd finished it would be reduced to the brown; he'd ruffle her perfect hair-do right enough.

It was a blissful dream; to have rampant sex with women who asked nothing in return. Yet as the action progressed and he saw Faber making a fool of himself, falling in love with this threepenny-'appeny temptress who wrapped her sexual manipulation in romantic clichés, his excitement began to wane. What a fool Faber was. A woman like that had nothing to do with love. She was outside all the business of shared hopes, joys and failures; she was destructive whether she knew it or not and she almost certainly didn't. She demanded attention and affection but only because she couldn't bear to see her friend happy. He'd never fall for a woman like that. He'd give her a good rutting which is what she deserved. Yet here was Faber, an educated, successful man with an obliging and loving wife, behaving like a virgin teenager in front of the first girl who bats her eyelids or waggles her tits.

Elsie was dismissive of Faber's obsession. She didn't reflect that all men weren't like her father who kept himself away from temptation as diligently as a bat avoids the light; she thought Faber was simply a fathead who put flattery before loyalty and pleasure before duty. What man in his right mind could prefer the flippant Leonora to the steady Barbara? It was true Barbara smoked and lived too easy a life: having people doing all the work for you was bound to fill your head with silly ideas; but at least she was a faithful wife. It would have shocked her to know that millions of men will disdain faithfulness if the opportunity of pleasure without demands comes their way; it would have left her bereft to learn that respect and devotion to women who adhere to the demanding ideal of married life can be swept away like a dead leaf in a torrent when careless, frivolous women open their legs and offer heaven with no possibility of hell.

When Faber met his tragic fate, Bert felt sorry for him but at the same time thought it was, in a way, deserved: he'd allowed himself to be led on by a woman who had nothing to offer but romantic posturing, neurotic demands and inconsequential sex. Did he think she was going to look after him? Did he imagine she had the makings of a loyal, reliable wife who would stay beside him through disaster and wreckage? No, he should have taken her for what she was or not at all; but Bert had trouble with the not at all. If a woman offered herself, why resist, so long as you weren't found out?

Elsie laid all the blame on Leonora. She was an evil woman. Of course, Faber was rotten. His wife was as good as sunshine. Elsie believed a respectable woman was the best thing a man could have; a wife who did her duty in the house and the bedroom should make a man grateful. To accept that and at the same time to dally with a fribble was enough to make her vomit. Though she despised and disdained Faber she didn't think him evil; he'd been tempted. He wouldn't have been unfaithful if Leonora hadn't manipulated him, and Elsie wasn't so immersed in her religious doctrine that she couldn't understand the exorbitant power of female sexuality.

She knew well enough there was barely a man on earth who would refuse a woman if she offered herself; that affection, respect and commitment were as flimsy as paper lanterns in a hurricane when the butcher's slab fact of sex presented itself free of any encumbrance. She knew that a man who offered sex to a woman had as much chance of being accepted as an atheist in the Vatican. Men were such hopeless dupes they would pay women for sex while women who would pay men for sex were as rare as life in the universe. It was odd but that's how it was and she knew it as instinctively as any woman. That was why she reserved her venom for Leonora; if women behaved like her, no marriage was safe. A woman who flaunted her sexuality must be despised; she must be dismissed as a baggage, a Jezebel. That was the way the status of respectable woman must be defended, and without that what was there but a chaos of vicious competition and a world drowned in lust, loneliness and recrimination?

"Did you enjoy it?" asked Bert as they emerged from the dark into the dazzling foyer.

"It was all right," she said.

"You could see where it was going from the start," he said.

"He should've 'ad more sense than get involved with a woman like that."

"You're right," said Bert.

"That's what you get if you play fast and loose."

"It is, but you've got to feel sorry for him."

"Yes, but not for her. She was evil."

Bert wanted to laugh. Evil? He couldn't see it. She was at odds with herself and spun like an ill-balanced wheel; but evil? Wasn't it more to do with the kind of conflicts in the mind Faber was supposed to be expert in? He liked the irony that the psychiatrist was the victim of his own obsession. He was fascinated by the reference in Faber's lecture to the *inferior function* and Dr Jung. He would like to read about that stuff.

"She led him on right enough."

"And he was daft enough to fall for it. A married man wi' a good wife. Rotten thing."

"You're right," said Bert, but he couldn't agree with her. Yes, there was no doubt Faber was in the wrong, but for a man to turn down a woman like Leonora was desperately hard. She was one of those women who know how to play on a man's sympathies; to make herself appear as vulnerable and helpless as a child; to awaken in him all his latent will to protect; to make him feel strong and capable and at the same time to undermine him fatally, rob him of his confidence and self-respect. She was everything that was subsumed by the cliché of the *femme fatale*; and though every man knew the danger of such a woman, that no more deterred most men than the risk of drowning would keep them from the breakers on the beach at St Ives on a scorching August day.

The pleasure was worth the risk. Bert knew if a Leonora came along, he would find it almost impossible not to get into bed with her. Yet he couldn't say that to Elsie. Was their relationship then based on lies? It troubled him but not so much as to disturb his cheerfulness. He was married. It was unlikely any such women would come his way. He would soon be a father. That was where his future lay. If a Leonora did appear, he would have to deal with it. Yet it was odd that he couldn't tell the truth about himself to Elsie. He loved her. He was committed to her. Yet what was true was true. He would have liked to discuss it with her and for her to laugh. He would have liked to have been accepted for what he was. He would have liked to hear her say: "Well, if a Leonora does come along, talk to me about it. Don't worry, I'll be a good enough wife to you for you not to be tempted." But such waving-in-the-wind ideas were impossible for Elsie. If he'd admitted what he thought she would have ordered him from the house and locked the door behind him.

Her ideas were as straight as a Roman road and as rigid as a girder and they constructed a little fortress behind which she lived in apparent safety.

When they lay in the slowly warming bed, he put his arm round her and pulled her to him. It was nice to nestle with her backside pushed against his groin. Yet as she stayed still and quiet he couldn't help thinking of Leonora and wondering if life might not be more exciting with a woman who smoked, drank and treated her sexuality as a toy.

A few weeks later, on a bright Tuesday morning, Harry Clow called him in. He sat behind his huge desk in the small office. Bert knew at once from his demeanour something was wrong. Yet his confidence didn't begin to melt; he knew he did his work well. He could defend himself against any criticism.

"There's a problem with these figures," said Clow.

"What's that?"

"Wages. Someone's been fiddling bonus."

"Really."

"You've put these figures together haven't you?"

Clow held up the sheets and Bert nodded.

"Then you must know what's going on."

"No, I don't."

"The men are claiming bonus they haven't earned. Somebody's splitting the money with them. Who could it be ?"

Bert sprang to his feet. The back street, ill-educated, socially gauche wretch came alive. He prided himself on his honesty. He'd never stolen a thing in his life. He had that powerful affiliation to *law and order* often found among the poor which springs from their sense that without it their vulnerability can be easily exploited. As he would have been outraged had anyone stolen from him, so he wouldn't offend anyone else's feeling. Clow was calling him a thief and a cheat. His instinct was to go at him with his fists but he wasn't the fool his grandfather was. A welter of ideas was forming in his mind but for the moment there was just the nuclear indignation of being accused.

"Are you calling me a thief?"

"I'm looking at the evidence."

"Let me see that," said Bert striding forward, but Clow pulled back the documents and took a defensive pose.

"Just sit down."

"I won't sit down," said Bert. "Not till you withdraw the accusation."

"I'm just telling you what's in the figures. They can't be right. Someone's on the fiddle and as you did these accounts you must know about it."

"You watch your tongue," said Bert, wagging his index finger before Clow's face. "Calling me a thief you'd better get the police."

"I don't need to."

"What d'you mean?"

"I'll take it to Mr Cropper. The figure speak for themselves."

"Let me see them then."

"You compiled them. You know what's in them."

Bert stood facing his boss, the desk between them. Suddenly into his head came the image of Clow with his arm round Johnny Speed. He stared into his eyes. The other man looked back at him with fixed disdain and superiority. Bert knew exactly what was going to happen. How would Cropper react? He hardly knew him. Would he give him the chance to defend himself? Did he have the right just to give him his cards? He thought of his father-in-law and wished he was in a union; but accountants didn't join unions. Bert had believed he was rising above the possibility of summary sacking; he was white collar; he was getting qualifications; he was moving into the sphere of secure jobs, decades of well-paid employment and a pension to follow; yet here he was, like any joiner or brickie the boss took a dislike to and sent packing without notice.

In the few seconds of silence between them Bert realised he had no means of defending himself. Was it possible to go to law? He had no idea but he knew he couldn't afford it. He was faced with the power of a boss. Clow was setting him up. Would Cropper take his word for it or investigate properly? In any case, Bert knew he was utterly dependent. He understood his grandfather's mad rage; he knew why he used his fists on strangers on a Saturday night. What could be more humiliating than this? To be employed was a humiliation. It was to be inserted in weakness and dependency. He despised himself. He felt like the child he'd been, standing in front of the priest waiting for the leather strap across his palm.

"You snake," he said.

Clow relaxed a little and smirked.

"Think that'll get you anywhere?"

"Keep your job, you've seen the last of me."

He turned and strode to the door.

"That's an admission of guilt in my book."

"Your book is corrupt. You can stick it up your backside, Clow."

"You'll not get another job in this town if I've anything to do with it."

"Think I need your help to get work?"

"No-one'll take you on without a reference."

"We'll see."

Bert was on the verge of making a cruel comment about Johnny Speed, but he held back, pulled open the door, took the stairs two at a time, grabbed his coat and was out in the fresh air.

A dread seized him as he walked: the descent into poverty. Tom Craxton wouldn't kick him out. He'd have a roof over his head and food to eat, but to rely on Tom's generosity would break him. He had to make his own way. What could he do? Maybe the Labour Exchange would find him something. He could scour the *situations vacant* in the paper. A man who wanted to work could find work. He wouldn't go under. He'd sweep floors if he had to till something better came along. Yet in spite of his fighting to convince himself, his mood darkened, the town looked grimmer in spite of the sunshine, people seemed to pass him as if they knew he was falling into potential misery and exclusion. How would he tell Elsie? And what about the child?

Clow's bit of power had done for him. It was terrible; men had power over men and made them suffer. Why? What was power? He sought an idea that could save him. He was walking into town. Where could he go? The only refuge he could think of was Slick Sticks Sam.

He rapped on the door whose green paint was badly faded and chipped. There was no reply or any sound. It was far too early for Sam to be out. He knocked more insistently till he heard a rustle and a thud. He leaned on the door frame with his hands in his pockets. A young woman opened to him. She was wrapped in a white dressing gown that she gripped at breast height. Her cleavage was visible. Her peroxide hair was a half-finished bird's nest. She had a bad squint in her right eye. He smiled and looked down at her legs. She pulled the gown a little tighter round her breasts but flicked her hips into a sensuous curve and bit her bottom lip like a confused child.

"Sam in?"

"He's in bed."

"I'd never've believed it."

"He says he'll have the rent tomorrow."

Bert laughed and the sound echoed in the stairwell like a portent of doom.

"Tell him it's Bert. Tell him I've just been sacked."

She looked at him with her big, apparently innocent eyes and closed the door. Seconds later Sam opened it. He was in his underpants and had a *Woodbine* in his mouth.

"Christ, Bert, what you doin' turnin' up in the middle o' the night?"

He went inside billowing smoke like a train and as Bert followed he glanced to the left through the open bedroom door and saw the delightful, naked backside of the young woman as she bent to pick her clothes from the floor. He was suddenly transported; wouldn't it be something to live like Sam? He was one of those men born without the capacity to worry. What happened, happened. He was as fatalistic as a medieval follower of Allah.

Yes, it was terrible to spend the rent on booze and fags, but what did you get for being provident? What had he got? He'd worked hard

301

and believed there was a place for him but Clow had quartered him. It was power, unadorned and vicious; and wasn't that how life worked? Didn't those with power use it against those who lacked it? Wasn't vulnerability an invitation to abuse? He wished, like Sam, he could play music a bit and earn enough from *gigging* here and there to avoid a steady job. He knew it was a romantic notion, that there wasn't much glamour in having to throw your drum kit into the guard's van to get to Manchester or sleep outside the station because you missed the last one home; but the consolation was the lovely arse he'd just seen.

How old was she? Eighteen? He'd chosen to say goodbye to that, as he'd chosen to work eight hours a day adding up because he thought it was the way to a good life; but it was a cheat. The whole damn system was a cheat. Cropper was driving his Bentley while he wouldn't be able to afford petrol for his *banger*. Everything was set up so the rich prospered, even marriage. There were only two ways out : either rise up against it and change the system, or duck under it, like Sam. The oaken will required to keep up the struggle for change had become sawdust and for the moment Sam's disaffiliation seemed the attractive route.

"Just walked out of my job."

"You must be crazy."

"Either that or get my cards."

"Why?"

"Clow."

They looked at one another. Sam drew on his *Woodbine* as if it gave him sustenance and scratched himself through his grey-white underwear. He shook his head.

"I told you to leave him alone. Can't trust his sort as far as you can spit."

"He claimed I'd been fiddling the blokes' bonus. He was going to report me to Cropper."

"The git."

"Know anyone who needs their accounts doing?"

Sam leaned forward to stub out his *dog-end* in the stolen ashtray on the wobbly coffee table. The young woman appeared in slacks and a sweater, backcombing her hair.

"Shall I put't kettle on?"

Bert had a cynical wish to say: "I'd rather you took your clothes off," but he smiled.

"Yeah, I'll have a coffee," said Sam.

"Me too," said Bert.

It was odd, he thought as he flopped on the sofa, Sam and his woman lazing around like this in the middle of the morning while people were busy at their jobs. It granted a sense of freedom simply by being a transgression. He felt as though the rest of world was in its office or factory while they alone were adrift; and why shouldn't life go on like this? Why should there be clocking on and off and timesheets and miserable bank holidays and two weeks in summer when everyone did the same things in Blackpool or Morecambe?

"Told Elsie?" said Sam.

"Not yet."

"She'll fryin'pan you."

"I'll get work," said Bert. "I was getting fed up at Cropper's in any case."

"Yeah. Bugger, all the same."

"If I had a bit of money I'd set myself up in something."

"Wouldn't we all."

"Work, eh? You've got it lucky, Sam."

"Sure, bashin' drums till midnight seven days a week for five quid. If I had your brain I'd be an accountant too. Get meself a big house in Fulwood and a nice motor."

"You wouldn't have that in the kitchen though."

"Wouldn't I?"

"Not if you were married."

"Who said anythin' about marriage?"

"It's expected," said Bert. "Got to have the little woman on your arm for the Christmas do at the *Bull and Royal*."

"Fuck the *Bull and Royal*."

Bert laughed like a man who'd just won a million on the pools. The young woman brought the mugs through.

"This is Pauline, by the way," said Sam.

"Nice to meet you, Pauline. How'd you get to know Sam?"

"I was dancin', he was drummin'," she shrugged her shoulders as she handed him his drink.

"You're a dancer then?"

"Stripper," said Sam.

"Artistic dance if you don't mind," she said, holding the steaming coffee towards him at arm's length.

"Everybody's got to make a living," said Bert.

"What do you do?" she said.

"I'm on the dole," he said.

"Oh, that's a shame."

"He's an accountant," said Sam. "Resting, as our friends in the theatre say. He'll be a millionaire one day. Play your cards right, Pauline, he'll take you for a dirty weekend at the Manchester *Midland* when he's flush."

She gave a little giggle, inclined her head to her shoulder, made one of those rapid wiggles with her hips only women are capable of and tripped back to the kitchen.

Bert watched her, thinking how empty she was compared to Elsie. It was odd how he could disdain such a woman for her lack of mental or moral strength, yet at the same time be powerfully physically aroused by her. That was a cheat too; nature was dissembling. Perhaps that was how it was meant to be; women attracted men simply by the bounce of their hips or the flicker of their eyelids; they didn't have to do anything; and maybe men were supposed to respond to that and have sex with as many women as they wanted. Then what was all the flummery about marriage for?

He thought of his son. He was loved. His existence made Laura and Gino more loving. Wasn't that better than a night or two with Pauline? Yet things weren't warmer between him and Elsie now their child was on the way. He couldn't fathom her moods. Why was she irritable and sharp? Why did she seem to push him away? Why was she always intent on some activity, however trivial: washing the windows or ironing vests? Why couldn't she find some fun in domestic tasks or take the time to relax and nestle? He wondered if he were to blame. In any case, the Craxtons had been good to him. He had a home. He felt he almost belonged; and Elsie was his wife. The word was full of serious resonance just as the words he'd have used to describe Pauline were replete with frivolity and flippancy. A wife was something worth having. Like a mother. He wished he could feel what he ought to. He longed for his ideas and his feelings to blend like the confluence of two gushing rivers; but his idea of himself as a husband didn't fit with the discomfort he felt at Elsie's behaviour. He asked himself if this was how most marriages were. He had no point of reference; he couldn't evoke the life of his parents. He'd made his choices. He was where he was. There was nothing to do but carry on.

"I could try Manchester," said Bert.

"Would Elsie go?" said Sam lighting another *Woodbine*.

"I doubt it."

"Women, eh?They either crave the exotic or cling to the domestic."

"Sometimes Sam, you're almost poetic."

"It's all those Gershwin and Hoagy Carmichael songs."

"I wish had an ear for music," said Bert. "Something creative. Figures are just bloody figures."

"Yeah. Thirty-six, twenty-four, thirty-six."

Pauline came through with her own mug and perched on the arm of the sofa as if she were about to be photographed.

"Six years in bloody Italy and Egypt and here I am, forced out of my job because my boss likes young men but wants to pretend he's respectable."

"I think it's disgusting," said Pauline sipping her drink as if it might contain arsenic or the elixir of youth.

"It's what you like to read about in *The News of The World*."

"A girl has to know what's going on."

"How's the national debt just now?" and Sam drew hard on his cigarette.

"Don't tease me, it's not gentlemanly."

"Bert's a gentleman, I have to play drums for my breakfast."

"I'm no gentleman. I'm as illegitimate as they come."

"It's not where you come from, Bert, it's where you're goin'."

"Yeah, and I'm going to the Labour Exchange."

"They get you by the bollocks one way or another," said Sam, "if it's not the boss it's the state. It's enough to turn a man to crime."

"There's work if people look for it," said Pauline, with a prim little bridle. "I don't think they should give them the dole for doing nothing."

"You could be Minister of Labour," said Sam. "The country'd be on it's feet in five minutes."

"There's no need to be nasty. I'm just expressing my opinion, it's a free country."

"'Course it is, you're free to take your clothes off for money every night and the dockers are free to get bad backs unloading bananas."

"I'm not ashamed of what I do. I entertain people. It's hard work. You wouldn't like standing naked on a draughty stage in February."

"Where would the country be without strip clubs? We should shut down the coal mines and make our living with g-strings and feather boas."

"It's not nice the way you make fun of me."

Bert laughed.

"She's right, Sam. It's not nice."

"I'm not a nice bloke. I'd sell your grandma for a packet of *Woodbines*."

"I wouldn't stop you," said Bert.

"Anyway," said Pauline, "I think it's disgusting, men doing it with men. It's not natural."

"Toothpaste isn't natural," said Sam. "Nature is a pain in the arse."

Bert laughed again. Pauline looked at him with a slightly superior expression. How odd it was a stripper could talk like a medieval monarch about the unemployed. Bert couldn't bring himself to argue with her because she seemed so mentally feeble. In any case, it would be ill-mannered, as he was a guest. Yet it disappointed his deepest feelings to the point of despair: the commonplace opinions of the lowliest and most morally dubious folk were enough to soak the earth in blood and heap it with corpses.

It seemed to him as obvious as rain that the dole was needed only because there wasn't enough work; no-one offered a half-way decent job would want to live on unemployment pay; and it wasn't the penny-pinching that was the worst, it was the humiliation. People didn't make choices about work; not real choices. Work was an imposition. If you lived where there were coal mines you'd probably be a miner; if you lived round the corner from a shipyard you'd be likely to be a riveter. Where was the choice? Of course, the fancy folk could choose; but no-one was free. Work was a fact of life. It was as given as breathing. All the talk of freedom was a trick; the truth was we are compelled to work; everyone must do what they can; Sam played the drums, Eddie joined wood and Bert added figures. What was so mystical about that? Everyone made their contribution and everyone should enjoy the fruits.

It seemed so unarguable he couldn't see why people didn't accept it. Yet somehow it was all entangled; Pauline believed people without jobs were just skivers. Where had she got such an idea? If she looked around her and used her common sense she'd know it wasn't like that. It was how work was organised. It was madness that so much wealth was created and so many were poor. It was lunacy that Tom Craxton laboured all week for a few shillings; if he worked on his own account he'd be well-off. It was all twisted; and now here he was facing the dole himself and with a baby on the way. The old fear of his childhood poverty rose like a hand that reached up from his intestines to grip his throat; the terrible loneliness of being mocked for his impoverishment, the shredding sense of being shunned by his fellows who took delight in his misery, made him want to walk away. He would gladly have left the town never to return. He wanted to make a new start. He wanted to be somewhere no-one had heard of Pongo.

"I'd best be going, look at the time," said Pauline sliding from the sofa arm.

"Can you get me some fags?" said Sam.

She turned and held out her hand.

"I'll give you the money later."

"I'm not as daft as your landlord," she said and minced into the kitchen reappearing in her red coat with the collar turned up and her high heels that clicked efficiently on the bare floorboards. "Nice to meet you, Bert." She looked at Sam. "I'll see you at the club."

"Yeah," said Sam, "and get us ten *Woodbine* will you?"

She walked out like a wife abandoning a cheating husband.

"I can give you the money for some cigarettes," said Bert.

"No, no. You've enough on your stove. I'll get an advance from the manager. Tell him I've had to pay for my mother's funeral, again."

"How are things with the lady in unfortunate circumstances?" said Bert, remembering his unfulfilled promise to help.

"I found a doctor. Cost me thirty quid. That's why I'm skint."

"Is she all right?"

"Far as I know."

Thirty quid and it was done. Better that than a child no-one wanted. Bert wondered if his own mother had thought of it. It was curious to think if she hadn't been a Catholic he might never have lived; though life had been hard, he wouldn't have liked to miss it; there were still plenty of years ahead, time to make amends.

Yet when he thought of the horrible misery of his early years, a dismal life he was lifted from by the mad fact of war, he found himself reflecting that putting a child through that was unforgivably cruel. He couldn't do it. Sam was right. He couldn't be a father; maybe the girl was hopeless too. How queer it was that people could fail in something so fundamental; why weren't people good parents by nature? The thought filled him with quiet terror. Bringing children into the world was as easy as getting drunk; any fool could do it; but bringing up a child was impossibly hard. What did he know about it? He couldn't imitate his grandparents or his mother. He supposed it was about love and discipline; but he admitted to himself he was as prepared to be a father as to navigate the Amazon in a bathtub.

Would he fail? Would his child suffer as he'd done? He fell back on the thought of the Craxtons; Elsie would be a good mother; Tom a reliable granddad; the child would be cared for. All the same, the thought of failing in something so essential hollowed out his insides.

He felt as if the fact of fatherhood was coming like an asteroid from space; it might blast a hole in his life and throw him out of orbit. On the other hand it might be his greatest fulfilment or another tragedy. Another? Was his own life tragic? He fought against the idea; it was stupid self-pity. Life had to be lived; get on with it; grapple with it. What else could he do? What else could Sam do?

There was no doubt Sam was a failure. By all the common definitions, he was lacking. Pauline, the moralistic stripper, would condemn him if he had to claim the dole. She represented society's priggish judgementalism. She was one of those people who congratulate themselves on their petty *success* and look down on those who are in trouble, as if their good fortune were of their own making; but a person succeeded as much by circumstance and luck as by character, and if the successful were supposed to congratulate themselves, what were the failures supposed to do? Sink into self-hatred? It was all too ridiculous. If he blamed himself for being without a job, it would drive him insane. Is that what society wanted, to drive the poor to madness? Maybe it was so; maybe there was a kind of murderousness behind respectable opinion; perhaps the middle-classes would be glad if the unemployed committed mass suicide; perhaps there wasn't too much distance between blaming the poor for their poverty and Hitler's gas chambers.

Bert knew his grandparents had made themselves poor by their drinking, but they'd had plenty of encouragement. It was futile to blame individuals for what society did to them. His grandparents were weak-minded people; whether by nature or education he didn't know; but if society makes drink freely available to the weak-minded, what does it expect? And how can society ban drink for everyone just because of a few catastrophic cases like his grandparents? Any simple answer was sure to be wrong; in fact any answer at all. There was no answer, there was only tolerance, kindness, generosity and the recognition that life, which some people ride like a surfer on an Atlantic breaker, casts others to the cold depths of the ocean where they kick and flounder and never find their way to the surface. There was no answer, there was just the duty always to give people another chance and never to twist their arms up their backs.

"Well," he said with a smile, "be careful in future."

"If only I could be careful in the past."

Bert laughed.

Out in the street where weeds grew between the flagstones and the shattered green glass of a wine bottle lay in the gutter, he wondered if he should go home; perhaps the best was to tell Elsie straight away. There'd be a row. She wouldn't understand. She'd blame him for walking out and compare him to her father who had worked for decades at demeaning, dirty, dangerous jobs. She wouldn't see how he was trapped nor appreciate that by leaving before they got the chance to sack him, he'd hung on to the shreds of his dignity.

She'd fear they'd report him to the police, but Bert knew Clow's game: he had no real evidence. He walked through the park down to the river and stood on the old tram bridge where he'd run with his mates as a boy. The brown river surged to the sea and the little eddies and whirlpools it formed as it struck the pillars were at once perilous and charming. There was no doubt the world was lovely. The trees and the carefully tended grass slope and lawns; the rare blue sky and the birds whose names he didn't know pecking on the banks or settling in the high foliage; it was all delightful, yet he couldn't help feeling it was doomed. The blackbirds, which to him were simply charming, were engaged in a struggle for life. Were they enjoying themselves? There must be a certain kind of pleasure which keeps creatures doing what they have to; rats must like the sewers; for them it must be like eating at *The Ritz*.

Pleasure was written into things. It wasn't God, as Elsie thought; it was the driving need to keep life going and out of that drive arose the terrible, various and everyday tragedies of human life. He was gut-wrenchingly afraid his life was going to tilt into tragedy. The one point of surety was the Craxtons. They were good people. They might be odd, taciturn, arrestingly stern, but even Henry with his foolish, thoughtless ways would give you a roof if you were homeless. The Craxtons were his luck. He knew his best chance in life was to cleave to them. He would have to unlock the cellar to Elsie. He would bear the blizzard of her disdain and anger. It would subside. Soon he'd be a father. He'd find a job. He'd work ever harder and come through. The comfortable semi in Fulwood and the status of a respectable, hard-working husband and father would come to him if he persevered, and in his circumstances, he could envisage nothing better.

He was careful to arrive home at the usual time. He would have to choose his moment; but as soon as he saw Elsie sitting at the kitchen table, her fingers knitted, he knew something was wrong. Had she found out? Who could have told her?

"What's the matter?" he said as he took off his coat.

She began to sob, her face contorting into that little girl's distress which always came over her if she was upset. Bert looked at Tom who stood by the mantelpiece smoking his pipe. Elsie muttered something through her weeping.

"What?" he stood opposite her leaning towards her trying to be sympathetic but not sure if he should touch her.

She spoke again but he couldn't make it out. She pulled her handkerchief from her sleeve, wiped her eyes and blew her nose. There was a momentary pause in the earthquake of her disturbance.

"Is it your mother?" he said.

She shook her head ferociously and before the disintegrating eruption could start again blurted the words. He stood as lifeless as Jupiter. He had come to break news and she had usurped him. What was he hearing? His mind was as featureless as the Arctic. It was as if a tap which fed his thinking had been turned off. The seconds before he spoke were longer than the years he'd lived.

"What about the baby?"

She blubbered and moaned. The words wouldn't form in his head. She might have been speaking some ancient tongue. She began shaking her head once more and looked up into his eyes. For a moment he thought he saw something like love. He turned to Tom.

"What is it?"

His father-in-law took the pipe from his mouth. He was still and quiet.

"Babby's not kickin'" he said. "She feels nowt."

Bert quickly straightened himself.

"It might be nothing," he said, smiling, "we'll get to the hospital and have you checked. We'll be there in ten minutes in the car."

She put her head in her hands and her moaning began to become a wail. Bert pulled his coat back on, ran to fetch hers from behind the door, put it over her shoulders and helped her up from the chair.

When he'd got her in the passenger seat, Tom appeared with a canvas shopping bag.

" 'Appen you'll need these," he said.

Bert looked inside and saw Elsie's nightdress, some underwear and her toothbrush. He faced Tom who was as calm as if he'd known all his life this moment would arrive.

"Thanks."

The three miles to the hospital might have been a journey half way round the world. They didn't speak. Bert was trying to convince himself all would be well. Why should the worst happen? But his efforts were subverted by a thought which marched as insistently as a line of ants, over every barrier, on to its fatal destination: she was a woman and her instinct would be right.

There was nothing he could do but be as kind as possible. He took her to the maternity ward but they said she should go to casualty which provided him the great relief of losing his temper. He berated the ward sister. He refused to take his wife away. She was given a bed and within an hour a doctor had seen her. There was no doubt. The baby must be born as soon as possible. They gave her a drug to bring it on. He wasn't allowed to be with her. In the corridor he paced like any expectant father. He'd anticipated this wait. He would be waiting for new life. His son or daughter would soon be in his arms. A new life would begin for him. Now, a new life was to begin, marked by a new tragedy. He was waiting for death. He'd never been at the bedside of a dying person. He could imagine attending as Elsie's mother gave up her limp grip on life; but now he was going to be brought the news of life dead before it had begun.

He dozed in the uncomfortable chair. He went outside to breath the early hours air. The night sky was a black, star-speckled cruelty. What was he doing here? What was the earth? What was this all for? He didn't know if he could bear it. His usual cheerfulness wasn't crushed; he could have whistled a Cole Porter tune. His immediate surroundings were as interesting as ever. Yet beneath that, his feelings had fallen away like a cliff of clay battered by the sea. No matter how he told himself his feeling would renew, he couldn't overcome the dreadful magnetism of despair. They could start again. They would have children. But it was no good; for now there was only this, the fact of death, the pain of loss and the terrible knowledge that for months he would be haunted by emptiness.

It was after dawn when they came for him. Elsie was pale, exhausted, remote. At least she wasn't crying. All the emotion had gone from her. She was as dried out as a parched African river bed. A nurse held a little bundle in front of him and quickly withdrew it saying: "All right?"

"No," he said. "Let me hold it."

The nurse looked at him in dismay but his demeanour was insistent. She hadn't even told him if it was a boy or girl. He took the little parcel from her and looked down at the tiny, crumpled face. At once he could see Elsie's features.

"Boy or girl?" he said looking the nurse hard in the eyes.

"Girl," she said.

He turned away. The nurse stayed at his shoulder, so he took a few paces away. He delicately pulled awry the little sheet to reveal the impossibly small perfection. He noticed her hands were like his own. He lifted her infinitely light, cold fingers. He expected her eyes to open any moment. He couldn't believe her mouth wasn't going to gape and the sweet cry of life emerge from her miniature lungs. How he would have loved to hear her cry of hunger. Yet she lay, silent, beautiful and unblemished. What a pretty girl she would have made. How he would have delighted to walk hand in hand with her and have people notice her loveliness. She would have been as attractive as her mother. He bent and kissed her forehead and each of her denied eyes. Turning to Elsie he said:

"What shall we call her?"

She stared blankly at him for a few moments.

"Judith," she said.

"Judith," he repeated. "Yes, my little Judy. Hey, daddy's here little one. Daddy's here."

The nurse tried to take the baby away but he moved her to his chest.

"Wait a minute," he said. "I'm talking to my daughter."

He wrapped her once more in the cool white sheet, then holding her to him he paced, repeating her name, kissing her forehead, rocking her as if to calm her, give her security, make her sleep. At length, the nurse stood before him. He stopped. She looked in his face and smiled. When she took his child from him he had no power to resist. The nurse left the room. He wanted to go with her. He wanted never to be separated from his little Judith.

"Is there anything you need?" he said to Elsie.

She shook her head. The sister arrived and asked him to leave. His wife was to go to theatre.

"I'll be back later," he said bending to kiss her forehead.

Outside, a new day was under way. He walked out of the hospital grounds. Cars passed him. A bus went by full of folk on their way to work. Not merely the town but the universe itself was too small for his grief. All significance was obliterated. What did these people think they were doing? What they took to be important was fluff. He broke out in a sweat and began to sob. He stopped and took his handkerchief from his pocket, dabbed his eyes and tried to control himself. A woman hurrying looked at him suspiciously. It took minutes for the paroxysm to pass.

He walked on, exhausted, hungry, thinking of Judith, wondering where she was now. His mind couldn't hold an idea. He felt he could walk the earth's circumference and still not find a word to say. He was heading home but he had no home. He needed to sleep, but what good was sleep? The day was clear and he noticed how clean the morning air smelled. It almost made him feel life was good. He'd taken the wrong route and found himself in town. He wondered if he should buy a paper, but what news could there be? Perhaps he should drink a cup of tea, but the idea of sitting down was impossible. His legs would hardly carry him.

When he turned into his street he stopped. His front door was twenty yards away. It was a small house, a poor house, but it would have welcomed Judith. He would have to meet Tom. What would he say to him? He walked on, put his key in the lock. He was home, but when he closed the door behind him he felt he was being nailed into his coffin and he stood in the tiny hallway, unable to take off his coat, unable to move, unable now even to cry.